**Praise for *New York Times* bestselling author
Lindsay McKenna**

"McKenna provides heartbreakingly tender romantic
development that will move readers to tears. Her military
background lends authenticity to this outstanding tale,
and readers will fall in love with the upstanding hero and
his fierce determination to save the woman he loves."
—*Publishers Weekly* on *Never Surrender*

"Talented Lindsay McKenna delivers excitement and
romance in equal measure."
—*RT Book Reviews* on *Protecting His Own*

"Lindsay McKenna will have you flying with the daring
and deadly women pilots who risk their lives… Buckle in
for the ride of your life."
—*Writers Unlimited* on *Heart of Stone*

NEW YORK TIMES BESTSELLING AUTHOR

LINDSAY McKENNA

&

CINDI MYERS

A HERO'S HONOR

2 Thrilling Stories
The Rogue & *The Guardian*

HARLEQUIN

 HARLEQUIN®

ISBN-13: 978-1-335-50835-5

A Hero's Honor

Copyright © 2023 by Harlequin Enterprises ULC

The Rogue
First published in 1993. This edition published in 2023.
Copyright © 1993 by Lindsay McKenna

The Guardian
First published in 2015. This edition published in 2023.
Copyright © 2015 by Cynthia Myers

Recycling programs
for this product may
not exist in your area.

For questions and comments about the quality of this book,
please contact us at CustomerService@Harlequin.com.

Harlequin Enterprises ULC
22 Adelaide St. West, 41st Floor
Toronto, Ontario M5H 4E3, Canada
www.Harlequin.com

Printed in U.S.A.

CONTENTS

THE ROGUE 7
Lindsay McKenna

THE GUARDIAN 245
Cindi Myers

Lindsay McKenna is proud to have served her country in the US Navy as an aerographer's mate third class—also known as a weather forecaster. She was a pioneer in the military romance subgenre and loves to combine heart-pounding action with soulful and poignant romance. True to her military roots, she is the originator of the long-running and reader-favorite Morgan's Mercenaries series. She does extensive hands-on research, including flying in aircraft such as a P3-B Orion sub-hunter and a B-52 bomber. She was the first romance writer to sign her books in the Pentagon bookstore. Visit her online at lindsaymckenna.com.

Books by Lindsay McKenna

Shadow Warriors

Running Fire
Taking Fire
Never Surrender
Breaking Point
Degree of Risk
Risk Taker
Down Range

The Wyoming Series

Out Rider
Night Hawk
Wolf Haven
High Country Rebel
The Loner
The Defender
The Wrangler
The Last Cowboy
Deadly Silence

Visit the Author Profile page
at Harlequin.com for more titles.

THE ROGUE

Lindsay McKenna

Prologue

"Killian, your next assignment is a personal favor to me."

Morgan Trayhern was sitting with his friend and employee in a small Philipsburg, Montana, restaurant. The situation with Wolf Harding and Sarah Thatcher had been successfully wrapped up, and now it was time to pack up and go home. Morgan grimaced apologetically, as Killian's features remained completely closed, only a glitter in his hard, intelligent blue eyes suggesting possible interest.

Morgan picked up a fork and absently rotated it between his fingers and thumb. They'd already ordered their meals, so now was as good a time as any to broach the topic. "Look," he began with an effort, purposely keeping his voice low, "whether I want to or not, I'm going to have to put you on an assignment involving a woman, Killian."

Killian sat relaxed, his long, spare hands draped casually on his thighs as he leaned back in the poorly padded metal chair. But anyone who knew him knew he was never truly relaxed; he only gave that appearance. He stared guardedly at Morgan. "I can't."

Morgan stared back, the silence tightening between them. "You're going to have to."

Killian eased the chair down and placed his hands on the table. "I told you—I don't deal with women," he said flatly.

"At least hear me out," Morgan pleaded.

"It won't do any good."

Exhaustion shadowed Morgan's gray eyes. "Just sit there and listen."

Killian wrestled with an unexpected surge of panic that left a bitter taste in his mouth. He held Morgan's gaze warningly, feeling suddenly as if this man who had been his friend since their days in the French Foreign Legion had become an adversary.

Morgan rubbed his face tiredly. "The assignment deals with Laura's cousin from her mother's side of the family," he began, referring to his wife, who'd managed to befriend Killian—at least as much as Morgan had ever seen him allow. "This is important to me—and to Laura—and we want to know that you're the one handling the situation. It's personal, Killian."

Killian's scowl deepened, and his mouth thinned.

"Laura's cousin, Susannah Anderson, came to visit us in D.C." Morgan's eyes grew dark and bleak. "From what we've been able to piece together, on the way home, Susannah was at the bus station in Lexington,

Kentucky, when a man came up and started a conversation with her. Moments later, he was shot right in front of her eyes. We think Susannah saw the murderer, Killian—and he shot her, too, because she was a witness. The bullet hit her skull, cracked it and exited. By some miracle, she doesn't have brain damage, thank God. But the injury's swelling left her in a coma for two months. She regained consciousness a month ago, and I was hoping she could give us a lead on her attacker, but she can't remember what he looked like. And another thing, Killian—she can't talk."

Morgan rubbed his hands together wearily, his voice heavy with worry. "The psychiatrists are telling me that the horror of the experience is behind her inability to speak, not brain damage. She's suppressed the whole incident—that's why she can't describe the killer. Laura went down and stayed with Susannah and her family in Kentucky for a week after Susannah was brought home from the hospital, in hopes that she'd find her voice again." Morgan shrugged. "It's been a month now, and she's still mute."

Killian shifted slightly, resting his hands on the knees of his faded jeans. "I've seen that mute condition," he said quietly, "in some of the children and women of Northern Ireland."

Morgan opened his hands in a silent plea to Killian to take the assignment. "That's not the whole story, Killian. I need you to guard Susannah. There's evidence to indicate that the killer will go after Susannah once he finds out she survived. I think Susannah was an innocent bystander in a drug deal gone bad, but so far we don't know enough to point any fingers.

Susannah's memory is the key, and they can't risk her remembering the incident.

"Susannah was under local police guard at the Lexington hospital while she was there, and I had one of my female employees there, too. Since her release, I've told Susannah to stay on her parents' fruit farm in the Kentucky hills. Normally she lives and works down in the small nearby town of Glen, where she teaches handicapped children."

Morgan grasped the edge of the table, and his knuckles were white as he made his final plea. "She's family, Killian. Laura is very upset about this, because she and Susannah are like sisters. I want to entrust this mission to my very best man, and that's you."

Glancing sharply at his boss, Killian asked, "I'd be a bodyguard?"

"Yes. But Susannah and her parents aren't aware of the possible continued threat to her, so I don't want them to know your true capacity there. They're upset enough after nearly losing their daughter. I don't want to stress them more. Relaxation and peace are crucial to Susannah's recovery. I've contacted her father, Sam Anderson, and told him you're a friend of mine who needs some convalescence. Sam knows the type of company I run, and has an inkling of some of the things we do. I told him you were exhausted after coming in off a long-term mission and needed to hole up and rest."

Killian shrugged. The story wasn't too far from the truth. He hardened his heart. "I never take assignments involving women, Morgan."

"I know that. But I need you for this, Killian. On the surface, this assignment may look easy and quiet, but it's not. Stay on guard. I'm trying to track the drug deal right now. All our contacts in South America are checking it out, and I'm working closely with the Lexington police department. There's a possibility it could involve Santiago's cartel."

Killian's jaw clenched at the name of José Santiago, the violent Peruvian drug kingpin they'd finally managed to extradite and get behind bars.

Morgan gave Killian a pleading look. "Susannah's already been hurt enough in this ordeal. I don't want her hurt further. I worry that her family could become a target, too."

Cold anger wound through Killian as he thought about the mission. "Picking on a defenseless woman tells you the kind of slime we're dealing with."

Morgan gave Killian a probing look. "So will you take this assignment?"

Morgan knew that Killian's weakness, his Achilles' heel, was the underdog in any situation.

"One more thing," Morgan warned as he saw Killian's eyes thaw slightly. "Susannah isn't very emotionally stable right now. Her parents are Kentucky hill people. They're simple, hardworking folks. Sam owns a two-hundred-acre fruit farm, and that's their livelihood. Susannah ought to be in therapy to help her cope with what happened to her. I've offered to pay for it, but she's refusing all help."

"Frightened of her own shadow?" Killian asked, the face of his sister, Meg, floating into his memory.

Morgan nodded. "I want you to take care of Susannah. I know it's against your guidelines for a job, but my instincts say you're the right person to handle this situation—and her."

His own haunted past resurfacing, tugging at his emotions, Killian felt his heart bleed silently for this woman and her trauma. Avoiding Morgan's searching gaze, he sat silently for a long time, mulling over his options. Finally he heaved a sigh and muttered, "I just can't do it."

"Dammit!" Morgan leaned forward, fighting to keep his voice under tight control. "I *need* you, Killian. I'm not *asking* you to take this assignment, I'm *ordering* you to take it."

Anger leaped into Killian's narrowed eyes, and his fist clenched on the table's Formica top as he stared at Morgan. "And if I don't take this assignment?"

"Then, whether I like it or not, I'll release you from any obligation to Perseus. I'm sorry, Killian. I didn't want the mission to come down to this. You're the best at what we do. But Susannah is part of my family." His voice grew emotional with pleading. "Whatever your problem with women is, put it aside. I'm begging you to help Susannah."

Killian glared at Morgan, tension radiating from him, every joint in his usually relaxed body stiff with denial. He *couldn't* protect a woman! Yet, as he stared at Morgan, he knew that if he didn't take the assignment his boss would release him from his duties with Perseus, and the money he made was enough to keep Meg reasonably well-off. If he hadn't come to work for Perseus, he'd never have been able to free her from the financial obligations brought on by her tragedy.

His need to help his sister outweighed the risk of his own pain. The words came out harshly, bitten off: "I'll do the best I can."

Relief showed on Morgan's taut features. "Good.

My conscience is eating me alive on this situation, Killian. But this is the only way I can make amends to Susannah for what's happened. She was innocent—in the wrong place at the wrong time."

"I'll leave right away," Killian rasped as he took the voucher and airline ticket Morgan proffered. No use putting off the inevitable. He'd pick up his luggage at the motel across from the restaurant and get underway. No longer hungry, he rose from the booth. Morgan appeared grateful, but that didn't do anything for him. Still angry over Morgan's threat to fire him, Killian made his way outside without a word. Walking quickly, he crossed the street to the motel, his senses as always hyperalert to everything around him.

What kind of person was this Susannah Anderson? Killian wondered. He'd noticed Morgan's voice lower with feeling when he'd spoken about her. Was she young? Old? Married? Apparently not, if she was staying with her parents. A large part of him, the part that suffered and grieved over Meg, still warned him not to go to Kentucky. His soft spot for a woman in trouble was the one chink in his carefully tended armor against the pain this world inflicted on the unwary.

Yet, as he approached the motel on this hot Montana summer morning, Killian felt an oblique spark of interest that he hated to admit. Susannah was a melodic name, suggestive of someone with sensitivity. Was she? What color was her hair? What color were her eyes? Killian could read a person's soul through the eyes. That ability to delve into people, to know them inside out, was his greatest strength. On the flip side, he allowed no one to know him. Even Morgan Trayhern, who had one of the most sophisticated security companies in America, had only a very thin background dossier on him. And Killian wanted it kept that way. He wanted no one to know the extent of the pain he carried within him—or what he'd done about it. That kind of information could be ammunition for his enemies—and could mean danger to anyone close to him. Still, his mind dwelled on the enigmatic Susannah Anderson. She could be in more danger with Killian around than from any potential hit man. Why couldn't Morgan understand that? Killian hadn't wanted to tell Morgan his reasons for refusing to take assignments involving women; he'd never told anyone. A frown worked its way across his brow. Susannah had been a victim of violence, just like Meg. More than likely, she was afraid of everything.

Arriving at his motel room, Killian methodically packed the essentials he traveled with: a long, wicked-looking hunting knife, the nine-millimeter Beretta that he wore beneath his left armpit in a shoulder holster, and his dark brown leather coat.

When he'd placed a few other necessary items in a beat-up leather satchel, Killian was ready for his next assignment. He'd never been to Kentucky, so he'd have a new area to explore. But whether he wanted to or not, he had to meet Susannah Anderson. The thought tied his gut into painful knots. Damn Morgan's stubbornness! The woman was better off without Killian around. How in the hell was he going to handle his highly volatile emotions, not to mention her?

Chapter 1

"We're so glad you've come," Pansy Anderson gushed as she handed Killian a cup of coffee and sat down at the kitchen table across from him.

Killian gave the woman a curt nod. The trip to Glen, Kentucky, and from there to the fruit farm, had passed all too quickly. However, the Andersons' warm welcome had dulled some of his apprehension. Ordinarily, Killian spoke little, but this woman's kindness made his natural reticence seem rude. Leathery-looking Sam Anderson sat at his elbow, work-worn hands clutching a chipped ceramic mug of hot black coffee. Pansy, who appeared to be in her sixties, was thin, with a face that spoke of a harsh outdoor life.

As much as Killian wanted to be angry at everyone, he knew these people didn't deserve his personal frustration. Struggling with emotions he didn't dare explore, Killian whispered tautly, "I'm glad to be here, Mrs. Anderson." It was an utter lie, but still, when he looked into Pansy's worn features he saw relief and hope in her eyes. He scowled inwardly at her reaction. He couldn't offer hope to them or to their daughter. More likely, he presented a danger equal to the possibility of the murderer's coming after Susannah. Oh, God, what was he going to do? Killian's gut clenched with anxiety.

"Call me Pansy." She got up, wiping her hands on her red apron. "I think it's so nice of Morgan to send you here for a rest. To tell you the truth, we could sure use company like yours after what happened to our Susannah." She went to the kitchen counter and began peeling potatoes for the evening meal. "Pa, you think Susannah might like the company?"

"Dunno, Ma. Maybe." Sam's eyes became hooded, and he stared down at his coffee, pondering her question. "My boy, Dennis, served with Morgan. Did he tell you that?"

"No, he didn't."

"That's right—in Vietnam. Dennis died up there on that hill with everyone else. My son sent glowing letters back about Captain Trayhern." Sam looked up. "To this day, I've kept those letters. It helps ease the pain I feel when I miss Denny."

Pansy sighed. "We call Susannah our love baby, Killian. She was born shortly after Denny was killed. She sure plugged up a hole in our hearts. She was such a beautiful baby…"

"Now, Ma," Sam warned gruffly, "don't go getting teary-eyed on us. Susannah's here and, thank the good Lord above, she's alive." Sam turned his attention to

Killian. "We need to warn you about our daughter. Since she came back to us from the coma, she's been actin' awful strange."

"Before the tragedy," Pansy added, "Susannah was always such a lively, outgoing young woman. She's a teacher over at the local grade school in Glen. The mentally and physically handicapped children are her first love. She used to laugh, dance, and play beautiful music." Pansy gestured toward the living room of the large farmhouse. "There's a piano in there, and Susannah can play well. Now she never touches it. If she hears music, she runs out of the house crying."

"And she don't want anything to do with anyone. Not even us, much of the time," Sam whispered. He gripped the cup hard, his voice low with feeling. "Susannah is the kindest, most loving daughter on the face of this earth, Killian. She wouldn't harm a fly. She cries if one of Ma's baby chicks dies. When you meet her, you'll see what we're saying."

"The violence has left her disfigured in a kind of invisible way," Pansy said. "She has nasty headaches, the kind that make her throw up. They come on when she's under stress. She hasn't gone back to teach, because she hasn't found her voice yet. The doctors say the loss of her voice isn't due to the blow on her head."

"It's mental," Sam added sadly.

"Yes… I suppose it is…" Pansy admitted softly.

"It's emotional," Killian rasped, "not mental." He was instantly sorry he'd spoken, as both of them gave him a strange look. Shifting in his chair, Killian muttered, "I know someone who experienced something similar." Meg had never lost her voice, but he'd suffered with her, learning plenty about emotional wounds. He saw the relief in their faces, and the shared hope. Dammit, they shouldn't hope! Killian clamped his mouth shut and scowled deeply, refusing to meet their eyes.

Pansy rattled on, blotting tears from her eyes. "You understand, then."

Pansy gave him a wobbly smile and wiped her hands off on the towel hanging up on a hook next to the sink. "We just don't know, Killian. Susannah writes us notes so we can talk with her that way. But if we try and ask her about the shooting she runs away, and we don't see her for a day or two."

"She's out in the old dilapidated farmhouse on the other side of the orchard—but not by our choice," Sam offered unhappily. "That was the old family homestead for over a hundred years 'fore my daddy built this place. When Susannah came home from the hospital last month, she insisted on moving into that old, broken-down house. No one's lived there for twenty years or more! It's about half a mile across the hill from where we live now. We had to move her bed and fetch stuff out to her. Sometimes, on a good day, she'll come join us for supper. Otherwise, she makes her own meals and stays alone over there. It's as if she wants to hide from the world—even from us..."

Killian nodded, feeling the pain that Pansy and Sam carried for their daughter. As the silence in the kitchen became stilted, Killian forced himself to ask a few preliminary questions. "How old is Susannah?"

Sam roused himself. "Going on twenty-seven."

"And you say she's a teacher?"

A proud smile wreathed Pansy's features as she washed dishes in the sink. "Yes, she's a wonderful teacher! Do you know, she's the only member of either of our families that got a college degree? The handicapped children love her so much. She taught art class." With a sigh, Pansy added, "Lordy, she won't paint or draw anymore, either."

"Nope," Sam said. "All she does is work in the orchard, garden and tend the animals—mostly the sick ones. That's what seems to make her feel safe."

"And she goes for long walks alone," Pansy added. "I worry. She knows these hills well, but there's this glassy look that comes into her eyes, Killian, and I sometimes wonder if she realizes where she's at."

"Have there been any strangers around, asking about Susannah?" Killian asked offhandedly. Now he understood why Morgan didn't want to tell these gentle, simple people the truth of the situation. But how the hell was he going to balance everything and keep a professional attitude?

"Oh," Pansy said with a laugh, "we get lots of folks up here to buy our fruits, nuts and fresh garden vegetables. And I'm known for my healin' abilities, so we always have folks stoppin' by. That's somethin' Susannah took to—using herbs to heal people with. She's a good healer, and the hill folk, if they can't get to me because I'm busy, they'll go to Susannah. We have a huge herb garden over by the old homestead, and she's making our medicines for this year as the herbs are ready for pickin'."

"That and using white lightning to make tinctures from those herbs." Sam chuckled. And then he raised his bushy eyebrows. "I make a little corn liquor on the side. Strictly for medicinal purposes." He grinned.

Killian nodded, reading between the lines. Although the Andersons were farm people, they were well-off by hill standards. When he'd driven up earlier in the brown Land Cruiser he'd rented at the airport, he'd noted that the rolling green hills surrounding the large two-story white farmhouse were covered with orchards. He'd also seen a large chicken coop, and at least two hundred chickens roaming the hundred acres, ridding the land of insect pests. He'd seen a couple of milking cows, a flock of noisy gray geese, some wild mallards that made their home in a nearby pond, and a great blue heron walking along the edge of the water, probably hunting frogs. In Killian's mind, this place was perfect for someone like him, someone who was world-weary and in need of some genuine rest.

"Why don't you go out and meet Susannah?" Pansy asked hopefully. "You should introduce yourself. Maybe what she needs is someone her own age to get on with. That might help her heal."

White-hot anger clashed with gut-wrenching fear within Killian. Anger at Morgan for forcing him to take this mission. Fear of what he might do around Susannah if he didn't maintain tight control over his emotions. Killian kept his expression passive. Struggling to keep his voice noncommittal, he said, "Yes, I'll meet your daughter. But don't get your hopes up about anything happening." His tone came out harder than he'd anticipated. "I'm here for a rest, Mrs. Anderson. I'm a man of few words, and I like to be left alone."

Pansy's face fell a little, but she quickly summoned up a soft smile. "Why, of course, Mr. Killian. You are our guest, and we want you to feel free to come and go as you please."

Kindness was something Killian had *never* been able to deal with. He stood abruptly, the scraping of the wooden chair against the yellowed linoleum floor an irritant to his taut nerves. "I don't intend to be lazy. I'll help do some work around the place while I'm here."

"I can always use a pair of extra hands," Sam said, "and I'd be beholden to you for that."

Relief swept through Killian, at least momentarily. Work would help keep him away from Susannah. Yet, as a bodyguard, he'd have to remain alert and nearby— even if it was the last thing he wanted to do. But work would also help him get to know the farm and its lay-out, to anticipate where a threat to Susannah might come from.

Sam rose to his full six-foot-five-inch height. He was as thin as a spring sapling. "Come meet our daughter, Mr. Killian. Usually, this time of day, she's out in the herb garden. It's best I go with you. Other-wise, she's liable to start 'cause you're a stranger."

"Of course," Killian said. Everything about the An-derson home spoke of stark simplicity, he noted as he followed Sam. The floors were covered with linoleum, worn but clean, and lovingly polished. The handmade furniture looked antique, no doubt crafted by Anderson men over the generations. A green crocheted afghan covered the back of the sofa. Pansy had mentioned when he arrived that it had been made by her mother, who had recently passed away at the age of ninety-eight. Evidently, a long-lived family, Killian mused as he followed Sam out the creaky screen door onto the large wooden porch, where a swing hung.

"Now," Sam warned him, "don't take offense if Su-sannah sees you and takes off for her house. Sometimes when folks come to buy our produce they mistakenly stop at the old house. She locks herself in and won't go near the door."

Not a bad idea, Killian thought, with her assailant still on the prowl. Sometimes paranoia could serve a person well, he ruminated. He looked at himself. He was paranoid, too, but with good cause. As they walked down a well-trodden path lined with fruit trees he wondered how much Susannah knew of her own situation.

"Now," Sam was saying as he took long, slow strides, "this here's the apple orchard. We got mostly Gravestein and Jonathan varieties, 'cause folks are always lookin' for good pie apples." He gestured to the right. "Over there is the Bartlett pears and Bing cherries and sour cherries. To the left, we got Alberta and freestone peaches. Ma loves figs, so we got her a row of them, too. Susannah likes the nut trees, so I ended up planting about twenty acres of black walnuts. Darn good taste to the things, but they come in this thick outer shell, and you have to wait till it dries before you can even get to the nut. It's a lot of work, but Susannah, as a kid, used to sit around for hours, shelling those things by the bucketful. The black are the best-tasting of all walnuts."

Killian nodded, his gaze never still. The surrounding rolling hills, their trees bearing nearly mature fruit, looked idyllic. A variety of birds flew through the many branches and he heard babies cheeping loudly for their parents to bring them food. Still, the serene orchard was forestlike, offering easy cover for a hit man.

After about a fifteen-minute walk up a gentle slope, Killian halted beside Sam where the orchard opened up into an oblong meadow of grass. In the center of the open area stood an old shanty with a rusted tin roof. The sides of the ramshackle house were grayed from years of weathering, and several windows needed to be repaired, their screens torn or rusted or missing altogether. Killian glanced over at Sam in surprise.

"I told you before—Susannah insists upon living in this place. Why, I don't know," Sam muttered. "It needs a heap of fixin' to be livable, if you ask me." He stuffed his hands into the pockets of his coveralls. "Come on. The herb garden is on the other side of the house."

Susannah sank her long fingers into the welcoming black warmth of the fertile soil. Then, taking a clump of chives, she placed it in the hole she'd dug. The inconstant breeze was dying down now that dusk had arrived. She heard the singing of the birds, a peaceful reminder that no one was nearby. A red-breasted robin flew to the white picket fence that enclosed the large herb garden. Almost immediately he began to chirp excitedly, fluttering his wings.

It was a warning. Susannah quickly looked around, feeling vulnerable with her back turned toward whoever was approaching. Her father rounded the corner of the house, then her heart began beating harder. There was a stranger—a man—with him.

Ordinarily Susannah would have run, but in an instant the man's steely blue gaze met and held her own, and something told her to stay where she was. Remaining on her knees in the soil, Susannah watched their progress toward her.

The man's catlike eyes held on hers, but instead

of the naked fear she usually felt at a stranger's approach since coming out of the coma, Susannah felt an odd sizzle of apprehension. But what kind? His face was hard-looking, revealing no hint of emotion in his eyes or the set of his mouth. His hair was black and military-short, and his skin was deeply bronzed by the sun. Her heart started to hammer in warning.

Her father greeted her with a smile. "Susannah, I've brought a friend to introduce to you. Come on, honey, come over and meet him."

The stranger's oddly opaque gaze held her suspended. Susannah gulped convulsively and set the chives aside. Her fingers were stained dark from the soil, and the jeans she wore were thick with dust. Slowly, beneath his continued inspection, Susannah forced herself to her bare feet. The power of the stranger's gaze, the anger she saw in the depths of his eyes, held her captive.

"Susannah?" Sam prodded gently as he halted at the gate and opened it. "Honey, he won't hurt you. Come on over..."

"No," Killian said, his voice hoarse. "Let her be. Let her get used to me."

Sam gave him a quizzical look, but said nothing.

Killian wasn't breathing. Air seemed to have jammed in his chest. Susannah was more than beautiful; she was ethereal. Her straight sable-colored hair flowed around her slender form, almost touching her breasts. Her simple white cotton blouse and jeans enhanced her figure. Killian could see no outward signs of the violence she'd endured, although at some point in her life her nose had been broken. The bump was prominent, and he wondered about the story behind it. Her lips were full, and slightly parted now. But it was her eyes—large, expressive, dove gray—that entranced him the most.

Who is he? Why is he looking at me like that? Susannah looked down at herself. Sure, her jeans were dirty, but she had been gardening all day. Her feet, too, were covered with soil. Automatically she raised a hand to touch the front of her blouse. Was one of her buttons undone? No. Again she raised her head and met those eyes that, though emotionless, nonetheless drew her. There was a sense of armor around him that startled her. A hard, impervious shell of self-protection. She'd often sensed the same quality around her handicapped children when they first started school—a need to protect themselves against the all-too-common hurts they were subjected to. But there was more than that to this man's bearing, Susannah realized as she allowed her intuition to take over. She also sensed a darkness, a sadness, around this tall, lean man, who was probably in his mid-thirties. He felt edgy to her, and it set her on edge, too. Who was he? Another police detective from Lexington, come to grill her? To try to jar loose her frozen memory? Susannah's hands grew damp with apprehension. This man frightened her in a new and unknown way. Maybe it was that unexpected anger banked in his eyes.

Killian used all his senses, finely honed over years of dangerous work, to take in Susannah. He saw her fine nostrils quiver and flare, as if she were a wary young deer ready for flight. He felt the fear rise around her, broadcast in every line of her tension-held body. Meg's once-beautiful face floated in front of him. The terror he'd felt as he stood at her hospital bedside as she became conscious for the first time since the blast slammed back into him. Smiling didn't come easily to him, but he'd forced one then for Meg's benefit, and it had made all the difference in the world. She'd reached out and weakly gripped his hand and begun to cry, but to Killian it had been a good sign, a sign that she wanted to live.

Now, for Susannah's benefit, Killian forced the corners of his mouth upward as he saw terror come to her widening eyes. Although he was angry at Morgan, he didn't need to take it out on her. Almost instantly he saw the tension on her face dissipate.

Fighting the screaming awareness of his emotional response to Susannah, Killian said to Sam in a low voice, "Go ahead and make the introduction, and then leave us. I don't think she's going to run."

Scratching his head, Sam nodded. "Darned if I don't believe you. For some reason, she ain't as afraid of you as all the rest."

Killian barely nodded as he continued to hold Susannah's assessing stare. Her arms were held tightly at her sides. Her fingers were long and artistic-looking. She seemed more like a girl in her teens—barefoot and in touch with the magic of the Earth—than a schoolteacher of twenty-seven.

"Honey, this is Mr. Killian," Sam said gently to his daughter. "He's a friend of Morgan's, come to stay with us and rest up for a month or so. Ma and I said he could stay. He's a friend, honey. Not a stranger. Do you understand?"

Susannah nodded slowly, never taking her eyes off Killian.

What is your first name? The words were there,

on the tip of her tongue, but they refused to be given voice. Frustration thrummed through Susannah. How she ached to speak again—but some invisible hand held her tongue-tied. Killian's mouth had curved into the barest of smiles, sending an odd heat sheeting through her. Shaken by his presence, Susannah could only nod, her hands laced shyly together in front of her. Still, she was wary. It wasn't something she could just automatically turn off.

Killian was excruciatingly uncomfortable, and he wanted to get the social amenities over with. "Thanks, Sam," he said brusquely.

Sam's gaze moved from his daughter to Killian and back to her. "Honey, supper's in a hour. Ma would like you to join us. Will you?"

Susannah felt her heartbeat picking up again, beating wildly with apprehension over this man named Killian—a male stranger who had come to disrupt the silent world where she'd retreated to be healed. She glanced down at her feet and then lifted her chin.

I don't know. I don't know, Pa. Let me see how I feel. Susannah was disappointed with herself. All she could do was shrug delicately. Ordinarily she carried a pen and paper with her in order to communicate with her folks, or friends of the family who stopped to visit. But today, not expecting visitors, she'd left her pad and pen back at the house.

"Good enough," Sam told her gruffly. "Maybe you'll let Killian walk you back afterward."

Killian stood very still after Sam disappeared. He saw the nervousness and curiosity reflected in Susannah's wide eyes—and suddenly he almost grinned at the irony of their situation. He was normally a person of few words, and for the first time in his life he was going to have to carry the conversation. He spread his hand out in a gesture of peace.

"I hope I didn't stop you from planting."

No, you didn't. Susannah glanced sharply down at the chives. She knelt and began to cover the roots before they dried out. As she worked, she keyed her hearing to where the man stood, outside the gate. Every once in a while, she glanced up. Each time she did, he was still standing there, motionless, hands in the pockets of his jeans, an old, beat-up leather jacket hanging loosely on his lean frame. His serious features were set, and she sensed an unhappiness radiating from him. About what? Being here? Meeting her? So many things didn't make sense to her. If he was one of Morgan's friends, why would he be unhappy about being here? If he was here for a vacation, he should be relaxed.

Killian caught Susannah's inquiring gaze. Then, dusting off her hands, she continued down the row, pulling weeds. The breeze gently blew strands of her thick hair across her shoulders, framing her face.

Although he hadn't moved, Killian's eyes were active, sizing up the immediate vicinity—the possible entrances to the shanty and the layout of the surrounding meadow. His gaze moved back to Susannah, who continued acting guarded, nearly ignoring him. She was probably hoping he'd go away and leave her alone, he thought wryly. God knew, he'd like to do exactly that. His anger toward Morgan grew in volume.

"I haven't seen a woman in bare feet since I left Ireland," he finally offered in a low, clipped tone. No, conversation wasn't his forte.

Susannah stopped weeding and jerked a look in his

direction. Killian crossed to sit on the grassy bank, his arms around his knees, his gaze still on her.

As if women can't go with their shoes off!

Killian saw the disgust in her eyes. Desperately he cast about for some way to lessen the tension between them. As long as she distrusted him, he wouldn't be able to get close enough to protect her. Inwardly Killian cursed Morgan.

Forcing himself to try again, he muttered, "That wasn't an insult. Just an observation. My sister, Meg, who's about your age, always goes barefoot in the garden, too." He gestured toward the well-kept plants. "Looks like you give them a lot of attention. Meg always said plants grew best when you gave them love." Just talking about Meg, even to this wary, silent audience of one, eased some of his pain for his sister.

You know how I feel! Weeds in her hands, Susannah straightened, surprised by the discovery. Killian had seen her facial expression and read it accurately. Hope rushed through her. Her mother and father, as dearly as they loved her, couldn't seem to read her feelings at all since she'd come out of the coma. But suddenly this lanky, tightly coiled stranger with the sky-blue eyes, black hair and soft, hesitant smile could.

Are you a psychiatrist? I hope not. Susannah figured she'd been through enough testing to last her a lifetime. Older men with glasses and beards had pronounced her hysterical due to her trauma and said it was the reason she couldn't speak. Her fingers tightened around the weeds as she stood beneath Killian's cool, expressionless inspection.

Killian saw the tension in Susannah's features dissolve for just an instant. He'd touched her, and he knew it. Frustrated and unsure of her reaction to him, he tried again, but his voice came out cold. "Weeds make good compost. Do you have a compost pile around here?"

Susannah looked intensely at this unusual man, feeling him instead of listening to his words, which he seemed to have mouthed in desperation. Ordinarily, if she'd met Killian on a busy street, he would have frightened her. His face was lean, like the rest of him, and his nose was large and straight, with a good space between his slightly arched eyebrows. There was an intense alertness in those eyes that reminded her of a cougar. And although he had offered that scant smile initially, his eyes contained a hardness that Susannah had never seen in her life. Since the incident that had changed her life, she had come to rely heavily on her intuitive abilities to ferret out people's possible ulterior motives toward her. The hospital therapist had called it paranoia. But in this case, Susannah sensed that a great sadness had settled around Killian like a cloak. And danger.

Why danger? And is it danger to me? He did *look* dangerous, there was no doubt. Susannah couldn't find one telltale sign in his features of humanity or emotion. But her fear warred with an image she couldn't shake, the image of the sad but crooked smile that had made him appear vulnerable for one split second out of time.

Chapter 2

Killian watched Susannah walk slowly and cautiously through the garden gate. She was about three feet away from him now, and he probed her for signs of wariness. He had no wish to minimize her guardedness toward him—if he could keep her at arm's length and do his job, this assignment might actually work out. If he couldn't...

Just the way Susannah moved snagged a sharp stab of longing deep within him. She had the grace of a ballet dancer, her hips swaying slightly as she stepped delicately across the rows of healthy plants. He decided not to follow her, wanting to allow her more time to adjust to his presence. Just then a robin, sitting on the fence near Killian, took off and landed in the top of an old, gnarled apple tree standing alone just outside the garden. Instantly there was a fierce cheeping, and

Killian cocked his head to one side. A half-grown baby robin was perched precariously on the limb near the nest, fluttering his wings demandingly as the parent hovered nearby with food in his beak.

Killian sensed Susannah's presence and slowly turned his head. She was standing six feet away, watching him pointedly. There was such beauty in her shadowed gray eyes. Killian recognized that shadow— Meg's eyes were marred by the same look.

"That baby robin is going to fall off that limb if he isn't careful."

Yes, he is. Yesterday he did, and I had to pick him up and put him back in the tree. Frustrated by her inability to speak the words, Susannah nodded and wiped her hands against her thighs. Once again she found herself wanting her notepad and pen. He was a stranger and couldn't be trusted, a voice told her. Still, he was watching the awkward progress of the baby robin with concern.

Unexpectedly the baby robin shrieked. Susannah opened her mouth to cry out, but only a harsh, strangulated sound came forth as the small bird fluttered helplessly down through the branches of the apple tree and hit the ground roughly, tumbling end over end. When the baby regained his composure, he began to scream for help, and both parents flew around and around him.

Without thinking, Susannah rushed past Killian to rescue the bird, as she had yesterday.

"No," Killian whispered, reaching out to stop Susannah. "I'll do it." Her skin was smooth and sunwarmed beneath his fingers, and instantly Killian released her, the shock of the touch startling not only him, but her, too.

Susannah gasped, jerking back, her mouth opened in shock. Her skin seemed to tingle where his fingers had briefly, carefully grasped her wrist.

Taken aback by her reaction, Killian glared at her, then immediately chastised himself. After all, didn't he want her to remain fearful of him? Inside, though, his heart winced at the terror he saw in her gaze, at the contorted shape of her lips as she stared up at him—as if he was her assailant. His action had been rash, he thought angrily. Somehow Susannah's presence had caught him off guard. Infuriated by his own blind re-actions, Killian stood there at a loss for words.

Susannah saw disgust in Killian's eyes, and then, on its heels, a gut-wrenching sadness. Still stunned by his swift touch, she backed even farther away from him. Finally the robin's plaintive cheeping impinged on her shocked senses, and she tore her attention from Killian, pointing at the baby robin now hopping around on the ground.

"Yeah. Okay, I'll get the bird," Killian muttered crossly. He was furious with himself, at the unexpected emotions that brief touch had aroused. For the most fleeting moment, his heart jumped at the thought of what it would feel like to kiss Susannah until she was breathless with need of him. Thoroughly disgusted that the thought had even entered his head, Killian moved rapidly to rescue the baby bird. What woman would be interested in him? He was a dark introvert of a man, given to very little communication. A man haunted by a past that at any moment could avalanche into his pres-ent and effectively destroy a woman who thought she might care for him. No, he was dangerous—a bomb ready to explode—and he was damned if he was going to put any woman in the line of fire.

As he leaned down and trapped the robin carefully between his hands, the two parents flew overhead, shrieking, trying to protect their baby. Gently Killian cupped the captured baby, lifting the feathered tyke and staring into his shiny black eyes.

"Next time some cat might find you first and think you're a tasty supper," he warned sternly as he turned toward the apple tree. Placing the bird in his shirt pocket, he grabbed a low branch and began to climb.

Susannah stood below, watching Killian's lithe progress. Everything about the man was methodical. He never stepped on a weak limb; he studied the situation thoroughly before placing each foot to push himself upward toward the nest. Yet, far from plodding, he had an easy masculine grace.

Killian settled the robin in its nest and quickly made his way down to avoid the irate parents. Leaping the last few feet, he landed with the grace of a large cat. "Well, our good deed is done for the day," he said gruffly, dusting off his hands.

His voice was as icy as his unrelenting features, and Susannah took another step away from him.

Thank you for rescuing the baby. But how can such a hard man perform such a gentle feat? What's your story, Killian? His eyes turned impatient under her inspection, and Susannah tore her gaze away from him. The man had something to hide, it seemed.

How much more do you know about me? What did my folks tell you? Susannah felt an odd sort of shame at the thought of Killian knowing what had happened to her. Humiliation, too, coupled with anger and fear—

the entire gamut of feelings she'd lived with daily since the shooting. Out of nervousness, she raised a hand to her cheek, which felt hot and flushed.

Killian noted the hurt in Susannah's eyes as she self-consciously brushed her cheek with her fingertips. And in that moment he saw the violence's lasting damage: loss of self-esteem. She was afraid of him, and part of him ached at the unfairness of it, but he accepted his fate bitterly. Let Susannah think him untrustworthy—dangerous. Those instincts might save her life, should her assailant show up for another try at killing her.

"I need to wash my hands," he said brusquely, desperate to break the tension between them. He had to snap out of it. He couldn't afford to allow her to affect him—and possibly compromise his ability to protect her from a killer.

Unexpectedly Susannah felt tears jam into her eyes. She stood there in abject surprise as they rolled down her cheeks, unbidden, seemingly tapped from some deep source within her. Why was she crying? She hadn't cried since coming out of the coma! Embarrassed that Killian was watching her, a disgruntled look on his face, Susannah raised trembling hands to her cheeks.

Killian swayed—and caught himself. Every fiber of his being wanted to reach out and comfort Susannah. The tears, small, sun-touched crystals, streamed down her flushed cheeks. The one thing he couldn't bear was to see a woman cry. A weeping child he could handle, but somehow, when a woman cried, it was different. Different, and gut-wrenchingly disturbing. Meg's tears had torn him apart, her cries shredding what was left of his feelings.

Looking down at Susannah now, Killian felt frus-

tration and disgust at his inability to comfort her. But
that edge, that distrust, had to stay in place if he was
to do his job.

Turning away abruptly, he looked around for a garden hose, for anything, really, that would give him an
excuse to escape her nearness. Spying a hose leading from the side of the house, he turned on his heel
and strode toward the faucet. Relief flowed through
him as he put distance between them, the tightened
muscles in his shoulders and back loosening. Trying
to shake pangs of guilt for abandoning her, Killian
leaned down and turned on the faucet. He washed his
hands rapidly, then wiped them on the thighs of his
jeans as he straightened.

He glanced back toward Susannah who still stood
near the garden, looking alone and unprotected. As he
slowly walked back to where she stood, he thrust his
hands into the pockets of his jeans. "It's almost time for
dinner," he said gruffly. "I'm hungry. Are you coming?"

Susannah felt hollow inside. The tears had left her
terribly vulnerable, and right now she needed human
company more than usual. Killian's harsh company
felt abrasive to her in her fragile emotional state, and
she knew she'd have to endure walking through the orchard to her folks' house with him. She forced herself
to look into his dark, angry features. This mute life of
pad and pencil was unbelievably frustrating. Normally
she believed mightily in communicating and confront-
ing problems, and without a voice, it was nearly impossible to be herself. The old Susannah would have
asked Killian what his problem with her was. Instead
she merely gestured for him to follow her.

Killian maintained a discreet distance from Susannah as they wound their way through the orchard on the well-trodden path. He wanted to ask Susannah's forgiveness for having abandoned her earlier—to explain why he had to keep her at arm's length. But then he laughed derisively at himself. Susannah would never understand. No woman would. He noticed that as they walked Susannah's gaze was never still, constantly searching the area, as if she were expecting to be attacked. It hurt him to see her in that mode. The haunted look in her eyes tore at him. Her beautiful mouth was pursed, the corners drawn taut, as if she expected a blow at any moment.

Not while I'm alive will another person ever *harm you,* he promised grimly. Killian slowed his pace, baffled at the intensity of the feeling that came with the thought. The sun shimmered through the leaves of the fruit trees, scattering light across the green grass in a patchwork-quilt effect, touching Susannah's hair and bringing red highlights to life, intermixed with threads of gold. Killian wondered obliquely if she had some Irish blood in her.

In the Andersons' kitchen, Killian noted the way Susannah gratefully absorbed her mother's obvious care and genuine concern. He watched the sparkle come back to her lovely gray eyes as Pansy doted over her. Susannah had withdrawn into herself on their walk to the farmhouse. Now Killian watched her reemerge from that private, silent world, coaxed out by touches and hugs from her parents.

He'd made her retreat, and he felt like hell about it. But there could be no ambiguity about his function here at the farm. Sitting at the table now, his hand around a mug of steaming coffee, Killian tried to protect himself against the emotional warmth that pervaded the kitchen. The odors of home-cooked food, fresh and lovingly prepared, reminded him of a far gentler time in his life, the time when he was growing up in Ireland. There hadn't been many happy times in Killian's life, but that had been one—his mother doting over him and Meg, the lighthearted lilt of her laughter, the smell of fresh bread baking in the oven, her occasional touch upon his shoulder or playful ruffling of his hair. Groaning, he blindly gulped his coffee, and nearly burned his mouth in the process.

Susannah washed her hands at the kitchen sink, slowly dried them, and glanced apprehensively over at Killian. He sat at the table like a dark, unhappy shadow, his hand gripping the coffee mug. She was trying to understand him, but it was impossible. Her mother smiled at him, and tried to cajole a hint of a reaction from Killian, but he seemed impervious to human interaction.

As Pansy served the dinner, Killian tried to ignore the fact that he was seated opposite Susannah. She had an incredible ability to communicate with just a glance from those haunting eyes. Killian held on tightly to his anger at the thought that she had almost died.

"Why, you're lookin' so much better," Pansy gushed to her daughter as she placed mashed potatoes, spareribs and a fresh garden salad on the table.

Susannah nodded and smiled for her mother's sake. Just sitting across from Killian was unnerving. But because she loved her mother and father fiercely she was trying to ignore Killian's cold, icy presence and act normally.

Sam smiled and passed his daughter the platter of

ribs. "Do you think you'll get along with Killian hereabouts for a while?"

Susannah felt Killian's eyes on her and refused to look up, knowing that he was probably studying her with the icy gaze of a predator for his intended victim. She glanced over at her father, whose face was open and readable, and found the strength somewhere within herself to lie. A white lie, Susannah told herself as she forced a smile and nodded.

Killian ate slowly, allowing his senses to take in the cheerful kitchen and happy family setting. The scents of barbecued meat and thick brown gravy and the tart smell of apples baking in the oven were sweeter than any perfume.

"I don't know what you did," Pansy told Killian, "but whatever it is, Susannah looks so much better! Doesn't she, Sam?"

Spooning gravy onto a heaping portion of mashed potatoes, Sam glanced up. "Ma, you know how uncomfortable Susannah gets when we talk as if she's not here."

Chastened, Pansy smiled. "I'm sorry, dear," she said, giving her daughter a fond look and a pat on the arm in apology.

Susannah wondered glumly how she could possibly look better with Killian around. Without a doubt, the man made her uncomfortable. She decided it was just that her mother wanted to see her looking better. Aching inwardly, Susannah thought how terribly the past three months had worn down her folks. They had both aged noticeably, and it hurt her to realize that her stupid, failed foray into the "big" world outside Kentucky had cost them, too. If only she hadn't been so naive about the world, it might not have happened, and her parents might not have had to suffer this way. Luckily, her school insurance had covered the massive medical bills; Susannah knew her folks would have sold the farm, if necessary, to help her cover expenses.

"Let's talk about you, Killian," Pansy said brightly, turning the conversation to him.

Killian saw Susannah's eyes suddenly narrow upon him, filled with curiosity—and some indefinable emotion that set his pulse to racing. He hesitated, not wanting to sound rude. "Ordinarily, Pansy, I don't open up to anyone."

"Whatever for?"

Sam groaned. "Honey, the man's got a right to some privacy, don't he?"

Pansy laughed. "Now, Pa…"

Clearing his throat, Killian moved the mashed potatoes around on his blue-and-white plate. He realized he wasn't going to be able to get around Pansy's good-natured probing. "I work in the area of high security." The explanation came out gruffly—a warning, he hoped, for her to stop asking questions.

"Surely," Pansy said, with a gentle laugh, "you can tell me if you're married or not. Or about your family?"

Tension hung in the air. Killian put down his fork, keeping a tight rein on his reaction to what he knew was a well-intentioned question. Sam shot him an apologetic look that spoke volumes, but Killian also saw Susannah's open interest. She'd stopped eating, and was waiting to hear his answer.

Killian felt heat creeping up his neck and into his cheeks. Pain at the memory of his family sheared through him. He dropped his gaze to the uneaten food on his plate and felt an avalanche of unexpected grief that seemed to suck the life out of him momentarily. Unwillingly he looked up—and met Susannah's compassionate gaze.

Killian shoved his chair back, and the scraping sound shattered the tension. "Excuse me," he rasped, "I'm done eating."

Susannah saw pain in Killian's eyes and heard the roughness of emotion in his voice as he moved abruptly to his feet. The chair nearly tipped over backward, but he caught it in time. Without a sound, Killian stalked from the kitchen.

"Oh, dear," Pansy whispered, her fingers against her lips. "I didn't mean to upset him…"

Susannah reached out and gripped her mother's hand. She might not be able to talk, but she could at least offer the reassurance of touch.

Sam cleared his throat. "Ma, he's a closed kind of man. Didn't you see that?"

Pansy shrugged weakly and patted her daughter's hand. "Oh, I guess I did, Sam, but you know me— I'm such a busybody. Maybe I should go after him and apologize."

"Just let him be, Ma, and he'll come around," Sam counseled gently.

"I don't know," Pansy whispered, upset. "When I asked him about his family, did you see his face?"

Susannah nodded and released her mother's hand. As she continued to finish her meal, she ruminated on that very point. Killian had reacted violently to the question, anguished pain momentarily shadowing his eyes. Susannah had found herself wanting to reach out and reassure him that all would be well. But would it?

Morosely Susannah forced herself to finish eating her dinner. Somehow she wanted to let her mother know that there had been nothing wrong with her questions to Killian. As she had so many times these past months, she wished she could talk. Pansy was just a warm, chatty person by nature, but Susannah understood Killian's discomfort over such questions. Still, she wanted to try to communicate with Killian. She would use the excuse that he could walk her home, since it would be nearly dark. Her father never allowed her to walk home alone at night. At the same time, Susannah felt fear at being alone with him.

What was there about him that made her want to know him? He was a stranger who'd walked into her life only a few hours ago. The fact that he was Morgan's friend meant something, of course. From what her cousin Laura had told her, she knew that Morgan Trayhern drew only loyal, responsible people to him. Still, they were hard men, mercenaries. Susannah had no experience with mercenaries. In fact, she had very little experience with men in general, and especially with men her own age. She felt she wasn't equal to the task of healing the rift between her mother and Killian, but she knew she had to try. Otherwise, her mother would be a nervous wreck every time Killian sat down to eat. No, something had to be done to calm the troubled waters.

Killian was sitting in the living room, pretending to watch television, when he saw Susannah come out of the kitchen. He barely met her gaze as she walked determinedly toward him with a piece of paper in her hand. He saw uncertainty in her eyes—and something else that he couldn't have defined. Knowing that his abruptness had already caused bad feelings, he tensed as she drew close enough to hand him the note.

Walk me home. Please?

Killian lifted his head and studied her darkly. There was such vulnerability to Susannah—and that was what had nearly gotten her killed. Killian couldn't help but respond to the silent plea in her eyes as she stood waiting for his answer.

Without a word, he crushed the note in his hand, got to his feet and headed toward the door. He would use this excuse to check out her house and the surrounding area. When he opened the door for her, she brushed by him, and he felt himself tense. The sweet, fragrant scent of her perfume momentarily encircled him, and he unconsciously inhaled the subtle scent.

It was dusk, the inky stains across the early-autumn sky telling Killian it would soon be dark. As he slowly walked Susannah back to her house, his ears were tuned in to the twilight for any out-of-the-ordinary sounds. He needed to adjust his senses to the normal sounds of this countryside, anyway. Until then, he would have to be even more alert than normal. There were no unusual odors on the fragrant air, and he couldn't ferret out anything unusual visually as he restlessly scanned the orchard.

When they reached her home, Killian realized that it had no electricity. He stood just inside the door and watched as Susannah lit a hurricane lamp filled with kerosene. She placed one lamp on the wooden table, another on the mantel over the fireplace, and a third in the living room. The floorboards, old and gray, creaked beneath her bare feet as she moved about. Uneasy at how little protection the house afforded against a possible intruder, Killian watched her pull open a drawer of an oak hutch.

Susannah located a notebook and pen and gestured for Killian to come and sit down with her at the table. Mystified, Killian sat down tensely at Susannah's elbow while she wrote on the notepad.

When she'd finished writing, she turned the notepad around so that Killian could read her question. The light from the kerosene lamp cast a soft glow around the deeply shadowed kitchen.

Killian eyed the note. "Is Killian my first or last name?" he read aloud. He grimaced and reared back on two legs of the chair. "It's my last name. Everyone calls me by my last name."

Susannah made a frustrated sound and penned another note.

What is your first name?

Killian scowled heavily and considered her request. Morgan's orders sounded demandingly in his brain. He was to try to get Susannah to remember what her assailant looked like. If he remained too cool and unresponsive to her, she wouldn't want to try to cooperate with him. Yet to reveal himself would be as good as opening up his horrifying past once again. That had happened once before, with terrible results, and he'd vowed it would never happen again. Dammit, anyway! He rubbed his mouth with his hand, feeling trapped. He had to gain Susannah's cooperation. Her trust.

"Sean," he snarled.

Susannah winced, but determinedly wrote another note.

Who do you allow to call you Sean?

Killian stared at the note. Despite Susannah's obvious softness and vulnerability, for the first time he noticed a look of stubbornness in her eyes. He frowned.

"My mother and sister called me by my first name. Just them," he muttered.

Susannah digested his admission. Maybe he used his last name to prevent people getting close to him. But evidently there were at least two women in his life who could reach inside those armored walls and get to him. There was hope, Susannah decided, if Killian allowed his family to use his first name. But she'd heard the warning in his voice when he'd spoken to her mother. She might be a hill woman, and not as worldly as he was, but surely it wasn't unreasonable to expect good manners—even from a mercenary. She held his blunt stare and felt the fear and anger seething around him. That cold armored cloak was firmly in place.

Grimly Susannah penned another note.

My mother didn't mean to make you uncomfortable. If you can find some way to say something to her to defuse the situation, I'd be grateful. She meant well. She didn't mean to chase you from the dinner table.

Killian stared at her printed note for a long time. The silence thickened. Susannah was right; he'd been wrong in his reaction to the situation. He wished he had the words, a way to explain himself. Frustration overwhelmed him. Looking up, he thought for a moment that he might drown in her compassionate gray gaze. Quirking his mouth, he muttered, "When I go back down tonight, I'll tell her I'm sorry."

Susannah smiled slightly and nodded her head.

Thank you. I know so little of Morgan's men.
None of us know anything about mercenaries. I
hope you can forgive us, too?

Steeling himself against Susannah's attempt to
smooth things over, Killian nodded. "Don't worry
about it. There's nothing to forgive." He started to get
up, but she made an inarticulate sound and reached
out, her hand closing around his arm. Killian froze.

Susannah's lips parted when she saw anguish replace
the coldness in Killian's eyes as she touched him. She
hadn't meant to reach out like that; it had been instinc-
tive. Somewhere in her heart, she knew that Killian
needed touching—a lot of it. She knew all too well
through her work the value of touching, the healing
quality of a hand upon a shoulder to give necessary support and courage. Hard as he appeared to be, was Killian
really any different? Gazing up through the dim light
in the kitchen, she saw the tortured look in his eyes.

Thinking that he was repulsed by her touch, she
quickly released him.

Killian slowly sat back, his heart hammering in his
chest. It was hell trying to keep his feelings at bay.
Whether he liked it or not, he could almost read what
Susannah was thinking in her expressive eyes. Their
soft gray reminded him of a mourning dove—and she
was as gentle and delicate as one.

My folks are simple people, Killian. Pa said you
were here for a rest. Is that true? If so, for how long?

Killian felt utterly trapped, and he longed to escape. Morgan was expecting the impossible of him. He didn't have the damnable ability to walk with one foot as a protector and the other foot emotionally far enough away from Susannah to do his job. The patient look on her face only aggravated him.

"I'm between missions," he bit out savagely. "And I want to rest somewhere quiet. I'll try to be a better house guest, okay?"

I know you're uncomfortable around me. I don't expect anything from you. I'll be staying up here most of the time, so you'll have the space to rest.

Absolute frustration thrummed through Killian. This was exactly what he *didn't* want! "Look," he growled, "you don't make me uncomfortable, okay? I know what happened to you, and I'm sorry it happened. I have a sister, who—"

Susannah tilted her head as he snapped his mouth shut and glared at her. He wanted to run. It was in every line of his body, and it was in his eyes. The tension in the kitchen had become a tangible thing.

Who what?

Agitated, Killian shot to his feet. He roamed around the kitchen in the semidarkness, seesawing back and forth about what—if anything—he should tell her. She sat quietly, watching him, without any outward sign of impatience. Running his fingers through his hair, he turned suddenly and pinned her with an angry look.

"My sister, Meg, was nearly killed in a situation

not unlike yours," he ground out finally. "She's disfigured for life, and she's scared. She lives alone, like a recluse. I've seen what violence has done to her, so I can imagine what it's done to you." He'd said enough. More than enough, judging from the tears that suddenly were shimmering in Susannah's eyes.

Breathing hard, Killian continued to glare at her, hoping she would give up. He didn't want her asking him any more personal questions. Hell, he hadn't intended to bring up Meg! But something about this woman kept tugging at him, pulling him out of his isolation.

I'm sorry for Meg. For you. I've seen what the violence to me has done to my folks. It's awful. It's forever.

As Killian read the note, standing near the table, his shoulders sagged, and all the anger went out of him. "Yes," he whispered wearily, "violence is wrong. All it does is tear people's lives apart." How well he knew that—in more ways than he ever wanted to admit.

If you're a mercenary, then you're always fighting a war, aren't you?

The truth was like a knife in Killian's clenched gut. He stood, arms at his sides, and hung his head as he pondered her simple question. "Mercenaries work in many capacities," he said slowly. "Some of them are very safe and low-risk. But they do deal with violent situations, too." He lifted his head and threw her a warning look. "The more you do it, the more you become it."

Are you always in dangerous situations?

He picked up the note, then slowly crushed it in his hand. Susannah was getting too close. That just couldn't happen. For her sake, it couldn't. Killian arranged his face into the deadliest look he could muster. "More than anything," he told her in a soft rasp, "you should understand that I'm dangerous to you."

It was all the warning Killian could give her short of telling what had happened when one woman *had* gotten to him, touched his heart, made him feel love. He'd sworn he'd never tell anyone that—not even Meg. And he'd vowed never to let it happen again. Susannah was too special, too vulnerable, for him to allow her to get close to him. But she had a kind of courage that frightened Killian; she had the guts to approach someone like him—someone so wounded that he could never be healed.

"I'll see you tomorrow morning," he said abruptly. He scanned the room closely with one sweeping gaze, then glanced down at her. "Because I'm a mercenary, I'm going to check out your house and the surrounding area. I'll be outside after I make a sweep of the house, and then I'll be staying at your folks' place, in the guest bedroom." He rubbed his jaw as he took in the poor condition of the window, which had no screen and no lock. "If you hear anything, come and get me."

I've been living here the last month and nothing has happened. I'll be okay.

Naiveté at best, Killian thought as he read her note. But he couldn't tell her she was in danger—good old

Morgan's orders again. His mouth flattening, he stared across the table into her weary eyes. "If you need help, come and get me. Understand?" As much as he wanted to stay nearby to protect Susannah, Killian knew he couldn't possibly move in with her without a darn good explanation for her and her parents. He was hamstrung. And he didn't want to have to live under Susannah's roof, anyway, for very different reasons. As much as he hated to leave her unprotected at the homestead, for now he had no choice.

At least Susannah would remain safe from him, Killian thought as he studied her darkly. His mind shouted that he'd be absolutely useless sleeping down at the Anderson house if the killer tried to reach her here. But what could he do? Torn, he decided that for tonight, he would sleep at the Andersons' and ponder the problem.

With a bare nod, Susannah took in Killian's vibrating warning. He had told her he was a violent man. She sensed the lethal quality about him, and yet those brief flashes she'd had of him without his defenses in place made her believe that deep down he longed for peace, not war.

Chapter 3

As she bathed and prepared to go to bed, Susannah tried to sift through her jumbled feelings. Killian disturbed her, she decided, more than he frightened her. Somehow she was invisibly drawn to him—to the inner man, not the cold exterior he held up like a shield. She pulled her light knee-length cotton gown over her head and tamed her tangled hair with her fingers. The lamplight cast dancing shadows across the opposite wall of the small bathroom. Ordinarily, catching sight of moving silhouettes caused her to start, but tonight it didn't.

Why? Picking up her clothes, Susannah walked thoughtfully through the silent house, the old planks beneath the thin linoleum floor creaking occasionally. Could Killian's unsettling presence somehow have given her a sense of safety? Even if it was an edgy kind of safety? Despite his glowering and his snappish words, Susannah sensed he would help her if she ever found herself in trouble.

With a shake of her head, Susannah dumped her clothes into a hamper in the small side room and made her way toward the central portion of the two-story house. At least four generations of Andersons had lived here, and that in itself gave her a sense of safety. There was something about the old and the familiar that had always meant tranquility to Susannah, and right now she needed that sense as never before.

She went into the kitchen, where the hurricane lamp still threw its meager light. Pictures drawn in crayon wreathed the walls of the area—fond reminders of her most recent class of children. Last year's class. The pictures suggested hope, and Susannah could vividly recall each child's face as she surveyed the individual drawings. They gave her a sense that maybe her life hadn't been completely shattered after all.

Leaning down, Susannah blew out the flame in the lamp, and darkness cloaked the room, making her suddenly edgy. It had been shadowy the night she'd walked from her bus toward the brightly lit central station—she could remember that clearly. She could recall, too, flashbacks of the man who had been killed in front of her. He'd been sharply dressed, with an engaging smile, and he'd approached her as if she were a longtime friend. She'd trusted him—found him attractive, to be honest. She'd smiled and allowed him to take the large carry-on bag that hung from her shoulder. With a shudder, Susannah tried to block the horrifying end to his brief contact with her. Pressing her fingers against her closed eyes, she felt the first signs of one of the massive migraines that seemed to come and go without much warning begin to stalk her.

As she made her way to her bedroom, at the rear of the house—moving around familiar shapes in the dark—Susannah vaguely wondered why Killian's unexpected presence hadn't triggered one of her crippling headaches. He was dangerous, her mind warned her sharply. He'd told her so himself, in the sort of warning growl a cougar might give an approaching hunter. As she pulled back the crisp white sheet and the worn quilt that served as her bedspread, Susannah's heart argued with her practical mind. Killian must have lived through some terrible, traumatic events to project that kind of iciness. As Susannah slid into bed, fluffed her pillow and closed her eyes, she released a long, ragged sigh. Luckily, sleep always cured her headaches, and she was more tired than usual tonight.

Despite her physical weariness, Susannah saw Killian's hard, emotionless face waver before her closed eyes. There wasn't an iota of gentleness anywhere in his features. Yet, as she searched his stormy dark blue eyes, eyes that shouted to everyone to leave him alone, Susannah felt such sadness around him that tears stung her own eyes. Sniffing, she laughed to herself. How easily touched she was! And how much she missed her children. School had started without her, and she was missing a new class of frightened, unsure charges she knew would slowly come out of their protective shells and begin to reach out and touch life.

Unhappily Susannah thought of the doctors' warnings that it would be at least two months before she could possibly go back to teaching. Her world, as she had known it, no longer existed. Where once she'd been trusting of people, now she was not. Darkness had always been her friend—but now it disturbed her. Forcing herself to shut off her rambling thoughts, Susannah concentrated on sleep. Her last images were of Killian, and the sadness that permeated him.

A distinct click awakened Susannah. She froze beneath the sheet and blanket, listening. Her heart rate tripled, and her mouth grew dry. The light of a first-quarter moon spilled in the open window at the head of her old brass bed. The window's screen had been torn loose years ago and never repaired, Susannah knew. Terror coursed through her as she lay still, her muscles aching with fear.

Another click. Carefully, trying not to make a sound, Susannah lifted her head and looked toward the window opposite her bed. A scream jammed in her throat. The profile of a man was silhouetted against the screen. A cry, rooted deep in her lungs, started up through her. Vignettes of the murderer who had nearly taken her life, a man with a narrow face, small eyes and a crooked mouth, smashed into her. If she hadn't been so frightened, Susannah would have rejoiced at finally recalling his face. But now sweat bathed her, and her nightgown grew damp and clung to her as she gripped the sheet, her knuckles whitening.

Breathing raggedly, she watched with widening eyes as the silhouette moved. It wasn't her imagination! The shriek that had lodged in her chest exploded upward. A sound, a mewling cry fraught with desperation, escaped her contorted lips. *Run!* She had to run! She had to get to her parents' home, where she'd be safe.

Susannah scrambled out of bed, and her bare feet hit the wooden floorboards hard. Frantically she tore at the bedroom door, which she always locked behind her. Several of her nails broke as she yanked the chain guard off and jerked the door open. Blindly she raced through the living room and the kitchen and charged wildly out the back door. Her bare feet sank into the dew-laden grass as she raced through the meadow. Her breath coming in ragged gulps, she ran with abandon.

The shadows of the trees loomed everywhere about her as she sped onward. As she sobbed for breath, she thought she heard heavy footsteps coming up behind her. Oh, God! No! *Not again!*

Killian jerked awake as someone crashed into the back door of the farmhouse. At the sound of frantic pounding he leaped out of the bed. Wearing only light blue pajama bottoms, he reached for his Beretta. In one smooth, unbroken motion he slid the weapon out of its holster and opened the door. Swiftly he raced from the first-floor guest room, through the gloomy depths of the house, to the rear door, where the pounding continued unabated.

The curtains blocked his view, but Killian knew in his gut it was Susannah. Unlocking the door, he pulled it open.

Susannah stood there, her face twisted in terror, tears coursing down her taut cheeks and her gray eyes huge with fear. Without thinking, he opened his arms to her.

She fell sobbing into his arms, her nightdress damp with perspiration. Killian held her sagging form against him with one hand; in the other was his pistol, safety off, held in position, ready to fire. Susannah's sobs were a mixture of rasps and cries as she clung to him. Killian's eyes narrowed to slits as he dragged her away from the open door, pressing her up against the wall, out of view of any potential attacker. Rapidly he searched the darkened porch beyond the open door, and the nearby orchard. His heart was racing wildly. He was aware of Susannah's soft, convulsing form trapped between him and the wall as he remained a protective barrier for her, in case the killer was nearby. But only moonlight showed in the quiet orchard and the countryside beyond.

Seconds passed, and Killian still could detect no movement. Susannah's sobs and gasps drowned out any chance of hearing a possible assailant. "Easy, colleen," he whispered raggedly, easing away from her. The feel of her trembling body beneath him was playing havoc with his carefully controlled emotions so much so, he'd called her colleen, an Irish endearment. Fighting his need to absorb the softness of her womanly form against him, Killian forced himself away from her. Shaken, he drew her into the kitchen and nudged the door closed with his foot. "Come on, sit down." He coaxed Susannah over to the table and pulled the chair out for her. She collapsed into it, her face filled with terror as she stared apprehensively at the back door. Killian placed a hand on her shoulder, feeling the terrible tension in her.

"It's all right," he told her huskily, standing behind her chair, alert and waiting. The kitchen had only two small windows, just above the counter and sinks, and the table was in a corner, where a shooter wouldn't be able to draw a bead on them. They were safe—for the moment. Killian's mind ranged over the options a gunman would have. He could barge into the kitchen after her, or leave and wait back at her house. Or he could leave altogether and wait for another opportunity to kill Susannah.

Susannah shook her head violently and jabbed her finger repeatedly toward the door. She glanced up at Killian's hard, shadowy features. Her eyes widened even more when she spotted the pistol that he held with such casual ease. He was naked from the waist up, she realized, the moonlight accentuating his deep chest and his taut, leanly muscled body. Gulping, Susannah tore her attention back to the door, waiting to hear those heavy footsteps that had been pursuing her like hounds from hell. Her breathing was still harsh, but Killian's hand on her shoulder made her feel safer.

Killian looked around, his hearing keyed to any strange noises. Surprised that the Andersons hadn't awakened with the amount of noise Susannah had made, he glanced down at her. Undiminished panic still showed in her eyes. One hand was pressed against her heaving breast. She looked as if every nerve in her body were raw from whatever she'd just experienced.

Leaning down, he met and held her wide, searching gray eyes. "Susannah, what happened? Was someone after you?"

She nodded her head violently. Her mother always had a pencil and paper on the kitchen table for her. She grabbed them and hastily scrawled a message.

A man! A man tried to get in the window of my bedroom!

Killian's eyes narrowed.

Susannah gasped raggedly as she held his burning, intense gaze.

He patted her shoulder, hoping the gesture would offer her some sense of security. "You stay put, understand? I'm going to try and find him. I'll go back to your house and have a look around."

Susannah gave a low cry, and the meaning of the sound was clear as she gripped Killian's arm and shook her head. *No! No, don't go! He's out there! He'll kill you! Oh, please, don't go! He's after me, not you!*

Killian understood her silent plea for him to remain with her. But it was impossible under the circumstances. "Shh... I'll be all right," he said soothingly. "I want you to stay here. You'll be safer."

Gulping unsteadily, Susannah nodded, unwillingly releasing him.

With a look meant to give her solace, Killian rasped, "I'll be right back. I promise."

Shaking badly in the aftermath of her terrified run, Susannah sat huddled in the chair, feeling suddenly chilled in her damp cotton gown. Killian moved soundlessly, like a cougar, toward the door. But as he opened it and moved out into the night, Susannah felt a new wave of anguish and fear. Killian could be murdered! Weaving in and around the fruit trees, the dew-laden grass soaking his bare feet and pajama legs, Killian quickly circled the Anderson house. If the killer was around, he wasn't here. Moving with the soundlessness of a shadow, he avoided the regular path and headed for Susannah's house. As he ran silently through the orchard, a slice of moon and the resulting silvery light allowed him to penetrate the night. Reaching the old homestead, his pistol held upward, Killian advanced toward the rear of the house, every sense screamingly alert. His nostrils flared, he inhaled, trying to get a whiff of any odor other than the sweet orchard fragrances.

Locating Susannah's bedroom at the rear, Killian saw nothing unusual. Remaining near a small grove of lilac bushes that were at least twenty feet tall, he waited. Patience was the name of the game. His original plan to remain at the Anderson house obviously wasn't a good one, he thought grimly as he waited. Frustration ate at him. He'd have to find a way to stay at Susannah's home in order to protect her. The chill of the predawn air surrounded him, but he was impervious to it.

His gaze scouted the surrounding area, his ears tuned in to pick up any sound. *Nothing.* Killian waited another ten minutes before moving toward the house. The killer could be inside, waiting for Susannah to return. His mouth dry, he compressed his lips into a thin line and quietly stole toward the homestead. His heart set up a sledgehammer pounding in his chest as he eased toward the open back door, the only entrance to the house. Wrapping both hands around the butt of his gun, Killian froze near the door frame. Susannah had left so quickly that the screen door was ajar, as well.

Still, there was no sound that was out of place. But Killian wasn't about to trust the potentially volatile situation. Moving quickly, he dived inside, his pistol aimed. Silence. His eyes mere slits, he remained crouched and tense as he passed through the gloomy kitchen, his head swiveling from side to side, missing nothing, absorbing everything. The living room was next. Nothing.

Finally, after ending the search in Susannah's bedroom, Killian checked the windows. Both were open to allow the fresh early-fall coolness to circulate. One window's screen was in place; the other screen, on the window behind her brass bed, was ripped and in need of repair. Going outside, Killian checked carefully for footprints around either of the bedroom windows, but the grass next to the house was tall and undisturbed. He noticed that as he walked distinct footprints appeared in the heavily dew-laden grass. There were no previous footprints to indicate the presence of an intruder.

Grimly Killian headed back toward the Anderson house, still staying away from the path, still alert, but convinced now that Susannah had experienced a nightmare about her assailant. Relief showered over him at the realization. Still, the incident had put him on notice not to allow the idyllic setting to relax him too much. Dawn was barely crawling onto the horizon, a pale lavender beneath the dark, retreating mantle of the night sky. A rooster was already crowing near the chicken coop as Killian stepped lightly onto the wooden porch.

Susannah met him at the screen door, her eyes huge with silent questions.

"There wasn't anyone," Killian told her as he entered the quiet kitchen. He noticed that Susannah had put a teakettle on the stove and lit the burner beneath it. He saw her eyes go wider with shock at his terse statement. Her gaze traveled to the pistol that was still in his hand, and he realized that it was upsetting her.

"Let me put this away and get decent. I'll be out in a moment. Your folks awake yet?"

Susannah shook her head. Despite her fear, she felt herself respond to the male beauty of Killian's tall, taut body. Black hair covered his chest in abundance, a dark strip trailing down across his flat, hard belly and disappearing beneath the drawstring of the pajamas that hung low on his hips. Susannah gulped, avoiding his narrowed, burning gaze.

In his bedroom, Killian quickly changed into jeans and a white short-sleeved shirt. He pulled on dark blue socks and slipped into a pair of comfortable brown loafers, then ran his fingers through his mussed hair, taming the short strands back into place. Then he strapped on his shoulder holster and slid the pistol into place.

Rubbing his hand across his stubbled jaw, Killian moved back to the kitchen, still amazed that the Andersons had slept through all the commotion. All the more reason, he warned himself, to stay alert for Susannah's sake.

When he entered the kitchen, he saw that she had poured him a cup of tea in a flowery china cup. She was sitting at the table, her hand gripping the notepad and pencil, as if she had been waiting for his return. Killian sat down next to her.

"You had a nightmare," he told her. "That was all."

Susannah rapidly wrote a note on the pad and turned it around for Killian to read.

Impossible! I saw his shadow!

Killian picked up the tea and sipped it, enjoying the

clean, minty taste. "There was no trace of footprints around either of your bedroom windows," he explained apologetically. "I searched your house carefully and found nothing. It was a dream, Susannah."

No! Susannah sat back, her arms folded across her breasts, and stared at his darkly etched features while he drank the tea. After a moment, she scribbled on the pad again.

I saw him! I saw the face of the man who nearly killed me!

Killian saw the bleak frustration, and fear in her gray eyes. Without thinking, he placed his hand over hers. "You remember what he looks like?" Before, she'd been unable to identify her assailant.

She nodded.

"Good. The police need an identification." Realizing he was gently cupping her cool hand, Killian pulled his back and quickly picked up his teacup. What the hell was going on? Couldn't he control his own actions? The idea frightened him. Susannah seemed unconsciously to bring out his softer side. But along with that softer side lurked the monstrous danger that could hurt her. He took a sip from the cup and set it down. His words came out clipped—almost angry.

"When you settle down over this, I want you to draw a picture of his face. I can take it to the police— it might give them a lead."

Hurt by his sudden gruffness, Susannah sat there, still taking in Killian's surprising words. *A nightmare?* How could it have been? It had been so *real*! Touching her forehead, which was now beginning to ache in earnest, Susannah closed her eyes and tried to get a grip on her rampant emotions. Killian's warm, unexpected touch had momentarily soothed her apprehension and settled her pounding heart—but just as quickly he'd withdrawn.

Opening her eyes, she wrote:

I'll draw a picture of him later, when I feel up to it.

Killian nodded, still edgy. One part of him was keyed to Susannah, the other to the door, the windows, and any errant sound. He knew his shoulder holster disturbed her. She kept glancing at him, then at the holster, a question in her eyes. How much could he tell her? How much *should* he tell her? He sensed her curiosity about him and his reasons for being here.

Feeling utterly trapped, Killian tried to think clearly. Being around Susannah seemed to scramble his emotions. He'd been too long without softness in his life. *And,* Killian lectured himself, *it would have to remain that way.* Still, he couldn't let go of the memory of the wonderful sensation of her pressed against him. He should have thrown her to the floor instead of using himself as a human shield to protect her, he thought in disgust. That way he wouldn't have had to touch her, to be reminded of all that he ached to have and never could. But he hadn't been thinking clearly; he'd reacted instinctively.

Grimly he held her gaze. "From now on, Susannah, you need to stay here, in your folks' home, where it's safer."

I will not stay here! I can't! If it was just a dream, then I'll be okay out there. I don't want to stay here.

He studied her in the silence, noting the set of her delicate jaw and the flash of stubbornness in her eyes. With a sigh, he set the cup down on the saucer.
"No. You'll stay here. In *this* house."
Susannah shook her head.

You don't understand! I tried to stay here when I got home from the hospital. I had awful dreams! If I stay in my room, I can't sleep. At the other house I feel safer. I don't have as many nightmares. I don't know why. I can't explain it, but I will not come and stay here.

Killian studied the scribbled note, utterly thwarted. No one knew better than he did about the night and the terrible dreams that could stalk it. He understood Susannah's pleading request, probably better than anyone else could. His heart squeezed at the pain in her admission, because he'd too long lived a similar life. With a sigh, he muttered, "All right, but then I'm staying at your place with you until we can get this settled. I need to know for sure whether this guy is real or just a dream."

Shocked, Susannah stared at him, her mouth dropping open. She felt the brutal hardness around him again and saw anger, touched with anxiety in his eyes. Her mind reeled with questions as the adrenaline left her bloodstream and left her shaky in its aftermath. With a trembling hand, she wrote:

Who are you? You carry a gun. I don't think you

are who you say you are. Morgan suspects something, doesn't he? Please, tell me the truth, even if you don't tell my parents. I deserve to know.

Killian fingered the note, refusing to meet her challenging gaze. Stunned by Susannah's intuitive grasp of the situation, he realized he had to tell her. Otherwise, she'd never allow him to stay at her house.

"All right," he growled, "here's the truth. Morgan suspects that the man who tried to kill you will come and hunt you down once he knows you survived. You can ID him, and he's going to try to kill you before you can do it." He saw Susannah's eyes grow dark with shock. Angry that he had to hurt her with the truth, Killian snapped, "I'm here on assignment. I'm to protect you. Please don't tell your parents my real reason for being here. Morgan feels they've been through enough. I wasn't going to tell you, dammit, but you're so stubborn, you didn't leave me any recourse. I can't have you staying alone at the other house."

Susannah felt Killian's anger buffet her. Despite her fear and shock, she felt anger toward him even more.

How dare you! How dare Morgan! You should have told me this in the first place!

Killian didn't like being put in the middle, and he glared at her. "Look, I do as I'm ordered. I'm breaking my word in telling you this, and I'll probably catch hell from my boss for doing it. I don't like this any more than you do. If you want all of the truth, I don't even want to be here—I don't take assignments that involve women. But Morgan threatened to fire me if

I didn't take this mission, so you and I are in the same boat. You don't want me here, and I damn well don't want to be here!"

Stunned, Susannah blinked at the powerful wave of feeling behind his harsh words. She sensed a desperation in Killian's anger, and it was that desperation that defused her own righteous anger.

I'm sorry, Killian. I shouldn't be angry with you.

He shook his head and refused to meet her eyes. The frightening truth was, every time he did, he wanted simply to find his way into her arms and be held. "Don't apologize," he muttered. "It isn't your fault, either. We're both caught between a rock and a hard place."

Without thinking, Susannah slowly raised her hand and placed it across Killian's clenched one on the table. His head snapped up as her fingers wrapped around his. The anger dissolved in his eyes, and for just a moment Susannah could have sworn she saw longing in his stormy gaze. But, just as quickly, it was gone, leaving only an icy coldness. She removed her hand from his, all too aware that he was rejecting her touch.

All she had wanted to do was comfort Killian. From her work, Susannah knew the healing nature of human touch firsthand. Killian had looked positively torn by the fact that he had to be here with her. Susannah had wanted to let him know somehow that she understood his dilemma. He didn't want anything to do with her because she was a woman. Her curiosity was piqued, but she knew better than to ask. Right now, Killian was edgy, turning the cup around and around in his long, spare hands.

You don't have to stay out there with me.

Killian made a muffled sound and stood up suddenly. He moved away from the table, automatically checking the window with his gaze. "Yes," he said irritably, "I do. I don't like it any more than you do, but it has to be done."

But it was a nightmare! You said so yourself. You can stay here with my folks.

Killian savagely spun on his heel, and when he spoke his voice was hoarse. "There's nothing you can say that will change my mind. You need protection, Susannah."

With a trembling hand, Susannah touched her brow. It was nerve-racking enough to stay by herself at the abandoned farmhouse. She was desperately afraid of the dark, of the terrors that came nightly when she lay down as her overactive imagination fueled the fires of her many fears. But Killian staying with her? He was so blatantly male—so quiet, yet so capable. Fighting her own feelings toward him, she sat for a good minute before writing on the notepad again.

Please tell my folks the truth about this. I don't want to lie to them about the reason you're staying out at the house with me. It would seem funny to them if you suddenly started living out there with me.

Killian couldn't disagree with her. He paced the room quietly, trying to come up with a better plan. He stopped and looked down at her exhausted features.

"I'll talk to them this morning."

Relief flowed through Susannah, and she nodded.

Morgan was trying to protect us, but this is one time when we should know the whole truth.

"I tried to tell him that," Killian said bitterly. He stood by the table, thinking. "That's all water under the bridge now," he said. "You saw the killer's face in your nightmare. I need you to draw a picture of him this morning so that I can take it to the police station. They'll fax it to Lexington and to Morgan."

Trying to combat the automatic reactions of fear, rage and humiliation that came with remembering, Susannah nodded. Her hand still pressed against her brow, she tried to control the cold-bladed anxiety triggered by the discussion.

It was impossible for Killian to steel himself against the clarity of the emotions he read in Susannah's pale face. "Easy," he said soothingly. "Take some deep breaths, Susannah, and the panic will start to go away." He watched her breasts rise and fall sharply beneath her wrinkled cotton gown, and he couldn't help thinking how pretty she looked in the thin garment with lace sewn around its oval neckline. She was like that lace, fragile and easily crushed, he realized as he stood watching her wrestle with her fear.

Miraculously, Susannah felt much of her panic dissolve beneath his husky-voiced instructions. She wasn't sure if it was because of the deep breaths or merely Killian's quiet presence. How did he know what she was experiencing? He must have experienced the very same thing, otherwise he wouldn't know how to help her. And he was helping her—even if he'd made it clear that he didn't want to be here.

"Good," Killian said gruffly as she became calm. He poured them more tea and took his chair again. "I'll sleep in the bedroom down the hall from yours. I'm a restless sleeper," he warned her sharply. "I have nightmares myself..." His voice trailed off.

Susannah stared at him, swayed by the sincerity in his dark blue eyes. There was such torment in them. Toward her? Toward the assignment? She just wasn't sure. Morning light was stealing through the ruffled curtains at the window now, softening his harsh features.

Nervously fingering the rectangular notepad, Susannah frowned, uncertain of her own feelings as she was every time he was with her.

"I won't bother you, if that's what you're worried about," he added when he saw the confusion on her face. He prayed he could keep his word—hoped against hope that he wouldn't have one of the terrible, wrenching nightmares that haunted him.

Agitated, Susannah got to her feet and moved to the window. The pale lavender of dawn reminded her of the color of her favorite flowers—the lilacs. Pressing and releasing her fingers against the porcelain sink, she thought about Killian's statement.

Killian studied Susannah in the quiet of the kitchen. Her dark hair lay mussed against her tense shoulders, a sable cloak against the pristine white of her nightgown. Killian ached to touch her hair, to tunnel his fingers through it and find out what it felt like. Would it be as soft as her body had been against his? Or more coarse, in keeping with the ramrod-straight spine that showed her courage despite the circumstances?

"Look," he said, breaking the tense silence, "maybe this will end sooner than I expect. I'll work on the house over there to stay close in case something happens. I'll paint and fix up the windows, the doors." *Anything to keep my mind off you.*

Turning, Susannah looked at him. He sat at the table, his long fingers wrapped around the dainty china cup on the yellow oilcloth. His body was hunched forward, and he had an unhappy expression on his face. She would never forget the look in his eyes, his alertness, or the sense of safety she'd felt when she'd fallen sobbing into his arms at the back door. Why was she hedging now about allowing him to be near her?

Licking her lips, she nodded. Suddenly more tired than she could remember ever being, she left the counter. It was time to go home. When she got to the screen door, Killian moved quickly out of his chair.

"I'll walk you back," Killian said, his tone brooking no argument. Opening the screen door, she walked out.

Although he wanted Susannah to believe he was relaxed, Killian remained on high alert as they trod the damp path through the orchard back to her home. The sky had turned a pale pink. It wouldn't be long before the sun came up.

Killian felt Susannah's worry as she looked around, her arms wrapped tightly around herself. He wanted to step close—to place a protective arm around her shoulders and give her the sense of security she so desperately needed and so richly deserved. Yet he knew that touching her would melt his defenses. That couldn't happen—ever. Killian swore never to allow Susannah to reach inside him; but she had that ability, and he knew it. Somehow, he had to strengthen his resolve and keep her at arm's length. At all costs. For her own sake.

"Maybe if I patch that torn screen in your bedroom and put some locks on the windows, you'll feel better about being there." He saw her flash him a grateful look. "I'll tell your folks what happened when they get up. Then I'll contact Morgan."

Susannah nodded her agreement. She longed simply to step closer to Killian, to be in his protective embrace again. She couldn't forget the lean power of his body against hers, the way he'd used himself as a barrier to protect her.

She wrestled with conflicting feelings. Why was Killian so unhappy about having to stay out at the house with her? She couldn't help how she felt. She knew that right now, if she went back to her old room at her folks' house, the nightmares would return. Her life had begun to stabilize—until tonight. If only Killian could understand why she had to be at the old homestead.

"I'll make sure your house is safe. Then I want you to get some sleep. When you get up, you can draw me the face you saw in the nightmare."

Killian saw Susannah's eyes darken.

"Don't worry, I'll be around. You may not know it, but I'll be there. Like a shadow."

Shivering, Susannah nodded. Her life had turned into nothing but a series of shadows. Killian's body against hers had been real, and never had she needed that more. But Killian didn't like her, didn't want to be with her. She swallowed her need to be held, still grateful that Killian would be nearby. Perhaps her mind was finally ready to give up the information it had seen, and that should help in the long run.

Touching her throat, she fervently wished her voice would come back. At least now she could make some noise, and that seemed a hopeful sign. She stole a glance up into Killian's grim, alert features. She'd welcome his company, even though he didn't want hers. Right now, she needed the human contact. Thinking back, she realized that the anger she'd sensed in Killian had been due to his not wanting to take the assignment. It hadn't really been aimed directly at her. Sometimes it was lonely out there at the homestead. He wasn't a willing guest, Susannah reminded herself. Still, if her attacker was really out there, she would feel a measure of safety knowing that Killian was nearby.

After thoroughly checking Susannah's home again, Killian allowed her into the farmhouse. He'd double-check around the house and quietly search the acreage around it just to make sure no one was hiding in wait. At the bedroom door, Susannah shyly turned and gave him a soft, hesitant smile. A thank-you showed clearly in her eyes, and it took everything Killian had for him to turn away from her. "I'll be over about noon," he rasped, more gruffly than he'd intended.

Susannah waited for Killian's promised noon arrival as she sat at her kitchen table. She questioned herself. Her real home was in town, near the school where she taught. Why didn't she have the courage to move back there? Glumly she admitted it was because she was afraid of being completely alone. At least this broken-down homestead was close to her parents.

Killian deliberately made noise as he stepped up on Susannah's porch, carrying art supplies under one arm. He knew all about being jumpy. He'd decked more than one man who had inadvertently come up behind him without warning. Wolf had been one of those men, on assignment down in Peru. The others on the team had learned from his mistake and had always let Killian know they were coming.

Susannah was waiting for him at the screen door. She looked beautiful, clothed in a long, lightweight denim skirt and a fuchsia short-sleeved blouse. She'd tied her hair back with a pink ribbon, and soft tendrils brushed her temples. Killian tensed himself against the tempting sight of her.

Stepping into the kitchen, Killian sniffed. "You've got coffee on?" He found himself wanting to ease the seriousness out of her wary eyes. The dark shadows beneath them told him she hadn't slept well since the nightmare.

Placing sketch pad, colored pencils and eraser on the table, Killian eased into a chair. Susannah went to the cupboard, retrieved a white ceramic mug and poured him some coffee. He nodded his thanks as she came over and handed it to him.

"Sit down," he urged her. "We've got some work to do."

Looking over the art supplies, Susannah sat down at his elbow. Somehow Killian looked heart-stoppingly handsome and dangerous all at once. His dress was casual, but she always sensed the inner tension in him, and could see some undefinable emotion in his blue eyes when he looked at her. But the anger was no longer there, she noted with relief.

"I'd like you to sketch for me the man you saw in your nightmare," Killian said.

Hesitant, Susannah fingered the box of colored pencils. Her throat constricted, and she closed her eyes for a moment. How could she make Killian understand that since the attack her love of drawing and painting had gone away?

"It doesn't have to be fancy, Susannah. Draw me something. Anything. I have a way to check what you sketch for me against police mug shots." He saw pain in her eyes, and her lower lip trembled as she withdrew her hand from the box of pencils. He cocked his head. "What is it?" He recalled his sister's pain, and the hours he'd spent holding her while she cried after realizing her once-beautiful face was gone forever. A powerful urge to reach out and give Susannah that same kind of help nearly overwhelmed him, but he reared back inwardly. He couldn't.

With a helpless shrug, Susannah swallowed against the lump and shakily opened up the sketch pad. She had to try. She believed in Killian, and she believed he could help her. Suddenly embarrassed, she took her pad and pencil and wrote:

I'm rusty at this. I haven't drawn since being wounded.

He grimaced. "I'm no art critic, Susannah. I can't draw a straight line. Anything you can do will look great to me. Give it your best try."

Susannah picked up a pencil and began to sketch.

She tried to concentrate on the task at hand, but she found her senses revolving back to Killian's over- whelming presence. All morning she'd thought about him staying here with her. It wasn't him she couldn't trust, she realized—it was herself! The discovery left her feeling shaken. Never had a man influenced her on all levels, as Killian did. What was it about him? For the thousandth time, Susannah ached to have her voice back. If only she could talk!

Quiet descended upon them. Killian gazed around the kitchen, keenly aware of Susannah's presence. It was like a rainbow in his dismal life. There were at least forty colorful drawings tacked to the kitchen walls, obviously done by very young children. Prob- ably her class. Peace, a feeling that didn't come often to Killian, descended gently around him. Was it the old-fashioned house? Being out in the country away from the madding crowd? Or—he swung his gaze back to Susannah and saw her brows drawn together in total concentration, her mouth pursed—was it her?

Unconsciously Killian's shoulders dropped, and he eased the chair back off its two front legs, loosely hold- ing the mug of coffee against his belly. Birds, mostly robins, were singing and calling to one another. The sweet scents of grass, ripening fruit and clean moun- tain air wafted through the kitchen window. Susan- nah had a small radio on in the corner, and FM music flowed softly across the room, like an invisible caress.

His gaze settled on Susannah's ponytail, and he noted the gold and red glints between the sable strands. Her hair was thick and luxurious. A man could drive himself crazy wondering what the texture of it was like, Killian decided unhappily. Right now, he knew his focus had to be on keeping her protected, not his own personal longings.

The sketch of the man took shape beneath Susannah's slender fingers over the next hour. Frequently she struggled, erasing and beginning again. Killian marveled at her skill as an artist. She might consider herself rusty, but she was definitely a professional. Finally her mouth quirked and she glanced up. Slowly she turned the sketch toward him.

"Unsavory-looking bastard," Killian whispered as he put the coffee aside and held the sketch up to examine it. "Brown eyes, blond hair and crooked front teeth?"

Susannah nodded. She saw the change in Killian's assessing blue eyes. A fierce anger emanated from him, and she sensed his hatred of her attacker.

He reminds me of a weasel, with close-set eyes that are small and beady-looking.

Killian nodded and put the sketch aside. "I'll take this to the police department today. I called Morgan. He knows you've remembered what your attacker looked like, so he's anxious to get this, too. He'll know what to do with it. If this bastard has a police record, we'll be on the way to catching him."

Chilled, Susannah slowly rubbed her arms with her hands.

Killian felt her raw fear. But he stopped himself from reaching out to give her a touch of reassurance. Gathering up the sketch, he rose. "I'll be back as soon as I can. In the meantime, you stay alert."

The warning made another chill move through her

as she looked up at him. Somehow, some of the tension around him was gone. The peace that naturally inhabited the farmhouse had always worked wonders on her own nervousness, and Susannah realized that it might be doing the same for him. She nodded in agreement to his orders.

"It would be best if you went down to your parents' house while I'm gone. They know the truth now, and they'll be more watchful for you. In the long run, it's best this way."

Susannah couldn't disagree with him. The more people who were on guard and watchful, the less chance of the killer's finding her. Rising, she left with him.

"Maybe," Killian told her as they walked across the top of the hill, "this will be over soon."

At his words, Susannah's eyes sparkled with such fierce hope, combined with gratitude, that Killian had to force himself to keep from reaching out to caress her flushed cheek.

He'd give his life for her, if necessary, he realized suddenly. Susannah was worth dying for.

Chapter 4

Susannah was helping her mother can ripe figs in the kitchen when she saw Killian return from Glen. She stood at the counter and watched him emerge from the four-wheel-drive Land Cruiser. The vehicle seeming fitting for a man like Killian, she thought, a man who was rugged, a loner, iconoclastic. Though his face remained emotionless, his roving blue gaze held her, made her feel an inherent safety as he looked around the property. Her heart took a skipping beat as he turned and headed into the house.

"Killian's home," Pansy said. She shook her head as she transferred the recently boiled figs to the jars awaiting on the counter. "I'm so nervous now." With a little laugh, she noted, "My hands haven't stopped shaking since he told us the truth this morning."

Wanting somehow to reassure her, Susannah put her arms around her mother and gave her a hug.

Killian walked into the kitchen and saw Susannah embracing her mother. He halted, a strange, twisting feeling moving through him. Mother and daughter held each other, and he remained motionless. It was Susannah who sensed his presence first. She loosened the hug and smiled shyly in his direction.

Pansy tittered nervously when she realized he was standing in the doorway. "I didn't hear you come in, Mr. Killian."

"I should have said something," he said abruptly. Killian felt bad for the woman. Ever since he'd told the Andersons the truth, it had been as if a shock wave had struck the farm. Sam Anderson had promptly gone out to the barn to fix a piece of machinery. Pansy had suddenly gotten busy with canning duties. Staying occupied was one way to deal with tension, Killian realized. His gaze moved to Susannah, whose cheeks were flushed. Her hair was still in a ponytail, the tendrils sticking to her dampened temples with the heat of the day and the lack of breeze through the kitchen. She looked beautiful.

"Did you tell the police?" Pansy asked, nervously wiping her hands on her checked apron.

"Yes. Everyone has a copy of the picture Susannah sketched. Morgan will call me here if they find out who it is. The FBI's in on it, so maybe we'll turn up something a little sooner."

Susannah heard her mother give a little moan, and she reached over and touched her shoulder and gave her a look she hoped she could decipher.

"Oh, I'm okay, honey," Pansy said in response, patting her hand in a consoling way.

Killian absorbed the soft look Susannah gave her worried mother. She had such sensitivity. How he wished he could have that in his life. A sadness moved through him, and he turned away, unable to stand the compassion on Susannah's features.

"Is Sam still out at the barn?" he demanded.

"Yes."

"I'll go help him," Killian said, and left without another word.

An odd ache had filled Susannah as she watched Killian's carefully arranged face give way to his real feelings. There had been such naked hunger in his eyes that it left her feeling in touch with herself as a woman as never before. She tried to help her mother, unable to get Killian's expression out of her mind—or her heart.

"That Mr. Killian's a strange one," Pansy said, to no one in particular, as she spooned the figs into a jar, their fragrant steam rising around her. "He's so gruff. Almost rude. But he cares. I can feel it around him. I wonder why he's so standoffish? It's hard to get close to him, to let him know how grateful we are for him being here."

Susannah nodded. Killian *was* gruff—like a cranky old bear. It was part of what he used to keep people at bay, she thought. Yet, just a few minutes ago, she'd seen the real Sean Killian—a man who had wants—and desires. And her heart wouldn't settle down over that discovery.

Around four o'clock, Pansy sent Susannah out with a gallon of iced tea and two glasses for the men, who were still laboring in the barn. The sunlight was bright and hot for an early-September day, and Susannah reveled in it. Chickens scattered out of her path as she crossed the dirt driveway to the barn, which sat off to one side of the green-and-white farmhouse.

As she entered the huge, airy structure, the familiar smell of hay and straw filled her nostrils. At one end of the barn, where the machinery was kept, Susannah spotted her father working intently on his tractor. The engine had been pulled up and out of the tractor itself and hung suspended by two chains looped around one of the barn's huge upper beams. She saw Killian down on his knees, working beneath the engine while her father stood above him. They were trying to thread a hose from above the engine to somewhere down below, where Killian leaned beneath it, his hand outstretched for it.

Killian had clearly shed his shirt long before, and his skin glistened with sweat from the hot barn air, accentuating his muscular chest and arms. A lock of black hair stuck damply to his forehead as he frowned in concentration, intent on capturing the errant hose.

Susannah slowed her step halfway to them. Her father turned away from the tractor, going to the drawer where he kept many of his tools. Just then, she heard a vague snap. Her eyes rose to the beam that held the heavy engine. Instantly her gaze shifted to Killian, who seemed oblivious of the sound, his concentration centered on threading the hose through the engine.

Sam Anderson was still bent over a drawer, rummaging for a tool.

Susannah realized that the chain was slowly coming undone. At any second it would snap free and that heavy tractor engine would fall on Killian! Without thinking, she cried out a warning. *"Look out, Killian!"*

Her scream shattered the barn's musty stillness.

Killian jerked his hand back and heard a cracking, metallic sound. He glanced to his left and saw Susannah, her finger pointing toward the beam above him. Sam had whirled around at the cry. In one motion, Killian leaped away from the engine.

Susannah clutched the jar of iced tea to her as she saw the chain give way. She screamed as the tractor engine slammed heavily down on the barn floor. But Killian was leaping away as the engine fell, rolling through the straw and dust on the floor.

Setting the iced tea aside, Susannah ran toward him, unsure whether he was hurt or not. He lay on his side, his back to her, as she raced up to him.

"Killian?" she sobbed. "Killian? Are you hurt?" She fell to her knees, reaching out to touch him.

"Good God!" Sam Anderson hurried to Killian's side. "Son? You all right?"

Breathing raggedly, Susannah touched Killian's hard, damp shoulder. He rolled over onto his back, his eyes narrowed and intense.

"Are—are you all right?" she stammered, quickly glancing down his body, checking for blood or a sign of injury.

"I'm fine," Killian rasped, sitting up. Then he grew very still. He saw the look in Susannah's huge eyes, saw her expressive fingers resting against her swanlike throat. Her face was pale. He blinked. Susannah had spoken. Her eyes still mirrored her fear for him, and he felt the coolness of her fingers resting on his dirty arm.

"You're sure?" Susannah demanded breathlessly, trading a look with her father, who knelt on the other side of Killian. "You could have been killed!" Badly shaken, she stared down into his taut face and held his burning gaze. Killian was like a lean, bronzed statue, his gleaming muscles taut from the hard physical labor.

Sam gasped and stared at his daughter. "Honey, you're talking!"

Gasping herself, Susannah reared back on her heels, her hands flying to her mouth. She saw Killian grin slightly. It was true! She had spoken! With a little cry, Susannah touched her throat, almost unbelieving. "Pa, I got my voice back…"

Killian felt Susannah's joy radiating from her like sunlight itself. He felt embraced and lifted by her joy at her discovery. And what a beautiful voice she had— low and husky. A tremor of warning fled through him as he drowned in her shining eyes. This was just one more thing to like about Susannah, to want from her.

Susannah's gaze moved from her father to Killian and back again. "I can speak! I can talk again!" Susannah choked, and tears streamed down her cheeks.

"Oh," Sam whispered unsteadily, "that's wonderful, honey!" He got to his feet and came around to where his daughter knelt. Leaning over, he helped her stand, then threw his arms around her and held her tight for a long, long time.

Touched, Killian remained quietly on the floor. The closeness of Sam with his daughter brought back good, poignant memories of his early home life, of his mother's strength and love. Slowly he eased himself to his feet and began to brush off the straw that clung to his damp skin. Sam and Susannah were laughing and crying, their brows touching. Tears jammed unexpectedly into Killian's eyes, and he quickly blinked them away. What the hell was happening to him?

Turning away from the happy scene, Killian went to retrieve his shirt. Disgruntled and shaken at his own emotional response, he tried to avoid looking at Susannah. It was *her*. Whatever magic it was that she wielded as a woman, it had a decided effect on him, whether he wanted it to or not. Agitated, Killian buttoned his shirt, stuffed the tail into his jeans and gathered up the broken chain, which lay across the floor and around the engine.

"Come on, honey, let's go tell Ma," Sam quavered, his arm around his daughter's shoulders. He gave Killian a grateful look. "You, too. You deserve to be a part of the celebration."

Killian shrugged. "No...you folks go ahead..."

Susannah eased out of her father's embrace and slowly approached Killian. How beautifully and dangerously male he was. Her senses were heightened to almost a painful degree, giving her an excruciating awareness of his smoldering, hooded look as she approached. His chiseled mouth was drawn in at the corners.

"You're okay?" Susannah breathed softly. Then she stepped back, blushing.

Shocked by her unexpected concern for him despite what had happened to her, Killian was at a loss for words. He gripped the chain in his hands. "I'm okay," he managed in a strangled tone. "Go share the news with your mother..." he ordered unsteadily. What a beautiful voice she had, Killian thought dazedly, reeling from the feelings her voice stirred within him.

Trapped beneath his sensual, scorching gaze, Susannah's lips parted. What would it be like to explore that mouth endlessly, that wonderful mouth that was now pursed into a dangerous, thin line of warning? Every nerve in her body responded to his look of hunger. It was the kind of look that made Susannah wildly aware that she was a woman, in all ways. It was not an insulting look, it was a look of desire—for her alone.

"Come on, honey," Sam said happily as he came up and patted her shoulder, "let's go share the good news with Ma. She's gonna cry a bucket of tears over this."

Killian remained still, nearly overwhelmed by his need to reach out and touch Susannah's mussed hair or caress her flushed cheek. He watched as father and daughter left the barn together. Their happiness surrounded him like a long-lost memory. Taking a deep, steadying breath, Killian began to unhook the ends of the chain from the engine. His mind was waging war with his clamoring heart and his aching body. Susannah could now tell them what had happened to her. His emotions were in utter disarray. Her voice was soft and husky, like a well-aged Irish whiskey.

Angrily Killian cleaned up the mess in the barn and put the chains aside. In a way, he felt chained to the situation at the farm, he thought—chained to Susannah in a connection he could neither fight nor flee. Never had a woman gotten to him as Susannah had. His relationships with women had been few and brief—one-night stands that allowed him to leave before darkness came and made an enemy out of anyone who dared get close to him. What was it about Susannah that was different? The need to explore her drove him out of the barn. He slowly walked toward the farmhouse, savagely jamming down his fiery needs. Maybe now he could talk to Susannah about the assault, he reasoned.

Pansy was serving up lemonade in tall purple glasses in celebration. Susannah felt Killian's approach at the screen door before he appeared. What was this synchronicity the two of them seemed to share? Puzzled, but far too joyous over her voice returning to spend time worrying, she gave him a brilliant, welcoming smile as he walked into the kitchen.

"Sit down, son," Sam thundered. "You've earned yourself a glass of Ma's special hand-squeezed lemonade."

Killian hesitated. He'd hoped to come into the house, go to his room, take a cold shower and settle his roiling emotions. But the looks on their faces made him decide differently. With a curt nod, he took a seat opposite Susannah. Her eyes sparkled like diamonds caught in sunlight. He felt himself becoming helplessly ensnared in the joy that radiated around her like a rainbow of colors.

Pansy gave him the lemonade, gratitude visible in every line of her worn face.

"Killian, we're glad you're all right," she said. "Thank goodness you weren't hurt." She reached over and patted Susannah's hand warmly. "Just hearin' Susannah's voice again is like hearin' the angels speakin'."

Killian sipped the icy lemonade, hotly aware of the fire within him, captive to Susannah's thankful gaze. "Your daughter saved me from a few broken bones," he muttered.

Sam hooted and said, "A few? Son, you would've had your back broken if my Susannah hadn't found her voice in time."

Killian nodded and stared down at the glass. If there was such a thing as an angelic woman, it was Susannah. Her skin glowed with renewed color, and her lips were stretched into a happy curve as she gripped her father's leathery brown hand. Killian absorbed the love and warmth among the family members. Nothing could be stronger or better than that, in his opinion. Except maybe the fevered love of a man who loved his woman with a blind passion that overrode the fear of death in him.

"I can't believe it! This is like a dream—I can talk again!" Susannah told him, her hand automatically moving to her throat.

Killian ruminated over the events. He was perfectly at ease with saving other people's lives—but no one, with the exception of his teammates in Peru, had ever saved him from certain death. And he had to admit to himself that Sam was correct: If not for Susannah he'd have a broken back at best—and at worst, he'd be dead. Killian was unsure how to feel about having a woman save his worthless hide. He had a blinding loyalty to those he fought beside, to those who saved him. He lifted his head and stared at Susannah. Things had changed subtly but irrevocably because of this event. No longer was Morgan's edict that he stay here and protect her hanging over his head like a threat.

Moving his fingers across the beaded coolness of the glass, Killian pondered the web of circumstances tightening around him. Perhaps his sense of honor was skewed. On one hand, Susannah deserved his best efforts to protect her. On the other hand, he saw himself as a danger to her each night he stayed at her home. What was he going to do? He could no longer treat her as a mere assignment—an object to be protected. Not that he'd been particularly successful with that tack before.

"Getting your voice back is going to be a big help," Killian offered lamely.

With a slight laugh, Susannah said, "I don't know if you'll feel that way or not, Sean. Pa says I talk too much." Susannah felt heat rise in her neck and into her face when his head snapped up, his eyes pinning her. She suddenly realized she'd slipped and used his first name. Vividly recalling that Killian had said that only his mother and sister used his first name, she groped for an apology. "I'm sorry, I forgot—you like to be called by your last name."

Killian shrugged, not wanting to make a big deal out of it. "You saved my life. I think that gives you the right to call me anything you want." His heart contracted at her husky, quavering words, and he retreated into silence, feeling that words were useless. Her voice, calling him Sean, had released a Pandora's box of deeply held emotions from his dark, haunted past. When she'd said his name, it had come out like a prayer. A beautiful, clean prayer of thanks. How little in his world was clean or beautiful. But somehow this woman giving him her lustrous look made him feel as if he were both. His head argued differently, but for once Killian ignored it.

With a happy smile, Pansy came over and rested her hands on her daughter's shoulders. "You two young'ns will stay for dinner, won't you? We have to celebrate!"

Killian wanted the safety of isolation. He shook his head. "I've got things to do, Mrs. Anderson." When he saw the regret in the woman's face, he got to his feet.

He felt Susannah's eyes on him, as if she knew what he was doing and why he was doing it. "Thanks anyway," he mumbled, and quickly left the kitchen. His job was to protect this family, not to join it. Killian was relieved to escape, not sure how long he could continue to hold his emotions in check. As he stalked through the living room and down the hall to his bedroom, all he wanted was a cold shower to shock him back to the harsh reality he'd lived with since leaving Ireland so many years before. And somehow, he was going to have to dredge up enough control to be able to sleep under the same roof with Susannah. Somehow...

Early-evening light shed a subdued glow around the kitchen of Susannah's small house. Killian sat at the kitchen table and watched as she made coffee at the counter. He had insisted he wasn't hungry, but Pansy had sent a plate of food with him when he'd escorted Susannah back to her homestead. The meal had been simple but filling. Tonight he was more tense than he could recall ever being. He felt as if his emotions were caught in a desperate tug-of-war.

Was it because of Susannah's whiskey laughter, that husky resonance that made him feel as if she were reaching out and caressing him? Killian sourly tried to ignore what her breathy voice did to him.

"You sure ate your share of Ma's cherry pie, Sean," she said with a teasing look over her shoulder. Killian sat at the table, his chin resting forward on his chest, his chair tipped back on its rear legs. His narrow face was dark and thoughtful.

"It was good."

Chortling, Susannah retrieved the lovely flowered

china cups and saucers from the oak cabinet. "You ate like a man who hasn't had too many home-cooked meals in his life."

Killian grudgingly looked at her as she came over and set the cups and saucers on the oilcloth. Her insight, as always, was unsettling to him. "I haven't," he admitted slowly.

Susannah hesitated. There was so much she wanted to say to him. She slid her fingers across the back of the wooden chair opposite him. "Sean, I need to talk to you. I mean really talk to you." Heat rushed up her neck and into her cheeks, and Susannah groaned, touching her flushed face. "I wish I didn't turn beet red all the time!"

Killian absorbed her discomfort. "In Ireland we'd call you a primrose—a woman with moonlight skin and red primroses for cheeks," he said quietly.

The utter beauty of his whispered words made Susannah stand in shocked silence. "You're a poet."

Uncomfortable, he muttered, "I don't think of myself in those terms."

She saw the wariness in his eyes and sensed that her boldness was making him edgy. "Is it a crime to say that a man possesses a soul that can see the world in terms of beauty?"

Relieved that Susannah had turned and walked back to the counter, Killian frowned. He studied her as he tried to formulate an answer to her probing question. Each movement of her hands was graceful—and each time she touched something, he felt as if she were touching him instead. Shaking his head, he wondered what the hell had gotten into him. He was acting like a man who'd been without a woman far too long. Well, hadn't he?

Clearing his throat, Killian said, "I'd rather talk about you than myself."

Susannah sat down, drying her hands on a green-and-white-checked towel. "I know you would, but I'm not going to let you." She kept her voice light, because she sensed that if she pushed him too hard he'd close up. She opened her hands to him. "I need to clear the air on some things between us."

Killian's stomach knotted painfully. The fragrant smell of coffee filled the kitchen. "Go on," he said in a warning growl.

Susannah nervously touched her brow. "I'm actually afraid to talk to you. Maybe it's because of what happened, getting shot by that man. I don't know…"

"The hurt part, the wounded side of you, feels that fear," Killian told her, his tone less gruff now. "It was a man who nearly killed you. Why shouldn't you be afraid of men in general?" He had to stop himself from reaching out to touch her tightly clasped hands on the tabletop. Her knuckles were white.

"You seem to know so much about me—about what I'm feeling." She gave him a long, scrutinizing look. "How?"

Shifting uncomfortably, Killian shrugged. "Experience, maybe."

"Whose? Your own?" After all, he was a mercenary, Susannah reminded herself. A world-traveled and world-weary man who had placed his life on the line time and again.

"No…not exactly… My sister, Meg, was—" His mouth quirked at the corners. "She was beautiful, and

had a promising career as a stage actress. Meg met and
fell in love with an Irish-American guy, and they were
planning on getting married." He cleared his throat and
forced himself to finish. "She flew back to Ireland to
be in a play—and at her stopover at Heathrow Airport
a terrorist bomb went off."

"Oh, no..." Susannah whispered. "Is she...alive?"

The horror of that day came rushing back to Killian,
and he closed his eyes, his voice low with feeling.
"Yes, she's alive. But the bomb... She's badly disfigured. She's no longer beautiful. Her career ended, and
I've seen her through fifteen operations to restore her
face." Killian shrugged hopelessly. "Meg cut off her
engagement to Ian, too, even though he wanted to stay
with her. She couldn't believe that any man could love
her like that."

"How awful," Susannah whispered. Reaching out,
she slid her hand across his tightly clenched fist. "It
must have been hard on you, too."

Wildly aware of Susannah's touch, Killian warned
himself that she'd done it only out of compassion. Her
fingers were cool and soft against his sun-toughened
skin. His mouth went dry, and his heart rate skyrock-
eted. Torn between emotions from the past and the
boiling heat scalding up through him, Killian rasped,
"Meg has been a shadow of herself since then. She's
fearful, always looking over her shoulder, has terrible nightmares, and doesn't trust anyone." Bitterly he
added, "She's even wary of me, her own brother." It
hurt to admit that, but Killian sensed that Susannah
had the emotional strength to deal with his first-time
admission to anyone about his sister.

Tightening her hand around his, Susannah ached

for Killian. She saw the hurt and confusion in his eyes. "Everyone suffers when someone is hurt like that." Forcing herself to release Killian's hand, Susannah whispered, "Look what I've put my parents through since I awakened from the coma. Look how I distrusted you at first."

He gave her a hooded look. "You're better off if you do."

"No," Susannah said fervently, her voice quavering with feeling. "I don't believe that anymore, Sean. You put on a tough act, and I'm sure you're very tough emotionally, but I can read your eyes. I can see the trauma that Meg went through, and how it has affected you." She smiled slightly. "I may come from hill folk, but I've got two good eyes in my head, and a heart that's never led me wrong."

Killian struggled with himself. He'd never spoken to anyone about his sister—not even to Morgan. And now he was spilling his guts to Susannah. He said nothing, for fear of divulging even more.

"I'm really sorry about your sister. Is she living in America?"

"No. She lives near the Irish Sea, in a thatched hut that used to belong to a fisherman and his wife. They died and left her the place. Old Dun and his wife, Em, were like grandparents to Meg. They took care of her when I had to be on assignment. Meg can't stand being around people."

"It's hard for most people to understand how it feels to be a victim of violence," Susannah mused. She looked over at the coffeepot. The coffee was ready to be served. Rising, she added, "I know that since I woke up from the coma I've been jumpy and paranoid.

If someone comes up behind me, I scream. If I catch sight of my own shadow unexpectedly I break out in a sweat and my heart starts hammering." She poured coffee into the cups. "Stupid, isn't it?"

Putting a teaspoon of sugar into the dark, fragrant coffee, Killian shook his head. "Not at all. I call it a survival reflex."

Coming back to the table and sitting down, Susannah gave him a weak smile. "Even now, I dread talking about what happened to me." She turned her hands over. "My palms are damp, and my heart is running like a rabbit's."

"Adrenaline," Killian explained gently, "the flight-or-fight hormone." He stirred the coffee slowly with the spoon, holding her searching gaze.

"Morgan only gave me a brief overview of what happened to you," he probed gently. "Why don't you fill me in on your version? It might help me do my job better."

Susannah squirmed. "This is really going to sound stupid, Sean. It was my idea to go visit Morgan and Laura." She looked around the old farmhouse. "I've never gone much of anywhere, except to Lexington to get my teaching degree. A lot of my friends teased me that I wasn't very worldly and all that. After graduating and coming back here, I bought myself a small house in Glen, near where I work at the local grade school. Laura had been begging me to come for a visit, and I thought taking a plane to Washington, D.C., would expand my horizons."

Killian nodded. In many ways, Susannah's country ways had served to protect her from the world at large. Kentucky was a mountainous state with a small population, in some ways insulated from the harsher realities that plague big cities. "Your first flight?"

She smiled. "Yes, my first. It was really exciting." With an embarrassed laugh, she added, "I know, where else would you find someone who hasn't flown on a plane in this day and age. I had such a wonderful time with Laura, with her children. Morgan took me to the Smithsonian Institution for the whole day, and I was in heaven. I love learning, and that is the most wonderful museum I've ever seen. On my way home I landed at Lexington and was on my way to the bus station to get back here to Glen." Her smile faded. "That's when all this happened."

"Were you in the bus station itself?"

Susannah shook her head. "No. I'd just stepped off the bus. There was a row of ten buses parked under this huge roof, and my bus was farthest away from the building. I was the last one off the bus. It was very dark that night, and it was raining. A thunderstorm. The rain was whipping in under the roof, and I had my head down and was hurrying to get inside.

"This man came out of nowhere and began talking real fast to me. At the same time, he was reaching for my shoulder bag and pulling it off my arm. He was smiling and saying he'd like to help me."

"Was he acting nervous?" Killian asked, noticing that Susannah had gone pale recounting the event.

"I didn't realize it at the time, but yes, he was. How did you know that?"

"Because no doubt he spotted you as a patsy, someone gullible enough to approach, lie to, and then use your luggage—probably to hide drugs or money for a later pickup. But go on. What happened next?" Killian leaned forward, his hands around the hot mug of coffee.

Susannah took in a ragged breath. She was amazed by Killian's knowledge. She was so naive, and it had nearly gotten her killed. "He said he'd take my bag into the station for me. I didn't know what to do. He seemed so nice—he was smiling all the time. I was getting wet from the rain, and I was wearing a new outfit I'd bought, and I didn't want it ruined, so I let him have the bag." She flushed and looked down. "You know the worst part?" she whispered. "I was flattered. I thought he was interested in me…" Her voice trailed off.

Susannah rubbed her brow and was silent for a long moment. When she spoke again, her voice came out hoarse. "He'd no sooner put the piece of luggage over his shoulder than I saw this other man step out of the dark and shoot at him. I screamed, but it was too late. The man fell, and I saw the killer move toward me. No one else was around. No one else saw it happen." Susannah shuddered and wrapped her arms around herself. "The next thing I knew, the killer was after me. I ran into a nearby alley. I remember thinking I was going to die. I heard shots—I heard bullets hitting the sides of the building and whining around me."

Closing her eyes, she whispered, "I was running hard, choking for air. I slipped on the wet street, and it was so dark, so dark…" Susannah opened her eyes. "I remember thinking I had to try to scream for help. But no one came. The next thing I knew, something hit me in the head—a hot sensation. That's it."

Glancing over at Killian, Susannah saw anger flash in his narrowed eyes. Her voice went off-key. "I woke up two months later. My ma was at my side when I came around, and I remember her crying."

"It was probably a drug deal gone wrong," Killian growled. He stared down at his hands. He'd like to wrap them around that bastard and give him back what he'd done to Susannah. "You were at the wrong place at the wrong time. There may have been drugs left in a nearby locker that the man who talked to you was supposed to pick up. Or the guy may have been on the run, using you as a decoy, hoping the killer wouldn't spot him if he was part of a couple." He looked at her sadly. "I'm sorry it happened, Susannah."

"At least I'm alive. I survived." She shrugged, embarrassed. "So much for my trying to become more worldly. I was so stupid."

"No," Killian rasped, "not stupid. Just not as alert as you might have been."

Shivering, Susannah slowly rubbed her arms with her hands. "Sean…the other night when I woke up?"

"Yes?"

"Please believe me. There *was* a man outside my bedroom window. I heard him. I saw his shadow against the opposite wall of my bedroom."

With a sigh, Killian shook his head. "There was no evidence—no footprints outside either window, Susannah. The grass wasn't disturbed."

Rubbing her head with her hands, Susannah sat there, confused. "I could have sworn he was there."

Killian wanted to reach out and comfort her, but he knew he didn't dare. Just her sharing the tragedy with him had drawn her uncomfortably close to him. "Let me do the worrying about it," he said. "All I need you to do is continue to get well."

Susannah felt latent power swirling around him as he sat tautly at the table. Anger shone in his eyes, but this time she knew it wasn't aimed at her; it was aimed at her unidentified assailant.

"I never thought about the killer coming to finish me off," she told him lamely. "That's stupid, too."

"Naive."

"Whatever you want to call it, it still can get me killed." She gave him a long look. "Would this man kill my parents, too?"

"I don't know," Killian said, trying to soothe her worry. "Most of these men go strictly for the target. In a way, you're protecting your parents by not being in their house right now."

"But if the killer got my address, he might think I was at my home in Glen, right?"

"That would be the first place he'd look," Killian agreed, impressed with her insight.

"And then he'd do what?"

"Probably discreetly try to nose around some of your neighbors and find out where you are," he guessed.

"It's no secret I'm here," Susannah said unhappily. "And if the killer didn't know I was out here at the homestead, he might break into my folks' home to find me."

"Usually," he told her, trying to assuage her growing fear, "a contract killer will do a good deal of research to locate his target. That means he probably will show up here sooner or later. My hunch is that he'll stake out the place, sit with a field scope on a rifle, or a pair of binoculars, and try to figure out the comings and goings of everyone here. Once he knew for sure where you were and when to get you alone, he'd come for you."

A chill ran up her spine, and she stared over at Killian. His blue eyes glittered with a feral light that frightened her. "All the trouble I'm causing…"

"I'm here to protect all of you," Killian said. "I'm going to try to get to the bottom of this mess as soon as possible."

With a sigh, Susannah nodded. "I felt it. The moment you were introduced to me, I felt safe."

"Well," Killian growled, rising to his feet, "I'd still stay alert. Paranoia's a healthy reaction to have until I can figure out if you're really safe or not," he said, setting the cup and saucer in the sink.

Grimly Killian placed his hands on the counter and stared out the window. The blue-and-white-checked curtains at the window made it homey, and it was tempting to relax and absorb the feeling. He'd been so long without home and family, and he was rarely able to go back to Ireland to visit what was left of his family—Meg. Sadness moved through him, deep and cutting. Being here with Susannah and her family had been a reprieve of sorts from his loneliness.

"Sean, I really don't feel good about going back to town, back to my house, knowing all this." Susannah stared at his long, lean back. He was silhouetted against the dusk, his mouth a tight line holding back unknown emotions, perhaps pain. Overcoming her shyness, she whispered, "Now that I know the real reason you're here, I'll take you up on that offer to stay with me at night. If you want…"

Slowly Killian turned around. He groaned internally as he met her hope-filled gaze, saw her lips part. The driving urge to kiss her, to explore those wonderful lips, was nearly his undoing.

Susannah took his silence as a refusal. A strange light burned in his intense gaze. "Well… I mean, you don't have to. I don't want you to feel like a—"

"I'll stay," he muttered abruptly.

Nervously Susannah stood and wiped her damp hands down her thighs. "Are you sure?" He looked almost angry. With her? Since the assault, she'd lost so much of her self-esteem. Susannah found herself quivering like jelly inside; it was a feeling she'd never experienced before that fateful night at the bus station.

"Yes," Killian snapped, moving toward the back door. "I'll get my gear down at your folks' place and bring it up here."

Feeling as if she'd done something wrong, Susannah watched him leave. And then she upbraided herself for that feeling. It was a victim's response, according to the woman therapist who had counseled her a number of times when she'd come out of the coma but was still at the hospital.

"Stop it," Susannah sternly told herself. "If he's angry, ask him why. Don't assume it's because of something you said." As she moved to the bedroom next to her own, separated by the only bathroom in the house, Susannah felt a gamut of insecurities. When Sean returned, she was determined to find out the truth of why he'd been so abrupt with her.

Chapter 5

"Are you angry with me?" Susannah asked Killian, the words coming out more breathless than forceful, to her dismay. He'd just dropped his leather bag in the spare bedroom.

Turning, he scowled. "No. Why?"

"You acted upset earlier. I just wanted to know if it was aimed at me."

Straightening, Killian moved to where Susannah stood, at the entrance to his bedroom. Twilight had invaded the depths of the old house, and her sober features were strained. It hurt to think that she thought he was angry with her. Roughly he said, "My being upset has nothing to do with you, Susannah."

"What does it have to do with, then?"

He grimaced, unwilling to comment.

"I know you didn't want this assignment from Morgan..."

Exasperated, he muttered, "Not at first." Killian refused to acknowledge that Susannah appealed to him on some primal level of himself. Furthermore, he couldn't allow himself to get involved emotionally with the person he had to protect. And that was why he had never before accepted an assignment involving a woman; his weakness centered around those who were least able to protect themselves—the women of the world. Emotions touched him deeply, and there was little he could do to parry them, because they always hit him hard, no matter what he tried to do to avoid them. Men were far easier to protect; they were just as closed up as he was, lessening the emotional price tag.

Susannah wasn't about to let Killian squirm out of the confrontation. "I learned a long time ago to talk out problems. Maybe that's a woman's way, but men can profit from it, too." She lifted her hands and held his scrutinizing gaze, gaining confidence. "I don't want you here if you don't want to be, Sean. I hate thinking I'm a burden to anyone."

The ache to reach out and tame a strand of hair away from her flushed features was excruciatingly tempting. Killian exhaled loudly. "I wish you weren't so sensitive to other people's moods."

She smiled a little. "Maybe it's because I work with handicapped children who often either can't speak or have trouble communicating in general. I can't help it. What's bothering you, Sean?"

He shoved his hands into the pockets of his jeans and studied her tautly. "It's my nature not to talk," he warned.

"It does take courage to talk," Susannah agreed, gathering her own courage, determined to get to the root of his problem with her. "It's easier to button up and retreat into silence," she said more firmly.

His mouth had become nothing more than a slash. "Let's drop this conversation."

Susannah stood in the doorway, feeling the tension radiating from him. He not only looked dangerous, he felt dangerous. Her mouth grew dry. "No."

The one word, softly spoken, struck him solidly. "I learned a long time ago to say nothing. I'm a man with a lot of ugly secrets, Susannah. Secrets I'm not proud of. They're best left unsaid."

"I don't agree," Susannah replied gently. She saw the terror lurking in the depths of Killian's eyes as he avoided her searching gaze. "My folks helped me through the worst of my reactions after I came out of the coma. They understood my need to talk about my fears by writing them down on a piece of paper when I couldn't speak." She blinked uncertainly. "I couldn't even cry, Sean. The tears just wouldn't come. The horrible humiliation I felt—still feel even now—was lessened because they cared enough to listen, to hold me when I was so scared. At least I had someone who cared how I felt, who cried *for* me when the pain was too much for me to bear alone."

Killian lifted his chin and stared deeply into her luminous gray eyes. The need to confide, to open his arms and sweep her against him, was painfully real. His whole body was tense with pain. "In my line of work, there aren't many therapists available when things start coming down—or falling apart. There are no safe havens, Susannah. To avoid trouble and ensure safety, I breathe through my nose. It keeps my mouth shut."

He'd said too much already. Killian looked around, wanting to escape, but Susannah stood stubbornly in the doorway, barring any exit. Panic ate at him.

Susannah shook her head. "I felt such sadness around you," she whispered, opening her hands to him. "You put on such a frightening mask, Sean—"

Angrily he rasped, "Back off."

The words slapped her. His tone had a lethal quality. Swallowing hard, Susannah saw fear, mixed with anguish, mirrored in his narrowed eyes. The words had been spoken in desperation, not anger. "How can I? I feel how uncomfortable you are here with me. I feel as if I've done something to make you feel like that." She raised her eyes to the ceiling. "Sean, I can't live like that with a person. How can you?"

Nostrils flaring, Killian stared at her in disbelief. Her honesty was bone deep—a kind he'd rarely encountered. Killian didn't dare tell her the raw, blatant truth—that he wanted her in every way imaginable. "I guess I've been out in the field too long," he told her in a low, growling tone. "I'm used to harshness, Susannah, not the softness a woman has, not a home. Being around you is…different…and I'm having to adjust." *A lot.*

"And," he added savagely, seeing how flustered she was becoming, "I'm used to bunking with men, not a woman. I get nightmares." When her face fell with compassion for him, he couldn't deal with it—almost hating her for it, for forcing the feelings out of him. "The night is my enemy, Susannah. And it's an enemy for anyone who might be near me when it happens. The past comes back," he warned thickly. Killian wanted to protect Susannah from that dark side of himself. He was afraid he might not be able to control himself, that terrorized portion of him that sometimes trapped him for hours in its brutal grip, ruling him.

Standing there absorbing the emotional pain contained in his admission, Susannah realized for the first time that Killian was terribly human. He wasn't the superman she'd first thought, although Morgan's men had a proud reputation for being exactly that. The discovery was as breathtaking as it was disturbing. She had no experience with a man like Killian—someone who had been grievously wounded by a world whose existence she could hardly fathom. The pleading look Killian gave her, the twist of his lips as he shared the information with her, tore at Susannah's heart. Instinctively she realized that Killian needed to be held, too. If only for a little while. He needed a safe haven from the stormy dangers inherent in his chosen profession. That was something she could give him while he stayed with her.

"I understand," she whispered unsteadily. "And if you have bad dreams, I'll come out and make you a cup of tea. Maybe we can talk about it."

He slowly raised his head, feeling the tension make his joints ache. He held Susannah's guileless eyes, eyes that were filled with hope. "Your naiveté nearly got you killed once," he rasped. "Just stay away from me if you hear me up and moving around at night, Susannah. *Stay away.*"

She gave him a wary look, seeing the anguish in his narrowed eyes even as they burned with desire. Desire for her? Susannah wished that need could be for her alone, but she knew Killian was the kind of man who allowed no grass to grow under his feet. He was a wanderer over the face of the earth, with no interest in settling down. Much as she hated to admit it, she had to be honest with herself.

Killian wasn't going to say anything else, Susannah realized. She stepped back into the hallway, at a loss. Lamely she held his hooded stare.

"It's as if you're saying you're a danger to me."

"I am."

Susannah shook her head. "I wish," she said softly, "I had more experience with the world, with men…"

Killian wanted to move to her and simply enfold Susannah in his arms. She looked confused and bereft. "Stay the way you are," he told her harshly. "You don't want to know what the world can offer."

Susannah wasn't so sure. She felt totally unprepared to deal with a complex man like Sean, yet she was powerfully drawn to him. "Should I follow my normal schedule of doing things around here tomorrow morning?" At least this was a safe topic of conversation.

"Yes."

"I see. Good night, Sean."

"Good night." The words came out in a rasp. Killian tasted his frustration, and felt a heated longing coil through him. Susannah looked crestfallen. Could he blame her? No. Darkness was complete now, and he automatically perused the gloomy area. Perhaps talking a little bit about himself hadn't been so bad after all. At least with her. He knew he couldn't live under the same roof without warning Susannah of his violent night world.

By ten, Killian was in bed, wearing only his pajama

bottoms. He stared blankly at the plaster ceiling, which was in dire need of repair. His senses functioned like radar, swinging this way and that, picking up nuances of sound and smell. Nothing seemed out of place, so he relaxed to a degree. And then, against his will, his attention shifted to dwell on Susannah. She had a surprisingly stubborn side to her—and he liked discovering that strength within her. Outwardly she might seem soft and naive, but she had emotional convictions that served as the roots of her strength.

Glancing at the only window in his room, Killian could see stars dotting the velvet black of the sky. Everything was so peaceful here. Another layer of tension dissolved around him, and he found himself enjoying the old double bed, the texture of the clean cotton sheets that Susannah had made the bed with, and the symphony of the crickets chirping outside the house.

What was it about this place that permeated his constant state of wariness and tension to make him relax to this degree? Killian had no answers, or at least none he was willing to look at closely. Exhausted, he knew he had to try to get some sleep. He moved restlessly on the bed, afraid of what the night might hold. He forced his eyes closed, inhaled deeply and drifted off to sleep. On the nightstand was his pistol, loaded and with the safety off, perpetually at the ready. Killian jerked awake, his hand automatically moving to his pistol. Sunlight streamed through the window and the lacy pale green curtains. Blinking, he slowly sat up and shoved several locks of hair off his brow. The scent of freshly brewed coffee and frying bacon wafted on the air. He inhaled hungrily and threw his legs across the creaky bed. Relief flowed through him as he realized that for once the nightmares hadn't come to haunt him. Puzzled, he moved to the bathroom. Not only had the nightmares stayed at bay, but he'd slept very late. Usually his sleep was punctuated by moments of stark terror throughout the night and he finally fell more heavily asleep near dawn. Still, he never slept past six—ever. But now it was eight o'clock. Stymied about why he'd slept so late, he stepped into a hot shower.

Dressed in a white shirt and jeans, Killian swung out of his room and down the hall, following the enticing smells emanating from the kitchen. Halting in the doorway, he drank in the sight of Susannah working over the old wood stove. Today she wore a sleeveless yellow blouse, well-worn jeans and white tennis shoes. Her hair, thick and abundant, cloaked her shoulders. As if she had sensed his presence, she looked up.

"I thought this might get you out of bed." She grinned. "So much for keeping up with me and my schedule. I was up at five-thirty, and you were still sawing logs."

Rubbing his face, Killian managed a sheepish look as he headed for the counter where the coffeepot sat. "I overslept," he muttered.

Taking the bacon out of the skillet and placing it on a paper towel to soak up the extra grease, Susannah smiled. "Don't worry, your secrets are safe with me."

Killian gave her a long, absorbing look, thinking how pretty she looked this morning. But he noted a slight puffiness beneath Susannah's eyes and wondered if she'd been crying. "I guess I'll have to get used to this," he rasped. The coffee was strong, hot and black—just the way he liked it. Susannah placed a stack of pancakes, the rasher of bacon and a bottle of maple syrup before him and sat down opposite him.

"'This' meaning me?"

Killian dug hungrily into the pancakes. "It's everything."

Susannah sat back and shook her head. "One- or two-word answers, Sean. I swear. What do you mean by 'everything'?"

He gave her a brief look. He was really enjoying the buckwheat pancakes. "It's been a long time since I was in a home, not a house," he told her between bites.

She ate slowly, listening closely not only to what he said, but also to how he said it. "So, home life appeals to you after all?"

He raised his brows.

"I thought," Susannah offered, "that you were a rolling stone that gathered no moss. A man with wanderlust in his soul."

He refused to hold her warm gaze. "Home means everything to me." The pancakes disappeared in a hurry, and the bacon quickly followed. Killian took his steaming cup of coffee and tipped his chair back on two legs. The kitchen fragrances lingered like perfume, and birds sang cheerfully outside the screen door, enhancing his feeling of contentment. Susannah looked incredibly lovely, and Killian thought he was in heaven—or as close as the likes of him was ever going to get to it.

Sipping her coffee, Susannah risked a look at Killian. "To me, a house is built of walls and beams. A home is built with love and dreams. You said you were from Ireland. Were you happy over there?"

Uncomfortable, Killian shrugged. "Northern Ireland isn't exactly a happy place to live." He shot her a hard look. "I learned early on, Susannah, the danger of caring about someone too much, because they'd be ripped away from me."

It felt as if a knife were being thrust down through Susannah. She gripped the delicate cup hard between her hands. "But what—"

With a shrug, Killian tried to cover up his own unraveling emotions. Gruffly he said, "That was the past—there's no need to rehash it. This is the present."

Pain for Killian settled over Susannah. She didn't know what had happened to him as a child, but his words "the danger of caring about someone too much" created a knot in her stomach.

Finishing her coffee, Susannah quietly got up and gathered the plates and flatware. At the counter, she began washing the dishes in warm, soapy water.

Killian rose and moved to where Susannah stood. He spotted a towel hanging on a nail and began to dry the dishes as she rinsed them.

"You're upset."

"No."

"You don't lie well at all. Your voice is a dead giveaway—not to mention those large, beautiful eyes of yours." No one could have been more surprised than Killian at what had just transpired. He hadn't meant to allude to the tragedy. Her empathy was touching, but Killian knew that to feel another person's pain at that depth was dangerous. Why didn't Susannah shield herself more from him?

Avoiding his sharpened gaze, Susannah concentrated on washing the dishes. "It's just that, well, you seem to carry a lot of pain." She inhaled shakily.

"I told you the secrets I carried weren't good ones," he warned her darkly.

"Yes, you did…" she agreed softly.

Disgusted with himself, Killian muttered, "Face it, life isn't very nice."

Susannah's hands stilled in the soothing water. Lifting her chin, she met and held his stormy gaze. "I don't believe that. There's always hope," she challenged.

With a muffled sound, Killian suppressed the curse that rose to his lips. Susannah didn't deserve his harsh side, his survival reflexes. "*Hope* isn't a word I recognize."

"What about dreams?"

His smile was deadly. Cynical. "Dreams? More like nightmares, colleen."

There was no way to parry the grim finality of his view of the world—at least not yet. Susannah softened her voice. "Well, perhaps the time you spend here will change your mind."

"A month or so in Eden before I descend back into hell? Be careful, Susannah. You don't want to invest anything in me. I live in hell. I don't want to pull you into it."

A chill moved through her. His lethal warning sounded as if it came from the very depths of his injured, untended soul. Killian was like a wounded animal—hurting badly, lashing out in pain. Rallying, Susannah determined not to allow Killian to see how much his warning had shaken her.

"Well," she went on with forced lightness, "you'll probably be terribly bored sooner or later. In the end, you'll be more than ready to leave."

Killian scowled as he continued to dry the flatware

one piece at a time. "We'll see" was all he'd say. He'd said enough. *Too much.* The crestfallen look in Susannah's eyes made him want to cry. Cry! Struck by his cruelty toward her, Killian would have done anything to take back his words. Susannah had gone through enough hell of her own without him dumping his sordid past on her, too.

"What's on the list this morning?" he demanded abruptly.

Susannah tried to gather her strewn, shocked feelings. "Weeding the garden. I try to do it during the morning hours, while it's still cool. We have to pick the slugs off, weed and check the plants for other insects. That sort of thing." Again, tension vibrated around Killian, and it translated to her. She knew there was a slight wobble in her strained tone. Had Killian picked it up? Susannah didn't have the courage to glance at him as he continued drying dishes.

A huge part of Susannah wanted to help heal his wounds. Her heart told her she had the ability to do just that. Hadn't she helped so many children win freedom from crosses they'd been marked to bear for life? She'd helped guide them out of trapped existences with color, paints and tempera. Each year she saw a new batch of special children, and by June they were smiling far more than when they'd first come to class. No, there was hope for Killian, whether he wanted to admit it or not.

Killian methodically pulled the weeds that poked their heads up between the rows of broccoli, cauliflower and tomatoes. A few rows over, Susannah worked, an old straw hat protecting her from the sun's intensity. He worked bareheaded, absorbing energy from the sunlight. Since their conversation in the kitchen that morning, she'd been suspiciously silent, and it needled Killian enormously.

He had to admit, there was something pleasurable about thrusting his hands into the damp, rich soil. Over near the fence, the baby robin that had previously fallen out of its nest chirped loudly for its parents to bring her more food. Killian wore his shoulder holster, housing the Beretta beneath his left arm. Susannah had given him a disgruntled look when he'd put on the shoulder harness, but had said nothing. Just as well. He didn't want her getting any ideas about saving him and his dark, hopeless soul. Let her realize who and what he was. That way, she'd keep her distance. He wasn't worth saving.

Susannah got off her hands and knees. She took the handful of slugs she'd found and placed them on the other side of the fence, under the fruit tree, below the robin's nest. Not believing in insecticides, she tried to use nature's balance to maintain her gardens. The robins would feed the slugs to their babies, completing the natural cycle.

Usually her work relaxed her, but this morning the silence between her and Killian was terribly strained, and she had no idea how to lessen it. She glanced over at Killian, who worked in a crouch, pulling weeds, his face set. Every once in a while, she could feel him surveying the area, his guarded watchfulness evident.

Susannah took off her hat, wiped her damp brow with the back of her hand and walked toward the house. She wanted to speak to him, but she felt that cold wall around him warning her to leave him alone.

Entering the kitchen, Susannah realized just how lonely was the world Killian lived in. It was sheer agony for him to talk. Each conversation was like pulling teeth—painful and nerve-racking. Tossing her straw hat on the table, Susannah poured two tall, icy glasses of lemonade.

Killian entered silently, catching her off guard. Susannah's heart hammered briefly. His face was glistening with sweat, but his mouth was no longer pursed, she noted, and his eyes looked lighter—almost happy, if she was reading him accurately.

"Come on, sit down. You've earned a rest," she said.

The lemonade disappeared in a hurry as he gulped it down and nodded his thanks.

"More?"

"Please." Killian sat at the table, his hands folded on top of it, watching Susannah move with her incredible natural grace.

With another nod of appreciation, he took the newly filled glass but this time didn't gulp it down. He glanced at his watch. "I hadn't realized two hours had gone by."

Susannah smiled tentatively. Casting about for some safe topic, she waved at the colorful pictures on the kitchen walls. "My most recent class did these. Some of the kids have intellectual disabilities, others have had deformities since birth. They range in intellectual age from about six to twelve. I love drawing them out of their shells." And then, deliberately holding his gaze, she added, "They find happiness by making the most of what they have." Susannah pointed again to the tempera paintings that she'd had framed. "I keep these because they're before-and-after drawings," she confided warmly.

"Oh?"

"The paintings on this wall were done when the children first came to class in September. The paintings on the right were done just before school was out in June. Take a look."

Killian rose and went over to the paintings, his glass of lemonade in hand. One child's first painting was dark and shadowy—the one done nine months later was bright and sunny in comparison. Another painting had a boy in a wheelchair looking glum. In the next, he was smiling and waving to the birds overhead. Killian glanced at Susannah over his shoulder. "Telling, aren't they?"

"Very."

He studied the others in silence. Finally he turned around, came back to the table and sat down. "You must have the patience of Job."

With a little laugh, Susannah shook her head. "For me, it's a wonderful experience watching these kids open up and discover happiness—some of them for the first time in their lives." Her voice took on more feeling. "Just watching them blossom, learn to trust, to explore, means everything to me. It's a real privilege for me."

"I guess some people pursue happiness and others create it. I envy those kids." Killian swallowed convulsively, feeling uncomfortably as if her sparkling eyes were melting his hardened heart—and his hardened view of the world. Her lower lip trembled under the intensity of his stare, and the overwhelming need to reach over, to pull Susannah to his chest and kiss her until she molded to him with desire, nearly unstrung his considerable control. If he stayed at the table, he'd touch her. He'd kiss the hell out of her.

Susannah wanted Sean to get used to the idea that he, too, could have happiness. "You know, what we did out there this morning made you happy. I could see it in your eyes. Your face is relaxed. Isn't that something?"

Leaving her side abruptly, Killian placed his empty glass on the counter, a little more loudly than necessary. "What's next? What do you want me to do?"

Shocked, Susannah watched the hardness come back into Killian's features. She'd pushed him too far. "I... Well, the screen in my bedroom could be fixed..." she said hesitantly.

"Then what?" A kind of desperation ate at Killian. He didn't dare stay in such close proximity to Susannah. The more she revealed of herself, the more she trusted him with her intimate thoughts and feelings, the more she threatened his much-needed defenses. Dammit, she trusted too easily!

"Then lunch. I was going to make us lunch, and then I thought we'd pick the early snow peas and freeze them this afternoon," she said.

"Fine."

Blinking, Susannah watched Killian stalk out of the kitchen. The tension was back in him; he was like a trap that begged to be sprung. Shakily she drew in a breath, all too clearly recognizing that the unbidden hunger in his eyes was aimed directly at her. Suddenly she felt like an animal in a hunter's sights.

Chapter 6

"Look out!" Killian's shriek careened around the darkened bedroom. He jerked himself upright, his hand automatically moving for the pistol. Cool metal met his hot, sweaty fingers. Shadows from the past danced around him. His breathing was ragged and chaotic. The roar of rifles and the blast of mortars flashed in front of his wide, glazed eyes as he sat rigidly in bed. A hoarse cry, almost a sob, tore from his contorted lips.

He made a muffled sound of disgust. With the back of his hand, Killian wiped his eyes clear of tears. Where was he? What room? What country? Peru? Algeria? Laos? *Where?*

His chest rising and falling rapidly, Killian narrowed his eyes as he swung his gaze around the quiet room. It took precious seconds for him to realize that he was here, in Kentucky. Cursing softly, he leaped out of bed, his pajama bottoms damp with sweat and clinging to his taut body. Shaking. He was shaking. It was nothing new. Often he would shake for a good hour after coming awake. More important, the nightmare hadn't insidiously kept control of him after waking. The flashbacks frightened him for Susannah's sake.

Laying the pistol down, Killian rubbed his face savagely, trying to force the remnants of the nightmare away. What he needed to shock him back into the present was a brutally cold shower. That and a fortifying cup of coffee. Forcing himself to move on wobbly legs, he made it to the bathroom. Fumbling for the shower faucet, he found it and turned it on full-force.

Later, he padded down the darkened hall in his damp, bare feet, a white towel draped low around his hips. His watch read 3:00 a.m.—the same time he usually had the nightmares. Shoving damp strands of hair off his brow, he rounded the corner. Shock riveted him to the spot.

"I thought you might like some coffee," Susannah whispered unsteadily. She was standing near the counter in a long white cotton nightgown. Her hands were clasped in front of her. "That and some company?"

Rubbing his mouth with the back of his hand, Killian stood tautly, his heightened senses reeling with impact. Moonlight lovingly caressed Susannah, the luminescence outlining her slender shape through her thin cotton gown. The lace around the gown's boat neck emphasized her collarbones and her slender neck. He gulped and allowed his hand to fall back to his side. Susannah's face looked sleepy, her eyes dreamy with a softness that aroused a longing in him to bury himself in her, hotly, deeply. She remained perfectly still as he devoured her with his starving gaze.

There was fear in her eyes, mixed with desire and longing. Killian not only saw it in the nuances of her fleeting expression, but sensed it, as well. Like a wolf too long without a mate, he ached to claim her as his own. And then, abruptly he laughed at himself. Who was he kidding? She was all the things he was not. She had hope. She believed in a future filled with dreams. Hell, she gave handicapped children back the chance to dream.

"It's not a good time to be around me," he rasped.

Inhaling shakily, Susannah nodded. "It's a chance I'll take." Never had she seen a man of such power, intensity and beauty as Killian. He stood in the kitchen doorway, the towel draped casually across his lean hips, accentuating his near nakedness.

Killian's shoulders were proudly thrown back, and his muscles were cleanly delineated. His chest was covered with hair that headed like an arrow down his long torso and flat belly. The dark line of hair disappeared beneath the stark whiteness of the towel, but still, little was left to the imagination. Susannah gulped convulsively.

Susannah's skin tingled where his hungry gaze had swept across her. Trying to steady her desire for him, she noticed that her hands shook as she turned to put the coffee into the pot.

It had taken everything for Susannah to tear her gaze from his overwhelming masculine image. "I—I heard you scream. At first I thought it was a nightmare

I was having, and then I realized it wasn't me screaming. It was you."

Killian remained frozen in the doorway. The husky softness of Susannah's voice began to dissolve some of the terror that seemed to twist within him like a living being.

She shrugged. "I didn't know what to do."

"You did the right thing," he said raggedly. He forced himself to move toward the table. Gripping the chair, he sat down, afraid he might fall down if he didn't. His knees were still weak from the virulent nightmare. He looked up at Susannah. "Didn't I tell you that I wasn't worth the risk? Look at you. You're shaking." And she was. He wanted desperately to reassure her somehow, but he couldn't.

Rubbing her arms, Susannah nodded. "I'll be okay."

Killian felt like hell. He'd scared her, triggered the fear she'd barely survived months ago, and he knew it. "I walk around in a living death every day of my life. You don't deserve to be around it—or me."

The sweat glistening on Killian's taut muscles spoke to her of the hell he was still caught up in. Susannah forced herself to move through her fear and cross to his side. She reached out and gently laid her hands on his shoulders.

Killian groaned. Her touch was so warm, so steadying.

"Just sit there," she whispered in a strained tone. "Let me work the knots out of your shoulders. You're so tense."

He opened his mouth to protest, but the kneading quality of her strong, slender hands as they worked his aching muscles stopped him. Instead of speak-

ing, he closed his eyes and gradually began to relax.
With each sliding, coaxing movement of her fingers
along his skin, a little more of the fear he carried with
him dissolved. Eventually he allowed himself to sag
against the chair.

"Lean on me," Susannah coaxed. She pressed her
hand to his sweaty brow and guided his head against
her.

How easy it was to have his head cushioned against
her as her hands moved with confidence on his shoulders and neck. A ragged sigh issued from him, and he
closed his eyes, trusting her completely.

"Good," she crooned softly, watching his short,
spiky lashes droop closed. Even his mouth, once a
harsh line holding back a deluge of emotions, gradually relaxed.

Susannah felt the steel-cable strength of his muscles
beneath her hands. He was built like a cougar—lean
and lithe. Her feelings were alive, bright and clamoring not only for acknowledgment, but for action. The
thrill of touching Killian, of having him trust her this
much, was dizzying and inviting. Susannah ached to
lean forward and place a soft kiss on his furrowed
brow. How much pain did this man carry within him?

As she stood in the moonlit kitchen with him, massaging his terror and tension away, Susannah realized
that Killian's life must have been one of unending
violence.

"Two years ago," she said unsteadily as she
smoothed away the last of the rigidity from his now-
supple muscles, "I had a little boy, Stevey, in my class.
He had intellectual disabilities and had been taken
from his home by Social Services. He was only eight

years old, and he was like a frightened little animal. The social worker told me that his father was an alcoholic and his mother was on drugs. They both beat up on him."

Killian's eyes snapped open.

"I'm telling you this for a reason," Susannah whispered, her hands stilling on his shoulders. "At first, Stevey would only crawl into a corner and hide. Gradually I earned his trust, and then I got him to draw. The pictures told me so much about what he'd endured, what he'd suffered through, alone and unprotected. There wasn't a day that went by that I didn't cry for him.

"Stevey taught me more about trust and love than any other person in my life ever has. Gradually, throughout the year that he was in my class, he came to life. He truly blossomed, and it was so breathtaking. He learned to smile, then to laugh. His new foster parents love him deeply, and that helped bring him out of the terror and humiliation he'd endured.

"I saw this frightened, beaten child have enough blind faith in another human being to rally and reach out just once more. Stevey had a kind of courage that I feel is the rarest kind in the world, and the hardest to acquire." Susannah reached out and stroked Killian's damp hair. "Stevey knew only violence, broken trust and heartache. But something in him—his spirit, if you will—had the strength to work through all of that and embrace others who truly loved him and accepted him for who he was."

Killian released a shaky breath, wildly aware of Susannah's trembling fingers lightly caressing his hair. Did she realize what she was doing? Did she know that if she kept it up he'd take her hard and fast, burying himself in her hot depths? Longing warred with control. He eased out of her hands and sat up.

"Why don't you get us that coffee?" he said. His voice was none too steady, and it had a sandpaper rasp. Glancing up as Susannah walked past him, he saw her face. How could she look so damned angelic when all he felt was his blood pounding like a dam ready to burst?

Miraculously, the nightmare and its contents had disappeared beneath Susannah's gentle, questing hands. Killian's eyes slitted as he studied her at the counter, where she was pouring the coffee. What was it about her? Grateful that she wasn't looking at him, Killian struggled to get his raging need back under control. Usually he had no problem disconnecting himself from his volcanic emotions, but Susannah aroused him to a white heat of desire.

With trembling hands, Susannah set the coffee before Killian, sharply conscious of his perusal of her. His words, his warning, kept thrumming through her. She felt danger and intensity surrounding them. Did she have the courage to stay? To be there for Killian? Forcing herself to look up, she met and held his blue gaze, a gaze that was hooded with some unknown emotion that seemed to melt her inwardly.

Gulping, she sat down at his elbow, determined not to allow him to scare her away. Right now, her heart counseled her, he needed a friend, someone he could talk with.

Killian sat there thunderstruck. Susannah couldn't be this naive—she must realize how he wanted her. Yet she sat down next to him, her face filled with determination as she sipped her steaming coffee. Angry, and feeling at war within himself, he snapped irritably, "Why don't you go back to bed?"

"Because you need me here."

His eyes widened enormously.

Prepared to risk everything, Susannah met and held his incredulous gaze. "You need a friend, Sean."

His fingers gripped his cup, and he stared down at the black contents. "Talking is the last thing I want to do right now."

She tried to absorb his brutal, angry words. "What, then?"

He snapped a look at her. "Get away from me, Susannah, while you can. Stop trying to get close. I'm not Stevey. I'm a grown man, with a grown man's needs. You're in danger. Stay, and I can't answer for what I might do."

There was such anguish in his raspy words, and she felt his raw need of her. She sat up, her fingers releasing the cup. "No, you aren't like Stevey," Susannah whispered unsteadily. "But you are wounded—and in need of a safe haven."

With a hiss, Killian jerked to his feet, the chair nearly tipping over from the swiftness of his movement. "Wounded animals can bite those who try to help them!" Breathing harshly, he walked to the other end of the kitchen. "Dammit, Susannah, stay away from me. You've already been hurt by a man who nearly killed you." He struck his chest. "I can hurt you in so many different ways. Is that what you want? Do you want me to take you, to bury myself in you, to make night and day merge into one until you don't know anything except me, my arms, my body and—"

With a muffled sound, Killian spun around, jerked

open the screen door and disappeared into the night. If he didn't go, he was going to take Susannah right there on the hard wooden floor. The primal blood was racing through him, blotting out reason, disintegrating his control. As he stalked off the porch, he knew she was an innocent in this. She was the kind of woman he'd always dreamed of—but then, dreams never could stand the test of harsh daylight.

Who was he kidding? Killian walked swiftly, his feet and ankles soon soaked from the trail he made through the dewy grass. Moonlight shifted across him in unending patterns as he continued his blind walk through the orchard. He had to protect Susannah from himself—at all costs. She didn't deserve to get tangled up with his kind. It could only end in disaster.

Gradually he slowed his pace as his head began to clear. The night was cool, but not chilly. He realized with disgust that he'd left without his weapon, and that he'd left Susannah wide open to attack if someone was prowling around. As he halted and swiftly shifted his awareness to more external things, he acknowledged that, although unarmed, he was never defenseless. No, he'd been taught to kill a hundred different ways without need of any kind of weapon.

He stood in the middle of the orchard, scowling. Bats dipped here and there, chasing after choice insects that he couldn't see. The old homestead was a quarter of a mile away, looking broken down and in dire need of paint, and also the love and care it would take to put it back in good repair. Killian laughed harshly. Wasn't he just like that old house? The only difference was that the scars he wore were mostly carried on the inside, where no one could see them. No one except

Susannah. Why couldn't she be like everyone else and see only the tough exterior he presented to the world?

Killian stood there a long time, mulling over the story she'd told him about the little boy named Stevey. The boy deserved Susannah's loving care. She was the right person to help coax him out of his dark shell of fear. Her words, soft and strained, floated back to him: "You are wounded—and need a safe haven."

How long he stood there thinking about their conversation, he didn't know. When he glanced at his watch, it was 4:00 a.m. Forcing himself, he walked slowly back to the homestead. As he walked, he prayed—something he rarely did—that Susannah had had enough sense to go back to bed. What would he do if she was still up and waiting for him? His mouth was dry, and he wiped at it with the back of his hand. He didn't know.

Susannah was out in the extensive rose garden, giving the colorful flowers the special food that helped them to bloom. It was nearly noon, and she was hot, even though she wore her straw hat, a sleeveless white blouse and a threadbare pair of jeans. Her mind and heart centered on Killian. She'd gone back to bed around four, and had promptly plummeted into a deep, restful sleep. When she'd gotten up this morning at six, his bedroom door had been shut. Was he in there? Had he gone somewhere else? Susannah didn't know, and she hadn't had the courage to find out.

Taking her one-gallon bucket and the box of rose food, she went back over to the hose to mix the ingredients for the next rosebush. The air was heavy with the wonderful fragrance of the flowering bushes. The rose garden sat on the southern side of the homestead, where there was the most light. There was no fence around it, and the bushes stretched for nearly a quarter of a mile.

Susannah hunched over the bucket and poured the rose food into the pooling water, stirring it with her hand. The water turned a pretty pink color. Pink always reminded her of love, she thought mildly. Then Killian's harsh warning pounded back through her. He *was* dangerous, she thought, feeling the heat of longing flow through her—dangerous to her heart, to her soul. Killian had the ability to touch her very essence. How, she didn't know. She only knew he had that capacity, and no other man she'd ever met had been able to touch her so deeply.

Shutting off the faucet, Susannah set the food aside and hefted the gallon bucket to carry it to the next rosebush, a beautiful lavender one with at least ten blossoms. No longer could she keep from entertaining the idea of loving Killian. Her dreams had turned torrid toward morning, and she vividly recalled images of his hands caressing her body, his mouth ravishing her with wild abandon, meeting her willing, equally hungry lips.

She poured the bucket's contents into the well around the rosebush. What did she want? *Killian.* Why? Because... Susannah straightened and put the bucket aside. She pulled out a pair of scissors and began pruning off old blooms. Was it to help him heal? Yes. To show him that another person could trust him fully, fearlessly, even if he didn't trust himself? Yes. To give him her love in hopes that he might overcome his own fear of loving and losing—and to love her? *Yes.*

Stymied, she stood there, her hands cupped around one of the large lavender roses. She leaned forward, inhaling the delicate fragrance. Life was so beautiful. Why couldn't Killian see that? As she studied the many-petaled bloom, Susannah ached for him. She knew she had the ability to show him the beauty of life. But what then? He would be in her life only long enough to catch the killer who might be stalking her. He'd repeatedly warned her that he wasn't worth loving.

But he was. With a sigh, Susannah pocketed the scissors, picked up the bucket and headed back to the faucet. Her stomach growled, and she realized that it was nearly lunchtime and she was hungry. Placing all the gardening tools near the spigot, Susannah walked back to the homestead. Would Killian be there? And if he was, would he be up yet? Fear mingled with need of him inside her. How would she handle their next confrontation?

Killian's head snapped up at the sound of someone's approach. He was at the kitchen cabinets, searching through them for something to eat. He'd just gotten up and taken a scaldingly hot shower to awaken, then gotten dressed in a dark blue short-sleeved shirt and jeans. He felt like someone had poleaxed him.

Susannah opened the screen door and took off her straw hat. When she saw him, she hesitated.

Killian glared at her.

"Hungry?" she asked, hoping to hide the tension she felt. She continued into the room and placed her hat on the table.

"Like a bear," he muttered, moving away from the counter.

Susannah kept plenty of distance between them. She noticed the stormy quality in his blue eyes, and her nerves grew taut. Scared, but aware that Killian needed courage from her, not cowardice, Susannah said firmly, "Have a seat and I'll fix you what I'm going to have: a tuna sandwich, sweet pickles and pretzels."

Sitting down, Killian tried to soften his growly bad humor. "Okay."

"Coffee or iced tea?"

"I don't care."

Gathering her dissolving courage, Susannah said, "I think you need a strong cup of coffee. Are you always like this when you wake up?" Killian looked fiercely unhappy, his eyes bleak, with dark circles under them. It was obvious he hadn't slept well after their verbal battle last night.

Killian refused to watch her as she moved to the icebox. "I told you I was a bastard."

She forced a laugh and brought bread and a bowl of prepared tuna to the counter. "You really aren't, you know. You're just grouchy because you lost some sleep last night and you haven't had your coffee yet."

"Maybe you're right." Killian watched her hungrily, every movement, every sway of her hips. Susannah had her sable hair swept into a ponytail, as usual, and it shone with each step she took. Her face glowed with the good health of a woman who loved the outdoors. Unhappily Killian folded his hands on the table. Why wouldn't Susannah heed his warning? Why didn't she believe that he was a bastard, someone capable of hurting her badly? He didn't want to hurt her—not her, of all people.

Humming softly, Susannah made coffee, prepared the sandwiches and put together a wholesome lunch. When she turned around, Killian's rugged profile still reflected his unhappiness. He sat tensely, his mouth pursed.

"Here, start on the sandwich. Bears don't do well on empty stomachs."

Grateful for her teasing, he took the sandwich and began eating. But he didn't taste it—all he was aware of was his own intense suffering, and Susannah's sunlit presence. She chased away his gloom, that terrible shadow that always hovered over him like a vulture ready to rip out what little was left of his heart.

Placing the coffee before him, Susannah took her usual seat at his elbow. Her heart was hammering so hard in her chest that she feared Killian might hear it. As she forced herself to eat, the kitchen fell into a stilted silence.

"Earlier, I went down to visit my parents," she offered after a moment, trying to lessen the tension. "They told me my school had called, that the principal wanted me to consider coming back to work sooner." She picked up a pickle and frowned. "I really miss teaching. I have a new class of kids that I've never seen." She watched Killian raise his head, his blue gaze settling on her. Her pulse raced. Trying to continue to sound nonchalant, she added, "So I called Mr. Gains back—that's the principal—and told him I'd like to return."

"When?" The word came out sharp.

Wiping her hands on a napkin, Susannah said, "Next Monday. I feel well enough now."

Relief shattered through Killian. That, and terrible disappointment. Some stupid part of him actually had held out hope that Susannah would stay, would persevere with him and reach into his heart. Putting down the sandwich, he reached for the coffee. Gulping down a swallow, he burned his mouth.

"Does that mean you're moving back into town? Into your house?"

"I—I don't know." Susannah managed a small shrug. "I really miss my kids, Sean. But I don't know if I'm ready to be alone. Do you know what I mean?"

He nodded and dropped his gaze. "Yeah, I know what you mean."

"I've been doing a lot of thinking this morning, and I guess I'll try to go to work full-time. Mr. Gains said if I have any problems I can split the class and work only half days for a while, until I get back into the swing of things."

"Half a day is enough for now."

She shrugged, not sure.

"Susannah, you're still healing."

And the other half of the day would be spent here, in Killian's intense presence, reminding her constantly of her need of him as a man, a lover. "I don't know," she confided in a low voice.

He set the coffee cup down a little more loudly than he'd intended. Susannah winced. "You aren't ready for all of that yet. You've got to pace yourself. Comas do funny things to people. What if you get flashbacks? Periods of vertigo? Or what if you blank out? All those things could happen under stress. And going back into that classroom *is* stress."

Susannah stared at him, feeling his raw intensity, his care. "Being here with you is stress, too, Sean."

Gripping the cup, he growled, "I suppose it is. I'm not the world's best person to be near. Around you, I shoot off my mouth, and look what it's done."

A soft smile touched her lips, and she leaned over and rested her hand on his arm. "Sean, some kinds of stress aren't bad. I like talking with you, sharing with you. I don't consider it bad or harmful. I feel shutting up and retreating is far more damaging."

"You would," Killian muttered, but he really didn't mean it. Just the cool, steadying touch of her fingers on his arm sent waves of need pulsing through him.

"Everyone needs someone," Susannah whispered. "Your needs are no different than anyone else's."

He cocked his head. "Don't be so sure."

She smiled a little, feeling danger swirling around her. "I'm betting your bark is worse than your bite."

"Oh? Was that the way it was with Stevey?"

Susannah forced herself to release him. "At first, every time I came near him, he lashed out at me."

"And what did you do?"

"I'd lean down, pull him against me and just hold him."

Killian shut his eyes and drew in a deep, shaky breath. "I don't know what to make of you, Susannah. Why would anyone put themselves in the line of fire just to let someone else know that they weren't going to be hurt again?" He opened his eyes, searching her thoughtful gray ones.

"I believe we're all healers, Sean. We not only have the ability to heal ourselves, but to heal others, too. Stevey wanted to be healed. Each time I approached him, he struck out less and less, until finally, one day, he opened his arms to me. It was such a beautiful, poignant moment."

"He trusted you," Killian said flatly.

"Yes, he did."

"You're a catalyst."

"So are you," she said wryly, meeting his wary eyes.

Uncomfortable, Killian wanted to shift the conversation back to her. "So you're going to try class for a full day next Monday?"

"Yes."

"All right, I'll drive you to work and hang around, if you don't mind. I want to get the layout of your school, your classroom. If they've got a contract out on you— and we still don't know if they do or not—I want to have that school, its entrances and exits, in my head in case something comes down."

She sat back, surprised. "Do you really think I'm in danger?"

"Until I can prove otherwise," Killian said roughly, "I'm assuming there's a hit man out there somewhere, just waiting for you. What you can't comprehend is that a contract means anytime, anywhere. A killer doesn't care where the hit takes place. He's been paid to do a job, and he's going to do it. He doesn't care if other lives get in the way."

The brutal harshness of his words sank into Susannah with a frightening chill. "What about my kids? Are they safe?"

Killian shrugged. "I don't know, Susannah. Hit men usually try for a clean one-shot deal. They don't like putting themselves in a messy situation where they could get caught." He saw the color drain from her face. "Look," he added harshly, "let me worry about the possibility of a hit man, okay? I know where to look, I know their usual methods. You'll be safe. And so will your kids," he added, softening his voice for her sake.

Getting up, Susannah moved to the counter. "I—I just didn't realize, Sean…"

"I didn't want you to," he muttered. "It's fairly easy

to watch you here, at the farm. But the moment you start driving to work, shopping and doing all the other things normal people do daily, you become more of a target-rich opportunity."

She shivered at the military jargon. *Target-rich opportunity.* Gripping the cool porcelain of the double sink, she hung her head. "I can't—I won't—live my life in fear, Sean."

"Well, then, there's a price to pay for that kind of decision. You deserve to know the chances you're taking. You could stay here, at the farm, and flushing out the hit man would be easier—but it would probably take longer."

Susannah turned around and held his searching gaze. Crossing her arms in front of her, she shook her head. "No. If there really is a contract out on me, let's find out. I'd rather get it over with."

Killian understood only too well. "You're courageous," he said, and he meant it.

"No," Susannah told him, her voice quavering, "I'm scared to death. But I miss the kids. I miss teaching."

Killian slowly rose and pushed back his chair. He brought over his now-empty plate and coffee cup. "Okay, Monday you go to work, but I'll be like a shadow, Susannah. Everywhere you go, I go. I'll explain the situation to your principal. He may decide not to let you come back after he knows the potential danger."

"Then I'll stay away," Susannah whispered. "I don't want to endanger my kids. They're innocent."

He set the dishes in the sink and turned to her. Placing his hands on her slumped shoulders, he rasped, "So are you."

Chapter 7

Uneasy, Killian walked the now-quiet halls of Marshall Elementary School, which was located near the edge of the small town of Glen. All of the children, from grades one through six, were in their classes, the wood-and-glass door to each room closed, and the teachers were busy with their charges. Killian's heart automatically swung back to Susannah, who was happily back at work. The meeting with the principal had gone well. Killian had actually expected him to turn down Susannah's request after hearing about the possibilities.

The principal obviously didn't believe there could be a contract out on Susannah. Nor did she. They didn't want to, Killian thought grimly as he padded quietly down the highly polished floor of an intersecting hall lined with metal lockers.

Dressed in jeans, a tan polo shirt and a light denim jacket that hid his shoulder holster, Killian had a small blueprint layout of the school and its adjacent buildings. He'd already been in Susannah's room and met her ten handicapped students. The children ranged in age from seven to twelve. He hadn't stayed long—he was more interested in the deadly possibilities of his trade.

At lunch, he planned to meet Susannah and her class in the cafeteria. A story had been devised to explain Killian's presence in Susannah's classroom: He was monitoring the course, a teacher from California who was going to set up a similar program out there. Everyone, including the faculty at the morning meeting, had accepted the explanation without reaction. Killian had discovered that Susannah had, from time to time, had teachers from other states come and watch how she conducted her class, because the children had developed more quickly than usual as a result of her unique teaching methods.

The lunch bell rang as Killian finished circling on the map in red ink those areas where a contract killer might hide. Luckily, there weren't many. He missed Susannah's presence, and he hoped to meet her on the way to the cafeteria with her charges.

Susannah's heart sped up at the sight of Killian moving slowly through the hall, which was filled with hundreds of laughing and talking children. She saw his dark eyes lighten as he met and held her gaze, and she smiled, feeling the warmth of his heated look.

Killian moved to the wall of lockers and waited for her.

"Hi," she said breathlessly.

Susannah's eyes shone with a welcome that reached through Killian's heavy armor and touched his heart. An ache began in his chest, an ache that startled Killian. How easily she could touch him with just a look and a soft smile. "How you doing?" Killian fell in step just behind her.

"Fine." Susannah beamed. "It's so good to be back, Sean! I feel like my life's finally coming back together again." Susannah looked tenderly at Freddy, a seven-year-old boy with Down syndrome who walked at her side, his hand firmly gripping hers. "I really missed my kids," she quavered, looking up at Killian.

Killian had his doubts about Susannah returning to work, about how it might affect her, but he said nothing. Freddy gave her a worshipful look of unqualified love. No wonder Susannah liked working with these special children. They gave fully, in the emotional sense, Killian noted with surprise.

"Are you done with your walk around the school?" Susannah asked as her little flock of children surrounded her. The double doors to the cafeteria were open. She guided her group through them and down the stairs.

"Yeah, I'm done. What can I do to help?"

She smiled and pointed to several long tables with chairs lined up on either side. "See that area?"

"Yes."

"After we get the kids seated, some of the help will bring over their lunches. You go ahead and go through the cafeteria line and meet me over there. I'm going to be pretty busy the next twenty minutes."

Killian sat with his back to the wall. For security reasons, he was glad that the cafeteria was in the basement with no windows. He didn't taste his food—chili, a salad and an apple—or the coffee he'd poured for himself. Instead, he watched Susannah. She wore a bright yellow cotton skirt today, a feminine-looking white short-sleeved blouse, and sandals. Her hair was loose, flowing over her back. She looked beautiful. And it was clear...that there wasn't one child who didn't adore her and positively glow when rewarded with her smile, a touch of her hand, or a brief kiss on the brow.

"Finally!" Susannah sat down with her tray of food. She tucked several stray strands of hair behind her ear and smiled across the table at him.

"You've got your hands full," Killian commented. Lunch was only forty-five minutes long, and Susannah had been up and helping her kids for close to half an hour. Now she'd have to gulp her food down.

"I love it! I wouldn't have it any other way."

Killian quietly suffered the din in the cafeteria, his senses heightened and pummeled at the same time. He nodded to Susannah, but his concentration was on the faculty. There was a possibility that the hit man could pose as a teacher, slip in and try to kill Susannah in the school. All morning he'd been committing faculty faces to memory, his gaze roving restlessly across the huge, noisy cafeteria.

"Well? Did you find what you were looking for?" Susannah asked, eating her chili.

"I located possible sites," Killian said, not wanting to refer directly to the topic for fear of scaring the attentive, listening children who surrounded them. "I'll discuss it with you tonight, when we get home."

With a sigh, Susannah smiled. "Home. It sounds so nice when you say that."

Avoiding her sparkling gaze, which sent a flush of heat sheeting through him, Killian nodded and paid attention to the apple he was eating but not tasting. Home anywhere with Susannah was a dream come true, he decided sourly. Four o'clock couldn't come soon enough because Killian realized he *wanted* time alone with Susannah. Each moment was a precious drop of a dream that, he knew, must someday come to an end. And, like a man lost in the desert, he thirsted for each drop that she gave him simply by being nearby.

"You're exhausted," Killian told Susannah as they worked in the kitchen preparing their dinner. He'd taken on the salad-making duties, and she was frying some steaks.

"Oh, I'm okay. First days are always that way. I'll adjust."

He glanced at her as he cut a tomato deftly with a knife. Susannah had changed into a pair of jeans and a pink sleeveless blouse. She was barefoot. He frowned as he studied her at the stove.

"Maybe you ought to switch to half days for now."

"No... I'll be okay, Sean. It's just that the first days are overwhelming. The children—" she glanced up and met his serious-looking face "—needed reassuring that I wouldn't abandon them. Handicapped children are so sensitized to possible loss of the people they rely on. They live in a very narrow world, and part of their stability is the fixedness of activity within it. If a teacher or a parent suddenly leaves, it's terribly upsetting to them."

"So you were applying Band-Aids all day?"

She grinned. "You might say that. You look a little tired yourself."

With a shrug, Killian placed the two salad bowls on the table near their plates. "A little," he lied. He'd hardly slept at all last night.

"Is the school a viable target?" she asked as she arranged their steaks on the plates.

Killian heard the quaver in her voice. He sat down and said, "There are pros and cons to it. The only place where you're really a target is the school-bus loading and unloading zone. The gym facility across the street is two stories tall—ideal for a hit man to hide in and draw a bead on you."

Trying to stay calm, Susannah sat down after pouring them each a cup of coffee. Taking a pink paper napkin, she spread it across her lap. "This is so upsetting, Sean."

"I know." The strain on Susannah's face said it all. Killian wished he wasn't always the bearer of such bad tidings.

"It's not your fault." She cut a piece of her steak and gave him a sidelong look. "Do these men hit quickly?"

"What do you mean?"

"Well, if a contract's been put out on me, will he try to get it done quickly, instead of waiting months to do it?"

"They like to get paid. They'll do it as quickly as possible to collect the balance of the money."

Susannah pushed some salad around with her fork. "Have you heard from the police about a possible identification from the sketch I gave you a few days ago?"

"Not yet. I was hoping Morgan or the Lexington

police would call me. With any luck," Killian said, eating a bite of the succulent steak, "we'll have more answers by tomorrow at the latest."

"And if you find out who my attacker is, you'll be able to know whether or not he's part of a larger drug ring?"

"Yes."

With a sigh, Susannah forced herself to eat. "I just wish it was over."

"So I'd be out of your life."

She gave him a tender look. "You're something good that's happened to me, Sean. I don't want you out of my life."

With a disgruntled look, he growled, "If I were you, I would."

As gently as possible, Susannah broached the subject of Meg with him. "Has your sister had any therapy to help her through the trauma she endured?"

Killian looked up. "A little." He frowned. "Not enough, as far as I'm concerned. Ian, her fiancé, wants to come back into her life, but Meg is afraid to let it happen."

Once again Susannah saw the anguish burning in Killian's eyes, anguish and love for his sister. There was no question but that he cared deeply about her. It was sweet to know that he now trusted her enough to reveal a small piece of his real self. Still, she knew she would have to tread lightly if Sean was to remain open and conversant. What had changed in him to make him more accessible? Possibly today at the school, she thought, cutting another piece of meat.

"Ian still loves her?"

Killian's mouth twisted. "He never stopped."

Susannah moved back to the stove. "You sound confused about that. Why?"

"Because Ian is letting his love for her tear him apart years afterward. He won't forget Meg. He refuses to."

"Love isn't something that dries up and goes away just because there's a tragedy," she said gently, passing him the platter of meat.

Killian placed another piece of steak on his plate, then handed the platter back to Susannah. "If you ask me, love is a special kind of torture. Ian twists in the wind waiting for Meg to take him back."

"He loves her enough to wait," Susannah noted. She saw Killian's eyes harden, the fork suspended halfway to his mouth.

Glancing at her, he snapped, "Love is nothing but pain. I saw it too many times, too many ways, growing up. I've watched Ian suffer. It's not worth it."

"What? Loving someone?" Susannah stopped eating and held his turbulent gaze.

"Yes."

Treading carefully, she asked, "Does Meg allow Ian back into her life in any form?"

"No, only me. She trusts only me."

"Why won't she allow Ian to help her recover?"

Flatly he responded, "Because Meg is disfigured. She's ugly compared to what she used to look like."

Suffering was all too evident on Killian's hard features. Susannah ached for both him and Meg. "She thinks that if Ian sees her he'll leave her anyway?"

"Yes, I guess so. But Ian knows she's no longer beautiful, and he doesn't care. I tried to tell Meg that, but she won't listen."

"Maybe Ian needs to go to Meg directly and confront her about it."

With a snort, Killian shook his head. "Let's put it this way. Our family—what's left of it, Meg and me—are bullheaded."

"She's not being bullheaded," Susannah said softly. "She's sticking her head in the sand and pretending Ian and his feelings don't count."

Killian moved around uncomfortably in his chair. "Sometimes," he muttered defiantly, "running away is the least of all evils."

Susannah met and held his dark blue gaze. "I don't agree. Having the courage to face the other person is always better. You should tell Ian to go to Meg and talk things out."

"If Ian knew where she lived, he'd have done that a long time ago."

She stared at him. "You won't tell him where she lives?"

"How can I? Meg begs me not to. Do you think I'm going to go against her wishes?"

"But," Susannah said lamely, "that would help heal the situation, Sean. Ian wouldn't be left feeling so tortured. Meg wouldn't feel so alone."

Smarting beneath her wisdom, Killian forced his attention back to his plate. He'd lost his appetite. "You're young, Susannah. You're protected. If you'd been kicked around like my family has been, gone through what we've gone through, you wouldn't be so eager for emotional confrontations."

She felt his panic—and his anger. "I know I'm naive," she whispered.

"Life makes you tired," Killian rasped. "Try getting

hit broadside again and again and see how willing you
are to get up and confront it again. Believe me, you'll
think twice about it. If Ian's smart, he'll get on with
his life and forget Meg."

The depth of his belief in running and hiding frightened Susannah. How many other women had wanted
to love Killian? How many had he left? Upset, she
could only say, "If I were Ian, I'd go to Meg. I'd love
her enough to find her on my own without your help."

Killian saw the flash of stubbornness in her eyes,
and felt it in her voice. He offered her a twisted, one-
cornered smile. "Idealism doesn't make it in this world,
and neither does hope. You've got too much of both,
Susannah. All they'll do is hurt you in the end."

Susannah was getting ready to take a bath around
ten that night when the phone rang. Killian was sitting
in the living room, reading the newspaper. His head
snapped up and his eyes narrowed. Forcing herself to
answer the phone, Susannah picked up the receiver.

"Hello?"

"Susannah?"

"Morgan! How are you?"

"I'm fine. Better question is, how are you doing
with Killian there?"

She flushed and avoided Killian's interested gaze.
"Better," she whispered, suddenly emotional. "Much
better."

"Good. Listen, I need to talk to Killian. Can you
put him on?"

"Sure. Give Laura and the kids my love, will you?"

"Of course. Are you doing all right physically?"

Susannah heard the guilt in Morgan's voice and

knew that he blamed himself in some way for her problems. Her hand tightened on the phone. "I'm improving every day," she promised.

"The headaches?"

Susannah thought for a moment. "Why," she breathed as the realization sank in, "I've had fewer since Killian arrived. Isn't that wonderful?"

"It is."

"I'll put Sean on the phone. Hold on." Susannah held the phone toward Killian. "It's Morgan. He wants to talk to you."

Unwinding from his chair, Killian put the newspaper aside.

Just the touch of Killian's fingers on her own as he took the receiver sent an ache throbbing through Susannah. Sensing that he wanted to be alone to talk to Morgan, Susannah left to take her bath.

Holding the receiver, Killian waited until Susannah was gone. "Morgan?"

"Yes. How's it going?"

"All right," Killian said noncommittally, keeping his voice low. He continued to watch the doorway that Susannah had disappeared through. If the conversation was disturbing, he didn't want her to overhear and become upset. "What's going on?"

"That sketch you sent that Susannah drew?"

"Yes?"

"We've got a positive identification from the FBI. His name is Huey Greaves, and he was a middleman stateside for Santiago's ring. So my hunch was correct—unfortunately. Greaves doubles as a hit man for Santiago whenever another cartel tries to encroach on his territory. The man who was killed was there to pick up drugs that were later found in one of the bus terminal luggage bins. He was from another drug ring—one that's been trying to move in on Santiago's territory."

Killian released a ragged breath, cursing softly. Susannah was in serious danger. "You've given this info to the Lexington police?"

"Yes. They've got an APB out on him. They've also alerted the county sheriff who covers Glen and the Anderson farm."

Grimly Killian gazed around the living room, which was dancing in the shadows created by the two hurricane lamps. "The bastard will hit Susannah."

Morgan sighed. "It's only a matter of time. Santiago—it figures."

"I've got to talk to her about this," Killian rasped. "She's got to know the danger involved. She started teaching today, and under the circumstances I don't think it's a good idea for her to go in tomorrow morning."

"No," Morgan agreed. "We know from experience that Santiago will go to any lengths. His people wouldn't care if there are children involved. Keep her at the farm, Killian. It's safer for everyone that way."

Killian almost laughed at the irony of the situation. No place was safe for Susannah—not even with him. "Yeah, I'll keep her here."

"You know Glen doesn't have much of a police department. The county sheriff is the only one who can help you if you get into trouble. Get the number and keep it handy. With budget cuts, they only have two patrol cars for the entire county, so don't expect too much. A two-hour delay wouldn't be unusual, Killian.

I'm afraid you're really on your own on this one. The county sheriff knows who you are and why you're there, and if they see this guy they'll call to let you know—and send a sheriff's cruiser in your direction as soon as humanly possible."

"Good." At least the police and the FBI were working together on this. Still, chances were that when the hit went down it would be Killian against the killer.

"Stay in touch," Morgan said.

"Thanks, Morgan. I will." Killian scowled as he hung up the phone. He wasn't looking forward to telling Susannah the bad news.

Susannah couldn't sleep. She was restless, tossing and turning on her ancient brass bed. The night air was warm, and she pushed off the sheet. Her watch read 2:00 a.m. It was the phone call from Morgan that had left her sleepless.

With a muffled sound of frustration, Susannah got up. She didn't want to wake Sean. Just the thought of him sent a flurry of need through her as she padded softly down the hall to the kitchen. Perhaps a cup of hot chamomile tea would help settle her screaming nerves so that she could sleep. But, she warned herself, tea wasn't going to stop the simmering desire that had been building in her for days.

Susannah ran a hand through her unbound hair, then opened the cabinet and took out a cup and saucer. Killian had warned her away from him—told her that he was no good for her. Why couldn't she listen to his thinly veiled threat?

"Susannah?"

Gasping, she whirled around, nearly dropping the

cup from her hand. Killian stood in the doorway, his drawstring pajamas barely held up by his narrow hips. His eyes were soft with sleep, and his hair was tangled across his brow. Her heart pounding, Susannah released a breath.

"You scared me."

"Sorry," he muttered, any remaining sleepiness torn from him as he studied her in the shadowy moonlight that crossed the kitchen. Her knee-length white gown gave her an angelic look, and the moonlight outlined her body like a lover's caress through the light cotton fabric. The dark frame of hair emphasized the delicateness of her features, especially her parted lips.

"I—I couldn't sleep." She gestured toward the kettle on the stove. "I thought I'd make some chamomile tea."

"Morgan's call upset you?"

"Yes."

Easing into the room, Killian crossed to the table and sat down. His head was screaming at him to go back to bed, but his heart clamored for her closeness.

"Make me a cup, will you?"

"Sure." Susannah's pulse wouldn't seem to settle down, and she busied herself at the counter, attempting to quell her nervousness. Killian's body was hard and lean. She wondered what it would be like to kiss him, to feel his arms around her.

As Susannah turned, the cups of tea in her hands, the window at the kitchen counter shattered, glass exploding in all directions.

"Get down!" Killian shouted. Launching himself out of his chair, he took Susannah with him as he slammed to the floor. More glass shattered, splintering in rainbow fragments all around them.

Susannah groaned under Killian's weight, her mind spinning with shock. She could hear Killian's harsh breathing, and his cursing, soft and strained. Almost instantly she felt his steely grip on her arms as he dragged her upward and positioned her against the corner cabinets for protection.

Her eyes wide, she took in the harshness in his sweaty features.

"The hit man," he rasped. *Dammit!* He'd left his pistol in the bedroom. He noticed small, bloody cuts on Susannah's right arm.

"But—how?"

Killian shook his head, putting his finger to his lips. Silence was crucial right now. The hit man had to be on the porch. But why the hell hadn't he heard him? Felt him? A hundred questions battered Killian. His senses were now screamingly alert. He had to get to his gun, or they were both dead!

Gripping Susannah's wrist, Killian tugged and motioned for her to follow him. If they couldn't make it to his bedroom, they were finished. The last thing he wanted was Susannah dead. The thought spurred him into action.

Gasping for breath, Susannah scrambled out of the kitchen on her hands and knees. In the darkened hall, Killian jerked her to her feet, shoving her forward and into his room. Instantly he pushed her onto the floor and motioned for her to wriggle beneath the bed and remain there.

Killian's fingers closed over the pistol on the nightstand. The feel of the cool metal was reassuring. Now they had a chance. His eyes narrowed as he studied the window near his bed and the open door to his room.

"Stay down!" he hissed. "Whatever happens, stay here!"

Tears jammed into Susannah's eyes as she looked up into his taut, glistening features. Here was the mercenary. The soldier who could kill. She opened her mouth, then snapped it shut.

"Don't move!" Killian warned. He leaped lightly to his feet, every muscle in his body tense with anticipation. He tugged at the blanket so that it hung off the bed and concealed Susannah's glaringly white nightgown. Swiftly he turned on his heel and moved to the door, his hands wrapped around the pistol that he held high and at the ready.

Killian was angry at himself—angry that he'd dropped his guard because he cared for Susannah. He pressed himself hard against the wall and listened. His nostrils flared to catch any unusual scent. Morgan Trayhern had called him a hound from hell on more than one occasion because of his acutely honed senses. Well, they'd saved his life more than once. Tonight, he had to count on his abilities to save Susannah.

As he ducked out of the entrance and quickly looked up and down the hall, Killian saw no evidence of the hit man. Then a creak of wood made him freeze. There! The kitchen! His heart was a thudding sledgehammer in his chest, his quiet breathing was ragged. The bastard was in the kitchen.

There! Killian heard the crunch of glass. How close to the kitchen doorway was he? He continued down the hall soundlessly, on the balls of his feet. His hands sweaty, beads of perspiration running down his temples, Killian focused like a laser on his quarry. Susannah's killer. Only two more feet and he'd have enough of an angle to peer into the darkened depths of the kitchen. Every muscle in his body stiffened with expectation.

Another crunch of glass. The sound was directional, giving away where the hit man stood. Instantly Killian launched himself forward, flattening himself against the hardwood floor, both hands in front of him, the snout of the Beretta aimed. Seeing the darkened shape of a man move, he squeezed off two shots. The sounds reverberated through the farmhouse. Damn! He'd missed!

The hit man fired back, a silencer on his gun cloaking the sound to light pops. Killian rolled to the left, the door jamb his shield. Wood cracked and splintered as bullets savagely tore at the barrier. His mind working rapidly, Killian counted off the shots. Six. More than likely the bastard had nine bullets in his clip. Then he'd have to reload.

The scrambling over glass continued. Killian kept low. He realized with terror that the bedroom where Susannah was hiding was directly behind the hit man. If Killian fired, his shots could go through the walls and hit her. Damn!

Breathing hard, his lips pulled away from clenched teeth, Killian grabbed a piece of wood near his bare feet, and threw it into the kitchen.

Two more shots were fired at it in quick succession.

Good! Only one more round before he'd have to take precious seconds to reload. Stinging sweat dripped into his eyes, and he blinked it away.

In those seconds, waiting for the hit man to make his move, Killian realized that he loved Susannah. Where had such a crazy idea come from? Tightening his grip on the Beretta, he rose onto one knee, ready to fire.

An explosion of movement occurred in the kitchen. Before Killian could fire, the table was tipped over, slamming against the doorway and spoiling his shot. The screen door was ripped off its hinges as a dark figure scrambled out. The thudding of running feet filled the air.

Cursing roundly, Killian leaped over the table. The son of a bitch! Sprinting onto the porch, Killian saw the hit man fleeing toward the road, where his car must be hidden. Digging his toes into the soft, wet grass, Killian started after him. The direction the hit man was running was in line with the Andersons' farmhouse, not more than a quarter mile away. Killian couldn't risk a stray bullet hitting the house or its occupants.

Running hard, he cut through the orchard. Ahead, he saw a dark blue car. The hit man jerked the door open, disappeared inside and hit the accelerator.

The nondescript car leaped forward, dirt and clods flying up, leaving a screen of dust in its wake. Killian memorized the license plate number before the car was swallowed up by the darkness. Lowering his pistol, he continued to run toward the Anderson residence. He wanted to report the car's license number to the sheriff and call Morgan. More than likely the vehicle was a rental car, and the hit man had signed for it with an alias at an airport—probably Lexington.

Killian's mind spun with options, with necessary procedures that would have to be instituted quickly.

Reaching the house, he wasn't surprised to find the Andersons still asleep, completely unaware of what had just occurred. Susannah's house was nearly a half mile away with plenty of orchard to absorb the sounds of battle.

Breathing hard, Killian entered the house via the kitchen and found the phone there on the wall. Setting his gun nearby on the counter, he shakily dialed the county sheriff. As he waited for someone to answer, his heart revolved back to Susannah. Was she all right? He recalled the cuts to her right arm, caused by the shattering glass. Anger with himself because he hadn't protected her as well as he should have filled Killian. As soon as he'd reported the incident, he'd get back to the house and care for Susannah.

Lying on her belly, Susannah had no idea how long she remained frozen. Her heart was beating hard, and her fingers were dug into the wooden floor. Sean! Was he all right? What had happened? Did she dare risk coming out from beneath the bed to find out? There had been no sound for about fifteen minutes. Her mind was playing tricks on her. Maybe Sean was bleeding to death on the kitchen floor and she didn't know it. Should she move from her hiding place? Should she stay?

She closed her eyes as tears leaked into them. Sean couldn't be dead! He just couldn't! The attack had ripped away her doubts. She loved Killian. It was that simple—and that complicated. Lying there, shaking badly as the adrenaline began to seep out of her bloodstream, she pressed her brow against her hands. Sean had ordered her not to move—no matter what. But how could she remain here? If he was lying wounded somewhere, how could she not move?

With a little cry, Susannah made her decision.

"Susannah?"

Killian! She gasped as he pulled the blanket away. Her eyes widened enormously as he got down on his hands and knees.

"Sean?"

He smiled grimly and reached for her. "Yeah. I'm all right, colleen. Everything's okay. The hit man got away. Come on, crawl out of there."

Susannah discovered how wobbly she was as she got to her feet. Killian gripped her hands.

"I—I don't think I can stand," she quavered, looking up into his dark, sweaty features.

"I'm not too steady myself," he answered with a rasp. He drew Susannah into his arms and brought her against him. The contact with her was shocking. Melting. Killian groaned as she leaned heavily against him, her arms around him, her head against his shoulder.

"Sweet," he whispered, holding her tightly— holding her so hard he was afraid he was going to crush her. The natural scent of her—a fragrant smell, like lilacs—encircled his nostrils. Killian dragged in that scent, life after the odors of death. He felt Susannah shift and lift her head. Without thinking, he cupped her chin and guided her lips to his mouth.

The meeting was fiery, purging. He felt the softness of her lips, felt them flow open, their heat, their moistness overwhelming his heightened senses. Time ceased to exist. All he was aware of, all he wanted, was her. The warmth of Susannah's breasts pressing softly against his chest, her softness against his hardness, shattered the last of his control.

He groaned, taking her mouth hungrily, sliding

against her, absorbing her warmth, her womanliness. His breathing grew chaotic, fevered, as she returned his inflammatory kiss. His fingers sliding into her hair, Killian gripped the silky strands, framing her face, holding her captive as he absorbed her into him like a starving man.

Susannah moaned, but it was a moan of utter surrender mingled with pleasure. She found herself pressed onto the bed, with Killian's tense body against her, driving her into the mattress. The near brush with death—the fear of losing him—overwhelmed her, and she sought blindly to reassure herself that he was alive, that he was safe. There was security in Sean's arms, those powerful bands that trapped her, holding her captive beneath him. With a fierce need, she returned his searching kiss.

"I need you, I need you," Killian rasped against her wet, soft mouth. "Now. I need you now..." He felt her arch beneath him, giving him the answer he sought. He'd nearly lost Susannah to an assailant's bullet. The warmth of her flesh, the eagerness of her beneath him, could have been destroyed in a split second. Sliding his shaky hands beneath her rumpled gown, he sought and found her slender rib cage, then moved upward. The instant his hands curved around her small breasts, he heard her cry out. But it was a cry of utter pleasure, not fear or pain. The husky sound coming from her throat increased the heat in his lower body. Never had he wanted a woman more. Never had he loved a woman as he loved Susannah.

The fierceness of his roiling emotions shattered Killian's ironclad control. He was helpless beneath her hands. They were gliding over his taut back and shoulders as he pulled the gown off her. In moments his pajamas were in a heap on the wooden floor. Her fingers dug convulsively into his bunched shoulders as he leaned down and captured the tight peak of her nipple with his insistent lips. She became wild, untamed, beneath him, moving her head from side to side, begging him to enter her.

The fever in his blood tripled, sang through him as he felt her thighs open to welcome him. He wanted to take it slow, to make it good for Susannah, but the fiery blood beating through him ripped away all but his primal need to plunge deep into her—to bury himself in her life, escaping the death that had stalked them less than an hour earlier.

Framing her face with his hands, Killian looked down into her dazed, lustrous eyes as he moved forward to meet her. He wanted to imprint Susannah's lovely features on his heart and mind forever. The moment he entered her hot, womanly confines, a low, vibrating growl ripped out of him. He couldn't stop his forward plunge—didn't want to. His need for this feverish coupling was like a storm that had waited too long to expend itself.

Killian's fingers tightened against Susannah's face and he stiffened as liquid fire encircled him, captured him, leaving him mindless, aware of nothing but a rainbow of sensations, each more powerful, more overwhelming, than the next. When Susannah moved her hips, drawing him even deeper inside her, he sucked in a ragged breath. Never had he experienced heaven like this. He leaned down, savoring her lips, drowning in the splendor of her sweet, fiery offering.

Then nothing existed but the touching and sliding

of their bodies against each other, satin against steel. Susannah was soft, giving, bending to Killian's needs with a sweet suppleness. He was hard, demanding—plunging and taking. Her lilac fragrance surrounded him as he buried his face in the silky folds of her hair. In moments, an explosive feeling enveloped him, freezing him into an immobility of such intense pleasure that he could only gasp in response. As she moved her hips sinuously against him, he could no more control himself than a rain storm could hold back from spending itself on the lush warmth of the earth.

Afterward, moments glided and fused together as Killian lay spent. He raised his head and realized that his fingers were still tightly grasping the thick strands of Susannah's hair, as if he were afraid she'd slip away from him—as if this were one of his fevered dreams, ready to flee when he opened his eyes. Susannah's lashes fluttered upward, and he held his breath, drowning in the glorious gray of her eyes.

The soft, trembling smile that curved her lips sent another sheet of heat through Killian. He felt her hot, wet tightness still around him, holding him, and he groaned.

"I feel like I've gone to heaven," he rasped against her lips. And then he added weakly, "Or as close as I'll ever get to heaven, because I'm bound for hell."

"You *are* heaven," Susannah managed huskily, held captive by him in all ways, luxuriating in his strength and masculinity.

Carefully Killian untangled his hand from her hair and touched her swollen lips. With a grimace, he whispered, "I'm sorry, colleen, I got carried away. I didn't mean to hurt you."

Susannah kissed his scarred fingers. "I'm fine. How could you hurt me?"

He shakily traced her smooth forehead and the arch of her eyebrow. "In a million ways," he assured her.

With a tender smile, Susannah framed his damp features. No longer was the man with the hard face staring down at her. No, this was the very human, vulnerable side of Sean Killian. And she reveled fiercely in his being able to shed his outer shell—to give himself to her in an even more important, wonderful way.

Gently Killian moved aside and brought Susannah into his arms as he lay on the bed. "Come here," he whispered, holding her tight for a long, long time. The moments ran together for him. Susannah's arm flowed across his chest, and one of her long, lovely legs lay across his own. He blinked his eyes several times, trying to think coherently. It was nearly impossible with Susannah in his arms.

"You're all a man could ever dream of having," he told her in a low, unsteady voice as he kissed her cheek, and then her awaiting lips. Lying there with her in his arms, he caressed her cheek.

Susannah melted within his embrace, savoring the feel of his fingers moving lightly across her shoulder, down her arm to her hip. He was stroking her as if she were a purring cat. And wasn't she? "I'll never be sorry this happened," she admitted breathlessly. "Never."

As Killian lay there, his mind finally beginning to take over from the lavalike emotions that had exploded in a volcano lain dormant too long, he tasted bitterness in his mouth. There was Susannah, innocent and trusting in his arms, her eyes shining with such adoration that it made him sick inside. She didn't know his sordid past, didn't know the ghosts that still haunted him.

"I shouldn't have done this to you," he rasped, frowning. Yet he couldn't stop touching her, sliding his hands across her satiny flesh and feeling her effortless response.

"No!" Susannah forced herself up onto one elbow. She reached out, her hand on his chest, where his heart lay. "We both wanted this, Sean. *Both* of us."

He grimaced. "It shouldn't have happened," he said, more harshly.

"Really?" Susannah couldn't keep the sarcasm out of her tone, and she was sorry for it.

Unable to meet her eyes, he shook his head and threw the covers aside. "I was to protect you, Susannah!"

"Loving someone isn't protecting them?"

He glanced at her sharply as he forced himself to get up and leave her side. If he stayed, he'd want to love her all over again, with the fierceness of a breaking thunderstorm.

"I was paid to protect you, dammit!" he flared, moving around the bed and going to the dresser. Jerking open the drawer, he retrieved jeans and a polo shirt.

Sitting up in bed, Susannah suddenly felt bereft. Abandoned. Quiet tension thrummed through the room, and a chill washed over her. Killian put on boxer shorts and the jeans. His face was hard again, his mouth set in a thin line.

"Sean, what's going on? I liked what we shared. I like you. Why are you so angry and upset about it?"

"You'd better get cleaned up, Susannah," he told her tautly, pulling the shirt over his head. "Take a shower and get dressed. The sheriff is sending out a cruiser to check out what happened with the hit man. He'll probably be here in a half hour or so."

Forcing herself to her feet, Susannah moved over to him. His movements were abrupt and tense. She gripped his arm.

"The police can wait," she said hoarsely, searching his dark, unfathomable eyes. "*We* can't."

Her fingers were like small, exquisite brands burning into his flesh. Killian pulled away from Susannah. "There is no 'we'!" he said harshly. It was pure, unadulterated hell looking down at her standing there naked and beautiful before him. "Look at you! Even now you can't protect yourself against the likes of someone like me. It shouldn't have happened, Susannah! It was my fault. I wanted—needed you so damned bad I could taste it." Aggravated, Killian ran his fingers through his mussed hair. "I broke a cardinal rule that I've never broken before—I got involved with the person I was supposed to protect." He gave her a sad look, his voice cracking with emotion. "I'm sorry. I'm sorry it happened. You didn't deserve this on top of everything else, Susannah."

Chapter 8

Susannah had barely stepped out of the shower when the sheriff's cruiser arrived. Going to her bedroom, she dressed in a sensible pair of dark green cotton slacks and a white short-sleeved blouse. Her hair was still damp, and she braided the strands together, fastening the ends with a rubber band. Her hands shook as she put on white socks and a pair of sneakers.

The terror of nearly being killed warred with Sean's reaction to their lovemaking, buffeting her weary senses. Each time she replayed the conversation, it made no sense to her. Why was he sorry he'd loved her? She wasn't. Touching her bangs with trembling fingers, she took one look in the mirror. Her face was pale, and her eyes were dark and huge. And her lips... Susannah groaned softly. Her mouth looked wonderfully ravished, slightly swollen and well kissed.

Entering the kitchen, Susannah saw the damage from the gunfire for the first time. Killian had set the table upright, and he and the two deputies sat at the table, their faces grim. Across the wooden floor, glass lay splintered and glinting in the lamplight.

Killian glanced up. Susannah stood poised just inside the room. He was struck by her beauty, her simple clothing—the luster in her gray eyes that he knew was meant for him alone. Trying to steel himself against his still-turbulent emotions, he got up.

"Come over here and sit down," he invited, his voice rough. "They've caught the guy who tried to kill us."

Gasping in surprise, Susannah came forward. "They did?"

"Yes, ma'am," a large, beefy deputy volunteered. "Thanks to Mr. Killian's quick reporting, we got him just as he was trying to leave the Glen town limits."

Killian pulled the chair out for her so that she could sit down. It hardly seemed possible, but Susannah looked even paler.

"You want some coffee?" he asked. Dammit, why did he have to sound so harsh with her? He was angry with himself, with his lack of control. It was he who had initiated their lovemaking.

"Please." Susannah tried to ignore Killian's overwhelming male presence—to concentrate on the deputy, whose name tag read Birch. But it was impossible. "Deputy Birch, what can you tell us about this hit man?" she managed to say, her voice unsteady.

"Not much. We're putting him through the paces right now back at the station. I do know he'll get put in jail without bail. The judge won't hear his case until nine this morning."

Susannah looked at the wall clock. It was 3:00 a.m., yet she felt screamingly awake. Was this how Sean felt all the time? Did a mercenary ever relax? As Killian moved around the counter, which was strewn with wood and glass debris, Susannah sensed an explosiveness around him.

"How may I help?" Susannah asked the deputies in a low, off-key voice.

"Just give us your statement, Miss Anderson." Birch threw a look at Killian. "I'd say your guardian angel here saved you."

She forced a smile that she didn't feel. "Yes, well, Mr. Killian is protective, if nothing else." Susannah saw him twist a look across his shoulder at her. His eyes were dark and angry. What had she done to deserve his anger? She hoped against hope that, when the deputies left, she and Sean could sit and talk this out.

Killian moved restlessly around the kitchen. It was 4:00 a.m., and the deputies were wrapping up their investigation. Susannah was looking exhausted, her adrenaline high clearly worn off, a bruised-looking darkness beneath her eyes.

"We'll be in touch shortly," Birch promised as the deputies stood up and ended their visit.

"Thank you," Susannah told them wearily, meaning it. She watched as Killian escorted the officers out to the porch, where they talked in low voices she couldn't overhear. Exhausted, she stood up, feeling as if she'd gone days without sleep. As much as she wanted to wait for Sean to return, to discuss whatever problem had sprung up between them, Susannah knew she didn't have the emotional strength for the confrontation. It would have to wait.

In her room, Susannah set the alarm for seven, so that she could call the principal and tell him she wouldn't be able to teach today. She lay down on the bed, not caring that she was still dressed, and fell asleep immediately. In her dreams, Killian loved her with his primal hunger all over again.

Susannah awoke with a start, her heart pounding. Sunlight was pouring in through the curtains at a high angle. What time was it? Groggily she looked at her watch. It was noon! She barely recalled getting up at seven to make the call and going straight back to bed.

Sitting for a moment, she allowed herself time to get reoriented. Had last night been some terrible combination of nightmare and dream? Killian's words about heaven and hell came back to her. That was what last night had been for her: tasting both extremes. It had been heaven loving Sean, feeling the intensity of his need for her. The hell had arrived earlier, in the form of a killer who'd wanted to take her life. Rubbing her brow, Susannah felt the beginnings of a headache. A heartache would be more appropriate. Why was Sean sorry he'd loved her?

When Susannah went to the kitchen, she found it almost as good as new. The only thing missing was the window over the sink. The floor had been swept clean of debris and mopped, the counters cleared of any evidence of the violent episode. She looked around. The splintered wood in the doorway had been removed. Either Killian or her father was busy making repairs.

What couldn't be repaired as quickly were the bullet holes along the kitchen wall. They were an ugly reminder, and Susannah stood there, rubbing her arms absently, feeling very cold.

"It's almost like new."

Gasping, Susannah turned at the sound of Killian's low voice. He stood at the screen door, a piece of wood in his hand. "You scared me to death!" She placed her hand against her pounding heart.

Entering, Killian scowled. Susannah looked sleepy, her eyes puffy, and her mouth—he groaned inwardly. Her mouth looked beautifully pouty, the force of his kisses last night still stamped there. The ache to kiss her all over again, to ease the fear lingering in her eyes by taking her into his arms, flowed through him. Savagely he destroyed the feeling.

"Sorry," he muttered. "I didn't mean to scare you." He stalked across the kitchen and placed the wood against the door jamb. It fit perfectly. Now all he had to do was nail it into place.

"That's okay," she reassured him, a little breathlessly, "I'm just jumpy right now."

"Now you know how a mercenary feels twenty-four hours a day." He gave her a cheerless look. Killian wanted to convey in every way possible the miserable life he led—no place for a decent human being like Susannah. He wished she'd quit looking at him like that, with that innocence that drove him crazy with need.

Forcing herself to move, Susannah poured herself some fresh coffee. "Has the sheriff called yet?"

"Yes. Greaves was the man. The same one that nearly killed you at the bus station. He isn't talking, but I spoke to Morgan earlier, and he's working with the sheriff. The FBI are still in on it, too." Killian placed the board against the wall and went to the icebox. He wasn't hungry, but he knew he had to eat.

Biting down on her lower lip, Susannah glanced over at Killian as he brought out whole wheat bread, lunch meat and mustard. "Is it over, then?"

"I don't know. Morgan is sending a message through a third party to Santiago's cartel in Peru. He's ordering him to lift the contract on you or we'll start extradition procedures against more of the cartel honchos."

"What makes you think they'll lift the contract?" Susannah watched him slap some mustard on the bread and top it with several pieces of lunch meat. His features were unreadable, as usual. What was he feeling? Hadn't their loving meant anything to him? He was acting as if it had never happened!

Killian moved to the table and sat down with his sandwich. "This particular drug family is in plenty of hot water already with the Peruvian government, so they don't need any more attention from the authorities. Besides, Greaves is one of their top men who does dirty work for them in this country. They don't want to risk him spilling the beans to the American authorities on what he knows about the drug shipments to the U.S. He's been in a position to know about a lot of things. No, they'll probably make the deal and take the heat off you."

Turning around so that her back rested against the counter, Susannah crossed her arms. Killian sat, frowning darkly while he munched on the sandwich. "How soon will we know?" she asked softly.

"Morgan says a day or two at the latest. He'll call us."

Her arms tightened against herself. "And if they agree to lift the contract, what will you do?"

Forcing himself to meet her gaze, Killian growled, "I'll leave."

The words plunged into her heart like a dagger. Susannah felt as if someone had just gutted her. Turning away, she realized she was out of sorts, still waking up, in no mental—or emotional—state to discuss last night. Killian was biting into his sandwich as if he were angry with it. His blue eyes were turbulent, and he was markedly restless. Misery avalanched Susannah.

"I'm going into town," Killian said abruptly, rising. He'd choked down the sandwich, not tasting it at all, and now it sat like a huge rock in his stomach. The suffering on Susannah's face was real, and he had no control over his response to it. He'd made her this way with one lousy indiscretion—with his selfish need of her. Killian stalked to the screen door, which he'd recently rehung with new hinges.

"I've got to pick up the new glass for that window. I'll be back later."

Hurt, Susannah nodded. When Killian had left, she remained where she was, her head bowed, her eyes shut. Forcing back tears, she realized that even though he'd made wild, passionate love to her this morning, it had been little more than that. She knew nothing of the mercenary type of man. Was this part of their pattern—loving a woman and then leaving her? Susannah laughed derisively as she opened her eyes. There were a lot of men out there like that, unwilling to commit to a real, ongoing relationship, so they used women, then left them. Was Killian like that?

Her heart cried no, but as Susannah moved around the kitchen, she couldn't come up with a more reasonable answer. Still, Killian just didn't seem the type not to be loyal. Perhaps, when he came back with the window this afternoon, both of them would be more settled after the frightening events of last night, and she could talk to him.

Killian stood back, pleased with the new window gracing the kitchen. He was wildly aware that Susannah was nearby. She'd taken care of the bullet holes, filling them with spackling compound. In a day or two, when they'd dried sufficiently, she would sandpaper them smooth and paint over them. No one would realize the bullet holes were there—no one except them. Some things, he thought with disgust, one never forgot.

As Killian poured himself some coffee and went to sit on the front porch swing, he knew he'd never forget loving Susannah. The swing creaked beneath his weight, the gentle back-and-forth motion taking the edge off his screamingly taut nerves and aching heart. Taking a sip of the hot, black liquid, he narrowed his eyes, seeing nothing in front of him. He loved Susannah. How had it happened? When? He shook his head as a powerful sadness moved through him.

It didn't matter. No woman had ever captured his imagination, his feelings, the closely guarded part of him that still knew how to dream, as she had. More than anything, he wanted to spend the whole day loving her, falling asleep with her supple warmth beside him—waking up to love her all over again. But this time he wanted to move slowly, to savor Susannah, to pleasure her. He doubted she'd gotten much pleasure the first time. He'd stolen from her like a thief, because he'd needed her so badly, he thought sourly.

Reality drenched Killian as he swung slowly back and forth. Susannah could never know how he loved her.

"Sean?"

He snapped his head up. Susannah stood uncertainly at the screen door.

"Yes?" He heard the brittleness in his voice and automatically steeled himself.

"I need to talk with you," Susannah said, and pushed the screen door open. "I was waiting for you to take a break."

His mouth thinning, he picked up his now-empty coffee cup in both hands. If he didn't, he would reach for Susannah, who had come to lean against the porch railing, near the swing.

"The window's in."

Susannah nodded, licking her dry lips. "Yes... It looks good as new." She shrugged. "I wish... I wish we could fix ourselves like that window—be brand-new all over again and not have a memory of what happened last night."

"That's what makes us human, I guess," he answered gruffly. The terrible suffering in Susannah's eyes was beginning to tear him apart.

Susannah nervously clasped her hands in front of her and forced herself to look at Killian. His face was closed and unreadable, his blue eyes narrowed and calculating. "We've got to talk," Susannah began hoarsely. "I can't go on like this."

"Like what?"

Taking in a ragged breath, Susannah whispered, "We loved each other last night, Sean. Doesn't that mean anything to you?"

Wincing inwardly, Killian saw tears forming in her eyes. His mouth going dry, a lump growing in his throat, he rasped, "Dammit, Susannah, it shouldn't have happened!"

"I'm not sorry, Sean, if that's what you're worried about."

He gave her a dark look. "Well, I am. We didn't use protection. For all I know, you could be pregnant."

Startled, Susannah allowed his growling words to sink in. "Is that what's bothering you? That I might be pregnant?"

With a disgusted sound, Killian lunged to his feet, tense. "Doesn't it worry you?" he snapped. Desperate for anything that might force her to understand that there was no possible future for them, he zeroed in on that argument.

Susannah cringed beneath his taunting words. It felt as if Killian could explode at any moment. He stood next to her, tense and demanding. "Well—"

"I didn't think you were looking ahead," he rasped.

"That isn't the issue," Susannah said, forcing herself to hold his angry gaze. "The real issue is whether or not we have something special, something worth pursuing—together."

No one loved her courage more than he did. For the first time, Killian saw the stubborn jut of her jaw and the defiance in her eyes. He told himself he shouldn't be surprised by Susannah's hidden strength.

With a hiss, he turned away. "There is no us!"

"Why? Why can't there be?"

Killian whirled on her, his breathing ragged. "Because there can't be, Susannah!" He glared at her. "There will be no relationship between us." It tormented him to add, "You got that?"

Her lips parting, Susannah took a step away from

Killian. Although his face was implacable, his eyes gave him away. Her womanly intuition told her that at least part of what he was saying was bluff.

"What are you afraid of?" she said, her voice quavering.

Stunned by her insight, Killian backed away. "Nothing!" he lied. His chest heaving with inner pain—and the pain he was causing Susannah—he added savagely, "Stick with your dreams and hopes, Susannah. I don't belong in your idealistic world. I can't fit into it. I never will." His voice deepened with anguish. "I warned you to stay away from me. I warned you that it wouldn't be any good if you got close to me."

Rattled, Susannah whispered, "But I did! And I don't regret it, Sean. Doesn't that make any difference?"

Killian shook his head, his voice cracking. "Listen to me. I told you, I'm out of your life. I'm here for maybe a day or two more at the most. I'm sorry I made love to you. I had no right. It was my fault." He gave a helpless wave of his arm.

Her eyes rounded. How callous, how cold, he sounded. "I don't believe you mean that," she said, her voice beginning to shake with real anger.

He stared at her, openmouthed. "Don't look at me like that, Susannah. I'm no knight on a white horse."

Hurting, fighting not to cry in front of him, Susannah stared up at him. "What man is?" she cried. "We're all human beings, with strengths and weaknesses. You try to keep people at arm's length by making them think you're cold and cruel. I know you're not! You're bluffing, Sean."

Startled, Killian felt panic as never before. But he

loved Susannah enough to allow her the freedom she didn't want from him. If only he could explain it to her... Moving forward, he gripped her arm with just enough force to let her know he meant what he was going to say. "Bluffing? When I leave and you don't hear from me again, that's no bluff, Susannah. I'm sorry I ever met you, because I've hurt you, and I never meant to do that. I swear I didn't." He gave her a little shake. When he spoke again, there was desperation in his voice. "Move on with your life after I leave. Find a good man here—someone who believes in dreams like you do. I've told you before—I'm bound for hell. Well, I got a little taste of heaven with you. It was damned good, Susannah. I'll never forget it, but I'm a realist." He released her and stepped back.

With a little sob, Susannah lifted her hand and pressed it against her mouth. Giving her a hopeless look, Killian spun on his heel and stalked back into the farmhouse.

Swaying, Susannah caught herself and sat down heavily in the swing, afraid her knees would give out entirely. Killian's words pummeled her, cut through her. She felt flayed by his anger. Hell was here, right now. It took a long minute for Susannah to wrestle with her unraveling emotions and force herself not to end up in a weeping heap. Miserably, she wiped the moisture from her eyes. In two days or less, they would know from Morgan whether or not the drug cartel would agree to the deal. If they did, Killian was out of her life in an instant. He wanted to run. He wanted to escape.

Killian slowly finished packing his bag. Morgan had just called to let him know the Peruvian cartel had agreed to lift the contract on Susannah. At least now she would be safe. His hand tightened around the handle of his satchel. The badly beaten leather bag had seen better days—like him, he thought wearily.

Right now, Susannah was out in the garden, barefoot, wearing her old straw hat, doing the weeding. Two of the most miserable days of Killian's life had somehow managed to pass. Never had he suffered so much, known agony as devastating as this. Every fiber of his being wanted to go out and say goodbye to Susannah. He hesitated, torn. If he did, he knew there was a good possibility he couldn't continue his charade. Last night, he'd heard Susannah sobbing softly, as if she were trying to hide her pain by crying into her pillow.

Tears jammed into Killian's eyes. With a disgusted sound, he forced them back. No, he didn't dare say goodbye to Susannah in person.

"Dammit," he rasped, his voice cracking. He scribbled a quick note, then went into the kitchen and left it on the table where Susannah would see it. He took one last look around the old, dilapidated farmhouse. Capturing the memories, he stored and locked them in the vault of his scarred heart.

Taking one last look toward the garden area, Killian saw Susannah down on her hands and knees, still weeding. Dragging in a deep, painful breath, Killian silently whirled around and left. Forever.

Susannah washed most of the dirt from her hands with water from the hose outside the garden fence. It was nearly four, and she knew she had to prepare supper. Where was Sean? She'd hardly seen him in the past two days. And why hadn't Morgan called? It hurt to think. It hurt to feel, Susannah thought as she slipped the straw hat off her head and entered the kitchen.

Almost immediately, she saw the note on the table. Next to it was a glass containing a freshly cut yellow rose. Frowning, her heart doing a funny skipping beat, Susannah went over to the table. Sitting down, she shakily unfolded the note.

Dear Susannah:

Morgan called about an hour ago to tell me that the drug cartel has promised to leave you alone. You're safe, and that's what is important.

By the time you get this note, I'll be gone. I'm sorry I couldn't say goodbye. Being with you was heaven, Susannah. And for a man bound for hell, it was too much to take. Cowardice comes in many forms, and I didn't have the courage to say goodbye to you. You deserve better than me, as I've told you many times before.

You were a rainbow in my life. I never thought someone like me would ever see one, much less meet one in the form of a woman. You deserve only the best, Susannah. I'm not a man who prays much, but I will pray for your happiness. God knows, you deserve it. Killian.

A sob lodged in Susannah's throat. She stared at the paper, the words blurring as tears rose then spilled out of her eyes and down her cheeks. She gripped the letter hard, reading it and rereading it. There were so many mixed messages. It hadn't been the hardened mercenary writing this. No, it had been the very human, hurting man beneath his warrior's facade.

Crying softly, Susannah put the note aside and buried her face in her hands. The school had given her another month's leave to recover from the shooting incident. Lifting her head, she wiped the tears from her eyes. She had a month… Gathering her strewn emotions, Susannah decided to call Morgan and talk to him about Sean. Outwardly, Killian was behaving like a bastard, but a bastard wouldn't have written about her being a rainbow in his life.

Susannah worked to compose herself. She'd gone through so much in such a short amount of time. A huge part of her didn't believe Sean's letter. Never had she felt this way toward a man. She'd been "in love" before, but that relationship hadn't matured. No man had made her feel so vibrant or so alive. Did she even know what real love was? Had Sean touched her heart with genuine love? Susannah didn't know, but one way or another she intended to find out.

She brought the glass containing the yellow rose forward. Touching the delicate petals with her fingers, the fragrance encircling her, Susannah realized that Killian might be tough in many ways, but, like this rose that he'd symbolically left her, he had a vulnerable, fragile underside.

That realization gave Susannah hope as nothing else could have. She'd call Morgan and begin an investigation into Sean and the world he called hell. There was a reason why he'd left her. Something he hadn't told her. Now Sean was going to have to realize that not everything in his life was destined for hell. Nor was every person going to allow him to run away when it suited his purposes—whatever they might be.

Chapter 9

Morgan stood and came around his large walnut desk as Susannah gave him a slight smile of welcome and stepped into his office. When his assistant, Marie, had shut the door, he opened his arms.

"I'm glad you came, Susannah."

Fighting back tears, Susannah moved into Morgan's comforting embrace. She gave him a quick squeeze of welcome and then stepped away from his towering presence.

"Thanks for seeing me, Morgan. I know how busy you are."

He gestured toward the creamy leather sofa in the corner of the spacious room. "You know you aren't getting out of here without staying at least overnight. Laura insists."

Nervously Susannah sat down. "Yes, I told her I'd

stay one night. But she must be terribly busy with this second baby. It's wonderful you have a boy and a girl now."

Morgan nodded, satisfaction in his voice. "A year apart. Katherine Alyssa Trayhern will have a big brother to grow up with. We're very happy about it. She's a real spitfire, too."

Susannah was truly happy for them. Dressed in a navy pin-striped suit, with a paisley silk tie and white shirt, Morgan looked professional, every inch the head of his flourishing company. Susannah and Laura had been close throughout the years, and she knew of Morgan's terrible, torturous past. "Well," she whispered, glancing up at him, "I'm going to need some of that spitfire personality your daughter has."

"I know this involves Killian. How can I help you?" Morgan sat down, alert.

Gripping her leather purse, Susannah held his curious gaze. "I know I was vague on the phone, but I didn't feel this was something I wanted to talk about in detail to anyone except you. And I wanted to do it in person. As I told you on the phone, the school is giving me a month to get my life back in order, and I intend to use it to do just that."

Morgan nodded. "I'm just glad the contract's been lifted. What's this about Killian?"

Susannah's heart contracted in grief. Unable to hold his warm, probing gaze, she felt a lump forming in her throat.

Morgan leaned over and slid his hand across her slumped shoulder. "What's going on, Susannah?"

Fighting to keep herself together, she whispered, "I don't know how it happened or when it happened, but

I've fallen in love with Sean." She gave him a pained look. "It happened so fast…"

Morgan nodded. "I fell in love with Laura the first moment I saw her, although I didn't know it then." He grimaced. "I fought the attraction, the love she brought out in me, for a long time. It was nearly my undoing. Luckily, she hung in there and refused to let me go my own way."

"Mercenaries must all be alike," Susannah muttered unhappily.

"There's probably a grain of truth to that. I met Killian in the Foreign Legion. Did you know that?"

"No, I didn't."

"He was a corporal in the company I helped run." Morgan shrugged. "Many of the men I employ here at Perseus are old contacts out of the Legion. The women who work for me all have a military background of some sort, too."

"What is Sean running from?"

"I don't know. Did he tell you anything about his past? He's always been more tight-lipped about it than most."

"No, it's like pulling teeth to get any kind of information out of him." Susannah sat quietly, staring down at her clasped hands. Softly she said, "Something happened to me when Sean was there protecting me from that hit man. The night we were almost killed, I discovered that I loved him. The fact that we might both lose our lives clarified my feelings for him."

Frowning, Morgan sat up. "I see…"

"Sean ran away from me, Morgan. He left me a note. He couldn't even face me to say goodbye, and that's not fair to me—or to him."

"Men who join the Foreign Legion are always running from something," Morgan said gently.

"I understand that now, but that's not an excuse for his behavior. I need some information," Susannah said firmly. "About Sean. About his past."

Morgan opened his hands. "When men come from the Legion, you don't ask many questions," he said gently. "Each of my employees signs a legal document saying that they aren't wanted criminals in another country before I'll hire them for Perseus. It's their word. I don't make inquiries unless I get a tip-off from Interpol or some other governmental body." He shrugged. "And Killian has been one of the most close-mouthed of my men. I know very little of his past."

"Then let me fill you in," Susannah whispered, "because when I'm done with my story I want you to tell me where he lives. He and I have some unfinished business to clear up."

Morgan was scowling heavily by the time Susannah had completed her story. He'd asked Marie to bring in hot tea and cookies, and the tray sat on the glass-topped coffee table in front of the sofa. He'd also had her stop all incoming calls—except for emergencies—and canceled the rest of the day's business.

Susannah couldn't eat, but she did sip some fragrant tea.

"I hate to tell you this," Morgan said, sitting down with her again, "but when Killian came in off your assignment he requested leave."

"Leave?"

"Yes. It's a program I devised when I set up this company. When an operative's out in the field, there are tremendous stresses on him or her. When they come in off a particularly demanding assignment, they can request time off from the company for as long as they need to recuperate. Killian came back from Kentucky and wanted leave. I granted it to him, no questions asked."

Susannah's heart beat a little harder. "Where is he, then?"

"Ordinarily, where our people live is top secret. We never give out addresses to anyone, for fear of the information leaking into enemy hands. But in this case, I'm going to make an exception."

Relief made her shaky. "He won't be expecting me to show up."

Morgan smiled grimly. "There's something about the element of surprise—you might catch him off guard enough to level with you."

"He never has leveled with me, Morgan."

Moving uncomfortably, he said, "Susannah, you're dealing with a lot of unknown factors here."

"He's hurting terribly, Morgan."

Rubbing his jaw, Morgan nodded. "I was hurting a lot when Laura met me," he murmured. "And I can't say I was the world's nicest person around her."

"But you hung in there—together. And look at you now. You're happy, Morgan."

Exhaling, he said, "Susannah, Killian's hurting in a lot of ways neither of us knows. I know you're an idealist, and I know you have a large, forgiving heart. But Killian may not have the capacity to reach out to you, even if he wants to. He may be too afraid, for whatever reason. You have to be prepared to accept that if it happens."

She hung her head and nodded. "I'm not so idealistic that I don't know when I'm not wanted, Morgan. But Sean never gave me that chance. He never had the courage to sit down and tell me the truth."

"I'm not saying what he did was right," Morgan said, frowning heavily. "We all run in our own way. Luckily, I had Laura's steadfast courage, her belief in me that helped me get a handhold on my own internal problems." Then, with a slight smile filled with sorrow, he added, "I still have problems that overflow into our personal life, our relationship. Mostly because of me, because of my past that still haunts me. It's not as bad now, but believe me, Laura has her hands full some days with me when the past hits me like a sledgehammer." He glanced at the gold watch on his wrist. "Come on, it's time to go home. Laura promised me a special meal because you were coming. Let's not be late."

The loneliness Susannah had felt since Killian's abrupt departure was somewhat ameliorated by Morgan and his happy family. Laura, beautiful as ever with her long blond hair, dancing eyes and ready smile, helped lift Susannah's spirits. Her son, Jason Charles Trayhern, had his father's dark black hair and gray eyes. On the other hand, three-month-old Katherine Alyssa was a duplicate of Laura's ethereal beauty. Just getting to hold her was a treat for Susannah.

After the meal was eaten and the children had been put to bed, Susannah lingered over a cup of coffee with Laura in the living room. Morgan discreetly excused himself and retired to his home office in the basement of their large home.

Laura curled up on the flowery print couch and smoothed her long pink cotton skirt.

"So tell me what's going on, Susannah! You barely ate any of that great supper I fixed!"

"I know, and I'm really sorry, Laura. The roast leg of lamb was wonderful. It's just that I've got a lot of things on my mind. Well…my heart, to be more honest." She smiled and leaned over, petting Sasha, the family's huge brown-and-white Saint Bernard, who had made herself at home next to Susannah's feet. She'd long since taken off her shoes and gotten comfortable—Laura and Morgan's home invited that kind of response.

"Killian, by any chance?"

"How did you know?"

With a slight smile, Laura said softly, "He's a man who's crying for a woman to help bring him out of his self-imposed exile."

"You've always had such insight into people."

Laura shrugged and smiled. "That's what helped me understand Morgan when I first met him. He was a man trapped in hell, although I didn't understand why for quite some time."

"Well," Susannah muttered. "That's exactly how Sean described himself."

"Chances are," Laura said gently, "he lives in an emotional hell on a daily basis." With a sigh, she sipped the coffee. "Susannah, men who go through a war like Morgan did are scarred for life. It kills a part of them, so they're crippled emotionally, in a sense. But that doesn't mean they can't make the most of what is still intact within them."

"Morgan had you to help him realize all of that."

"We had our love, our belief in each other," Laura agreed quietly. "Sometimes it's still not easy. For Morgan, the war will never really be over. There are days when there's a lot of tension between us." She smiled softly. "Fortunately, we love each other enough to sit down and discuss what's bothering him. Morgan has slowly been opening up more with each year that passes, but it's never easy for us, Susannah."

"You have his trust," Susannah pointed out. "I never had time to get Sean's trust. It all happened so fast, so soon..."

"I understand better than most," Laura whispered. "Men like Killian and Morgan need a woman with strength, with steadiness, because they've lost those things emotionally within themselves. I hope you're prepared for the kind of uphill battles a man like that will put you through."

Susannah glanced at her. "You're not scaring me off, Laura, if that's what you're trying to do."

Reaching over, Laura touched her shoulder. "No one believes in the power of love more than I do. I've seen it work miracles with Morgan—and with me." She lifted her head and looked toward the darkened hall that led to the bedrooms, her eyes misty. "And we have two beautiful babies that reflect that love."

"Ma didn't raise me to think life was easy," Susannah said. "I know the hell I went through with Sean while he was there. He just wouldn't—couldn't—talk."

"And that's going to be the biggest stumbling block when you see him again. Men like that feel as if they're carrying such a horrendous amount of ugliness within them. They're afraid that if they start to talk about it, it will get out of control."

"So they get tight-lipped about it?"

Laura nodded. "Exactly."

With a sigh, Susannah shrugged. "I don't have a choice in this, Laura. I don't want one, anyway. Sean is worth it."

"Well, tomorrow morning, Morgan's driver will take you to the airport, and you'll fly to Victoria, British Columbia, where he lives. It's on a lovely island off the west coast of Canada. There's quite a British flavor to the place. And flowers!" Laura smiled fondly. "The island is a riot of color and fragrance. I've never seen so many roses! You'll love the island."

As she listened, Susannah hoped that her lack of worldliness wouldn't be her undoing. She sat tensely, her hands clasped in her lap. All she had to lead her through this tangled web that Sean lived within was her heart. What would he do when she showed up at his doorstep? As Morgan had said, the element of surprise might work for her—but, she thought, it could also work against her.

Susannah had never needed the kind of strength she knew she would need in order to face Sean Killian bravely. Only Sean could show her if what she felt for him was love. But even if it was, there was no guarantee that he would have the courage to admit it.

Kneeling in the triangular flower bed, Killian stared glumly down at the bright yellow marigold in his hands. The gold, red and yellow flowers assaulted the air with their rather acrid odor. Like the flower in his hand, surrounded by the moist, rich soil, he was alone. Alone and bitter.

Resolutely he dug a small hole with the trowel, and

placed the marigold in it. With dirt-stained hands, he pressed the moist earth securely over the roots. Gardening had always helped soothe him. *Until now.*

Looking up from the garden, Killian stared at the calm blue of the ocean, three hundred feet away. His green manicured lawn contrasted beautifully with the glassy water. The pale azure of the sky was dotted with fleecy white clouds. Summer in Victoria was his favorite time. Luckily, the money he'd earned over the years had gotten him this small English-style cottage when the couple who'd owned it, up in years, could no longer keep up with its landscaping and gardening demands and sold it to him.

Susannah. Her name hung in front of Killian as he caressed the tiny, frilly petals of a pale yellow marigold. The color reminded him of the hope that always burned in her eyes. Hope. He had none. The feeling had been utterly destroyed so long ago. Closing his eyes, he knelt there, surrounded by the lonely cries of the sea gulls that endlessly patrolled the beach and, off in the distance, the hoarse barks of sea lions.

Killian opened his eyes, feeling the terrible loneliness knife through him as never before. Slowly he looked around. He was surrounded by the ephemeral beauty of many carefully constructed flower beds, all geometrically shaped and designed by him, their rainbow colors breathtaking. But Killian could feel none of his usual response to them. Only Susannah could make him feel.

What was wrong? What had happened to him? He opened up his hands and studied them darkly. He'd made love to other women off and on throughout his life, but never had the act—or more truthfully, the feelings—continued to live like a burning-hot light within his body and heart as they did now.

With a shake of his head, Killian muttered under his breath and got to his feet. Brushing off the bits of soil clinging to his jeans, he straightened. The three tiers of flower gardens culminated with at least a hundred roses of various colors. Their fragrance was heavy in the area nearest the rear sliding glass doors to his house.

And it was a house, Killian reminded himself harshly. Susannah's ramshackle, broken-down old place was a *home*. She'd made it feel homey, comfortable and warm with her life and presence. Killian savored the hours spent with her in that antiquated kitchen. Every night when he lay down to try to sleep, those scenes would replay like a haunting movie across his closed eyelids. And when he finally did sleep, torrid, heated dreams of loving Susannah drove him to wakefulness, and a clawing hunger that brought him to the verge of tears. Tears! He never cried!

Stopping at the rose garden, a long, rectangular area bordered with red brick, Killian barely brushed a lavender rose with his fingertips. *Susannah*. No longer did Killian try to escape her memory. The doorbell rang, pulling his attention from his morbid reverie. Who could it be? His housekeeper and regular gardener, Emily Johnston, had left earlier to buy the week's groceries, and she wouldn't be back until tomorrow morning.

Automatically Killian dropped into his natural mode of wariness. Although his address and phone number were known only to Meg and Morgan, he didn't trust his many enemies not to track him down.

As careful as Killian was about masking his movements to preserve his sanctuary, he never fooled himself. Someday one of his more patient and vengeful enemies might locate him.

Padding through the fully carpeted house, Killian halted at the front door and peered through the one-way glass. *Susannah!* His heart thumped hard in his chest. What the hell was she doing here? Could he be dreaming? His mind spun with questions. His heart began an uneven pounding. As he closed his hand over the brass doorknob, Killian felt a surge of hope tunnel through him. Just as quickly, he savagely destroyed the burgeoning feeling.

The door swung open. Susannah looked through the screen at Killian. As usual, his features were set—but his eyes gave away his true feelings. Her palms were sweaty, and her heart was thundering like a runaway freight train. She girded herself for his disapproval.

"What are you doing here?" Killian demanded in a rasp. He glanced around, checking out the surrounding area. Luckily, the street ended in a cul-de-sac, and he knew who his neighbors were and the cars they drove. The white Toyota out front must be a rental car that Susannah had driven.

"We've got some unfinished business," Susannah whispered. It was so hard to gather strength when she felt like caving in and stepping those precious few feet to fall into Killian's arms. The terrible light in his eyes told him he was no less tortured by her unexpected appearance than she was.

"Get in here," he growled, and gripped her by the arm.

Susannah didn't resist. She could tell that Killian

was carefully monitoring the amount of strength he applied to her arm. She entered his home. A dusky-rose carpet flowed throughout the living room and hall area, which was decorated with simple, spare, carefully placed furniture. The walls were covered with floor-to-ceiling bookcases. Killian must be a voracious reader.

There were so many impressions she wanted to absorb, to investigate. Each one would give her another clue to Killian. But she didn't have that kind of time. Every word, every gesture, counted. She turned as he closed the door with finality. The grimness in his face made her feel cold. Alone.

"How did you find me?"

"I flew to Washington and talked with Morgan. He told me where you lived." Susannah saw his eyes flare with disbelief.

Killian took a step back, because if he didn't he was going to sweep Susannah uncompromisingly into his arms. And then he was going to take her to his bedroom and make wild, hungry love with her until they were so exhausted that they couldn't move.

Killian looked down at her vulnerable features. There was real hope in Susannah's eyes, a kind of hope he'd never be able to claim as his own. She was dressed in a summery print blouse—pink peonies against a white background—and white slacks, with sandals outlining her feet. Her lovely sable hair was trapped in a chignon, and Killian had to stop himself from reaching forward to release that captive mass of silk into his hands. His mouth had grown dry, and his heart was beating dangerously hard in his chest.

"All right, what's going on?"

"You and me." Susannah felt her fear almost overwhelming her, but she dared not be weak now. She saw a slight thawing in Killian's narrowed eyes, a slight softening of his thinned mouth. "What made you think," Susannah said in a low, strangled voice, "that you could walk out on me just like that? We made love with each other, Sean. I thought—I thought we meant something to each other." She forced herself to hold his hardening gaze. "You ran without ever giving me the opportunity to sit down and talk to you. I'm here to complete unfinished business." Her voice grew hoarse. "One way or another."

Killian stood stunned. It took him a long time to find his voice. "I told you—I didn't mean to hurt you," he rasped. "I thought leaving the way I did would hurt you less."

Susannah's eyes went round, and anger gave her the backbone she needed. "Hurt me less?" Susannah forced herself to walk into the living room. She dropped her purse and her one piece of luggage on the carpet. Turning, she rounded on Killian. "I don't call running out on me less hurtful!"

Nervously Killian shoved his hands into the pockets of his jeans. "I'm sorry, Susannah. For everything."

"For loving me?"

Killian dropped his gaze and stared at the floor. He heard the ache in her husky tone; her voice was like a lover's caress. He was glad to see her, glad that she was here. "No," he admitted. He raised his chin and forced himself to meet her large, tear-filled eyes. "But I am sorry for the hurt I've caused you."

"You walk around in your silence and don't communicate worth a darn. I'm not a mind reader. Do you

know how awful I felt after you left? Do you know
that I blamed myself? I asked myself what I did wrong.
Was it something I said? Did?" Grimly, her eyes flash-
ing, she said, "I don't have a lot of worldly ways like
you. I know I'm a country woman, but I don't question
the way of my heart, Sean. You had no right to leave
the way you did. It wasn't fair to me, and it wasn't fair
to you, either."

Pain knifed through him and he moved into the
living room with her. He halted a foot away from her,
aching to put his hands on her shoulders, but not daring to. "I was to blame, not you."

To her amazement, Susannah saw Killian thawing.
Perhaps Laura was right: He needed a woman to be
stronger than him so that he could feel safe enough to
open up. Had he never had a woman of strength to lean
on? If not, it was no wonder he remained closed, protecting his vulnerability. The discovery was as sweet as it
was bold—and frightening. Susannah was just coming
out of her own trauma. Did she have enough strength for
the both of them? She simply didn't know, but the glimmer in Killian's eyes, the way his mouth unconsciously
hinted at the vulnerability he tried so hard to hide and
protect, made her decide to try anyway.

"I hope you've got a guest bedroom."

He blinked.

Susannah drilled him with a fiery look. "Sean, I
happen to feel that we meant a lot to each other when
you were in Kentucky. And after we made love, you
ran. I don't know your reasons for running, and that's
what I'm here to find out. I intend to stay here, no matter how miserable you make it for me, until we get to
the bottom of this—together."

Dread flared through Killian. No woman had ever challenged him like this. "You don't know what you're saying," he warned.

"Like heck I don't! Give me some credit, Sean. I work with special children. I've got to have a lot of insight into them to reach them, to touch them, so that they'll stop retreating."

Killian took another step away, terror warring with his need for Susannah. "You're biting off too much. You don't know what you're getting into," he snapped.

Tilting her chin, Susannah rasped, "Oh, yes I do."

"Now look," he said in a low, gravelly voice, "I don't want to hurt you, Susannah. If you stay here, it'll happen. Don't put yourself on the firing line for me. I'm not worth it."

Tears stung her eyes, but Susannah forced them back. Killian would read her tears as a sign of weakness. "You're wrong. You're a good man, Sean. You've been hurt, and you're hiding. I'm here to show you that you don't need to keep running. You're allowed to laugh, you know. And to cry. How long has it been since you've done either?"

Killian lunged forward blindly and gripped her by the arm. "Dammit," he rasped off-key, "get the hell out of here while you still can, Susannah! I'm a monster! A monster!" He savagely poked a finger at his belly. "It's in here, this thing, this hell that I carry. It comes out and controls me, and it will hurt whoever is around. You've got to understand that!"

She held his blazing gaze, seeing the horror of his past reflected in his eyes, hearing the anguish in his tone. "No," she said. "I'm not afraid of you," she rattled, "or that so-called monster inside of you. For the first time in your life, Sean, you're going to be honest, not only with yourself, but with someone else—me."

Killian took a step back, as if she'd slapped him. He stared down at her as the tension swirled around them like a raging storm. Frightened as never before, he backed away. In place of the panic came anger. He ground out, "If you stay, you stay at your own risk. Do you understand that?"

"I do."

He glared at her. "You're naive and idealistic. I'll hurt you in ways you never thought possible! I won't mean to, but it'll happen, Susannah." He stood there, suddenly feeling very old and broken. His voice grew hoarse. "I don't want to, but I will. God help me, I don't want to hurt you, Susannah."

Swallowing hard, a lump forming in her throat, she nodded. "I know," she replied softly, "I know…"

"This is hopeless," Killian whispered, looking out one of the series of plate-glass windows that faced the flower gardens and the ocean. "I'm hopeless."

Grimly Susannah fought the desire to take Killian into her arms. Intuitively she understood that it would weaken her position with him. He was wary and defensive enough to strike out verbally and hurt her for fear of getting hurt again. As she picked up her luggage, Susannah realized that her love for Sean was the gateway not only to trust, but also to a wealth of yet-untapped affection that lay deep within her.

"You're not hopeless," Susannah told him gently. "Now, if you'll show me where the guest bedroom is, I'll get settled in."

Killian gaped at her. His mouth opened, then closed.

"First door on the right down the hall," he muttered, then spun on his heel and left.

Her hands shaking, Susannah put her week's worth of clothes away in the closet and the dresser. Her heart wouldn't steady, but a clean feeling, something akin to a sense of victory, soared within her. She took several deep breaths to calm herself after having established a beachhead in the initial confrontation. Killian's desperation told her, she hoped, how much he was, indeed, still tied to her. Perhaps Morgan and Laura were right, and Killian did love her after all. That was the only thing that could possibly pull them through this storm together. Any less powerful emotion would surely destroy her, and continue to wound Killian.

Straightening up from her task, Susannah took in the simple, spare room. A delicate white Irish lace spread covered the double bed. The carpet was pale lavender, and the walls cream-colored. A vibrant Van Gogh print of sunflowers hung above the bed. The maple dresser was surely an antique, but Susannah didn't know from what era. The window, framed by lavender drapes and ivory sheers, overlooked a breathtaking view of the ocean.

"Well, Susannah, keep going," she warned herself. As much as she wanted to hide in the bedroom, she knew it wasn't the answer. No, she had to establish herself as a force in Killian's isolated world, and make herself part of it—whether he wanted her to or not. And in her heart she sensed that he did want her. The risk to her heart was great. But her love for Killian was strong enough to let her take that risk. He was always risking his life for others; well, it was time someone took a risk for him.

* * *

Killian stole a look into the kitchen. Susannah had busied herself all afternoon in his spacious modern kitchen. Although he'd hidden out most of the time in the garage, working on a wood-carving project, the fragrant odors coming from the kitchen couldn't be ignored. As upset as he was, the food she was cooking made him hungry. But it was his other hunger for Susannah that he was trying to quell—and he wasn't succeeding.

"What's for dinner?" he asked with a frown.

Susannah wiped her hands on the dark green apron she had tied around her waist. "Pot roast with sour-cream gravy and biscuits. Southerners love their biscuits and gravy," she said with pride.

"Sounds decent. Dessert?" He glanced at her.

"You really push your luck, don't you?"

He wanted to smile, but couldn't. "Yeah, I guess I do."

"I didn't come here to be a slave who cooks you three meals a day and cleans your house," Susannah pointed out as she gestured for him to sit down at the table. "This food is going to cost you."

"Oh?" Thinking he should leave, Killian sat down. Susannah seemed to belong in the kitchen—her presence was like sunshine. The bleakness of his life seemed to dissolve in her aura.

Susannah served the meat and placed the pitcher of gravy on the table with a basket of homemade biscuits. Sitting down, she held his inquiring gaze. "My folks and I always used to sit and talk after meals. It was one of the most important things I learned from them—talking."

With a grimace, Killian offered her the platter of meat first. "I'm not much of one for talking and you know it."

"So you'll learn to become a better communicator," Susannah said lightly. She felt absolutely tied in knots, and she had to force herself to put food on her plate. Just being this close to Killian, to his powerful physical presence, was making her body betray her head. When his lips curved into that sour smile, Susannah melted inwardly. She remembered how hot, how demanding and sharing, that mouth had been on hers. Never had she wanted to kiss a man so much. But she knew if she bowed to her selfish hunger for him as a man, she'd lose not only the battle, but the war, as well.

"Okay," he said tentatively, "you want me to talk." He spooned several thick portions of the roast onto his plate, added three biscuits and then some gravy. "About what?"

"You," Susannah said pointedly.

"I'm willing to talk about anything else," he warned her heavily.

With a shrug, Susannah said, "Fine. Start anywhere you want."

The food was delectable, and Killian found himself wolfing down the thick, juicy meat. Still in wonder over this strong, stubborn side of Susannah that he hadn't seen before, he shook his head.

"I didn't realize you were this persistent."

Susannah grinned. "Would it have changed anything?"

The merest shadow of a smile touched Killian's mouth, and the hesitant, pain-filled attempt sent a sheet of heat through Susannah. Taking a deep breath, she said, "I want to know about you, your past, Sean. I don't think that's too much to ask. It will help me understand you—and, maybe, myself, and how I feel toward you."

Again her simple honesty cut through him. He ate slowly, not only hearing, but also feeling her words. He saw Susannah's hands tremble ever so slightly. She was nervous, perhaps even more nervous than he was. Still, his heart filled with such joy that she was here that it took the edge off his terror. "So, if I open up, maybe you'll give me some of that dessert you made?"

Susannah laughed, feeling her first glimmer of hope. She felt Killian testing her, seeing if she was really as strong as he needed her to be. "That coconut chiffon pie is going to go to waste if you don't start talking, Sean Killian."

Her laughter was like sunlight in his dark world. In that moment, her eyes sparkling, her lush mouth curved, Killian ached to love her, ached to feel her take away his darkness. Hope flickered deep within him, and it left him nonplussed. Never had he experienced this feeling before. Not like this. Giving her an annoyed look, he muttered, "I'd rather talk about my flower gardens, and the roses."

"Enough about the roses," Susannah said as she stood up and cleared away the dishes. She saw his eyes darken instantly. Tightening her lips, she went to the refrigerator, pulled out the pie and cut two slices.

"I want you to tell me about your childhood."

Moodily he sat back in the chair, unable to tear his gaze from her. "It's not a very happy story" was all he said.

Susannah gave him a piece of pie and a fork. She sat back down, grimly holding his hooded gaze. "Tell me about it."

With a sigh, Killian shrugged and picked up the fork. "I was the runt. The kid who was too small for his age. I was always scrapping with older boys who thought they could push my younger sister, Meg, around." He pointed to his crooked nose. "I had this busted on three different occasions in grade school."

"Did you have anyone to hold you?"

Killian flashed her an amused look. "Scrappers didn't fall into their mothers' arms and cry, Susannah."

"Is your mother alive?"

He winced inwardly and scowled, paying a lot of attention to his pie, which he hadn't touched. "Mother died when I was fourteen."

"What did she die of?" Susannah asked softly.

Rearing back in the chair, and wiping his hands absently on his jeans, Killian replied, "A robbery."

She heard the rising pain in Killian's tone, and saw it in the slash of his mouth. "Tell me about it."

"Not much to tell," he muttered. "When I was thirteen, my parents emigrated to America. They set up a grocery store in the Bronx. A year later, a couple of kids came in to rob them. They took the money and killed my parents," he concluded bluntly. Killian bowed his head, feeling the hot rush of tears in his tightly shut eyes. Then he felt Susannah's hand fall gently on his shoulder. Just that simple gesture of solace nearly broke open the wall of grief he'd carried so long over his parents' harsh and unjust deaths.

Fighting to keep her own feelings under control, Susannah tried to understand what that experience would do to a fourteen-year-old boy, an immigrant. "You were suddenly left alone," she said unsteadily. "And Meg was younger?"

"Yes, by a year."

Susannah could feel the anguish radiating from him. "What did you do?"

Killian fought the urge to put his hand over hers where it lay on his shoulder. If he did, he'd want to bury his head blindly against her body and sob. The lump in his throat grew. So many unbidden, unexpected feelings sheared through him. Desperate, not understanding how Susannah could so easily pull these emotions out of him and send them boiling to the surface, Killian choked. With a growl, he lunged away from the table, and his chair fell to the tiled floor.

"You have no right to do this to me. None!" He turned and jerked the chair upright.

Susannah sat very still, working to keep her face neutral. She battled tears, and prayed that Killian couldn't see them in her eyes. His face was pale and tense, and his eyes were haunted.

"If you're smart," he rasped as he headed toward the garden, "you'll leave right now, Susannah."

Stubbornly she shook her head. "I'm staying, Sean."

His fingers gripped the doorknob. "Damn you! Damn you—"

She closed her eyes and took a deep, ragged breath. "You aren't going to scare me off."

"Then you'd better lock the door to your bedroom tonight," he growled. "I want you so damned bad I can taste it. I can taste you." He jabbed his finger warningly at her. "You keep this up, and I don't know what will happen. You're not safe here with me. Don't you understand?"

Susannah turned in her chair. When she spoke, her voice was soft. "You're not even safe with yourself, Sean."

Wincing, he stalked out of the house. Maybe a walk, a long, brutal walk, would cleanse his agitated soul and his bleeding heart. He loved Susannah, yet he feared he'd hurt her. No woman had ever unstrung him as easily and quickly as she did. He strode through the beauty of his flower gardens, unseeing.

Chapter 10

Susannah got ready for bed. She hadn't heard Killian return, and it was nearly eleven. Her nerves were raw, and she was jangled.

Lock the door.

Did she want to? Could she say no if Killian came into her bedroom? Where did running and hiding end? And where did freedom, for both of them, begin? Perhaps it would be born out of the heat of their mutual love... Her hands trembling, Susannah pulled down the bed covers. The room was dark now. Slivers of moonlight pierced the curtains, lending a muted radiance to the room.

Lock the door.

Dressed in a simple knee-length cotton gown, Susannah pulled the brush through her hair. Her own emotions were jumbled and skittish. What if Sean walked through that door? She stared hard at the doorknob. She hadn't locked it—yet. Should she? Was she hesitating for herself or for Sean?

Lock the door.

Trying to recall the nights with Killian at her farmhouse, Susannah realized that she'd been in such turmoil herself that, except for that one night, she had no idea if he generally slept, had terrible nightmares or experienced insomnia. Making a small sound of frustration, she set the tortoiseshell brush on the dresser. No. No, she had to leave the door open. If she locked it, it was a symbol that she really didn't trust him—or herself. Taking a deep, unsteady breath, she slipped between the cool sheets. Getting comfortable, she lay there, her hands behind her head, for a long, long time—waiting. Just waiting.

Lock the door.

Killian moved like a ghost through his own house. All the lights were out, but the moon provided just enough light to see. He was sweaty and tired, having walked miles along the beach in order to purge himself of the awful roiling emotions that were flaying him alive. The forced hike had taken the edge off him, but he hadn't dealt at all with his feelings.

Susannah.

Killian stood frozen in the hallway and finally faced the full realization: He loved her. His hand shook as he touched his forehead. When? Making a sound of disgust, he thought that from the moment he'd seen Susannah his heart had become a traitor to him. Yes, he'd made love to women in his life, but never had he wanted truly to love them. With Susannah, he wanted to give. He wanted to see that velvet languor in her eyes, and the soft curve of her lips as he pleasured her, loved her so thoroughly that they fused into melting oneness.

His nerves raw, more exhausted than he could recall ever having been, Killian forced himself to go to his room for a cold shower. But as he passed Susannah's room, he stopped. His eyes narrowed on the doorknob. Had she done as he ordered and locked her door against him? Sweat stood out on his tense features as his hand slowly moved forward. For an instant, his fingers hovered. A part of him wanted her to have the door locked. He didn't want to hurt her—didn't want to take from her without giving something back. But how could he give, when he didn't even know how to give to himself after all those years?

His mouth tightening, Killian's hand flowed around the doorknob. He twisted it gently. It was unlocked! He stood there, filled with terror and hope, filled with such hunger and longing that he couldn't move. Susannah trusted him. She trusted him to do the right thing for both of them. Just as quietly, he eased the doorknob back to its original position.

Her heart beating wildly, Susannah sensed Killian's presence outside her room. She lay there gripping the sheet, her eyes wide, as she watched the doorknob slowly turn, trying to prepare herself emotionally. If he entered her room, she wasn't sure what she'd do. Her heart whispered to her to love him, to hold him, to allow him to spend himself within her. Loving was healing, and Susannah knew that instinctively. Her head warned her sharply that he'd use her up and eventually destroy her emotionally, just as he'd been destroyed himself over the years.

The seconds ticked by, and Susannah watched the doorknob twist back into place. Killian knew now that she was accessible, that she would be here for him, for whatever he needed from her. The thought was as frightening as it was exhilarating. On one level, Susannah felt as if she were dealing with a wild, unmanageable animal that would just as soon hurt her as stay with her. That was the wounded side of Sean. The other side, the man who possessed such poignant sensitivity and awareness of her as a woman, was very different. Somewhere in the careening thoughts that clashed with her overwrought feelings, Susannah was counting on that other part of Sean to surface. But would it? And in time?

When the door didn't open, she drew in a shaky breath of air and gradually relaxed. At least Killian had come home. She'd worried about where he'd gone, and indeed whether he'd return. Forcing her eyes closed, Susannah felt some of the tension drain from her arms and legs. Sleep. She had to get some sleep. Tomorrow morning would be another uphill battle with Sean. But the night was young, her mind warned her. What were Killian's sleeping habits? Was he like a beast on the prowl, haunted by ghosts of the past, unable to sleep at night? Susannah wished she knew.

Sometime later, her eyelids grew heavy, her heart settled down, and she snuggled into the pillow. Almost immediately, she began to dream of Sean, and their conversation at the table—and the look of pain he carried in his eyes.

Susannah jerked awake. Her lips parting, she twisted her head from one side to the other. Had she been dreaming? Had she heard a scream? Or perhaps more the sound of an animal crying out than a human scream? Fumbling sleepily, she threw off the sheet and the bedspread. Dream or reality? She had to find out. What time was it? Stumbling to her feet, Susannah bumped into the dresser.

"Ouch!" she muttered, wiping the sleep from her eyes. Her hair, in disarray, settled around her face as she glanced at the clock. It was 3:00 a.m. The moonlight had shifted considerably, and the room was darker now than before. Reaching for her robe, Susannah struggled into it.

She stepped out into the hall, but only silence met her sensitive hearing. Killian's room was across the hall. The door was partly open. Her heart starting a slow, hard pounding, Susannah forced herself to move toward it.

Just as she reached it, she heard a muffled crash in another part of the house. Startled, she turned and moved on bare feet down the carpeted hall toward the sound. In the center of the gloom-ridden living room, she halted. Her nerves taut, her breathing suspended, Susannah realized that the sounds were coming from the garage. Killian did woodworking out there. More crashes occurred. Fear snaked through her. She knew he was out there. She had to go to him. She had to confront him. Now Susannah understood what an animal trainer must feel like, facing a wild, untamed animal.

Her mouth dry, her throat constricted and aching, Susannah reached for the doorknob. A flood of light from the garage momentarily blinded her, and she stopped in the doorway, her hand raised to shade her eyes.

* * *

Killian whirled around, his breathing raspy and harsh. His eyes narrowed to slits as he picked up the sound of the door leading to the house being opened. He'd prayed that his shrieks wouldn't wake Susannah, but there she stood, looking sleepy yet frightened. Sweat ran down the sides of his face.

"I told you—get the hell out of here!" The words, more plea than threat, tore out of him. "Go! Run!"

Susannah's mouth fell open. Killian's cry careened off the walls of the large woodworking shop. Despite her fear, she noted beautifully carved statues— mostly of children, mothers with children, and flying birds. Some had been knocked off their pedestals and lay strewn across the concrete floor. Were those the crashes she'd heard? Susannah's gaze riveted on Killian. He was naked save for a pair of drawstring pajama bottoms clinging damply to his lower body. His entire torso gleamed in the low light, and his hair was damp and plastered against his skull. More than anything, Susannah saw the malevolent terror in his dark, anguished eyes.

She whispered his name and moved forward.

"No!" Killian pleaded, backing away. "Don't come near me! Damn it, don't!"

Blindly Susannah shook her head, opening her arms to him. "No," she cried softly. "You won't hurt me. You won't…" And she moved with a purpose that gave her strength and kept her fear in check.

Stumbling backward, Killian was trapped by the wood cabinets. There was no place to turn, no place to run. He saw blips of Susannah interspersed among the violent scenes that haunted him continuously. In one, he saw the enemy coming at him, knife upraised. Another flashback showed his torturer coming forward with a wire to garrote him. He shook his head, a whimper escaping his tightened lips. He was trying desperately to cling to reality, to the fact that Susannah was here with him. He heard her soft, husky voice. He heard the snarl and curse of his enemies as they leaped toward him.

"No!" He threw his hands out in front of him to stop her. Simultaneously the flashback overwhelmed him. His hands were lethal weapons, honed by years of karate training, thickened by calluses, and he moved into position to protect himself. Breathing hard, he waited for his enemy to come at him with the knife as he met and held his dark, angry eyes.

Susannah saw the wildness in Killian's eyes, and she reached out to touch his raised hand. His face was frozen into a mask devoid of emotion; his eyes were fathomless, intent and slitted. Fear rose in her, but she knew she had to confront it, make it her friend and reach Killian, reach inside him.

Just as she grazed his hand, he whimpered. Her eyes widened as she saw him shift.

"Sean, no!" She threw out one hand to try to stop him. "No," she choked out again.

Where was he? He heard Susannah's cry. *Where?* Slowly the flashbacks faded, and Killian realized she was gripping his arm, her eyes wide and brimming with tears.

"No…" he rasped, and quickly jerked away from Susannah's touch. "God… I'm sorry." Bitterness coated his mouth, and he dragged in a ragged breath. "I could have hurt you. My God, I nearly—"

"It's all right. I'm all right, and so are you," Susannah whispered. Dizziness assailed her. She stood very still. When he reached out to touch her, his hand was trembling. The instant Killian's fingers touched her unbound hair, Susannah wanted to cry. There was such anguish in his eyes as he caressed her hair, as if to make sure she wasn't a part of whatever nightmare had held him in its thrall. Gathering what courage she had left, Susannah lifted her hand and caught his. His skin was sweaty, and the thrum of tension was palpable in his grip.

"It was just a nightmare," she quavered, lifting her head and meeting his tortured eyes.

Killian muttered something under his breath. "You shouldn't have stayed," he rasped. "I might have hurt you…" He gently framed her face and looked deeply into her tear-filled eyes. "I'm so afraid, Susannah."

Whispering his name, Susannah slid her arms around him and brought him against her. She heard a harsh sound escape his mouth as he buried his face against her hair, his arms moving like steel bands around her. The air rushed from her lungs, but she relaxed against him, understanding his need to hold and be held.

"I love you," she whispered, sliding her fingers through his short black hair. "I love you…"

Her words, soft and quavering, flowed through Killian. Without thinking, he lifted his head to seek her mouth. Blindly he sought and found her waiting lips. They tasted sweet, soft and giving as he hungrily took her offering. His breathing was chaotic, and so was hers. Drowning in Susannah's mouth and feeling her hands moving reassuringly across his shoulders took away the terror that had inhabited him. Her moan was of pleasure, not pain.

In those stark, naked moments, Killian stopped taking from her and began to give back. Her mouth blossomed beneath his, warm, sweet and hot. How badly he wanted to love her; his body was aching testimony to his need. Tearing his mouth from hers, he held her languorous gray gaze, which now sparkled with joy.

"It's going to be all right," he promised unsteadily. "Everything's going to be all right. Come on…"

Susannah remained beneath his arm, his protection, as he led her through the silent house. In the living room, he guided her to the couch and sat down with her. Their knees touched, and he held both her hands. "You're the last person in the world I'd ever want to hurt," he rasped.

"I know…"

"Dammit, Susannah, why didn't you run? Why didn't you leave me?"

She slowly looked up, meeting and holding his tear-filled eyes. "B-because I love you, Sean. You don't leave someone you love, who's hurting, to suffer the way you were suffering."

Killian closed his eyes and pulled her against him. The moments of silence blended together, and he felt the hotness of tears brim over and begin to course down his cheeks. His hands tightened around her as he gathered her into his arms. Burying his face in her sable hair, he felt a wrenching sob working its way up and out of his gut. The instant her arms went hesitantly around his shoulders, the sob tore from him. His entire body shook in response.

"Go ahead," Susannah whispered, tears in her

eyes. "Cry, Sean. Cry for all the awful things you've seen and had to do to survive. Cry. I'll hold you. I'll just hold you…" And she did, with all the womanly strength she possessed.

Time drew to a halt, and all Susannah could feel were the terrible shudders racking Killian's lean body as he clung to her, nearly squeezing the breath from her. He clung as if he feared that to let go would be to be lost forever. Susannah understood that better than most. She tightened her grip around his damp shoulders, whispering words of encouragement, of love, of care, as his sobs grew louder and harsher, wrenching from him.

Susannah was no longer feeling her own pain, she was experiencing his. She held Killian as if she feared that to release him would mean he would break into a million shattered pieces. His fingers dug convulsively into her back as the sobs continued to rip through him. Her gown grew damp, but she didn't care. His ability to trust her, to give himself over to her and release the glut of anguish he'd carried by himself for so long, was exhilarating.

Gradually Killian's sobs lessened, and so did the convulsions that had torn at him in her arms. Gently Susannah stroked his hair, shoulders and back. His spine was strong, and the muscles on either side of it were lean.

"You're going to be fine," Susannah whispered, pressing a kiss against his temple. "Just fine." She sighed, resting her head against his, suddenly exhausted.

Killian flexed his fingers against Susannah's back. Never had he felt more safe—or loved—than now. Just the soft press of her lips against his temple moved him to tears again. He nuzzled deeply into her hair, pressing small kisses against her neck and jaw.

Words wouldn't come. Each stroke of Susannah's hand took a little more of the pain away. The fragrance of her body, the sweetness of it, enveloped him, and he clung to her small, strong form, absorbing the strength she was feeding him through her touch and voice.

Susannah had been hurt by his abruptly leaving her life without an explanation, yet now she was strong, when he had never felt weaker. Her fingers trembled against his hair, and he slowly lifted his head. She gave him a tremulous half smile, her eyes huge with compassion and love for him.

Love. He saw it in every nuance of her expression, in her hand as it came to rest against his jaw. How could she love him? When she reached forward, her fingers taking away the last of the tears from his cheeks, he lowered his lashes, ashamed.

"Tears are wonderful," Susannah whispered, a catch in her voice. "Ma always said they were liquid crystals going back to Mother Earth. I always liked that thought. She said they were the path to the heart, and I know it's true." She smiled gently into Killian's ravaged eyes. "You were brave enough to take the biggest step of all, Sean."

"What do you mean?" he asked, his voice thick, off-key.

"You had the ability to reach out and trust someone with your feelings."

"Crying is a weakness."

"Who taught you that?"

"Father. Men don't cry."

"And they aren't supposed to feel. Oh, Sean—" Susannah stroked his cheek gently. "Men have hearts, too, you know. Hearts that have a right to feel as deeply and widely as any woman's."

He shakily reached over and touched her cheek. "I was afraid that if my nightmares came back and you were around, I'd hurt you." Hanging his head, unable to meet her compassionate gaze, he said, "When I was in the Foreign Legion, I met an Algerian woman, Salima, who loved me. I loved her, too." He shook his head sadly. "I kept having nightmares out of my violent past with the Legion, and it scared her. Finally, I left her for good. I feared that one night I might lash out and strike her." Miserable, Killian held Susannah's gaze. "After that, I swore never to get involved with a woman. I didn't want to put anyone through the hell I put Salima through. I saw what it did to her, and I swore I'd never do it again. And then you walked into my life. I've never felt such strong emotions for a woman before, Susannah. Those old fears made me leave to protect you from what I might do some night. My God, I couldn't stand it if I hurt you. I nearly did tonight."

She caressed his jaw. "You could have, but you didn't. Some part of you knew it was me, Sean. That's what stopped you, darling."

He lowered his gaze, his voice cracking. "I—I had a nightmare about Peru, about one of our missions. Wolf and I got caught and tortured by a drug lord, and the rest of our team had to go into the estate and bust us out." He squeezed his eyes shut. "That was last year. It's too fresh—that's why I get these nightmares, the flashbacks…"

"And you were having flashbacks after you woke up?" Susannah guessed grimly.

His mouth quirked and he raised his head. "Yes. I was hoping…" He drew in a ragged sigh. "I started screaming in my bedroom, and I got up, hoping I hadn't awakened you. I went out to the garage, where I always go when these things hit. It's safer that way. A lot safer. I'm like a wild animal in a cage," Killian added bitterly, unable to meet her lustrous gaze. His hands tightened around hers.

"A wounded animal, but not a wild one," she whispered achingly as she cupped his cheek. Killian's eyes were bleak; there was such sadness reflected in them, and in the line of his mouth. "Wounds can be bound up to heal, Sean."

He managed a soft snort. "At what cost to the healer?"

Susannah stroked his damp, bristly cheek. The dark growth of beard gave his face a dangerous quality. "As long as you're willing to get help, to make the necessary changes, then I can stay with you, if you want."

He turned to her. "Look at you. Look at the price you've already paid."

Susannah nodded. "It was worth the price, Sean. *You're* worth the effort. Don't you understand that?"

"I don't know what kind of miracle was at work when you reached out for me," he rasped. Killian held up his hands. "I've killed with these, Susannah. And when I mean to defend myself, I do it. The other person doesn't survive."

A chill swept through Susannah as she stared at his lean, callused hands. Swallowing convulsively, she whispered, "Some part of you knew I wasn't your enemy, Sean."

He wanted to say, *I love you, that's why*, but stopped himself. Just looking at her pale, washed-out features told him that he had no right to put Susannah on the firing line. A terrible need to make love with her, to speak of his love for her courage, her strength, sheared through Killian. He gazed down at her innocent, up-turned face.

"You're a beautiful idealist," he whispered unsteadily. "Someone I don't deserve, and never will."

"I'll decide those things for myself."

He gave her a strange look, but said nothing. Placing his hand on her shoulder, he rasped, "Let's get you to bed. You need some sleep."

"And you? What about you?"

He shrugged. "I won't sleep."

"You slept like a baby after we made love to each other," Susannah whispered. She reached over and gripped his hand.

"I guess I did."

Susannah held his misery-laden eyes. "Then sleep with me now."

Killian stared at her, the silence lengthening between them. His throat constricted.

"Come," she whispered. "Come sleep at my side."

Chapter 11

A ragged sigh tore from Killian as he felt Susannah's weight settle against him. The darkness in her bedroom was nearly complete. Everything was so natural between them that it hurt. Despite how badly he'd frightened Susannah, she laid her head in the hollow of his shoulder, and her body met and melded against the harder contours of his. Her arm went around his torso, and Killian heard a quivering sigh issue from her lips. To his alarm, after he'd drawn up the sheet and spread, he felt Susannah trembling. It wasn't obvious, but Killian sensed it was adrenaline letdown after the trauma she'd endured.

"This is heaven on earth," he whispered roughly against her hair, tightening his grip around her. Susannah was heaven. A heaven he didn't deserve.

"It is." Susannah sighed and unconsciously moved

her hand across his naked chest. The hair there was soft and silky. His groan reverberated through her like music. Stretching upward, Susannah placed her lips softly against the hardened line of his mouth. Instantly Killian tensed, and his mouth opened and hungrily devoured hers. She surrendered herself to the elemental fire that leaped between them wherever their bodies touched.

Sean needed to understand that no matter how bad the terror that lived within him was, her love—and what she hoped was his love for her—could meet and dissolve it. Susannah's fleeting thought was quickly drowned in the splendor of his mouth as it captured hers with a primal hunger that sent heat twisting and winding through her. His hands tangled in her thick hair, and he gently eased her back on the pillow, his blue eyes narrowed and glittering.

"Love sets you free," she said, and reached up and drew him down upon her. Just the taut length of his body covering hers made her heart sing. The gown she wore was worked up and off her. The white cotton fell into a heap beside the bed, along with his pajama bottoms. As Killian settled back against her, he grazed her flushed cheek.

"You're so brave. So brave…" And she was, in a way Killian had never seen in a woman before. Knowing gave him the courage to reach out and love her as he'd torridly dreamed of doing so many times. As he slid his fingers up across her rib cage to caress her breast, he felt her tense in anticipation. This time, Susannah deserved all he could give her. There was no hurry now, no threat of danger. His mouth pulled into a taut line, somewhere between a smile of pleasure and a grimace of agony, as she pressed her hips against him.

The silent language she shared with him brought tears to his eyes. Susannah wasn't passive. No, she responded, initiated, and matched his hunger for her. When her hands drifted down across his waist and caressed him, he trembled violently. His world, always held in tight control, began to melt as her lips molded against his and her hands ignited him. He surrendered to the strength of this woman who loved him with a blinding fierceness that he was only beginning to understand.

As he slid his hand beneath her hips, Susannah closed her eyes, her fingers resting tensely against his damp, bunched shoulders. Her world was heat, throbbing heat, and filled with such aching longing that she gave a small whimper of pleading when he hesitated fractionally. The ache intensified. Without thinking, guided only by her desire to give and receive, Susannah moved with a primal timelessness that enveloped them. They were like living, breathing embers, smoldering, then blazing to bright, hungry life within each other's arms.

As Killian surged powerfully into her, he gripped her, as if she represented his one tenuous hold on life. In those spinning, molten moments when they gave the gift of themselves to one another, he felt real hope for the first time since he had lost his family. Glorying in his burgeoning love for Susannah, Killian sank against her, breathing raggedly.

Gently he tamed several strands of her sable hair away from her dampened brow. His smile was vulnerable as she opened her eyes and gazed dazedly up into his face. What right did he have to tell Susannah he loved her? Did he dare hope that she could stand the brutal terrors that plagued him night after night? Was he asking too much of her, even though she was willing to try?

Tasting again her wet, full mouth, Killian trembled. He didn't have those answers—as badly as he wanted them. There was so much to say to Susannah, to share with her. He lost himself in her returning ardor, for now unwilling to look beyond the moment.

With a groan, Killian came to her side and brought her into his arms. "You're sunlight," he rasped, sliding his fingers through her tangled hair. "Hope and sunlight, all woven together like some kind of mystical tapestry."

The words feathered through Susannah. Sean held her so tightly—as if he were afraid that, like the sun, she would disappear, to be replaced by the awful darkness that stalked him. With a trembling smile, she closed her eyes and pressed the length of herself against him. He'd used the word *hope.* That was enough of a step for now, she thought hazily. The word *love* had never crossed his lips. But she had to be patient and wait for Sean to reveal his love for her, if that was what it was after all. Susannah didn't try to fool herself by thinking that, just because they shared the beauty of loving each other physically, it meant that Sean came to her with real love. She would have to wait and hope that he loved her in return. Whispering his name, she said, "I'm so tired…"

"Sleep, colleen. Sleep," he coaxed thickly. As much as he wanted to love her again, to silently show her his love for her, Killian knew sleep was best. He might be a selfish bastard, but he wasn't that selfish. Refusing to take advantage of the situation, he absorbed her wonderful nearness, wanting nothing more out of life than this exquisite moment.

Lying awake for a good hour after Susannah had quickly dropped off to sleep, Killian stared up at the plaster ceiling. How could she have known that he needed this? Needed her in his arms? Her soft, halting words, laced with tears, haunted him. Susannah loved him—without reserve. Didn't she know what she was getting into? He was a hopeless mess of black emotions that ruled his nights and stalked his heels during the day.

His mouth tightening, Killian absently stroked her silky hair, thinking how each strand, by itself, was weak. Yet a thick group of strands was strong. Maybe that was symbolic of Susannah. She was strong right now, while he'd never felt weaker or more out of control.

Sighing, Killian moved his head and pressed a chaste kiss to her fragrant hair. He'd cried tonight, for the first time in his life. Oddly, he felt cleaner, lighter. His stomach still ached from the wrenching sobs that had torn from him, and he absently rubbed his abdomen. The tears had taken the weight of years of grief away from him. And Susannah had paid a price to reach inside him to help him.

Closing his eyes, his arms around Susannah, Killian slid into a dreamless sleep—a sleep that was profoundly deep and healing. His first such sleep since the day he'd become a soldier in the French Foreign Legion.

Killian awoke with a start. *Susannah?* Instantly, he lifted his head and twisted it to the right. She was

gone! Sunlight poured in through the ivory sheers—
a blinding, joyous radiance flooding the room and
making him squint. Quickly he sat up. The clock on
the dresser read 11:00. *Impossible!* Killian muttered
an exclamation to himself as he threw his legs across
the bed and stood up. How could it be this late?

Fear twisted his heart. *Susannah.* Where was she?
Had she left him after awaking this morning? Had she
realized just how much of a liability he would be in her
life? Bitterness coated his mouth as he quickly opened
the door and strode across the hall to his bedroom. He
wouldn't blame her. What woman in her right mind
would stay around someone like him?

Killian hurried through a quick, hot shower and
changed into a pair of tan chino slacks and a dark blue
polo shirt. He padded quickly down the hall and realized that not only were the heavily draped windows
in the living room open, they were raised. A slight
breeze, sweet and fragrant, filled the house.

"Susannah?" His voice was off-key. Killian quickly
looked around the living room and found it empty. He
heard no sound from the kitchen, but hurried there
anyway. Each beat of his heart said, *Susannah is gone.*
A fist of emotion pushed its way up through his chest,
and tears stung his eyes. Tears! Killian didn't care as
he bounded into the kitchen.

Everything looked in order. Nothing out of place—
and no Susannah. Killian stood there, his hand pressed
against his eyes, and gripped the counter for support.
She was gone. The shattering discovery overwhelmed
him, and all he could do was feel the hot sting of tears
entering his closed eyes as he tasted her loss.

The laughter of women vaguely registered on his

spinning senses. Killian snapped his head toward the window. Outside, down by the lawn leading to the oceanfront, Susannah stood with his gardener, Mrs. Johnston.

His fingers whitened against the counter, and it took precious seconds for him to find his balance. Susannah hadn't left! She'd stayed! Killian stood rooted to the spot, his eyes narrowing on the two women. Susannah wore a simple white blouse, jeans, and sensible brown shoes. Her glorious hair was plaited into one long braid that hung between her shoulder blades. She stood talking animatedly with the gray-haired older woman.

Relief, sharp and serrating, jagged down through Killian. Susannah was still here. He hung his head, feeling a mass of confused emotions boiling up within him. He loved Susannah. He loved her. As he raised his head, he felt many things becoming clear. Things he had to talk to Susannah about. What would her reaction be? He had to tell her the truth, and she had to listen. What then? Killian wasn't at all sure how Susannah would judge him and his sordid world. What he did know was what he wanted: to wake up with this woman every morning for the rest of his life. But could he ask that of her?

Susannah waved goodbye to Mrs. Johnston as she left. Turning, she went through the front door of the beautifully kept cottage. In the living room she came to a startled halt.

"Sean."

He stood near the couch. The surprise on her features turned to concern. Killian searched her face ruthlessly for any telltale sign that she had changed her mind about him since last night. He opened his hand.

"When I got up, you were gone. I thought you'd left."

Susannah saw the suffering in his dark eyes. "Left?" She moved toward where he stood uncertainly.

"Yeah, forever." Killian grimaced. "Not that I'd blame you if you did."

Susannah smiled softly as she halted in front of him. Killian was stripped of his worldly defenses, standing nakedly vulnerable before her. Sensing his fragile state, she gently reached out and touched his stubbled cheek.

"I'm in for the long haul," she said, holding his haunted gaze. "If you'll let me be, Sean."

A ragged sigh tore from him, and he gripped her hand in his. "Then we need to sit down and do some serious talking, Susannah."

"Okay." She followed him to the couch. When he sat down facing her, she tucked her legs beneath her. Her knees were touching his thigh. His face was ravaged-looking, and his eyes were still puffy from sleep.

"Last night," Killian began thickly, reaching out and grazing her skin, "I could have hurt you." He felt shaky inside, on the verge of crying again as he rested his hand on her shoulder. "After my parents were murdered, Meg and I were given to foster parents to raise. I guess we were lucky, because we had no family left back in Ireland, so Immigration decided to let us stay. Our foster parents were good to us. Meg really blossomed under their love and care."

"And you?"

Sean shrugged. "I was angry and moody most of

the time. I wanted to kill the two boys who had murdered our parents. I didn't do well at school. In fact, I skipped it most of the time and got mixed up in gang activities. Meg, on the other hand, was doing very well. She began acting in drama classes at high school, and she was good. Really good."

Susannah saw the pain in Sean's features. No longer did he try to hide behind that implacable, emotionless mask. His eyes were raw with uncertainty and his turbulent emotions. Reaching out, she covered his hand with hers. "How did you get into the Foreign Legion?"

"I joined the French Foreign Legion when I was seventeen, after running away from home. I had a lot of anger, Susannah, and no place to let it go. I was always in fights with other gang members. I saw what I was doing to my foster parents, to Meg, and I decided to get out of their lives.

"The Legion was hard, Susannah. Brutal and hard. It kills men who don't toughen up and walk a straight line of harsh discipline. By the time they found out my real age, I'd been in a year and survived, so they didn't kick me out. Most of my anger had been beaten out of me by that time, or released in the wartime situations we were called in to handle.

"I was only in a year when my company was sent to Africa to quell a disturbance." Killian withdrew his hand and stared down at the couch, the poisonous memories boiling up in him. "I won't tell you the gory details, but it was bloody. Tribesmen were fighting one another, and we had to try and intercede and keep the peace. For three years I was in the middle of a bloodbath that never stopped. I saw such inhumanity. I thought I knew what violence was, because I'd grown up in Northern Ireland, where it's a way of life, but this was a hundred times worse."

"And a hundred times more haunting?"

Her soft voice cut through the terror, through the revulsion that dogged him. When she slid her hand into his, he gripped it hard. "Yeah—the basis for most of my nightmares.

"The Legion has no heart, no feelings, Susannah. No one in the company slept well at night—everyone had nightmares. To combat it, to try to find an escape, I took up karate." He released her and held up his hand, his voice bleak. "All I did was learn how to kill another way. I was a natural, and when my captain realized it, he promoted me and made me an instructor to the legionnaires stationed with me. Just doing the hard physical work took the edge off my time in Africa.

"And then, *Sous-Lieutenant* Morgan Trayhern was transferred into my company as an assistant company commander. He had a lot of problems, too, and we just kind of gravitated toward each other over a period of a year. We both found some solace in each other's friendship. Morgan kept talking about creating a private company of mercenaries like ourselves. He wanted to pursue the idea once his hitch was up with the Legion.

"I liked the idea. I hated the Legion, the harsh discipline. Some of the men needed that kind of brutality, but I didn't. I was getting out after my six-year obligation was up, so I began to plan my life for the future. I told Morgan I'd join his company if he ever wanted to try it." Gently he recaptured Susannah's hand, grateful for her silence. She was absorbing every word he said.

"Then we had trouble in Africa again, and my company parachuted into a hot landing zone. It was the same thing all over again—only the tribes' names had changed. But this time both tribes turned on us and tried to wipe us out."

Susannah gasped, and her fingers closed tightly over Killian's scarred hand.

His mouth twisted. "Morgan was facing a situation similar to the one he had in Vietnam. We lost eighty percent of our company, Susannah. It was a living hell. I thought we were all going to die, but Morgan pulled us out. I saved his life during that time. Finally, at the last moment, he got the air support he'd requested. We were all wounded. It was just a question of how badly. Before both tribes hit us with a final assault, we were lifted out by helicopter." His voice grew bitter. "All the rest, every last valiant man who had died, were left behind."

"How awful…"

Killian sighed raggedly. "Last night I lay awake a long time with you in my arms, reviewing my life." He gently turned her hand over in his, realizing how soft and feminine she was against him. "I was born into violence, colleen. I've done nothing but lead a violent life. Last year, Morgan sent three of us down to work with the Peruvian police to clean up a cocaine connection. Wolf, a member of our team, got captured by the local drug lord. I went in to save him, and I ended up getting captured, too."

Susannah's eyes widened. "What happened?"

"The drug lord was real good at what he did to us," was all he would say. He still wanted to protect Susannah, somehow, from the ugliness of his world. "He had us for a month before Jake, the third member of our team, busted in and brought down the drug lord. Wolf was nearly dead, and I wasn't too far behind him. We got flown stateside by the CIA, and we both recuperated in a naval hospital near the capital. As soon as Wolf regained consciousness, he told Morgan he wanted out, that he couldn't handle being a mercenary any longer."

With a little laugh, Killian said, "At the time, I remember thinking Wolf had lost the edge it takes to stay alive in our business. He's part Indian, so he stayed pretty much to himself. So did I. But I admired his guts when he told Morgan 'no more.' Morgan didn't call him a coward. Instead, he saw to it that Wolf got a job as a forest ranger up in Montana."

With a shake of his head, Killian whispered, "I envied Wolf for having the courage to quit. I wanted to, but I thought everyone would see me as a coward."

Hope leaped into Susannah's eyes, and it was mirrored in her voice. "You want to quit?"

"I can't," Killian said quietly, searching her glowing features, clinging to the hope in her eyes. "Part of my check goes to pay for my sister's massive medical bills. But..."

"What?"

He gripped his hands, thinking how small, yet how strong, she was. "I'm messed up inside, Susannah. Maybe I've done this work too long and don't know any other way." His voice grew thick. "Last night, when I held you, I realized that I needed to get help—professional help—to unravel this nightmare that's eating me alive from the inside out. I swore I'd never put you in that kind of jeopardy again."

With a little cry, Susannah threw her arms around

Killian's shoulders. "I love you so much," she whispered, tears squeezing from her eyes. She felt his arms slide around her and bring her tightly against him. Killian buried his face in her hair. "It can be done, Sean. I know it can."

He shook his head, and when he spoke again his voice was muffled. "I don't know that, Susannah."

She eased away just enough to study his suffering features. "I'll be here for you, if you want..."

The words, sweet and filled with hope, fell across his tightly strung nerves. He searched her lustrous eyes. "I don't know..." How badly he wanted to confess his love to her, and yet he couldn't. "Let me feel my way through this."

"Do you want me to leave?" She hated to ask the question. But she did ask it, and then she held her breath.

"I— No, not really." He held her hand tightly within his. "That's the selfish side of me speaking. The other side, the nightmares... Well, you'd be better off staying at a nearby hotel—just in case."

Susannah had faith that Killian would never harm her, no matter how virulent his nightmares became, but she knew it wasn't her place to make that decision. "I have the next three weeks off, Sean. My principal gave me the time because he felt after all the trauma I'd gone through I needed time to pull myself together again."

Killian's heart thudded, and he lifted his head. "Three weeks?" Three weeks of heaven. There was such love shining in her eyes that he clung to the tenuous shred of hope that had begun burning in his chest when he loved Susannah last night.

"Yes…"

He compressed his lips and studied her long, slender fingers. The nails were cut short because she did so much gardening, Killian realized. Susannah had hands of the earth, hands that were in touch with the primal elements of nature—and her touch brought out so much in him that was good. "I'll take you to a hotel in downtown Victoria," he told her quietly. "I want you to stay these three weeks if you want, Susannah." He lifted his gaze and met hers. "No promises."

She shook her head, her mouth growing dry. "No… no promises. A day at a time, Sean."

Susannah gave him a trembling smile and framed his lean, harsh face between her soft hands. "You slept the whole night last night without those dreams coming back?"

Killian nodded. "It was the first night I've slept that hard. Without waking up." He knew there was awe in his voice at the revelation.

Susannah gave him a tender smile. "Because you trusted yourself on some level. The situation was important enough for you to reach out and try to change it."

There was food for thought in her assessment. A little more of the tension within him dissolved. "I want to live now, in the present," he told her, capturing her hands. "I want to take you sailing this morning, if you'd like." He gestured toward the wooden dock at the edge of the water. "I've got a forty-foot yacht that I've worked on for the past eight years, between assignments. I've always been good with wood, so I began to build the boat as something to do when I got back here."

"Because you couldn't sleep?" Susannah's heart broke for him.

"Partly." He managed to quirk a smile. "Then I put in the rose garden around the house. I find keeping busy keeps me from remembering."

"Then let's go sailing. I've never done it before, but I'm willing to try."

Sunlight glanced off the dark blue of the ocean as the yacht, the *Rainbow,* slipped cleanly through the slight swells of early afternoon. Susannah sat with Killian at the stern of the yacht. He stood proudly at the helm, his focus on the sails as the wind filled them, taking them farther away from the coast of the island. The first time the yacht had heeled over on her side, Susannah had let out a yelp of fear and surprise, thinking the boat would flip over and drown them. But Killian had held her and explained that the yacht would never tip over. Over the past two hours, Susannah had relaxed and enjoyed his company, the brilliant sunlight and the fresh salt breeze that played across the Strait of Juan de Fuca, where they were sailing.

"Here, hold the wheel," he said. Killian saw the surprise in her wide eyes. He smiled and held out his hand. Just being on the water helped to clear his mind and emotions.

"But—"

"I need to change the sails," he explained, reaching down and gripping her fingers. "Don't you want to learn about sailing?" he said teasingly as he drew her to her feet and placed her beside him at the wheel.

"Sure, but—"

Killian stood directly behind her, his body providing support and shelter for her as he placed her hands on the wheel. His mouth near her ear, he said, "I'm going to shift the sails from port to starboard. Be sure and duck when the boom comes across the cockpit. Otherwise, you'll be knocked overboard, and I don't want that to happen."

"Are you sure I can do this?" Susannah was wildly aware of Killian's body molded against hers. The feeling was making her want him all over again. As she twisted a look up at him, she felt her heart expand with a discovery that nearly overwhelmed her. His hair was ruffled by the breeze, and there was real joy in his deep blue eyes. For the first time, she was seeing Sean happy.

"Very sure." He leaned down and pressed his lips to her temple. The strands of her hair were silky beneath his exploration. Susannah invited spontaneity, and Killian reveled in the quick, hot kiss she gave him in answer.

"All right, I'll try," she said, her heart beating hard from his closeness.

"Just remember to duck," he warned, and left her in charge of guiding the yacht.

At two o'clock, they dropped anchor in a small crescent-shaped bay. Thrilled with the way the day was revealing itself, Susannah helped Sean tuck the sails away before the anchor was dropped. He motored the vessel into the dark blue bay, which was surrounded by tall evergreens on three sides. A great blue heron with a seven-foot wing span had been hunting frogs or small fish in the shallows, and it took off just as their anchor splashed into the water.

Susannah watched in awe as the magnificent bird

swept by, just above the mast, and headed around the tip of the island. She turned just in time to see that Killian was watching the huge crane, too.

"She was breathtaking," Susannah confided as she moved toward the galley. Killian had promised her lunch, and she was hungry.

Sean nodded. "What I'm looking at is breathtaking," he murmured, and he reached out and captured her. The yacht was very stable at anchor; the surface of the bay smooth and unruffled. Susannah came willingly into his arms, closed her eyes and rested against his tall, lean form. His voice had been low and vibrating, sending a wonderful sheet of longing through her.

Killian absorbed Susannah against him, her natural scent, the fragrance of her shining sable hair, intoxicating him. "I feel like a thief," he murmured near her ear, savoring the feel of her arms tightening around him. "I feel like I'm stealing from you before I get thrown back into the way things were before you stepped into my life."

Gently disengaging from him, just enough that she could meet and hold his gaze, Susannah nodded. Her love for him was so fierce, so steadfast, that she wasn't threatened by his admission. "I remember a number of times in my folks' marriage when they went through stormy times," she confided. "They love each other, Sean, and Ma often told me when I'd grown up and we talked about those stormy periods that love held them together. I like the way Ma sees love, Sean. She calls it a fabric that she and Pa wove together. Some threads were very strong. Others were weak and sometimes frayed or even broke. She saw those weak times as fix-it times. It didn't mean they weren't afraid. But the one thing they clung to throughout those times was the fact that they loved each other."

He rested his jaw against her hair, absorbing her story. "I've never thought of love as a fabric."

"Look at your parents," Susannah said. "Were they happy together?"

He nodded and closed his eyes, savoring her nearness and allowing her husky voice to touch his heart. "Very happy."

"And did they fight from time to time?"

"Often," he chuckled, suddenly recalling those times. "My mother was a red-haired spitfire. My father was dark-haired and closed up tighter than the proverbial drum. When she suggested we emigrate to America, my father balked at the idea. My mother was the explorer, the person who would take risks."

"And your father was content to remain conservative and have the status quo."

Killian nodded and grazed her flushed cheek. Susannah's sparkling gray eyes made him aware of just how much she loved him. "Yes. But in the end, my mother pioneered getting us to America. It took many years to make her dream for all of us come true, but she did it."

Susannah asked soberly, "Do you blame your mother for what happened a year after you emigrated?"

Killian shook his head. "No. I wanted to move as much as she did."

"You're more like your mother?"

"Very much."

"A risk-taker."

"I guess I am."

Susannah held his thoughtful gaze. She could feel

Sean thinking, weighing and measuring things they'd spoken about from the past and placing them like a transparency on the present—perhaps on their situation. Did he love her? He'd never said so, but in her heart, she felt he must—or as close as he could come to loving someone in his present state.

"I like," she said softly, "thinking about a relationship in terms of a tapestry. Ma always said she and Pa wove a very colorful one, filled with some tragedy, but many happy moments, too."

Gently Killian moved his hands down her slender arms, and then back up to rest on her shoulders. "A tapestry is a picture, too."

"Yes, it is."

"How do you see the tapestry of your life?" he asked quietly.

She shrugged and gave a slight smile, enjoying his rough, callused hands caressing her. "I see teaching handicapped children as important to my life. I certainly didn't see getting shot and being in a coma or having a contract put out on me, but that's a part of my tapestry now." She frowned. "I guess, having that unexpected experience, I understand how precious life is. Before, Sean, I took life for granted. I saw myself being a teacher, someday meeting a man who would love me, and then marrying. I want children, but not right away. I saw my folks' wisdom in not having children right away. It gave them a chance to solidify and work on their marriage. By the time Denny came along, they were emotionally ready for him. By the time I came along, they were more than ready." She smiled fondly. "I had a very happy childhood compared to most children. But I feel part of it was my parents' being older and more mature, more settled and sure of who they were."

"A tapestry that had the scales of life woven into it," he mused, holding her softened gaze.

"I never thought of it in symbolic terms, but yes, a balancing between doing something I love and having a husband and children when we're both ready for them, for the responsibility of raising them the best we can."

"You've brought balance into my life," Killian admitted, watching her eyes flare, first with surprise, then with joy. "I fought against it."

"Because you were scared."

"I still am," he told her wryly, and eased away.

Susannah followed him into the tight little galley below. There was a small table with a wraparound sofa, and she sat down to watch him fix their lunch at the kitchen area.

"I was scared to come and see you," she admitted.

Twisting a look over his shoulder as he prepared roast beef sandwiches, he said, "I couldn't believe you were standing there, Susannah."

"Your head or your heart?"

Her question was as insightful as she was about him. His mouth curved faintly as he forced himself to finish putting the sandwiches together. Placing the plate of them on the table, he brought over a bag of potato chips. "My head."

Susannah watched as he brought two bottles of mineral water from the small refrigerator built into the teakwood bulkhead. His entire face was relaxed, with none of the tension that was normally there. Even his mouth, usually a hard line holding back some emotional barrage, was softer.

"And your heart?" she asked in a whisper as he sat down next to her.

"My heart," he sighed, "in some way expected to see you." As he passed the sandwich to her, he met and caught her gaze. "I'm finding out that talking about how I feel isn't so bad after all."

With a little laugh, Susannah said, "Silence is the bane of all men. This society has bludgeoned you with the idea that you shouldn't feel, shouldn't cry and shouldn't speak of your emotions. It's a learned thing, Sean, and it's something you can change. That's the good news."

As he bit into his sandwich, Killian felt another cloak of dread dissolve around his shoulders. "You make it easy to talk," he admitted. "It's you. Something about you."

Melting beneath his intense, heated gaze, Susannah forced herself to eat the sandwich she didn't taste. Would Sean make good on his decision to send her away tonight? Or would he have the courage to let her remain? Her heart whispered that if he would allow her to stay with him tonight, his trust in himself and in her was strong enough that he could come to grips with his nightmare-ridden nights very quickly.

Nothing was ever changed in one day, Susannah reminded herself. But life demanded some awfully big steps if one genuinely wanted to heal. If Sean could trust in her love for him, never mind the fact that he might not return her love in the same measure, he could use her support in healing his past.

Only tonight would tell, Susannah ruminated.

Being a victim of violence had taught her about the moment, the hour, the day. She would take each moment with Sean as a gift, instead of leaping ahead to wonder what his decision might be.

Just as they entered Sean's home, his phone rang. Susannah saw him frown as he hurried to the wall phone in the kitchen to answer it.

"Hello? Meg?" Killian shot a glance over at Susannah, who stood poised at the entrance to the living room. Surprised that his sister had called, he saw Susannah smile and disappear. She didn't have to leave, but it was too late to call her back. Wrestling with his shock over his sister's call, Killian devoted all his attention to her.

Susannah wisely left the kitchen. Going to her bedroom, she slowly began to pack her one and only bag to leave for the hotel in Victoria. She'd seen shock and puzzlement register on Sean's face over Meg's call. Didn't they talk often? Her heart wasn't in packing her clothes. The bed where they had lain, where they had made love, still contained the tangle of covers. Susannah ached to stay the night, to show Sean that two people could help his problem, not make it worse.

Killian was just coming out of the kitchen after the call when he saw Susannah placing her suitcase by the door. He shoved his hands into his pockets and moved toward her.

Straightening, Susannah felt her heartbeat pick up as Killian approached her. He wore a quizzical expression on his face, and she sensed that something important had occurred. She curbed her questions. Sean had to trust her enough to share, and not make her pull everything out of him.

"The funniest thing just happened," he murmured as he came to a halt in front of her. "Meg just called. I can't believe it." He shook his head.

"Believe what?"

"Meg just told me that she contacted Ian. She's asked him to fly to Ireland to see her." He gave Susannah a long, intense look.

"Wonderful!" Susannah clapped her hands together. "That's wonderful!"

"Yes…it is…"

"What led her to that decision?" she asked breathlessly, seeing the hope burning in Killian's dark eyes.

"She said he'd somehow found out where she was living and sent her a long letter. He talked about his love being strong enough to support both of them through this time in her life. All along, Meg loved Ian, but she was afraid he'd leave her as soon as he saw her disfigurement." Again Killian shook his head. "I'll be damned. The impossible has happened. I'm really glad for her. For Ian. They're both good people, caught in a situation they didn't make for themselves."

Reaching out, Susannah gently touched his arm. "The same could be said of you. Of us, Sean."

He stood very still, hearing the pain, the hope, in Susannah's voice, and seeing it reflected in her eyes.

Risking everything, she whispered, "Sean, you could send me away, just as Meg sent Ian away. Only you would be sending me away just for the night hours that you fear so much. She sent him away for several years, because of her fear that she would be rejected. In a way," she said, in a low, unsteady voice, "you're doing the same thing to me. You're afraid if I stay, you'll hurt me."

Her fingers tightening around his arm, Susannah stepped closer. "I know it isn't true, but you don't. At least not yet. But if you're searching for proof, Sean, look at last night. You didn't have nightmares haunt you after we slept in each other's arms, did you?"

"No... I didn't..." He stood there, assimilating the urgency in her heartfelt words. Realization shattered him in those moments. Meg had finally realized that Ian's love for her was steady—that it wasn't going to be pulled away from her, no matter how bad the situation appeared. He studied Susannah intently. He wasn't really questioning her love for him; he was questioning his ability to love her despite his wounding. Just as Meg had done, in a slightly different way.

Running his fingers through his hair, he muttered, "Stay tonight, Susannah. Please?"

Her heart leaped with joy, but she remained very quiet beneath his inspection. "Yes, I'd like that, darling, more than anything..."

With a groan, Killian swept her into his arms. He buried his face in her hair. "I love you, Susannah. I've loved you from the beginning, and I was too stupid, too scared, to admit it to myself, to you..."

The words, harsh with feeling, flowed across Susannah. Murmuring his name over and over again, she sought and found his mouth. The courage to admit his love for her was, perhaps, the biggest step of all. Drowning in the heated splendor of his mouth, being held so tightly that the breath was squeezed from her, Susannah returned his fire. Tears leaked from beneath her closed eyes, dampening her lashes and then her cheeks.

As Killian eased from her lips, he took his thumbs and removed those tears of happiness. His own eyes were damp, and the relief he felt was sharp and deep. "I want to try," he rasped as he framed her upturned face. "It isn't going to be easy."

"No," she quavered, "it won't be. But our tapestry will be strong, because of our courage to grow— together, darling."

"I'm afraid of tonight, colleen."

"We'll be afraid together. We'll hold each other. We'll talk. We'll do whatever it takes, Sean."

She was right. "One day at a time. One night at a time." Never had Killian wanted anything to work as much as he did this. He'd never admitted loving another woman. He'd been too fearful to do that. Susannah's strength, her undiluted belief in him, was giving him the courage to try.

"There will be good nights and bad ones, I'm sure," Susannah warned. "We can't expect miracles."

He smiled a little. "You're the miracle in my life. I'll do whatever I have to in order to keep you."

His commitment was more than she'd ever dreamed of hearing from him. Somehow Meg's courage to release her past had helped him see his own situation differently. "Just trying is enough," Susannah told him simply. And it was.

Epilogue

Susannah's heart wasn't in her packing. Her three weeks on Vancouver Island had fled by like a blink of the eye. Killian was quieter than usual as he helped her take her clothes out of the closet.

He was thinking about something important, and she could feel it. The days had been wonderful days of discovery, of joy and exploration. The nights had been a roller-coaster ride of good and bad. Together they had managed to confront Killian's nightmare past, and with some success.

More than anything, Killian knew he needed professional help to completely change for good. They'd talked about it and agreed that Susannah couldn't be the linchpin of his healing. He saw her as a loving support, his primary cheerleader. But it wasn't her responsibility to heal him. It was his.

The suitcase was packed, and she snapped it shut. As she turned around, Killian brought her into his arms.

"I've got a few phone calls to make before I take you to the airport."

"Okay." One day at a time, she reminded herself. Sean had not spoken of anything beyond her three weeks at his house. As badly as Susannah wanted to know his future plans and how they included her, she didn't ask.

"I want you to be there when I make the call."

She searched his shadowed face. "Who are you going to talk to?"

"Morgan."

Her heart thudded once. "Morgan?"

"Yes."

"Why?"

Killian cupped her face and looked deep into her wide, loving eyes. "To tell him I'm asking for permanent reassignment to the U.S. only. I'm also telling him I want jobs that don't involve violence. He's got some of those available. Mercenaries are more than just men of war. Sometimes a mercenary is needed just to be eyes and ears. I'm going to tell him I want low-risk short-term assignments." He smiled uncertainly. "That way, I can make my home in Glen, Kentucky, and keep putting my life back together with you."

Tears jammed into her eyes. "Oh, Sean…" She threw her arms around his shoulders.

"It's not going to be easy," he warned her grimly, taking her full weight.

"We'll do it together," Susannah said, her voice muffled against his chest.

Killian knew it could be the worst kind of hell at times, but Susannah's unwavering support, her love for him, had made the decision easy. He held her tightly. "Together," he rasped thickly. "Forever."

* * * * *

Cindi Myers is the author of more than fifty novels. When she's not plotting new romance story lines, she enjoys skiing, gardening, cooking, crafting and daydreaming. A lover of small-town life, she lives with her husband and two spoiled dogs in the Colorado mountains.

Books by Cindi Myers

Alpha Tracker

Eagle Mountain: Search for Suspects

Disappearance at Dakota Ridge
Conspiracy in the Rockies
Missing at Full Moon Mine
Grizzly Creek Standoff

The Ranger Brigade: Rocky Mountain Manhunt

Investigation in Black Canyon
Mountain of Evidence
Mountain Investigation
Presumed Deadly

Eagle Mountain Murder Mystery: Winter Storm Wedding

Ice Cold Killer
Snowbound Suspicion
Cold Conspiracy
Snowblind Justice

Visit the Author Profile page
at Harlequin.com for more titles.

THE GUARDIAN

Cindi Myers

For Katie

Chapter 1

Abby Stewart was not lost. Maybe she'd wandered a little off her planned route, but she wasn't lost.

She was a scientist and a decorated war veteran. She had GPS and maps and a good sense of direction. So she couldn't be lost. But standing in the middle of nowhere in the Colorado wilderness did have her a little disoriented, she could admit. The problem was, the terrain around Black Canyon of the Gunnison National Park tended to all look the same after a while: thousands of acres of rugged, roadless wilderness covered in piñon forests, and scrubby desert set against a backdrop of spectacular mountain views. People did get lost out here every year.

But Abby wasn't one of them, she reminded herself again. She took a deep breath and consulted her handheld GPS. There was the shallow draw she'd just

passed, and to the west were the foothills of the Cim-
arron Mountains. And there was her location now.
The display showed she'd hiked three miles from her
car. All she had to do was head northeast and she'd
eventually make it back to her parking spot and the
red dirt two-track she'd driven in on. Feeling more
reassured, she returned the GPS unit to her backpack
and scanned the landscape around her. To a casual ob-
server, the place probably looked pretty desolate—a
high plateau of scrubby grass, cactus and stunted juniper. But to Abby, who was on her way to earning a
master's degree in environmental science, the Black
Canyon of the Gunnison was a treasure trove of more
than eight hundred plant species, including the handful she was focusing on in her research.

Her anxiety over temporarily losing her bearings
vanished as she focused on a gray-green clump of vegetation in the shadow of a misshapen piñon. She bent
over, peering closer, and a surge of triumph filled her.
Yes! A terrific specimen of *Lomatium concinnum*—
desert parsley to the layman. Number four on the list
of species she needed to collect for her research. She
knelt and slipped off her pack and quickly took out a
digital camera, small trowel and collecting bag.

Intent on photographing the parsley in place, then
carefully digging it up, leaving as much of the root
system intact as possible, she missed the sounds of
approaching footsteps until they were almost on her.
A branch crackled and she started, heart pounding.
She peered into the dense underbrush in front of her,
in the direction of the sound, and heard a shuffling
noise—the muffled swish of fabric rubbing against
the brush. Whoever this was wasn't trying to be par-

ticularly quiet, but what were they doing out here, literally in the middle of nowhere?

In the week Abby had been camped in the area she'd seen fewer than a dozen other people since checking in at the park ranger station, and all of those had been in the campground or along the paved road. Here in the backcountry she'd imagined herself completely alone.

Stealthily, she slid the Sig Sauer from the holster at her side. She'd told the few friends who'd asked about the gun that she carried it to deal with snakes and other wildlife she might encounter in the backcountry, but the truth was, ever since her stint in Afghanistan, she felt safer armed when she went out alone. Flashes of unsettling memories crowded her mind as she drew the weapon; suddenly, she was back in Kandahar, stalking insurgents who'd just wiped out half her patrol group. As a woman, she'd often been tasked with going into the homes of locals to question the women there with the aid of an interpreter. Every time she stepped into one of those homes, she wondered if she'd come out alive. This scene had the same sense of being cut off from the rest of the world, the same sense of paranoia and danger.

Heart racing, she struggled to control her breathing and to push the memories away. She wasn't in Afghanistan. She was in Colorado. In a national park. She was safe. This was probably just another hiker, someone else who appreciated the solitude and peace of the wilderness. She inched forward and pushed aside the feathery, aromatic branches of a piñon.

A small, dark woman bent over the ground, deftly pulling up plants and stuffing them into the pockets of her full skirt. Dandelions, Abby noted. A popular edible wild green. She replaced the gun in its holster and stood. "Hello," she said.

The woman jumped and dropped a handful of dandelions. She turned, as if to run. "Wait!" Abby called. "I'm sorry. I didn't mean to frighten you." She retrieved the plants and held them out to the woman. She was young, barely out of her teens, and very beautiful. Her skin was the rich brown of toffee, and she had high cheekbones, a rosebud mouth and large black eyes framed by lacy lashes. She wore a loose blue blouse, a long, full skirt and leather sandals, with a plaid shawl draped across her body.

She came forward and hesitantly accepted the dandelions from Abby. *"Gracias,"* she said, her voice just above a whisper.

Latina, Abby thought. A large community of Mexican immigrants lived in the area. She searched her mind for what schoolgirl Spanish she could recall. *"Habla inglés?"*

The woman shook her head and wrapped her arms around what Abby had first assumed to be a bag for storing the plants she collected, but she now realized was a swaddled infant, cradled close to the woman's torso with a sling made from the red, blue and green shawl. "You have a baby!" Abby smiled. "A *niño*," she added.

The woman held the baby closer and stared at Abby, eyes wide with fear.

Maybe she was an illegal, afraid Abby would report her to the authorities. "Don't worry," Abby said, unable to remember the Spanish words. "I'm looking for plants, like you." She broke a stem from the desert parsley and held it out. *"Donde esta este?"* she asked. *Where is this?*

The woman eyed Abby warily, but stepped forward to study the plant. She nodded. *"Si. Yo conozco."*

"You know this plant? Can you show me where to find more? *Donde esta?"*

The woman looked around, then motioned Abby to follow her. Abby did so, excitement growing. So far, specimens of *Lomatium* had been rare. Having more plants to study would be a tremendous find.

The woman moved rapidly over the rough ground despite her long skirts and the burden of the baby. Her black hair swung behind her in a ponytail that reached almost to her waist. Where did she live? The closest homes were miles from here, and the only road into this section of the park was the one Abby had come in on. Was she collecting the dandelions because she had an interest in wild food—or because it was the only thing she had to eat?

The woman stopped abruptly beside a large rock and looked down at the ground. Desert parsley spread out for several feet in every direction—the most specimens Abby had ever seen. Her smile widened. "That's wonderful. Thank you so much. *Muchas gracias."* She clasped the woman's hand and shook it. The woman offered a shy smile.

"Mi nombre es Abby."

"Soy Mariposa," the woman said.

Mariposa. Butterfly. Her name was butterfly? *"Y su niño?"* Abby nodded to the baby.

Mariposa smiled and folded back the blanket to reveal a tiny dark-haired infant. *"Es una niña,"* she said. "Angelique."

"Angelique," Abby repeated. A little angel.

"Usted ha cido harido." Mariposa lightly touched the side of Abby's face.

Abby flinched. Not because the touch was painful, but because she didn't like being reminded of the scar there. Multiple surgeries and time had faded the wound made by shrapnel from a roadside bomb, but the puckered white gash that ran from just above her left ear to midcheekbone would never be entirely gone. She wore her hair long and brushed forward to hide the worst of the scar, but alone in the wilderness on this warm day she'd clipped her hair back to keep it out of the way while she worked. She had no idea what the Spanish words Mariposa had spoken meant, but she was sure they were in reference to this disfigurement. *"Es no importante,"* she said, shaking her head.

She turned away, the profile of her good side to the woman, and spotted a delicate white flower. The three round petals blushed a deep purplish pink near their center. Half a dozen similar blooms rose nearby on slender, leafless stems. Abby knelt and slipped off her backpack and took out her trowel. She deftly dug up one of the flowers, revealing a fat white bulb. She brushed the dirt from the bulb and handed the plant to the woman. *"Este es comer. Bueno."* Her paltry Spanish frustrated her. "It's good to eat," she said, as if the English would make any more sense to her new friend.

Mariposa stroked the velvety petal of the flower and nodded. "It's called a mariposa lily," Abby said. *"Su nombre es Mariposa tambien."*

Mariposa nodded, then knelt and began digging up a second lily. Maybe she was just humoring Abby—or maybe she really needed the food. Abby hoped it was the former. As much as her studies had taught her about wild plants, she'd hate to have to depend on them for survival.

She turned to her pack once more and took out another collection bag, then remembered the energy bars stashed on the opposite side of the pack. They weren't much, but she'd give them to Mariposa. They'd at least be a change from roots. She found three bars and pressed them into the woman's hands. *"Por usted,"* she said.

"Gracias." Mariposa slipped the bars into the pocket of her skirt, then watched as Abby took out the camera and photographed the parsley plants. On impulse, she turned and aimed the camera at Mariposa. *Click.* And there she was, captured on the screen of the camera, face solemn but still very beautiful.

"You don't mind, do you?" Abby asked. She turned the camera so that the woman could see the picture.

Mariposa squinted at the image, but said nothing.

For a few minutes, the two women worked side by side, Mariposa digging lilies and Abby collecting more specimens of parsley. Though Abby usually preferred to work alone, it was nice being with Mariposa. She only wished she spoke better Spanish or Mariposa knew English, so she could find out more about where her new friend was from and why she was here in such a remote location.

Though the army had trained Abby to always be attuned to changes in the landscape around her, she must have gotten rusty since her return to civilian life. Mariposa was the first to stiffen and look toward the brush to the right of the women.

Abby heard the movements a second later—a group

of people moving through the brush toward them, their voices carrying in the still air, though they were still some distance away.

She was about to ask Mariposa if she knew these newcomers when the young woman took off running. Her sudden departure startled Abby so much she didn't immediately react. She stared after the young woman, trying to make sense of what she was seeing.

Mariposa ran with her skirt held up, legs lifted high, in the opposite direction of the approaching strangers, stumbling over the uneven terrain as if her life depended on it. Abby debated running after her, but what would that do but frighten the woman more? She watched the fleeing figure until she'd disappeared over a slight rise, then glanced back toward the voices. They were getting louder, moving closer at a rapid pace.

Abby slipped on the pack and unholstered the weapon once more, then settled into the shade of a boulder to wait.

The group moved steadily toward her. All men, from the sound of them. The uneven terrain and stubby trees blocked them from view, but their voices carried easily in the stillness. They weren't attempting stealth; instead, they shouted and crashed through the underbrush with a great crackling of breaking twigs and branches. As they neared she thought she heard both English and Spanish. They seemed to be searching for someone, shouting, "Come out!" and, "Where is he?"

Or were they saying, "Where is *she*?" Were they looking for Mariposa? Why?

The first gunshots sent a jolt of adrenaline to her heart. She gripped the pistol more tightly and hunkered down closer to the boulder. For a moment she was back in Afghanistan, pinned down by enemy fire, unable to fight back. She closed her eyes and clenched her teeth, fighting for calm. She wasn't over there anymore. She was in the United States. No one was shooting at her. She was safe.

A second rapid burst of gunfire shattered the air, and Abby bit down on her lip so hard she tasted blood. Then everything went still. The echo of the concussion reverberated in the air, ringing in her ears. She couldn't hear the men anymore, though whether because they were silent or because she was momentarily deaf, she didn't know. She opened her eyes and reached into the pocket of her jeans to grip the small ceramic figure of a rabbit she kept there. She'd awoken in the field hospital with it clutched in her hand; she had no idea who had put the rabbit there, but ever since, she'd kept it as a kind of good-luck charm. The familiar feel of its smooth sides and little pointed ears calmed her. She was safe. She was all right.

The voices drifted to her once more, less agitated now, and receding. They gradually faded altogether, until everything around her was silent once more.

She waited a full ten minutes behind the boulder, clutching the pistol in both hands, every muscle tensed and poised to defend herself. After the clock on her phone told her the time she'd allotted had passed, she stood and scanned the wilderness around her. Nothing. No men, no Mariposa, no dust clouds marking the trail of a vehicle. The landscape was as still as a painting, not even a breeze stirring the leaves of the stunted trees.

Still shaky from the adrenaline rush, she holstered the pistol and settled the backpack more firmly on her shoulder. She could return to her car, but would that increase her chances of running into the men? Maybe it would be better to remain here for a while longer. She'd go about her business and give the men time to move farther away.

She returned to the parsley plants. Digging up the specimen calmed her further. She cradled the uprooted plant in her fingers and slid it into the plastic collection bag, then labeled the bag with the date, time and GPS coordinates where she'd found it, and stowed it in her pack. Then she stood and stretched. Her muscles ached from tension. Time to head back to camp. She'd clean up, then stop by the ranger station and report the men and the shooting—but not Mariposa. She had no desire to betray the woman's secrets, whatever they were.

She checked her GPS to orient herself, then turned southwest, in the direction of her car and the road. She had no trail to follow, only paths made by animals and the red line on the GPS unit that marked her route into this area. On patrol in Kandahar she'd used similar GPS units, but just as often she'd relied on the memory of landmarks or even the positioning of stars. Nothing over there had ever felt familiar to her, but she'd learned to accept the unfamiliarity, until the day that roadside bomb had almost taken everything away.

She picked her way carefully through the rough landscape, around clumps of prickly pear cactus and desert willows, past sagebrush and Mormon tea and dozens of other plants she identified out of long habit. She kept her eyes focused down, hoping to spot one of the other coveted species on her list. All the plants were considered rare in the area, and all held promise of medical uses. The research she was doing now might one day lead to cultivation of these species to treat cancer or Parkinson's or some other crippling disease.

So focused was she on cataloging the plants around her that she didn't see the fallen branch until she'd stumbled over it. Cursing her own clumsiness, she straightened and looked back at the offending obstacle. It stuck out from beneath a clump of rabbitbrush, dark brown and as big around as a man's arm. What kind of a tree would that be, the bark such a dark color— and out here in an area where large trees were rare?

She bent to look closer and cold horror swept over her. She hadn't fallen over a branch at all. The thing that had tripped her was a man. He lay sprawled on the ground, arms outstretched, lifeless eyes staring up at her, long past seeing anything.

Chapter 2

Lieutenant Michael Dance had a low tolerance for meetings. As much as they were necessary to do his job, he endured them. But he'd wasted too many hours sitting in conference rooms, listening to other people drone on about things he didn't consider important. He preferred to be out in the field, doing real work that counted.

The person who'd called this meeting, however, was his boss, Captain Graham Ellison, aka "G-Man." Though Graham was with the FBI and Dance worked for Customs and Border Protection, Graham headed up the interagency task force charged with maintaining law and order on this vast swath of public land in southwest Colorado. And in their short acquaintance, Graham struck Michael as being someone worth listening to.

"National park rangers found an abandoned vehicle at the Dragon Point overlook yesterday," Graham said. A burly guy with the thick neck and wide shoulders of a linebacker and the short-cropped hair and erect stance of ex-military, Graham spoke softly, like many big men. His very presence commanded attention, so he didn't need to raise his voice. "The Montrose County sheriff's office has identified it as belonging to a Lauren Starling of Denver. Ms. Starling failed to show for work this morning, so they've asked us to keep an eye out. Here's a picture."

He passed around a glossy eight-by-ten photograph. Michael studied the studio head shot of a thirtysomething blonde with shoulder-length curls, violet-blue eyes and a dazzling white smile. She looked directly at the camera, beautiful and confident. "Do they think she was out here alone?" he asked, as he passed the photo on to the man next to him, Randall Knightbridge, with the Bureau of Land Management.

"They don't know," Graham said. "Right now they're just asking us to keep an eye out for her."

"Hey, I know this chick," Randall said.

Everyone turned to stare. The BLM ranger was the youngest member of the task force, in his late twenties and an acknowledged geek. He could rattle off the plots of half a dozen paranormal series on television, played lacrosse in his spare time and wore long-sleeved uniform shirts year-round to hide the colorful tattoos that decorated both arms. He didn't have a rep as a ladies' man, so what was he doing knowing a glamour girl like the one in the picture?

"I mean, I don't know her personally," he corrected, as if reading Michael's thoughts. "But I've seen her on TV. She does the news on channel nine in Denver."

"You're right." Simon Woolridge, with Immigration and Customs Enforcement, grabbed the picture and gave it a second look. "I knew she looked familiar."

"Like one of your ex-wives," quipped Lance Carpenter, a Montrose County sheriff's deputy.

"Lauren Starling is the evening news anchor for channel nine," Graham confirmed. "Her high profile is one reason this case is getting special attention from everyone involved."

"When did she go missing?" Marco Cruz, an agent with the DEA, asked.

"The Denver police aren't treating it as a missing person case yet," Graham said. "The car was simply parked at the overlook. There were no signs of a struggle. She took a week's vacation and didn't tell anyone where she was going. Nothing significant is missing from her apartment. That's all the information I have at the moment."

"Are they thinking suicide?" asked Carmen Redhorse, the only female member of the task force. Petite and dark haired, Carmen worked with the Colorado Bureau of Investigation.

No one looked surprised at her suggestion of suicide. Unfortunately, the deep canyon and steep drop-offs of Black Canyon of the Gunnison National Park were popular places for the despondent to end it all. Four or five people committed suicide in the park each year.

"There's no note," Graham said. "The Denver police are on the case right now. They've simply asked us to keep an eye on things. If you see anything suspicious, we'll pass it on to the local authorities." He consulted the clipboard in his hand. "On to more pressing matters. State police impounded a truck carrying a hundred pounds of fresh marijuana bud at a truck stop in Gunnison last night. The pot was concealed inside a load of coffee, but the drug dogs picked up the scent, no problem."

"When will these rubes learn they can't fool a dog's nose?" Randall leaned down to pet his Belgian Malinois, Lotte, who'd stretched out beneath his chair. She thumped the floor twice with her plume of a tail, but didn't raise her head.

"The logbook indicates the truck passed through this area," Graham continued. "That's the second shipment that's been waylaid in as many months, and another indication that there's an active growing operation in the area. We know from experience that public lands are prime targets for illegal growers."

"Free land, away from people, limited law enforcement presence." Carmen ticked off the reasons wilderness areas presented such a temptation to drug runners. "I read the first national parks had problems with bootleggers. Now it's pot and meth."

Graham turned to the large map of the area that covered most of one wall of the trailer that served as task force headquarters. "We're going to be flying more surveillance this week, trying to locate the growing fields. We'll be concentrating on the Gunnison Gorge just west of the park boundaries. The counters we laid last week show increased vehicle traffic on the roads in that area."

In addition to the more than thirty thousand acres within the national park, the task force was charged with controlling crime within the almost sixty-three thousand acres of the Gunnison Gorge National Conservation Area and the forty-three thousand acres of the Curecanti National Recreation Area. It was a ridiculous amount of land for a few people to patrol, much of it almost inaccessible, roadless wilderness. In recent years, drug cartels had taken advantage of short-staffed park service to cultivate thousands of acres of public land. They dug irrigation canals, built fences and destroyed priceless artifacts with impunity. This task force was an attempt to stop them.

A pretty feeble attempt, Michael thought. He thumbed a butterscotch Life Saver from the roll he kept in his pocket and popped it into his mouth. They were wasting time sitting around talking about the problem, instead of being out there doing something about it.

"If we want to find the crops, look for the people who take care of the crops," Simon said.

"You mean the people who plant the weed?" Randall asked.

"The people who plant it and water it and weed it and guard it from predators—both animal and human," Simon said. "Illegals, most likely, shipped in for that purpose. We find them and put pressure on them, we can find the person behind this. The money man."

Here was something Michael knew about. "Human trafficking in Colorado is up twenty percent this year," he said. "Some sources suggest a lot of victims who end up in Denver come from this area. We could be looking at a pipeline for more than drugs."

"So the guys in charge of drugs offer a free pass into the country to people who will work for them?" Lance asked.

"More likely they work with coyotes who charge people to bring them into the country, but instead of going to their cousin in Fort Collins or their aunt in Laramie, they end up prisoners of this drug cartel," Michael said. "And once they've worked the fields for a while or learned to cook up meth or whatever the drug lords need them to do, they take the women and the younger men to Denver and turn them out as prostitutes. It's slavery on a scale people have no idea even exists anymore."

"So in addition to drugs, we may be dealing with human trafficking," Carmen said.

"We don't know that." Simon's voice was dismissive. "It's only speculation. We do know that if these people have workers, they're probably illegals. Deport the workforce and you can cripple an operation. At least temporarily."

"Only until they bring in the next load of workers." Michael glared at the man across the conference table. "Rounding up people and deporting them solves nothing. And you miss the chance to break up the trafficking pipeline."

"End the drug operation and you remove the reason they have to bring in people," Simon countered.

"Right. And now they take them straight to Denver, where no one even notices what's going on."

"Back to the discussion at hand." Graham cut them off. He gave each of them a stern look. "As a task force, our job is to address all serious crime in this region, whether it's human trafficking or drugs or money laundering or murder. But I don't have to tell you that in this time of budget cuts, we have to be able to show the politicians are getting their money's worth. A high-profile case could do a lot to assure we all get to keep working."

And drugs were worth more to federal coffers than people, Michael thought grimly. The law allowed the Feds to seize any and all property involved in drug crimes, from cash and cars to mansions.

"Tomorrow we'll begin five days of aerial patrols, focused on these sectors." Graham indicated half a dozen spots on the map. "These are fairly level spots with access to water, remote, but possible to reach in four-wheel-drive vehicles."

"What about the private property in the area?" Michael asked. Several white spots on the map, some completely surrounded by federal land, indicated acreage owned by private individuals.

"Private property could provide an access point for the drug runners, so we'll be looking at that. Most of the private land is unoccupied," Graham said.

"Except for Prentice's fortress," Simon said.

Michael didn't ask the obvious question. If he waited, someone would explain this mystery to the new guy; if not, he'd find out what he needed to know on his own.

"Richard Prentice owns the land here." Graham pointed to a white square closest to the park—almost on the canyon rim. "He's built a compound there with several houses, stables, a gated entrance, et cetera."

"But before that, he tried to blackmail the government into buying the place at an exorbitant price," Carmen said. "He threatened to build this giant triple-X theater with huge neon signs practically at the park entrance." Her lip curled in disgust.

"He's had success with those kinds of tactics before," Graham said. "He threatened to blow up a historic building over near Ouray until a conservation group raised the money to buy the place from him."

"At an inflated price," Carmen said. "That's how he operates. If he can figure out a way to exploit a situation for money, he will."

"But the government didn't bite this time?" Michael asked.

"No," Lance said. "And the county fought back by passing an ordinance prohibiting sexually oriented businesses. He built a mansion instead, and spends his time filing harassment complaints every time we drive by or fly over."

"So do we think he has anything to do with the crime wave around here?" Michael asked. Greed and a lust for power were motivation enough for all manner of misdeeds.

Graham shook his head. "Prentice likes to thumb his nose at the government, but we have no reason to suspect he's guilty of any felonies."

"Which doesn't mean he isn't guilty," Carmen said. "Just that we can't prove it—yet."

Michael studied the map again. First chance he got, he'd check out this Prentice guy.

"Next on the list." Graham scanned the clipboard again, but before he could continue, a knock sounded on the door.

"Come in," Graham called.

The door opened and a woman stood on the threshold, eyes wide with surprise. A fall of long honey-blond hair obscured most of her face, but she appeared young, and pretty, with dark eyes and a well-shaped nose and chin. She wore canvas cargo pants, hiking boots and a long-sleeved canvas shirt, open at the throat to reveal a black tank top trimmed in lace, and a hint of tanned cleavage. Michael's gaze locked on the holstered weapon at her side—a .40-caliber Sig Sauer. He had one like it at his hip. So was she some kind of law enforcement? A new member of the team no one had mentioned?

"I, uh, I didn't mean to interrupt," she said. "I was looking for the park rangers. Their office was closed, and I saw the cars over here..."

"The park rangers go home at four," Graham said. "They'll be in at nine in the morning if you need help with camping permits or something."

Her eyes narrowed, focused on the tan uniforms, then on the name badge pinned to Graham's shirt pocket. "Captain Ellison. Are you a law enforcement officer?"

"Yes. Can I help you?"

She pressed her lips together, as if debating her next move, then nodded. "I need to report a crime. A murder."

The temperature in the room dropped several degrees, Michael was sure, and the group around the table leaned forward, all eyes—including the dog's—focused on the petite woman in the doorway.

"Why don't you come in and give us a few more details." Graham motioned the woman forward.

As she moved past him, Michael caught the scents of wood smoke and sweat and something lighter and more feminine—a floral perfume or shampoo. An awareness stirred in his gut, a sense of familiarity, and the hair rose on the back of his neck. Where had he seen this woman before?

"I'm a biologist," she said, speaking primarily to Graham, but casting nervous glances at the rest of them. "Or rather, I'm working on my master's degree in biology. I'm studying several plant species found in the park for my thesis. I was out collecting specimens this morning when I heard people approaching. They were shouting in English and in Spanish, and they appeared to be searching for someone."

"Did you get close to them?" Simon asked. "Did you talk to them?"

She shook her head. As she did so, her hair swung away from her face, revealing a jagged scar diagonally bisecting one cheek. The scar was bizarrely out of place on such a beautiful face, like a crack in an otherwise pristine china plate. Michael's gut tightened, and he struggled to control his breathing. He was sure he knew her now, but maybe his mind was playing tricks on him. Post-traumatic stress throwing up some new, bizarre symptom.

"They were some distance away—maybe two hundred yards," she continued. "I hid behind a large boulder and waited for them to leave."

"Why did you do that?" Simon asked.

"Because she's smart," Carmen said. "A woman alone in the middle of nowhere sees a group of rowdy men? Of course she hides."

Simon flushed, like a kid who's been reprimanded. "She looks as though she can take care of herself." He nodded to the weapon at her side. "You got a permit for that thing?"

"Yes." She turned away from him. "I couldn't see what they were doing—the terrain is rough out there. But I heard gunshots. Then they quieted down and left."

"You're sure they were gunshots?" Graham asked.

She nodded. "I was in the army, stationed in Kandahar. I know what gunfire sounds like. This was a semiautomatic. A rifle, not a handgun."

Michael gripped the underside of the conference table until his fingers ached. This was no trick of a war-stressed mind. This was *her*—the woman who'd lingered in the back of his mind for the better part of five years. The one he could never forget.

"All right." Graham leaned against the table, his pose deceptively casual. "What happened next?"

"I waited ten minutes to make sure they were gone, then I resumed collecting the specimens I'd come for. I headed back toward the road where I'd parked my car. I had walked less than half a mile when I stumbled over something." Her face paled and she swallowed hard, her lips pressed tightly together, holding in emotion. "It was a body," she said softly. Then, in a stronger voice, "A young man. Latino. He'd been shot in the chest."

"He was dead?" Randall asked.

"Oh, yes. But not for long. The body was still warm."

"So you think the men you heard shot him." Simon couldn't keep quiet long. Clearly, he liked playing the role of interrogator.

"It's your job to decide that, not mine," the woman said, a sharp edge to her voice. Good for her, Michael thought. Put Simon in his place.

"Can you show us where the body is?" Graham asked.

She nodded. "I think so. I was collecting specimens near there and I made note of the GPS coordinates. I should have noted the coordinates for the body, too, but seeing it out there was such a shock…" She looked down at the floor, hair falling forward to obscure her face once more. But Michael didn't need the visual confirmation anymore. This was *her*. And to think he'd thought he'd never see her again.

What were the odds that he'd run into her now—in this place half a world away from where they'd last met? Then again, his mother always said everything happened for a reason. Michael told himself he didn't believe in that kind of divine interference—in fate. But maybe some of his mother's superstition had rubbed off on him.

"We'll want a full statement from you later." Graham pulled out a pen and turned to a fresh sheet on his clipboard. "Right now, if you'll just give me your name and tell me where you're camped."

"Abigail Stewart."

Only when the others turned toward him did Michael realize he'd spoken out loud. Abby stared at him, too, her mouth half-open, a red stain coloring her previously pale cheeks. "How did you know my name?" she demanded.

He stood, forcing himself to relax, or at least to look as if he didn't have all these turbulent emotions fighting it out in his gut. "Hello, Abby," he said softly. "I'm Michael Dance."

"I don't know a Michael Dance," she said.

"No, you probably don't remember me. It's been a while. Five years."

She searched his face, panic behind her eyes. He wanted to reach out, to reassure her. But he remained frozen, immobile.

"You knew me in Afghanistan?" she asked. "I don't remember."

"There's no reason you should," he said. "The last time I saw you, you were pretty out of it. Technically, you were dead—for a while, at least."

He'd been the one to bring her back to life, massaging her heart and breathing in her ravaged mouth until her heart beat again and she'd sucked in oxygen on her own. He'd saved her life, and in that moment forged a connection he'd never been quite able to sever.

Chapter 3

Having a total stranger announce to a bunch of other strangers that you'd come back from the dead didn't rank high on Abby's list of experiences she wanted to repeat—or to ever have in the first place. From the moment she'd entered the trailer parked alongside the park ranger's office, she'd felt the tall, dark-haired officer's gaze fixed on her. She couldn't decide if he was rude or just overly intense; she hadn't spent a lot of time around law-enforcement types, so what did she know?

And what did she care? Except that the agent—Michael Dance—had made her care. He knew things about her she didn't. He knew what had happened in the hours and days she'd lost to unconsciousness and trauma. That he'd seen her ripped open and clinging to life by a thread felt so personal and intimate. She both resented him and wanted to know more.

As for Michael Dance, he seemed content to keep staring at her, and when she'd agreed to take the officers to the body she'd found, he'd slipped up beside her and insisted she ride with him.

"You could ride with me and Graham if you'd rather," Carmen, the only other woman in the room, offered, perhaps sensing Abby's unease.

"No, that's all right. I can ride with Lieutenant Dance." Alone in a vehicle, maybe she could ask him some of the questions that troubled her.

But now, as they cruised along the paved South Rim Road through the park, she felt tongue-tied and awkward.

He took a roll of Life Savers from the pocket of his uniform shirt and held it out to her. "Want one?"

"Okay." She took one of the butterscotch candies, then he did the same and returned the roll to his pocket.

"I'm addicted," he said. "I quit smoking last year and took up the candy as a substitute."

"Good for you for quitting," she said. "I knew a lot of soldiers who smoked, but I never took it up."

"Smart woman." He settled back in the driver's seat, gaze fixed on the curving ribbon of blacktop that skirted the park's main attraction—the deep, narrow Black Canyon.

Abby tried to relax, too, but curiosity needled her, overcoming her natural shyness. "How do you possibly remember me after all this time?" she blurted. "It's been years, and you must have only seen me for a few hours, at most." Had he been an orderly in the field hospital, a medic or a pilot, or simply a grunt tasked with transporting the wounded?

"I was a PJ. We saw hundreds of casualties during

my tour—but you were the only woman. And you were my first save. It made an impression."

PJs—pararescuers—were bona fide superheroes. Members of the US Air Force's rescue squadron swooped into the thick of danger in Pave Hawk helicopters, often under heavy enemy fire, to snatch wounded soldiers from almost certain death. They performed critical lifesaving procedures in the air, long before their patients reached the doctors at field hospitals. Abby remembered none of this, but she'd seen a special on TV and watched with sick fascination, trying to imagine what it was like when she was the patient, being patched together by young men she'd likely never see again.

"I… I don't know what to say." She plucked at the seat belt harness, feeling trapped as much by her own emotions as by the confining cloth strap. "Thank you doesn't seem like enough."

"I was glad you made it. We lost too many soldiers over there, but losing a woman would have been worse. I know it shouldn't be that way, but it was—I won't lie."

She nodded. Though women weren't authorized for combat roles back then, the army needed female soldiers to interrogate native women and to fill a variety of noncombat roles, from resupply to repairing equipment that constantly broke down. Women soldiers stood guard and went on patrol, and sometimes got caught up in battles, in a war with no clearly defined front line, where every peasant could be friend or foe. But for all the roles they filled, women made up only about 10 percent of the ground forces in Afghanistan. As a female soldier, Abby hadn't wanted to stand out from her fellow grunts, but she couldn't help it.

"I still can't believe you remembered my name," she said.

He winced. "I made it a point to remember it. Later, I tried to look you up—just to see how you were doing. I'm not a stalker or anything. I just wanted to know."

"But you didn't find me?"

"I found out you'd gotten transferred stateside, but that was about it." He adjusted his grip on the steering wheel of the FJ Cruiser he drove. A second Cruiser followed a few car lengths behind, with Graham and Carmen; for all Abby knew half a dozen other vehicles full of more law-enforcement agents came after that. "But now I know. You look good. I'm glad."

She resisted the urge to touch the scar. "Thanks for not qualifying the compliment."

He frowned. "I don't get it."

"Thanks for not saying, 'You look good, considering what you've been through.'"

"People really tell you that?"

"Sometimes. I also get 'That scar is hardly noticeable,' which I know is a lie, since if it was so unnoticeable, why are they bothering to point it out?" Had she really just said that? To this guy she didn't even know? She didn't talk about this stuff with anybody. Not even the therapist the Army had sent her to. Waste of money, that.

"So you're studying botany?" Maybe sensing her uneasiness, he smoothly changed the subject.

"Environmental science. And to answer your next question, which I know from experience is, 'What do you do with a master's degree in environmental science?' I'll probably end up teaching ungrateful undergrads somewhere. But all that is just to support the research I want to do into developing medicines from plants."

"You mean, like herbal remedies and stuff?"

"I mean, like cancer drugs and medicine to cure Parkinson's or diabetes. Plants are a tremendous resource we've scarcely begun to explore."

"So there are plants in this park that can cure diseases?" He motioned to the scrubby landscape around them.

"This might look like desert to you, but there are hundreds of plants within the park and surrounding public lands. It's the perfect place for my research."

"A big change from the war," he said.

"Everything is a big change from the war," she said. "Didn't you feel it, after you came home? That sense of not knowing what to do next? Of being a little out of place? Or was that just me?"

"It wasn't just you," he said. "Every day over there you had a mission—a purpose. Life over here isn't like that." He stared at the road ahead for a long moment, then added, "I thought about going back to school after I got out, but sitting in a classroom all day—that wasn't for me."

She shifted toward him, feeling more comfortable scrutinizing him for a change. He was good-looking—no doubt about that—with dark eyes and olive skin and a hawk nose and square chin. His broad shoulders filled out his short-sleeved tan shirt nicely, and slim-fit khakis showed off muscular thighs. "How did you end up working for border patrol?"

"They were at a job fair for veterans and it looked like interesting work. It was a lot of independent work, outdoors. I liked that."

She nodded. She understood that desire to be out-doors and alone, away from other people. After the noise, chaos and crowds of the war, the wilderness felt healing.

"It's great that you found work that's important," he said. "I mean, what you're doing could make a big difference in peoples' lives someday."

"Someday, maybe. But yeah, I do feel as though it's important work. Don't you think what you're doing is important?"

"Sometimes I do. Sometimes I'm not so sure." He checked his mirrors and crunched down on the candy. "You said this guy you found is Mexican?" he asked.

Back to the reason she was here. Guess they couldn't avoid that subject forever. "Well, Latino. He had dark hair and brown skin—like you."

"My mom is from Mexico. My dad's from Denver."

"Do you speak Spanish?"

"I do. Comes in handy on the job sometimes."

"Do you run into a lot of people from Mexico in the park?" she asked, thinking of Mariposa and Angelique.

"Some." He slowed as they reached the end of the paved road and bumped onto a rougher gravel surface. "How much farther from here?" he asked.

She checked her GPS. "About nine miles."

"You weren't kidding—remote."

"The best specimens are usually where they haven't been disturbed by people or grazing animals."

"Right. You haven't seen anything else suspicious while you were out and about this week, have you?"

She stiffened, again thinking of the Mexican woman and child. "What do you mean, suspicious?"

"A bunch of marijuana plants, for instance? Or a portable meth lab?"

"No. Should I have seen those things?"

"Probably not, if you want to stay safe."

"Is that why border patrol and the FBI and BLM and who knows who else are meeting in a trailer at park headquarters?" she asked. "To go after drugs in the park?"

The seat creaked as he shifted his weight. "We're an interagency task force formed to address rising crime in the park and surrounding lands—much of it drug related." He cut his eyes to her. "Just be careful out there. Good idea to carry that Sig."

"When I applied for my backcountry permit at the ranger station, they told me to watch out for snakes. No one said anything about drug dealers or murderers."

"Most tourists will never know they're there. And how many people who visit the park ever step off the main road or popular trails?"

"Not many," she said. "I almost never see anyone when I'm out in the backcountry." Which had made her encounter with Mariposa all the more remarkable. "If I do see anything suspicious, I'll stay far away," she said. "All I want to do is collect some plant specimens and get back to my research."

They both fell silent as the Cruiser bumped over the rutted, sometimes muddy road. Though it was already early June, most of the usually dry arroyos trickled with snowmelt, and grass that would later turn a papery brown looked green and lush. Abby spotted several small herds of deer grazing in the distance, and a cluster of pronghorn antelope that exploded into life as the vehicles trundled past, bouncing away in stiff-legged leaps.

Finally her GPS indicated they were near the area where she'd found the body. "Pull over anywhere," she said. "We'll have to walk in from here."

Michael stopped the Cruiser alongside the road and Graham slid his vehicle in behind them. The officers opened up the backs of the Cruisers and pulled out packs, canteens and, in Graham's case, a semiautomatic rifle. They were going in loaded for bear, she supposed in case they ran into any of the bad guys.

Graham indicated she should lead the way. GPS in hand, she set out walking. The officers fell in behind in classic patrol formation. Abby's heart raced. She slipped her hand into the front pocket of her jeans and wrapped it around the rabbit charm. *Nothing to worry about*, she reminded herself. *You're in Colorado. In a national park. No snipers here.*

But of course, the dead man she'd found earlier reminded her that the serene landscape was not as safe as it seemed.

They walked for an hour before they came to the patch of desert parsley she'd harvested earlier. She noted the freshly turned earth where she'd dug up her specimen. "There's the boulder I hid behind." She pointed to the large rock, then walked over to it, trying to remember everything she'd done in those moments before she discovered the body. "I started walking this way."

She led the way, the other three moving silently behind her. A few minutes later she spotted the pink bandanna she'd left tied to the branch of a piñon. "There." She pointed. "The body is by that tree."

She stopped and let the three officers move past.

She watched from a distance as they surveyed the body. Carmen took a number of photographs, then they fanned out, searching the ground—for clues, she supposed. She stood in the shade of the piñon, wishing she were anywhere else. She'd thought she'd put killing and bodies behind her when she left Afghanistan. The wilderness was supposed to be a place of peace, not violence.

Michael returned to her side. "You doing okay?" he asked.

She nodded. "I'll be fine."

She felt his gaze on her, but he didn't press, for which she was grateful. "Which direction did the men you saw come from?" he asked after a moment.

"From over there, near that wash." She nodded in the direction of the shallow depression in the terrain.

Graham joined them. "We'll need to seal off this area and send a team out to collect evidence."

"We need to figure out where he came from," Michael said. "There might be a camp somewhere nearby."

"Where are you camped, Ms. Stewart?" Graham asked.

"I'm in the South Rim Campground."

"Let us know if you decide to move into town or return to your home, in case we have questions," Graham said.

"I'd planned to stay here for another week to ten days," she said. "I've only just begun collecting the specimens I need."

"This part of the park will be off-limits to the public

for most of that time, I'm afraid," Graham said. "Until we determine it's safe."

He was going to close the backcountry? "That really isn't acceptable," she said. "I'm not some naive tourist, stumbling around, but I really need to collect these specimens to complete my research."

"You'll have to find them somewhere else. Until I decide it's safe, this section of the park is closed."

The three officers studied her, expressions impassive, implacable. She turned away, and her gaze fell on the body on the ground. All she could see was the feet, but they lay there with the stillness of a mannequin. Lifeless, a cruel joke played out in the desert.

She hated having her plans thwarted, but she knew Graham and the others were right. Until they knew who had killed this man and why, they had to err on the side of caution. "Fine. There are other places in the backcountry where I can look for specimens."

"Let us know…"

But Graham never finished the sentence. Bark exploded from the trunk of a tree beside her. "Get down!" Michael yelled, and shoved her to the ground as bullets whistled over their heads.

Chapter 4

In the silence that followed the burst of gunfire, the drum of Michael's pulse in his ears was so loud he was sure everyone could hear it. He slowed his breathing and strained his ears, alert for any clue about the shooter. Beneath him, Abby shifted, and he became aware of her ragged breathing. She shoved and he realized he was crushing her. Better crushed than shot, he thought, but he eased up a fraction of an inch, putting more of his weight on his hands, braced on the ground beneath his shoulders, and his knees, straddled on either side of her.

They lay in a depression in the ground, a shallow wash pocked with rocks and low scrub and a few stunted piñons. Turning his head, Michael spotted Graham and Carmen about five feet away. His eyes met Graham's. The supervisor looked angry enough to chew nails.

"Who's shooting at us?" Abby whispered, her voice so low he wondered at first if he'd imagined the question.

"Sniper," Graham answered. "I make his hide site about three hundred yards to the south, on that slight rise."

Michael turned his head, but he couldn't see anything except grass and dirt and the trunk of a piñon. They were too exposed here for him to even lift his head.

"He must be wearing a ghillie suit," Carmen said. "I can't see a thing." Michael turned back to look at her and realized she was half sitting behind a boulder. She'd pulled binoculars from her pack and was scanning the area.

"What's someone out here doing with a ghillie suit?" Abby asked.

Michael had been wondering the same thing. In a training course he'd taken, he'd seen men in the cumbersome camouflage suits covered with twigs and leaves so that when the wearer froze, he blended in completely with the surrounding landscape. It wasn't something you could pick up at your local outdoor supplier.

"They could have stolen one from the military, or made their own," Graham said. "These drug operations spare no expense to protect their business. That sniper rifle he's got is probably military issue, or close to it."

Graham shifted, reaching for his radio; the movement was enough to draw another blast of gunfire, bullets spitting into the dirt in front of them. Abby flinched, jolting against Michael. "Are you okay?" he whispered.

"Just a rock on my cheek. It's nothing."

More gunfire exploded, this time to their right. From her vantage point behind the boulder, Carmen had returned fire. "He's too far away," she said, lowering the weapon.

"Ranger Two, this is Ranger One, do you copy?" Graham had used the distraction to retrieve the radio from his utility belt and key the mike.

"Ranger Two. I copy." Simon's voice crackled through the static.

"We're pinned down by a sniper in the backcountry." He recited the GPS coordinates Abby had given them for her plant find. "Looks like one shooter. His hide site is approximately three hundred yards south of our position. He's on a small rise, maybe wearing a ghillie suit."

"We're on it. We'll try to come in behind him."

"Roger that. Over." Graham laid the radio on the ground beside his head. "Now we wait," he said.

Michael tried to ignore the cramping in his arms. If he let up, he'd crush Abby again, but any movement was liable to draw the sniper's fire. "Sorry," he said to her. "I know this isn't the most comfortable position."

She didn't answer. Instead, she started to tremble, tremors running through her body into his. She made a muffled sound, almost like...sobbing.

The sound tore at him. The sight of the dead man hadn't moved him, and while the sniper's fire got his adrenaline pumping, it didn't shake him the way Abby's sorrow did. "Hey." He slid one hand to her shoulder and turned his head so that his mouth was next to her ear.

He spoke softly, not wanting the others to hear. "It's okay," he said. "Our team is good. They'll nail this guy."

She tensed, her fingers digging into the dirt beneath them. Her breathing was ragged, and he could sense panic rising off her in waves. Was she having some kind of flashback? How could he help her—comfort her?

He'd been shot at plenty of times as a PJ, but they always had the Pave Hawks to swoop them out of danger. He'd always been too focused on the mission, on saving lives, to worry much about his own. It must have been worse for troops on the ground, like her.

He tried to lift more of his weight off her. "Hey," he said again. "Abby, talk to me. You're going to be okay."

She sucked in a ragged breath, her body rising and falling beneath him. "I hate this," she said after a minute.

"I hate it, too." The words sounded lame, even to him, but he'd say anything to keep her talking. "But you'll be okay. The cavalry is on its way."

The muscles of her cheek against his shifted; he hoped she was smiling at his lame joke. "This is probably the last thing you expected when you came out here to dig plants," he said.

"Yeah." The shaking wasn't as violent now—only a tremor shuddering through her every now and then. Her hands had relaxed, no longer gripping the dirt. He resisted the urge to smooth his hand along her back; she might take it the wrong way. As it was, he was becoming all too aware of the feel of her body beneath his, the side of her breast nestled beside his arm, the soft curve of her backside against his groin.

"This is just a little too familiar," she said.

He realized she wasn't talking about the feel of their bodies pressed together. "You've been pinned down by a sniper before?"

"Oh, yeah. That was the thing about being over there—the unpredictability of it all—not knowing when an IED would explode or a sniper would fire, not knowing who you could trust."

You can trust me, he wanted to say. But he didn't. Trusting him didn't change the fact that there was somebody they couldn't see determined to kill them if they so much as lifted their heads. He hadn't done a very good job so far of protecting her. The best he could hope for was to provide a distraction. "Have you always been interested in plants?" he asked. "Did you always plan to study biology?"

"I was going to be a television news anchor," she said. "Or a model. This scar on my face put an end to that."

Only a deaf man would miss the bitterness in her words. She was certainly pretty enough to be a model—but she probably didn't want to hear that, either. He tried once more to get the conversation back on track. "What you're doing now—finding plants that could cure cancer. That sounds a lot more rewarding."

"Yeah." She fell silent again. Okay, so she didn't want to talk. At least she'd stopped shaking.

"Mostly, I like the solitude," she said after a moment. "It's so peaceful out here. Usually."

"Yeah. Usually it is. You just got lucky."

She actually chuckled then—the sound made him feel about ten feet tall, as if he'd done something a lot more heroic than make lame jokes.

"Why do you think he's shooting at us?" she asked. "Is it because we found the dead man?"

"I doubt it's that. My guess is the dead guy's an illegal. He won't have any ID on him, or anything to tie him to anyone or anything. Most likely the sniper is protecting something. A meth lab or something like that."

"But doesn't firing at us give away the fact that there's something out here worth protecting?"

"Yeah, but it keeps us from getting too close and buys them time to move the operation. When we finally make it out to investigate, whatever is going on will be long gone."

"What happens after that?"

"We have a starting place for our search. From there we try to track them to their new location."

"Like in the war," she said.

"Yeah. A lot like in the war."

"Just my dumb luck that I come out here to get away from all that and end up in the middle of it. Do you ever feel that way?" she asked.

"Yeah," he said. "I thought my job would mostly be inspecting shipments and checking passports—looking for drugs and illegals, for sure. I knew I'd carry a weapon, but I didn't expect to ever have to use it. But then I think, maybe I'm exactly where I'm supposed to be. Maybe my military training can help me put an end to some of the violence, at least."

"Do you really believe that?" she asked. "That things happen for a reason?"

"Yeah. I mean, don't you think it's more than coincidence that we met up again after all this time?" Five years in which he'd never really forgotten about her. "I mean, what are the odds?"

"That's why it's called a coincidence," she said. "It's random. Just like me ending up out here in the middle of your little drug war. It's the way life works, but it doesn't mean anything."

Michael didn't say anything after Abby shot down his theory that the two of them were meant to meet up again. Well, sorry, but she didn't believe in fate. She wasn't meant to be flat on her stomach, squashed by some big guy in fatigues while another guy took potshots at her, any more than she was meant to disappoint her family by becoming a recluse who wandered the desert in search of rare plants. Life was life. Things happened and you rolled with the punches. She liked looking for plants in the desert, and she hoped the work she did now would help somebody else someday. But that didn't mean she'd been guided by fate. She made her own choices and accepted the consequences.

She closed her eyes, thinking she might as well catch a nap while she waited for whatever Michael's partners were doing out there. But closing her eyes was a mistake. As soon as her eyelids descended, she was back in Kandahar, pinned down by a sniper, her face in the dirt just like it was now. Only back then, there had been no cavalry to come to the rescue—the rest of her unit had been pinned down by enemy fire or already wiped out. For six hours she'd lain there with her face in the dirt while the guy next to her silently bled out and the guy on her other side freaked out, sobbing like a baby until every nerve in her was raw. In the end, the shooter must have decided they were all dead and moved on. Her own company thought the same thing—she woke up with two men slinging her onto a stretcher and someone shouting, "Hey, we've got a live one here!"

She opened her eyes again. Time to think about something else. Mariposa. Where were she and Angelique right now? Was she safe? Was she somehow mixed up in whatever illegal operation the sniper was protecting? What was she—somebody's wife or girlfriend, along for the ride, in over her head now? Was she as surprised by the violence that intruded on such peaceful surroundings as Abby was?

"When you were out here before, collecting your plants, did you see anybody else?" Michael asked. "Besides the men who were after our dead guy?"

What was he, a mind reader or something? "No, I didn't see anybody," she lied.

"No other hikers or campers?"

"I saw two hikers three days ago. They were tourists from Australia. And I pass people on the roads and see campers in the campground."

"That's it?"

"Why? Don't you believe me?"

"In interrogation training, they tell you that if you ask the same question in several different ways, you sometimes get different answers."

"So now you're interrogating me?" What she wouldn't give to be able to look him in the eye when she spoke. Instead, she was forced to address the ground while he lay on top of her. She appreciated that he was doing his best to hold himself off her, but still, the guy was big and solid. An easy one hundred and eighty pounds.

"It's a harsh word for questioning," he said. "A lot of law enforcement is just asking the right questions, of victims, or witnesses, or suspects."

"Well, you're not going to get different answers from me." She saw no reason to betray Mariposa to him. "Do you think you could just slide off me?" she asked.

"I don't think we'd better risk it. Movement seems to set off our shooter."

"Why did you throw yourself on top of me in the first place?"

"I'm trained to protect civilians. And I don't care how politically incorrect it is, my instincts are to keep women and children out of harm's way."

"How chivalrous of you." She hesitated, then added, "But thanks, all the same." The one thing she'd missed about the military was that sense that her buddies had her back.

"You're welcome. Sorry we couldn't have gotten reacquainted under better circumstances."

"Now that he's not actually shooting at us and we're just waiting, it's pretty boring," she said. "Like most of the time in the war."

"Are all our conversations going to come back to that?" he asked.

"Does it bother you, talking about the war?"

"Not really. I thought it bothered you."

"Sometimes it does," she admitted. When other people asked about her experiences in Afghanistan, she deflected the questions or changed the subject. "It's easier with you. You were over there. You understand."

"I guess I do relate to what you went through. A little bit anyway."

The radio's crackle made them both flinch. Abby turned her head toward the sound. Graham keyed the mike. "What have you got?" he asked.

"All clear here," one of the team members—maybe the sour-faced guy, Simon—said.

"No sign of the shooter?" Graham asked.

"Somebody was here, all right. There's broken brush and we found some shell casings. Looks like a .300 Win Mag. The dirt's a little scuffed up, but the ground's too hard to leave much of an impression."

"Get Randall and Lotte on it."

"They're here. The dog picked up a scent, but it died at the road. We found some tire tracks that look like a truck. We figure someone was waiting to pick up our guy. We never saw signs of a vehicle, so he probably left not long after he fired the last shots at y'all."

Graham swore under his breath and shoved up onto his knees. No gunshots split the air. Abby let out the breath she hadn't even realized she'd been holding.

Michael rolled off her and popped to his feet, then reached out a hand to help her up. She let him pull her up, her limbs stiff and sore from so long being prone. Clearly, she wasn't in as good a shape as she'd thought. "You're bleeding," he said, and gently touched the side of her face.

She flinched as his fingers brushed against the scar, but then she felt the stickiness of already drying blood. "A rock ricocheted off the ground," she said. "It's nothing."

"Here." He handed her a black bandanna, then offered a bottle of water. "You should clean it up."

Head down, she accepted the water and dampened the bandanna. The square of cloth was clean and crisp, like something a businessman would carry tucked into his pocket. She turned her back to the others as she cleaned off the blood and dirt from the side of her face.

"Let me have a look." Michael moved around in front of her. "You may need stitches."

"It's nothing." She tried once more to turn away, but he put his hand on her shoulder and took her chin in his other hand. "It's okay," he said softly. "I promise I don't faint at the sight of blood."

The teasing quality of the words almost made her smile. If anyone had seen her at her worst, it had been this guy. She had no idea what she'd looked like when the PJs had hauled her onto that helicopter, but the doctors had told her the shrapnel from the IED had torn through the side of her face, narrowly missing her eye. As much as she hated the scar, it was nothing compared to how she might have ended up.

She let him lift her chin and study the side of her face.

"It's just a little cut, pretty shallow. When we get back to the truck I'll get a bandage for it."

"Thanks." She turned away and combed her hair down to cover the side of her face again.

"Get Marco to help you with recon," Graham said. "I'll notify the park rangers that the backcountry is closed indefinitely. No more permits, and they'll need to round up anyone out with a permit now. Over."

"You mean just the backcountry within the park, right?" Abby asked.

"I mean all the park, the recreation area and Gunnison Gorge. If these people have a sniper looking after their interests, they have some real money and muscle behind it. Until we know the scope of their operation, we can't risk the safety of the public."

"You can't expect to keep people out of an area that large," she said.

"We can't prevent all unauthorized access, but we can stop issuing permits and close all the roads leading into the area. I'm sorry, but that means you won't be able to continue your research in the area."

His tone of command left little room for argument. He looked past her to Michael. "Take her back to headquarters, then meet up with Simon and the others. Ms. Stewart, we may have more questions for you later."

She doubted she'd have any useful answers, but she only nodded and turned to follow Michael back to the Cruiser. By the time they reached the vehicle, she was fuming.

"Sorry about your research," Michael said as he started the truck. "Maybe you can come back and finish up next summer. Hopefully, things will have calmed down by then."

"I don't have next summer," she said. "My grant is for this summer. Next summer I'll have to find a job and start paying off my student loans."

"Is there someplace else you can research—another park, or another part of the state?"

"My grant is to explore this area. Shifting my focus requires a new grant application. Your commander is overreacting. He doesn't have to close off all one hundred and thirty thousand acres of public land. That's ridiculous."

"Can you blame him? He's already under the gun from politicians who think this task force is a waste of money—can you imagine the fallout if some tourist gets taken out by a sniper? We've already got one murder on our hands. Your plants will still be there when this investigation is over."

"Don't patronize me."

"I'm not patronizing. I'm just trying to get you to calm down."

His words only made her more furious. She did not need to calm down. She'd just been shot at and forced to lie on her stomach on the ground for over an hour, and suffered the humiliation of almost flaking out in front of a bunch of strangers—if she didn't give vent to the tornado of emotions inside of her she might explode. "Shut up," she said. "Whatever you have to say, I don't want to hear it."

He glared at her for a long moment, then turned his attention to the road. The truck rocketed forward, bouncing over the rough two-track so that she had to grip the handle mounted at the top of the door to steady herself. Dust boiled up behind them, and rocks pinged against the undercarriage like BBs. She clenched her jaw to keep from shouting at him to slow down and not be so reckless. But that was what he wanted from her—another reaction. She wouldn't give him the satisfaction.

She'd already let him affect her emotions too much, his combination of brashness and consideration, strength and tenderness, touching vulnerable places inside her she hadn't let anyone see. She never talked about the war with anyone, and yet she'd confided in him. She didn't willingly let others see her scars, but she'd turned her face up to him with only a moment's hesitation. She didn't like how open and undefended he made her feel, with all his talk of fate and meaning behind what had to be only coincidence.

After a few miles, he slowed down enough that she could relax back in the seat. She hugged her arms across her chest and stared out at the landscape. Most people probably thought the land was ugly, with its scraggly vegetation and covering of rock and thin dirt. The real treasure lay beneath eye level, in the startlingly deep, narrow canyon that cut a jagged swatch through the high desert, its walls painted in shades of red and orange and gray. People long ago had dubbed it the Black Canyon, since sunlight seldom reached its depths. The silvery ribbon of the Gunnison River rushed through the bottom of the canyon, nurturing lush growth along its rocky banks, creating a world of color and moisture far below the parched landscape above.

But that stark desert held as much interest for Abby as the canyon below. She'd enjoyed discovering the secrets of the twisted piñons and miniature wildflowers, learning about the deer, rabbits, foxes and other wildlife that thrived there. She thought of herself like them—someone who had learned to survive amid bareness, to find the beauty in hardship.

They pulled up in front of headquarters. Her car was the only one in the lot now. She unsnapped her seat belt and her hand was on the door when Michael spoke. "Look. It isn't safe for you to go into the back-country by yourself, but what if I went with you? You can look for your plants while I patrol. I can square it with Graham."

She could only imagine the pushback he'd get from his supervisor when he made that suggestion. Captain

Graham Ellison struck her as a man who wasn't into bending the rules. "Why would you do that?"

He shrugged. "I kind of feel responsible for you."

Wrong answer. She didn't want anyone—she especially didn't want this man—to be responsible for her. She was responsible for herself. She climbed out of the truck and turned to face him. "I get that you saved my life," she said. "And I'm grateful for that. But that doesn't give you any kind of special claim on me."

He held up both hands. "I'm not making any claim on you. I'm just trying to help."

"I don't need your help. Thanks anyway." She turned and stalked away, though she could feel his gaze burning into her all the way to her car.

Chapter 5

"We got nothing." Simon slapped a thin file folder onto the conference room table and sank into a chair, a look of disgust on his face.

Graham, seated at the head of the table, frowned and reached for the folder. "What do you mean, you've got nothing?" he said. "We've got a dead body. We've got shell casings from a gun—tire tracks. All of that must lead to something." He leveled his stern gaze on the others around the table. Michael unwrapped another Life Saver and popped it into his mouth. Already, this meeting was off to a bad start. Twenty-four hours in and they had no more to go on than they had when Abby had walked into their office yesterday afternoon.

"It leads nowhere," Simon said. "The man had no ID. His fingerprints aren't in any database. We sent in DNA, but I doubt it will come up with anything—

he's obviously an illegal. We're not even sure where he's from. Could be Mexico, Central America, South America…" He shook his head.

"Where he's from may not be important," Graham said, tapping the file, which he hadn't bothered to open. "I want to know why he was shot in the middle of nowhere like that, and who shot him."

"Somebody wanted to shut him up."

All heads turned toward Marco, who had spoken. "Shut him up why?" Graham asked.

"I think he was trying to escape and they silenced him," Marco said.

"Why not bring him back?" Randall asked. "If our theory is these illegals are brought here to work in some drug operation, why lose a good worker?"

"A man who wants to get away badly enough to take off across the wilderness on foot isn't a good worker," Marco said.

"With this level of security, I'd say we're definitely looking at a drug operation," Simon said. "So why can't we find it?"

"If it's meth, it could be in a little trailer camouflaged on the back of beyond," Michael said. "Even if it's a grow op, they can hide acres of the stuff in remote canyons."

"Our aerial patrols haven't spotted anything suspicious." Graham's chair creaked as he leaned back in it. "Did Lotte pick up any scent?"

The Belgian Malinois raised her head, alert. Randall dropped his hand to idly stroke her head. "She worked for a couple of hours yesterday, but none of the trails she picked up led to anything."

"What about Abby Stewart?"

Michael realized Graham had addressed him. "What about her?" he asked.

"She's the one who found the body, and she was with us when the sniper fired," Graham said. "What's her link to all this?"

"She was in the wrong place at the wrong time," Michael said. "No link."

"What do we know about her?" Simon asked. "Is she really who she says she is?"

"She's who I say she is." Michael tried to suppress his annoyance and failed. "I knew her in Afghanistan. She was wounded over there, came home to recuperate and now she's a student at University of Colorado, earning her master's in biology."

"Her story checks out," Carmen said. "She came to the park five days ago and requested a backcountry permit. The park rangers told me she goes out every morning and comes back in the evening with her notebooks, pack and specimens she's collected."

"She could be meeting with anyone in that time," Simon said.

"You checked her out?" Michael's stomach churned, as if he'd been the subject of their snooping.

"We check everyone out," Graham said. "How was she when she left you yesterday?"

She'd been furious with him. If looks could kill, he'd be seriously wounded right now. "She was upset about not being able to continue her research," he said. "She has a grant that runs out at the end of the summer."

"What's she researching anyway?" Randall asked.

"Plants that grow in this area that have medicinal purposes," Michael said. "She says stuff that grows out there could be used to treat or cure cancer and other diseases."

"Sounds like a good excuse to spend time in the backcountry," Simon said. "Maybe the plant she's really interested in is marijuana."

"There are a lot of plants that have medicinal uses," Carmen said. "My people have known that for centuries. You palefaces are just now figuring it out."

Simon ignored the dig and leaned across the table toward Michael. "Even if she's not involved with our killers, that sniper saw her with us yesterday. He'll report that to his handlers."

"If they think she witnessed something out there, they'll want to shut her up, too," Marco said.

Michael felt as if he'd swallowed ice. "She could be in danger."

"It's a possibility," Graham said. "We'll need to keep an eye on her."

"I offered to take her out on patrol with me," Michael said. "That way, she could collect her plants and I could make sure she didn't wander into anything dangerous."

"Not a bad idea," Graham said. "What did she think?"

"She was still pretty shaken up by the sniper thing." No sense admitting he'd blown it by coming on too strong. "She had some bad experiences in the war."

"You said she almost died?" Carmen asked.

"She did die." Michael didn't have to close his eyes to see her lying on that stretcher, pale as the sheets. "She coded in the helicopter on the way to the hospital. We brought her back, but she was pretty messed up."

"She was hit in the face?" Carmen stroked the side of her own face.

"She was hit all over, but the head wound was the worst."

"And you saved her life," Carmen said.

He looked away. "I did my job."

"Then you have a connection with her, whether she acknowledges that or not," Graham said. "Go talk to her. Tell her we want to offer her protection, in exchange for her help."

"What kind of help?" The idea surprised him.

"I have a sense she knows something she's not telling us," Graham said. He opened the file. "Now let's see if there's anything else in here we can go after."

"I'm doing fine, Dad. The research is going well." Abby held the phone tightly to her ear and paced the length of the travel trailer she'd rented for the summer. Four steps toward the bedroom at one end, turn and four steps back to the dinette at the other end, passing the galley kitchen in between. The research had been going well, until Michael Dance and his friends had thrown a wrench in her plans.

"Have you thought any more about coming home when you've wrapped things up there?" Her dad's voice, the velvety, well-modulated bass that was familiar to sports fans and channel-four viewers all over Milwaukee, seemed to fill up the trailer. "I've been talking to some people I know at the station. We've got a vacancy for a weekend anchor job. They'd love to give you a tryout."

Abby squeezed her eyes shut and suppressed a groan. "That wouldn't be a good idea, Dad." Any tryout they gave her would be because her dad—Brian Stewart, the voice of Milwaukee sports—had called in favors. Or worse, because they were playing the wounded-vet card. She wanted no part of it.

"Nonsense! You were always a natural in front of the camera. And if you're worried about your scar— it really isn't that bad. Stage makeup can cover a lot, you know, and you could have more plastic surgery."

How many times had he said the same thing? Did he not hear her when she talked? "No more surgery," she said. "And no makeup. This is who I am."

"At least think about it. You know it would mean a lot to me."

And of course, this is all about you. She didn't say the words out loud. She wasn't that cruel. Practically since she could talk, her father had built the dream of her following in his footsteps. All the beauty pageants, the voice lessons and drama camps, had been part of his plan to turn her into an even bigger celebrity than he was.

"Are you sure you're okay, honey?" he asked. "You sound tired."

Maybe because she'd hardly slept last night, kept awake by memories of the day's events, mingled with flashbacks to the war. In the dark hours of the early morning, it had been hard to differentiate between the two. But she mentioned none of this to her father. He'd freak out and it would only prove what he had been saying for months now—that she was crazy to throw her life away on plants. Not when she had so much talent.

But did she really have talent? She had spent so many years getting by on her good looks. When you were blessed with beauty, people never looked any deeper or expected anything more. Their impression of you stayed on the surface. At least now when she made a discovery, she knew it was because she'd used her brain. "I'll be fine, Dad. It was good talking to you. I'd better go now. I have work to do."

"Goodbye, sweetheart. I love you. Your mom sends her love, too."

"I love you, too, Dad. Talk to you soon." She clicked off the phone and slid it into her pocket, then stared out the window at the distant mountains, the peaks still capped with snow. Maybe when she won the Nobel Prize for her work with medicinal plants, her father would give up his dream of making her a star, though she doubted it.

Knocking on the door of the little trailer startled her. She glanced at the gun, in its holster on the counter by the door, within easy reach if she needed it, then peeled back a corner of the blinds in the window beside the door.

Michael Dance stood on the ground below the steps, eyes shaded by dark sunglasses. He rocked back on his heels and glanced around the campsite, then leaned forward to knock again. She pulled open the door. "Good afternoon," she said.

"Good afternoon to you, too." His smile dazzled. It hit her like a spotlight, or maybe more like a laser beam, warmth blossoming in her chest.

"Come on in." She stepped back to let him pass her.

He stood in the middle of the trailer's one room and looked around—at the compact dinette with the padded bench seats all around that she used as a desk, at the half-size refrigerator and compact stove, microwave and sink, and back to the closed door of the bathroom and the queen-size bed. He nodded in approval. "This is nice. Cozy."

"It serves its purpose." She slid past him, the narrow space forcing them to brush together, the brief contact sending another wash of heat through her. She sat at the dinette, shoved her laptop to one side and motioned to the seat across from her. "Make yourself at home."

He eased his big frame onto the bench. "I didn't mean to interrupt your work," he said, nodding to the laptop.

"I was just compiling the notes I've made so far. And cataloging my specimens, since I don't know when I'll be able to collect more."

"Listen, about yesterday—" he began.

"I'm sorry I went off on you like that," she said. "I was still upset about the sniper and finding that dead man and...and everything. I shouldn't have taken it out on you."

She was touched by how relieved he looked. "I understand," he said. "It was a lot to take in. Most people would be overwhelmed."

"I should have handled it better." After all, she'd had plenty of practice dealing with death and violence in her short time in the military.

"The offer to come with me on patrol is still open," he said.

Relief washed over her. She'd been prepared to beg if she had to, in order to continue her research. "Then, I accept."

"Great." He drummed his fingers on the table and looked around the trailer once more, avoiding her gaze.

"Is there something else?" she asked.

His eyes shifted back to her. "The G-Man— Graham—thinks there's something you're not telling us. About yesterday, when that man was shot."

So much for her acting ability. Or maybe it was just that she was having second thoughts about keeping her secret. What if Mariposa was somehow tied up with whatever was going on out there in the parkland? By not telling about her, was Abby endangering other peoples' lives?

"Before I tell you anything else, answer a few questions for me first," she said.

He sat back, hands flat on the table between them. "All right."

She couldn't look into that intense gaze anymore, so she studied his hands. He had long fingers and neatly trimmed nails, and he wore a silver-and-onyx ring on his right hand. They were masculine, capable hands— she remembered the feel of them at her back yesterday. Reassuring. Protective. "You work for Customs and Immigration, right?"

"US Customs and Border Protection."

"So when you encounter someone who's in this country illegally, your job is to deport them?"

"That's more Simon's territory. He's with ICE— Immigration and Customs Enforcement. They're part of Homeland Security, too. My job is more about protecting our borders, though we work with ICE sometimes. Why?"

She shifted in her seat. How to admit to this man that she'd been lying to him? "I did see someone else yesterday—before the man was shot. There was a woman. She was out collecting plants, too, but for food, not for scientific specimens. She spoke only

Spanish and she had a baby with her. She told me
her name was Mariposa. She was so young—and gorgeous. I wouldn't have stood a chance if I'd competed
in a pageant with her. Here, I have a picture." She
pulled her phone from her pocket and found the photo
she'd snapped of Mariposa. She handed the phone to
him.

"She looks young," he said. "A teenager."

"Maybe," Abby said.

He returned the phone to her. "She trusted you
enough to let you take her picture."

"I didn't ask, I just snapped it in between shots of
the plants I was gathering. She seemed surprised, but
she didn't object."

"We'll run the photo by authorities, but I doubt we'll
find anything," he said. "Still, you never know. Did she
say where she lived? What she was doing out there?"

"No. Like I said, she didn't speak English and I
don't know much Spanish. I gave her a couple of pro-
tein bars and she seemed grateful. She heard the people
who shot that man shouting and she took off. I mean,
she panicked and was running for her life."

"So she knew who they were?"

"That's what I think. Or at least what they were up
to." She touched the back of his hand. "Do you think
she's mixed up in all this somehow? Maybe she's being
held prisoner by these people or something?"

"She's probably one of the workers. These drug operations bring illegals in to work their grow operations
or make meth. They're as good as prisoners, isolated
out here, kept under guard."

"Is that what happened to that man—he tried to
escape?"

"We don't know for sure, but that's a likely scenario."

"No wonder she panicked and ran."

"Did she say anything else?"

"She said the baby was a girl named Angelique. And she showed me where to find some of the plants I was looking for. She seemed very familiar with the plants in the area. I got the impression she was hungry." She blinked back tears, thinking of the beautiful woman and the baby, alone and in danger.

"Maybe we can find her and help her. Even if we send her back to her home, that would be better than the way she's living now."

"I guess so." Better to return to home and family than to live with the threat of danger.

"You competed in beauty pageants?" Michael asked.

Of course he'd picked up on that. Why had she even mentioned it? "Don't sound so shocked. I was Miss Milwaukee my freshman year in college."

"How did a beauty queen end up in Afghanistan?"

"It's a long story."

"I've got time."

She sighed. She could try to blow him off, but he struck her as someone who wouldn't give up questioning her. It was probably a trait that made him good at his job. "I thought it would be a good way to get money for grad school," she said. "My parents thought I was wasting my time with more schooling, so they wouldn't pay. And I didn't expect them to. I was willing to do it on my own."

"So the beauty queen wanted to be a biologist all along," he said.

"I didn't know what I wanted to do," she said. "My undergrad degree is in communications. But I needed to get away from home. My father is a local celebrity. He does sports for the number one news station in the city, plus he does a lot of voice-over work—ads and public service announcements and things. Everybody knows him. He wanted me to follow in his footsteps, but I wanted the chance to prove myself doing something that was just mine. I never thought it would turn out the way it did."

"No one does," he said. "I mean, you couldn't, right? No one would enlist if the first thing that came to mind was dying or being injured."

"My parents were horrified—first with my enlistment, then when I went overseas. When I was injured they freaked out. My mother burst into tears the first time she saw the scar. She still can hardly bear to look at me." She swallowed past the tightness in her throat. "My dad is always trying to fix me. He wants me to have more surgery, to try special makeup. He can't let go of the hope that I'll go into television after all. They think I'm wasting my time trying to be a scientist."

"Do you think it's a waste of time?"

"No. I'm happier doing this—something that's all mine—than I would have been competing with my dad. And I would have been competing, at least subconsciously. This is a chance to prove myself on my own terms. I guess it's what I was looking for in the military all along."

"Funny sometimes, how life has a way of working out."

"If you're talking about fate, I still don't believe in that. Things just happen for no reason."

"Hey, I didn't say anything." He grinned. "Is tomorrow soon enough for us to go out?"

"Go out?" She blushed, and hated that she did so.

"On patrol. You said you wanted to come with me, right?"

On patrol—of course. What was she, some sixteen-year-old expecting the class jock to ask her out on a date? "Oh, yeah. Sure. When can we go?"

"I'll pick you up about eight." He stood, and she rose, also, and followed him to the door. "Thanks for telling me about Mariposa," he said. "We'll try to find her and help her."

"I should have trusted you earlier, but…"

"Yeah, I know. It's hard to trust sometimes."

She followed him out the door, reluctant to say goodbye. Now that she'd confided in him, she felt closer somehow. As if she finally had a friend who really understood her. "What's that on your car?" he asked.

She followed his gaze to the box sitting on the hood of the Toyota Camry. "I don't know. I've never seen it before."

They walked to the car and she started to reach for the box, but he put out his arm to stop her. "Don't touch it yet. Let's take a closer look."

Following his example, she leaned over and read the writing on the outside of the small brown cardboard box. *Abby Stewart* was written in marker in block letters. "I don't see anything that says who it's from," she said.

"So you're not expecting a package from anyone?"

"No." She wrapped her arms across her stomach, fighting back a wave of nausea at the idea that a stranger had walked into her camp and left this.

Michael pulled out his radio. "Let's get Randall and Lotte over to take a look."

"The dog? Do you really think that's necessary?" She eyed the box. It looked both innocent and sinister.

"Better to be safe."

He made the call and Randall said he'd be right over. They retreated to the shade of the trailer's awning to wait. Abby fidgeted, but Michael leaned against the trailer, relaxed. "It's probably nothing," she said. "Maybe we should just open it."

"Let's wait," he said, and she didn't argue.

Randall pulled in beside Michael's Cruiser a few minutes later. He got out of the truck, then released Lotte. She trotted forward, eyes bright, tail waving. Randall showed her the box. "Lotte, *such*," he commanded.

The dog braced her front paws on the bumper of the car and stretched toward the box, ears flattened, tail low. She retreated quickly, whining, and circled the vehicle, clearly agitated. She paced, panting and whining, looking from the box to Randall and back again. "She doesn't look too happy about whatever is in there," Michael said.

"She's not alerting for bombs or explosives," Randall said. "But she doesn't like whatever she's smelling. Lotte, *komm*."

The dog came and lay at Randall's side. Michael took out a knife. "Let's see what we've got."

He picked up the box and balanced it in his hands. "It's heavy," he said. "Maybe three or four pounds." He opened out a blade on the knife and slit the tape along the sides of the box, then set it on the ground. "Better play it safe." He picked up a stick from beside the campsite's picnic table. "Stand back."

Abby retreated a few steps, chewing her lip nervously. They were probably going through all this drama for nothing, but the dog's behavior worried her. Whatever was in that box, it had upset Lotte, who still stared at it, her brow wrinkled.

Michael slid the tip of the stick under the edge of the box lid, and with a jerk, flipped it off. The box tilted to its side, the contents pouring out in a rippling, fluid motion. Lotte barked, and Abby screamed as she stared at the huge rattler, coiled and ready to strike.

Chapter 6

Michael pulled out his service weapon and squeezed off two shots. The rattler writhed and thrashed, then lay still. Lotte barked again and whined. Despite the heat, Abby felt chilled through. She stared at the dead snake, shaken more by the idea that someone had intended it for her than by the snake itself.

A gust of wind rattled the branches of the piñons that surrounded the campsite, and tugged at the awning of the trailer. "It's got to be five feet long." Randall picked up the stick Michael had used to open the box and lifted the snake.

"Careful," Abby said. "They still have venom in them, even when they're dead."

Randall nodded and glanced around. "Think we should bag it for evidence?"

"Photograph it, then bag it and tag it," Michael said. "The box, too. Maybe we can pick up some prints."

"I doubt it," Randall said. He let the snake drop again. It lay coiled in the dust, still menacing despite its lack of life. "Someone goes to all the trouble to box up a snake and leave it as a present, they're probably smart enough to wear gloves."

"Why would someone do this?" Abby asked.

"They're sending a message." Michael's expression was grim. "Warning you off."

"Warning me off what? I haven't done anything."

"You found that dead man and got us involved," Randall said. "We were close enough to something that sniper fired on us. Maybe they're trying to frighten you out of the backcountry altogether, in case you stumble onto anything else."

"I'm frightened, all right." She shuddered. "I could have been killed."

Michael rested a hand on her shoulder. "You might have been scared half to death. And you'd probably be pretty sick for a while," he said. "But the hospitals around here probably carry antivenin, so chances are good you'd have survived. But whoever did this probably doesn't care one way or another. You're a threat to them, so they're threatening back."

"I haven't done anything to anyone," she protested again.

"You witnessed an execution," he said.

She shuddered at the word. But that was what the murder of that man had been. They'd hunted him down and killed him, like predators hunting prey. "But I didn't see anything. I couldn't identify anyone."

"They can't be sure of that."

"But...how did they know my name?" She shook her head, the reality of what had happened refusing to sink in. "I hardly know anyone in the area—no one who would do anything like this."

"It would be easy enough to learn your name," Randall said. "They could look up your car registration, or get it off your camping permit at the park rangers' office. Using your name makes something like this more personal. More threatening."

She shuddered. She felt threatened, all right. And a little sick.

Michael squeezed her shoulder, then dropped his hand. "You can't stay here," he said.

"No, I can't." This time, whoever hated her had left a snake. What would they do next time? "But where can I go?"

"We'll find you a hotel in town," Randall said. "Register you under an assumed name. One of us can stay with you."

"One of you?"

"I'll stay with you," Michael said.

"You don't have to do that." She straightened her shoulders. "I have a weapon, and I know enough to be careful now. I can look after myself." She'd fought so hard to be independent. She couldn't let this faceless stranger or strangers take that from her.

Michael set his mouth in the stubborn line she was beginning to recognize. "Until we determine how big a threat these people are, I'm going to stay with you," he said.

"I don't need a babysitter." She especially didn't need him hovering. Just because he'd saved her life once didn't mean he was responsible for her the rest of her life. Now that the shock of what had happened was starting to fade, she could think more clearly. "Like you said, this was a warning. If someone had really wanted to hurt me, they wouldn't have bothered gift-wrapping the snake—they'd have turned it loose inside the car." She shuddered at the idea.

"I'm not going to give them a chance to get that close again." His dark eyes met hers, their previous warmth replaced by cold determination.

"You might as well give up," Randall said. "He's stubborn."

"Fine," she said. "But I'm not sharing a room with you." Having him that close, that…intimate…would be too much.

"I can get a room next door to yours."

"All right." She'd have to learn to live with that.

Randall pulled out a camera and began taking pictures. "Let me see that box," he said. "Maybe Lotte can pick up a scent trail."

But the dog found nothing. Abby went into the trailer to pack while the two officers collected evidence and disposed of the snake. She came out with a suitcase in one hand, her laptop bag and purse in the other, her backpack on her back. "All right, I'm ready," she said. "But in the morning, can I still go out on patrol with you?"

"If you still want to." He took the suitcase from her.

"I want to. Working is better than sitting around brooding about the fact that someone I don't even know hates me enough to attack me with a snake. Besides, I have a lot of territory to cover and only a few weeks to do it. I can't let a threat from a stranger stop me."

* * *

Michael told himself he shouldn't have been surprised by Abby's toughness. She'd already proved she was a survivor. He glanced at her as they negotiated the winding road that led away from the park. The afternoon sun slanted across her face like a spotlight, glinting on the silver earrings she wore. She definitely looked like a beauty queen, or a movie star. "Can I ask you a personal question?"

She turned toward him, her dark blue eyes wary. "You can ask. I don't promise I'll answer."

He focused on the road again. "What happened after you came back to the States—after you were wounded?" he asked. "I mean, how long were you in the hospital? Did you have any kind of rehab, or did they just send you home?"

"I went to a hospital in Germany first. They did surgery there to remove shrapnel, and the surgeons saved my eye. They had to repair my broken cheek." She touched the scar. "I have a titanium plate holding everything together."

He winced. "Sounds brutal."

"I guess it was, but I was in a fog a lot of the time— partly from the drugs, partly from the trauma itself."

"I think that's a protective mechanism the mind has—blocking out trauma that way." In his PJ training, he'd been taught that the wounded seldom remembered what happened on the helicopters.

"I guess, but it bothers me sometimes that I can't remember," she said. "After I was transferred back to the States, to a hospital in Milwaukee, people came to see me and I have no memory of it. And yet the silliest things stay with me."

"Like what?"

"Like I remember I asked my mom to bring me some clothes to wear besides the hospital gown—sweats and things like that. She brought me this yellow blouse I'd always hated. I yelled at her for bringing it and she started to cry. My dad yelled at me for hurting her feelings and then *I* started to cry." She shook her head. "It was just so stupid—what did it matter what color the blouse was?"

"I don't know if it's so stupid," he said. "It makes sense to me. There were so many things happening to you that you couldn't control. The clothes you wore were one little thing you could control. And the medications, not to mention the brain injury, probably made it more difficult to manage your emotions. Your doctors should have told your parents that."

"They probably did. But my mom and dad's way of coping with this whole mess was to pretend nothing was wrong. We'd have these surreal conversations, where Mom would talk about boys I used to date who would be so glad to see me again, and Dad would tell me I should try out for a summer job with the community theater group. After a while, I couldn't stand it anymore and I'd say something horrible, like no one wanted a freak on stage. Then Mom would start to cry again. It was awful."

His hands tightened on the steering wheel. "You're not a freak, you know."

"I know. But I'm not who I was. I'm still coming to terms with that. I don't even want that old life anymore—I'm not sure I ever wanted it. But I'm still figuring out what my new life will look like." She shifted in the seat. "But right now, I'm more focused on figuring out where I'm going to be staying tonight."

"Carmen made reservations at a motel on the other side of town. We figured the farther from the park, the better."

The motel turned out to be one of those old-fashioned lodges with rooms lined up in two low-slung wings on either side of the A-frame lobby. "We have reservations for Ricky and Lucy," Michael told the desk clerk, a fleshy older man with skin the color of raw dough.

He handed over the keys and accepted Michael's credit card, then they drove down to a room on the end and parked. "Ricky and Lucy?" Abby asked. "Why those names?"

"Ricky and Lucy Ricardo? From *I Love Lucy*. I love those old shows. When I had to come up with a couple's names, that popped into my head."

His reply made her feel a little off balance—as if he really was a mind reader. "I love those old shows, too," she said. "When I was in the hospital, I watched a lot of them." Lucille Ball had been a beauty queen who wasn't afraid to make a fool of herself to get a laugh. Watching her had given Abby hope; maybe she could be more than a pretty face herself. But how could Michael know that?

He unlocked the door to the room next to the one on the end and did a quick tour of the space, then looked into the bathroom and checked out the closet. "What are you searching for?" she asked.

"Any sign that anyone's been here ahead of us."

"Why would they have been?"

"Someone might have heard about our plans to stay here. It's not likely, but it pays to be careful."

He unlocked the door to the adjoining room on the end of this wing. "Just to make it easier to reach each other in an emergency," he explained. "You can stay in this room. I'll take the one next door."

His room was a copy of hers, right down to the blue-and-green quilted spread and the bottle of water on the dresser. "What now?" she asked.

"Want to order pizza?"

She almost laughed. After everything that had happened today, pizza seemed so ordinary. So safe. "That sounds like a good idea."

He pulled out his phone. "What do you like?"

"Anything but anchovies and onions."

He made a face. "Right."

She returned to her room and arranged her few things on the bed and table, then combed her hair and splashed water on her face. She hadn't bothered to do more than apply sunscreen this morning and it showed, her brows and lashes pale and unadorned. She thought about putting on makeup, but she didn't want Michael to get the wrong idea. Circumstances had thrown them together, but it wasn't as if they were dating or anything.

If she was ready to be in a relationship, he wouldn't be her first choice. She was glad he was with her now, and that men like him were hunting down whoever had killed the man in the desert, but he was too intense. Too protective. All his talk of fate and seeing meaning in random happenings unsettled her.

She booted up her laptop and tried to focus on the notes she'd made about desert parsley and its habitat. But that only made her think of Mariposa. She pulled out her phone and studied the picture of the beautiful young woman. Where was she right now? Were she and Angelique safe?

When Michael knocked on the door between their rooms and announced that the pizza had arrived, she gratefully shut down the computer and joined him in his room. The smell of spicy pepperoni and sausage, sauce and cheese made her a little dizzy, and she realized she was starving. "This was a great idea," she said, helping herself to a slice.

"Just what the doctor ordered." He filled his own plate and sat across from her at the little table in front of the window. He'd drawn the drapes, shutting out the setting sun, and turned on the too-dim lamp behind him. The interior felt cool and cozy.

"Speaking of doctors," she said, "you seem to know a lot about medicine. Did you consider becoming a doctor?"

"Early on, I thought about it. That's why I signed up for the PJs. I thought I wanted a career in trauma medicine. I pictured excitement and the adrenaline rush and saving people's lives." He fell silent and picked a slice of pepperoni off his pizza.

"What is it?" she asked. "Is something wrong?"

"They don't tell you that you lose more than you save." He looked into her eyes. "You were my first save—that's another reason I remember you."

She wanted to look away from the intensity of his gaze, but she couldn't. This man had saved her life; she couldn't turn away from him. "I wish I remembered you," she said. If she did, would she feel that connection between them that he seemed to feel?

He shrugged his shoulders, as if shrugging off bad memories. "Anyway, by the time my tour was up, I'd decided I wasn't cut out for that line of work. I bummed around for a few months, not sure what I wanted to do. After the constant adrenaline rush of the war, civilian life was an adjustment. When my uncle suggested border patrol, I figured I'd give it a shot."

"Do you like it?"

"I like working outdoors, doing something different all the time. I'm not so crazy about the bureaucracy. And sometimes I question whether I'm really doing much good."

"You saved me from that snake." She smiled, letting him know she was teasing.

"If I hadn't gotten to it, Randall would have shot it." He took another bite of pizza and chewed, then swallowed. "Or you'd have killed it yourself. You're tough."

The words made her feel lighter—taller. She smiled. "You couldn't give me a better compliment."

"Is that all it takes?" He grinned, his teeth very white against his olive skin. "Maybe I'll try that line out on other women. I've been doing it all wrong, telling them they were pretty. Not that you aren't— pretty, that is."

Her smile faded. "I heard how pretty I was my whole life. And then I woke up and that was gone. At least something like toughness can't be taken away so easily."

"You talk as though you're horribly disfigured. It's one scar. With your hair down or in profile, it isn't even visible."

"I know it's there, and that affects the way I think about it. I can't help it. I'm not complaining, it's just my reality now."

"Well, just so you know, I think you're beautiful."

"You just admitted you say that to all the girls."

He was about to reply when his phone rang. He set down his slice of pizza and answered it. "Dance."

"Hey, you and Abby get settled in?" Randall's voice was hearty, audible from where she sat.

"We're fine. What's up?"

"I took that snake by the park rangers' office and let them have a look at it," he said. "One of the guys there is a wildlife biologist. He told me something interesting about it."

"Hang on a minute, I'm going to put you on speaker." Michael glanced at Abby. "It's Randall. He found out something about your snake."

"It's not my snake." She made a face.

"Okay, go ahead," Michael told Randall.

"The snake you killed was a western diamondback," Randall said. "A common desert species, one responsible for most of the deaths from rattlesnake bites in the United States and Mexico."

Michael's eyes met hers across the table. She hugged her arms around herself, her appetite gone. "Why is that so interesting?" he asked.

"They don't have diamondbacks at this elevation," Randall said. "They don't have them at any elevation in Colorado. The only rattlesnakes around her are prairie rattlers—smaller and not as venomous as the diamondback. Whoever boxed up that fellow imported him from somewhere south or west of here."

Michael frowned. "Could you buy something like that at a pet store—you know, one that sells pythons and tarantulas and stuff?"

"It's against the law to sell venomous snakes. No,

somebody caught this one in the wild and was keeping it around for special purposes."

"That's sick," Abby said.

"I heard about a drug dealer in Tucson who kept his stash in an aquarium with a venomous snake," Randall said. "It discouraged theft."

Michael sat back in his chair, legs stretched out in front of him. "So what do you make of this?"

"It tells us something about the people we're after," Randall said.

"Yeah, they're twisted."

"Twisted, and they won't stop at anything to protect what's theirs—or to make a point."

"Yeah, well, thanks for the information. I'll talk to you later."

"I'll let you know if anything new develops."

"Yeah. Do that." He hung up the phone and stuffed it back into the pouch on his utility belt.

"What point are they making with me?" Abby asked.

"You must have gotten way too close to something they want very much to hide," he said. "First the sniper, then the snake."

"What are we going to do about it?" She wasn't going to sit here, waiting to be a target.

"Tomorrow, I want to go back out to where we found the body and look around some more."

"I want to come with you."

He shook his head. "I know I said you could go on patrol with me, but this probably isn't safe."

"I've been in unsafe situations before. I want to go. I want to see if we can help Mariposa and her baby."

He paused, considering.

"You said I was tough," she said. "I won't hold you back or get in the way. And if these people are as dangerous as they seem, you shouldn't be out there alone. I can watch your back."

"All right. If I told you no, you'd probably follow me anyway."

"I probably would."

"At least this way I can keep you close, and maybe a little safer."

She started to protest that she didn't need him to protect her, but the words died in her throat. So far, she had needed him. The idea wasn't as disturbing now as it had been earlier. Maybe leaning on someone for help wasn't so bad—if it was the right someone.

Chapter 7

Belted into the passenger seat of Michael's Cruiser, Abby couldn't shake the feeling that she was headed out on a mission, just like the missions in Afghanistan. The darkness here was like the darkness over there, deepest black, unsullied by the lights of houses or businesses. The nearest city, Montrose, was a dim glow on the horizon.

She leaned forward, straining against the seat belt, trying to see farther into the blackness. Her heart pounded and her nerves twitched with the same jumpy anticipation that had defined every trip she'd made off base during the war. They'd often left early in the morning, to take advantage of the cover of darkness. But their enemies had favored darkness, too, which had made every expedition fraught with danger.

The Cruiser's headlights cut narrow cones into the

blackness, enough to illuminate the scraggly trees, jutting rocks and grasses of the park's backcountry. Once, a pair of silvery eyes looked back at them, and as they drew closer, a coyote stared at them, frozen against a backdrop of reddish rocks.

She shivered and pulled her jacket more tightly around her. Even in summer, it was chilly at this altitude without the sun's warmth.

"You okay?" Michael asked.

"I'm fine." She slipped her hand into her pocket and rubbed her fingers across the little ceramic rabbit. Maybe it was silly for a grown woman to put faith in a good-luck charm, but the rabbit had gotten her through a lot of tough times since her injury. She wasn't ready to give up on it yet.

Michael leaned forward and switched the Cruiser's heat to high. "Tell me more about the research you're doing," he said. "What happens after you gather all these plants and leave here?"

"I'll take them to the lab and experiment with distilling certain compounds from them, and show the effect of those compounds on cells. For instance, if something inhibits cell mutation, it could help fight cancer, or if a substance encourages nerve cells to regenerate, or nerves to build new pathways, it could combat diseases like Parkinson's. I'll have to narrow my research to a single possibility for now, but the prospects for the future are endless."

"That's exciting, that you could be helping so many people. I'd like to do something like that."

She didn't miss the regret in his voice. "You're protecting people from danger," she said. "Making the park safer for visitors, trying to capture people who are hurting others."

"In theory I'm doing those things," he said. "But so far I haven't seen that anything I've done has directly made anyone's life better."

"Except mine," she said. "I wouldn't be here today if it wasn't for you."

He reached across the seat and took her hand and squeezed it. "Yeah. I'm glad about that."

She held his hand for a moment, letting the warmth and reassurance of his touch seep into her. But she couldn't let sentiment overwhelm common sense. Michael Dance was a good guy, but she scarcely knew him. He wasn't a knight in shining armor, and she definitely wasn't a princess who needed rescuing. She pulled away and focused her gaze out the windshield, on the faint band of gray on the horizon. "The sun will be up soon," she said.

If her sudden coolness caught him off guard, he didn't show it. "Check the GPS," he said. "We should be getting close."

She leaned over to glance at the dash-mounted GPS unit. "Looks like maybe another two miles."

"I'm going to cut the lights," he said. "Just in case anyone's watching." He switched off the headlights, plunging them into a disorienting void. She blinked, then he pressed a button and a dim glow illuminated the few inches of ground in front of the Cruiser's bumper. "Sneak lights," he said. "Mounted under the bumper."

She laughed nervously. "Good name."

The Cruiser crawled across the landscape. They'd left the road and followed what was little more than an animal trail—maybe even the same path Abby had followed when she was searching for specimens for her research.

Suddenly, Michael slammed on the brakes. She lurched forward against the shoulder harness. "What's wrong?" she whispered.

"I saw something out there. Movement." He waited a moment and she squinted, trying to make out anything. Though the eastern sky showed a faint blush of pink, it was impossible to make out details in the dim light. "Over there." He pointed up ahead and to the left. He eased his foot off the brake and angled the Cruiser in that direction, and turned on the headlights again. An animal ran in front of the vehicle, and then another.

"Coyotes," she said, and breathed a sigh of relief.

"They're feeding on something." His expression darkened. "We'd better check it out."

"Why? I mean, it's just a bunch of coyotes."

"They're scavengers. They eat whatever they find. For that many of them to be in one place, it must be something good-size."

Her stomach lurched and she swallowed past the sudden bitter taste in her mouth. "Like a body?"

He stopped the vehicle again and turned to her. "I have to check this out, but you can stay in the truck."

"Do you think it's another illegal, like the man we found day before yesterday?" she asked.

"It may not even be a person." The Cruiser rolled forward again.

"But you think it might be."

"It could be. But maybe not an illegal."

"Who, then?"

"A woman went missing in the park a few days ago.

At least, she's missing and they found her car abandoned at one of the overlooks. She's a news anchor from a station in Denver—Lauren Starling."

The name sounded vaguely familiar, but Abby couldn't put a face with it. "What would she be doing way out here?" She looked toward the spot ahead where one lone coyote stood guard, his eyes glittering in the Cruiser's headlights.

"She might have stumbled into something she shouldn't have," he said.

The way Abby herself almost had. "I hope not," she said.

"She also might not be connected to this case at all," Michael said. "Some people see the park as a good place to take their own life."

"Suicide? But why in a park?"

"Maybe they think it will be easier on their families, not having to clean up the mess." He braked again, and the lone coyote trotted off. In the glow of the headlights she could make out a brown shape on the ground. There was definitely something there. Her stomach roiled again, and she gritted her teeth against a wave of nausea.

Michael shifted into Park and unfastened his seat belt. "Stay here," he said.

He didn't have to tell her twice. As soon as he opened the door she caught the scent of decay. Of death. She looked away, out the side window, but felt her gaze pulled back to him as he made his way to the formless shape on the ground. He stepped cautiously, his shoulders tensed, one hand on the weapon at his side.

Then he stopped and relaxed. He crouched down

and studied the scene a moment longer, then stood and hurried back to the Cruiser. "It's a deer," he said. "There's not enough left to tell how it died. It could have been poachers, or maybe the coyotes managed to separate one from the herd."

She sagged against the seat, weak with relief. "A deer," she repeated. "I was so afraid…"

"I should have just checked it out and not said anything to upset you." He put the Cruiser into gear and turned back toward the track they'd been following.

"I'd have been more upset if you'd clammed up and refused to tell me anything," she said.

"I figured I could count on you to keep a cool head," he said. "I'm not sure how many other civilians would hold it together as well as you have, considering all that has happened."

Since coming to the park she'd stumbled over a dead body and been shot at by a sniper and threatened with a deadly rattlesnake. "I'm not exactly sleeping like a baby, but I'm okay," she said. "Maybe it's similar to being in battle—you do what you have to do at the time, then fall apart later."

He glanced at her. "I hope you don't fall apart."

"Maybe I'm stronger now." Despite a few flashbacks, she did feel stronger. Maybe the man beside her even had something to do with that.

"Give me the GPS coordinates on this spot." He took a small notebook from his shirt pocket.

She read off the coordinates. "Why do you need them?"

He shrugged. "You never know when someone might want to check this out. Maybe we suddenly have a rash of poaching and we need to document it."

"And to think I always pictured national parks as such peaceful, safe places."

"For most people, they are."

She stared out the windshield, at the expanding glow on the horizon. The gray light allowed her to make out more details in the landscape now—the silhouettes of trees and the distant mountains. "We're only a mile or so from the place where the sniper ambushed us," she said.

"I'm going to cut the lights again," he said. "It's getting light enough to see to drive, and if someone's watching, they'll have a harder time spotting us."

She watched the GPS as they crawled forward again. After a few more minutes, she held up her hand. "This is where I parked to hike into the area where we found the body, and where I saw Mariposa."

"And where the sniper fired at us." He put the Cruiser into four-wheel drive and turned off the faint track. "We'll drive a little farther into the backcountry, then get out and have a look around."

She pulled the zipper of her jacket up higher. "What exactly are we looking for?"

"Anything that looks out of place. They'll probably have used camouflage, but a building is tough to conceal. Look for a grouping of trees or rocks that stand out from the rest. Or they could set up a compound in a gully or canyon, where it's harder to detect." He tapped the console between them. "In here is a topo map. I highlighted some places they might try to conceal an operation. There's a Mini Maglite in there, too."

She found the map and light and when he stopped the vehicle she spread the heavy plastic-coated map between them. Yellow highlighter circled a box canyon, a dry wash and a small woodland. She studied the lines indicating elevation. "This wash is closest," she said, pointing to the area he'd circled. "And there's a seasonal creek nearby. This time of year, it will still have water from snowmelt. If I was going to set up a compound out here, that's what I'd choose."

"Let's give it a look, then."

She read out the GPS coordinates, and he turned the Cruiser toward them. "What do we do if we find something?" she asked.

"We call for backup. There's no sense going in alone when we don't even know how many people we're up against. This morning, we're just out sightseeing."

"I'm glad to hear it."

"But you were prepared to go in with just me?" He glanced at her, though she couldn't read his expression in the shadowed interior of the vehicle.

"I guess I trust your judgment," she said. "Is that a mistake?" After all, he didn't strike her as reckless. And he'd saved her life before—she couldn't imagine he'd be eager to throw it away now.

"You can trust me," he said. "Just like I trust you."

"Trust me how?"

"If we do get in a tight spot, I trust you to have my back."

"Of course." The words were casual, but the feeling in her chest was anything but lighthearted. Even the soldiers she'd worked with in Afghanistan weren't all so willing to rely on a woman for help. Michael's high opinion of her meant more than she was ready to say.

"What's that?" He hit the brake and leaned forward, gripping the steering wheel.

"What's what?" She saw nothing in the grayness ahead.

"I thought I saw a light." He switched off the sneak lights and the interior instrument lights. She stared out the windshield at a landscape of gray smudges, backlit by the first rays of the rising sun to their left. But she didn't see the light that had made him stop.

Michael opened the car door. "We better go in on foot," he said. "Stay close to me."

She slipped on her backpack and put one hand to the reassuring heft of the gun at her side. She was back on patrol again, minus the heavier pack and body armor. Even after so much time, the absence of that familiar weight made her feel vulnerable. Exposed.

She shut the door of the Cruiser without making a sound. But there was no way to move across the rugged ground without the occasional scrape of a shoe on rock, or the snapping of a twig that sounded as loud as a slamming door to her ears. Every sense felt heightened—sounds louder, sights clearer, the dawn breeze on her cheeks and the backs of her hands colder. She sniffed the air and grabbed Michael's arm. "Stop."

He halted. "What is it?"

"Do you smell that?"

He inhaled sharply through his nose. "Wood smoke."

"A campfire," she whispered. "I think we're getting very close."

"Which direction do you think it's coming from?"

She considered the question, then pointed ahead and to the right. "Over there."

They moved forward silently, slowly. The sky changed from gray to dusky pink to pale blue. The smell of wood smoke grew stronger, too, and with it came the scent of food—corn, maybe, or baking bread. Soon they were close enough to hear muffled voices, and the scrape of cutlery and clink of glassware.

Michael dropped to his belly and indicated she should do the same. They crawled on their stomachs, dragging themselves forward on elbows. She winced as a sharp rock dug into her forearm. At least here they didn't have to worry about land mines. Probably. She wished she hadn't thought of mines. Someone who'd employ a sniper, and maybe had access to a ghillie suit and military-grade weapons, might decide to use land mines, too.

She started to suggest as much to Michael when they moved around a clump of bushes and suddenly the whole camp was laid out in front of them, tucked into a wash, the depression deep enough so that the surrounding stunted piñons provided cover. Whoever had built the compound had piled brush between the trees to act as a privacy fence. They'd even pulled camouflage netting over the tops of the buildings, making the compound more difficult to detect from the air.

The camp itself wasn't impressive—four old camping trailers in a semicircle around a campfire ring and three warped wooden picnic tables. A brown tarp stretched between poles formed a crude shelter over the tables, where a dozen men and women sat, eating a breakfast of tortillas and beans.

A woman worked at the fire, baking more tortillas on a piece of tin balanced over the coals. When she turned to deliver a fresh batch of the flatbreads to another woman, Abby pinched Michael's arm. "That's Mariposa," she said. She wore the same plaid shawl she'd had on the other day, the baby wrapped securely in its folds.

Michael rose to squat on his heels and indicated they should leave. Reluctantly, she turned to go. She would have liked to talk to Mariposa again, to make sure she was all right. But staying here wasn't safe.

But as they prepared to emerge from the screen of bushes into more open ground, headlights suddenly cut through the darkness. Michael jerked her back into the underbrush and they crouched there, breathing hard and watching a truck make its way toward them.

The truck was bigger than a pickup, with a canvas-covered bed, similar to ones sometimes used by the military to transport troops. It lumbered into camp and stopped not far from the picnic tables. Abby and Michael crept to the edge of the brush once more and watched as two men, carrying semiautomatic rifles, climbed out and spoke to the men and women around the table in Spanish. But they were too far away to make out exactly what they were saying.

Suddenly, the camp sprang to life. The two men with rifles began directing the others to load the picnic tables into the back of the truck. A second truck arrived, and then a third. One man, who wore a white shirt and white straw cowboy hat, and who seemed to be in charge, picked up a bucket and thrust it at Mariposa. She spoke to him, clearly agitated, but he shoved the bucket into her hand and gave her a push. She turned and started walked toward the edge of the compound.

"He told her to get some water and put out the fire," Michael whispered. "They're ordering everyone to load the trucks and prepare to leave."

"I'm going around to the creek to see if I can talk to her and find out more."

Before he could stop her, she was on her feet, headed for the little creek that gurgled a few dozen yards from the camp. She moved cautiously, keeping the screen of brush between her and the activity in the camp. By the time she reached the water, Mariposa was already there, squatting on the bank and dipping the bucket in the shallows.

"Mariposa!" Abby called softly.

The woman looked up, startled. She dropped the bucket and it rolled away, under some bushes.

"Don't run. It's me." Abby moved closer, so the other woman could see her clearly.

Mariposa's expression changed to one of alarm. She spoke softly in rapid Spanish. The only word Abby could make out was *peligroso*—dangerous.

"I want to help you." Why couldn't Abby remember the word for help? She slipped off her pack and started looking for her phone. If she could get a signal out here, she could use a translator on the web to get her message across.

The shouting from camp grew louder. Mariposa glanced over her shoulder, then stood, the bucket abandoned in the creek.

Abby gave up the search for her phone. She dropped the pack and stood, also. "Come with me." She held out her hand. "I can help you."

Mariposa shook her head and started to back away. "No," she said—a word whose meaning was the same in Spanish and English.

"Por favor," Abby said. "Please."

Mariposa looked back toward camp. The shouting

sounded closer now. She clutched the baby to her, and Abby was sure she was about to turn and run.

But instead, she untied the shawl and thrust it— and the baby—into Abby's arms. Then she whirled and fled, back toward camp.

Abby stared, stunned, the unfamiliar weight and warmth of the infant in her hands. The child stirred and whimpered, and Abby felt a primal response, a fierce desire to keep this tiny, helpless life safe. She cradled the child to her chest and turned to go back to Michael.

She collided with him just as she turned. For a second they were frozen, his arms steadying her, the baby cradled between them. She fought the instinct to lean into him, to draw strength and comfort from his solid presence. "What happened?" he asked.

"I saw Mariposa. I talked to her. But we couldn't understand each other. I don't know enough Spanish and she doesn't speak English. I think she told me it was dangerous for me to be here."

"She's right. We have to get out of here. They brought another truck in and they're breaking down the camp. We have to get back to the Cruiser and radio for help." He looked down at the bundle in her arms. "What is that?"

"This is Mariposa's baby." She folded back the shawl to reveal the infant's face. The child stared up at them with solemn brown eyes. "Angelique. Mariposa handed her to me, then she ran away. I think she wanted me to keep her safe."

"Come on, we've got to go." He put his arm around her and urged her forward.

They only traveled a few yards before they spotted

the line of men and trucks in between them and the Cruiser. Michael swore under his breath. "We'd better risk a call for backup," he said. Huddled in the meager cover at the edge of the woods, he took out first his radio, then his cell. He swore under his breath. "The radio doesn't work this far out, and my phone can't get a signal," he said. "Try yours."

Abby felt sick to her stomach. "My phone is in my pack, back there by the stream. I was so busy with the baby…"

"I'll get it." He started toward the creek once more, but just then a man stepped out in front of him and leveled a rifle at them. He wore a white shirt, a white hat and a menacing expression.

"You're in the wrong place, amigo," he said.

Chapter 8

"Abby, run!" Michael shouted.

The last thing she wanted to do was abandon him to the man with the gun, but instinct compelled her to protect the child in her arms. Propelled by the urgency in Michael's voice, she turned and fled, running hunched over to shield the baby, darting and weaving, waiting for the gunshots she was sure would follow. She had no idea where she was headed, but every instinct told her she had to put as much distance as possible between herself and the camp. She could hide in the underbrush and wait until her pursuers were gone.

As for Michael, she prayed he'd find some way to escape. If she could think of any way to come back and help him without endangering the baby, she would.

She stumbled over rocks and brush, her lungs burning. The baby never made a sound. In her short life was she already so familiar with fear and flight? She ran until she was gasping for breath, fighting a painful stitch in her side. The infant was heavier than she looked. Abby stumbled and feared she might drop the child. She'd have to stop and rest for a moment. She needed to get her bearings and figure out her next move.

She huddled behind a pile of rocks, letting her breathing return to normal and her pounding heart slow its frantic racing. The rocks still held the chill of the evening, and she pressed her back against a boulder, letting the coolness seep into her and dry her sweat. She strained to hear any hint of approaching danger. She hadn't heard any gunshots from the camp, but would she have even noticed in her panic to escape?

She peered out from behind the rocks. No one appeared to be coming after her. She couldn't even make out the camp from this distance, but she could see the trucks on the edge of the wash and the bustle of activity around them. If only she had a pair of binoculars.

She needed to get to the truck. Michael probably had supplies and tools in there, maybe even a spare radio. If she could figure out how to start the vehicle, she could drive back to park headquarters and summon help.

She tried to orient herself. The rising sun had been on their left when they'd parked, and they'd walked straight ahead—south. She squinted in the direction she thought the Cruiser should be, but saw nothing. Michael had made a point of parking amid a grove of trees. She'd just have to set out walking in that direction and hope her instincts were right.

Cautiously, she moved out of her hiding place. Now that the sun was fully up, she felt exposed and more vulnerable than ever. But she'd seen no signs of pursuit. And no signs of Michael. Had the man in the white hat shot him and left his body beside the creek?

She pushed the thought away. She had to focus on Angelique now. She folded back the blanket and studied the child, who stared up at her with solemn brown eyes. She stroked the baby's soft cheek with her little finger and Angelique grasped it, holding on tightly. A wave of emotion rose up from deep inside Abby—a fierce protectiveness, longing and love. She would do whatever she had to in order to keep this child safe.

Keeping to the shelter of rocks and trees, she started moving north, on a trajectory she hoped would take her to the parked Cruiser but be well out of the way of the men at the camp. Every few yards she looked back toward the camp, but no one sounded an alarm that they had noticed her.

When she was confident she was well out of sight and sound of the camp, she increased her pace to a ragged trot over the rough ground. With the sun up it was getting warmer, and she wished she'd had some way to collect water back at the creek. If she didn't find the truck, she and Angelique were going to be in trouble.

She stopped to rest a moment and look around. Still no sign of the truck. She should have reached it by now. She couldn't see the camp, either, which made her uneasy. She wanted to be away from it, but she didn't want to accidentally stumble back onto it. She'd read that people who wandered off marked trails in the wilderness tended to walk in circles. Without a map or compass to guide her, she might be doing the same.

A movement somewhere to her right made her freeze. Slowly, she turned her head. Yes, there it was again, a subtle shifting of the brush. A shadow where a shadow shouldn't be. She wrapped her hand around the grip of the Sig Sauer and worked on controlling her breathing. A deep breath in...let it out slowly. She wouldn't shoot unless she had to, but if whoever was out there came too close... She clutched the baby tightly and slid the gun from the holster.

"Abby! Abby, it's me!"

She leaned forward and stared at the man loping toward her. Michael covered the distance quickly, with no sign of injury. She took a few steps toward him, only her grip on the pistol and the baby in her arms keeping her from greeting him with a hug. "How did you get away?" she asked when he stopped beside her.

He bent over, a rifle clutched in both hands, gasping for breath. A moment passed before he could speak, and in that moment she searched for any sign of injury, but he seemed whole and healthy.

He straightened. "When I shouted at you, it distracted the guy enough I was able to kick the gun out of his hands. We struggled for a bit, but I got away."

She nodded to the weapon he was holding. "With the gun."

He hefted the weapon. "He's probably not very happy about that, but I didn't give him any choice."

She glanced over his shoulder at the empty desert. "Are they coming after us?"

"I don't think so," he said. "Not right now anyway.

They seemed pretty anxious to clear out." He nodded to the bundle in her arms. "How's the baby?"

"Good. She's very quiet. I'm not sure if that's a good thing or not." She adjusted the blanket to shield Angelique from the sun. "I was trying to get back to the Cruiser," she said.

"Good idea. But first, I want to get a closer look at their trucks before they leave." He turned back toward the camp.

"Wait." She grabbed his arm. "You can't go back there."

"I want to get pictures before they leave—of the trucks and the people." He pulled his phone from his utility belt. "I can't get a signal, but the camera still works."

"It's too dangerous," she said.

"They won't expect me to come back. You can wait here with the baby."

"No, I'm coming with you." The two of them together, both armed, seemed a better idea than splitting up and forming separate targets. He might think no one was after them, but how could he be sure?

He didn't argue. "We'll follow the creek back to the camp," he said. "The trees will provide cover. We'll keep low and out of sight and just watch and take photographs."

"All right." She didn't like the plan, but she liked being left alone out there less.

They intersected with the creek farther up the wash and followed it down toward the camp. Soon, the slamming of vehicle doors and murmur of voices in Spanish filled the air. Michael stopped about a hundred yards from all the activity and crouched down. She huddled behind him, peering over his shoulder.

The men with guns stood guard as the other men and women filed into the trailers. Abby counted six people filing into one of the campers, which was smaller even than the one she'd rented for the summer. When all the people were inside, the guard reached up and locked the door, then pocketed the key.

"What are they doing?" she whispered, her lips against Michael's ear.

"I think the trucks are going to tow the trailers out of here."

Before he had even finished speaking, one of the trucks had backed up to the trailer and begun the process of hooking on to the camper. Michael pulled out his camera and snapped picture after picture. Abby searched the camp for any sign of Mariposa, but couldn't find her. Was she already locked into one of the crowded trailers?

The man in the white shirt and hat who'd confronted them by the creek stood to one side. He'd found another rifle and held it across his chest, barking orders at the others. Within a quarter of an hour, the camp was clear. The man in the white shirt surveyed the area and seemed satisfied. He climbed into the vehicle at the front of the line and the trucks—four of them now, each with a trailer in tow—pulled away from the campsite. Two set out toward the main road, while the other two started cross-country.

When the vehicles were too far away for anyone to see them, Michael crawled out of their hiding place and stood to get a better look. "Where are they going?" Abby asked.

"There are a lot of old ranch roads and two-tracks cutting across this property. They're probably taking a roundabout way to the highway. My guess is the other two will turn off at some point, too. They won't want to risk being seen on the main park road by one of the park rangers or one of our team."

"What do we do now?" she asked.

"I'd like to get some people out here to comb this place for evidence."

"Are they going to find anything?" Except for an area bare of vegetation where the fire and picnic tables had been, there was little sign of the compound that had been here only an hour before. Even the rocks that had been used to make the fire ring had been cleaned and scattered, the footprints of those who had been here smoothed over with a branch of juniper.

"You never know." He stared at his phone. "Still no signal."

"Maybe mine will work," she said. "Now that they're gone, I can retrieve my pack."

"Good idea. Where is it?"

"Back this way." She led the way along the creek to the spot where she'd talked to Mariposa. She scanned the creek bank. "I don't see it," she said. "I could have sworn it was right in here."

"It was blue, right?"

She nodded. "Bright blue. It shouldn't be hard to spot." She walked along the bank, looking into the water and underbrush, even though she knew she had dropped it in the open. He searched, also.

"One of them must have seen it and taken it," he said. "What was in there besides your phone and the GPS?"

"Water, food, a first-aid kit. A space blanket, another

pair of socks, a whistle, compass and fire starter." She ticked off the items in a standard backcountry emergency list—all things they could have used right now.

"They didn't leave anything behind," he said, looking around.

"Except this." She reached under a bush and started to pull out the metal bucket Mariposa had carried to the creek. "Though I don't see what good it's going to do us."

"Don't touch it." His hand on her arm stopped her and he moved up beside her. "We might get good prints off it that could help us identify some of the people involved."

"What should we do with it?" She stepped back.

"Leave it here. We'll want to get a team in here to go over the place—they can pick it up then." He tied his bandanna to a nearby tree branch to mark the spot.

"We just have to find our way back to headquarters," she said. "And find our way here again after that."

He straightened and looked around them, as if studying the terrain—the low hills and more distant mountains. "Which way is the canyon from here?" he asked. "Black Canyon." If they could find the canyon, they'd find the road that led to the headquarters.

"I don't know." She turned slowly in a circle, looking around them. "That's the thing about this place. The canyon isn't something you see from ground level. You have to be right up on it before you know it's there."

"What do we do now?" she asked.

"We can try to find the truck."

Her expression lightened. "I do know which direction the truck was in. All we have to do is walk right through there." She pointed to a cut in the fringe of trees along the edge of the wash, then set off at a brisk pace, Michael close behind her.

After twenty minutes of walking and backtracking, they didn't find the Cruiser. But they did find the tracks where it had been parked, and the tracks of the other vehicles that had passed. "What happened?" she asked.

"They stole it," he said. "Trucks don't just vanish, so one of them must be driving it."

"If they found the truck, they must know we're still out here," she said.

He nodded, his expression grim. "They'll probably send someone back to find us. We need to get out of here before that happens." He pulled out his phone and tried it, but it continued to show no signal. "We need higher ground." He looked around and spotted a low hill. "Up there."

She cradled Angelique in her arms as she climbed up the hill, praying that someone didn't have her in the sights of a rifle's scope as she climbed. She felt too exposed up here on the side of this hill. Anyone who looked in this direction would be able to spot them. She picked up her pace, anxious to find cover once more.

At the top of the rise, she ducked behind a low piñon and struggled to catch her breath. Michael stood a little ways from her, holding up his phone. "I think this is going to work," he said. "I'm getting a signal." He started walking backward, watching the screen, the phone in one hand, the radio in the other. "Almost there."

And then he was gone, dropping over the edge, a cascade of falling rocks and a single startled cry the only indication he had ever been there.

Chapter 9

Michael scrabbled for a hold on the crumbling shale that continued to give way beneath his feet and slip from his hands. He dropped the phone and the radio—the radio somersaulting into the air and out of sight, the phone bouncing like a thrown rock as it, too, disappeared into the canyon. He kicked out his feet and found only air, and an image of his body, broken and bleeding, at the bottom of the gully flashed through his mind.

Frantic, he hurled himself toward a ragged piñon that jutted from the canyon wall. His fingers grasped the prickly needles, and he swung his other hand up to grip a branch. The tree bent and creaked, but held.

He hung there for a long moment, struggling to breathe and to slow the pounding of his heart. He found a toehold for one foot in the rock below and supported his weight partially on one leg, with the other resting uncomfortably against the slick, steep canyon wall.

He'd fallen about ten feet, though it had seemed farther. His instinct was to shout for help, but he checked it. All of the men from the camp might not have left in the trucks. He didn't know who was up there, looking for him.

And looking for Abby and the baby. He had to keep quiet for their sake.

Just then, Abby's face appeared above him. She was kneeling at the edge of the drainage into which he'd fallen, looking down at him, her forehead creased in a worried frown. "What happened?" she asked, her voice carrying to him in the clear air, though she didn't shout.

"I must have slipped. Stupid move." He should have known to be more careful on this unpredictable terrain, but it was too late to berate himself now.

"Can you climb up?"

He considered the almost vertical wall above him, lined with brittle shale and slick mud. Here and there tufts of grasses or wildflowers clung to the side— feeble handholds for a man who weighed one-eighty. "I don't suppose you have a rope," he said.

"Sorry. I'm fresh out."

"Yeah, I thought so." Already his arms were beginning to feel as if they'd pull out of their sockets. He couldn't hang here much longer. "What's happening up there?" he asked.

"Angelique is fussy—I think she's hungry. I've got her here beside me."

Of course her first concern was for the child. "No sign of the bad guys?"

"No sign of them. What can I do to help?"

"Maybe say a prayer." He focused on a clump of grass three feet overhead. "What do you know about native grasses?" he asked.

"Um, a lot, actually. What do you want to know?"

"Do they have very deep roots?"

"It depends. Some of them have very deep roots. That helps them find scarce water, and also prevents erosion."

And maybe they'd save his life. He took a deep breath, stretched up and took hold of the clump of grass. He lost his toehold and scrabbled for a new one, plastered against the side of the canyon, cool mud against his cheek, the scent of wet earth and sage filling his nostrils.

He clawed at the canyon wall and dug in with fingers, knees, toes—anything to keep from falling. Agonizing inch by agonizing inch, he crept toward the top, muscles screaming, mind fighting panic. Whenever he dared look up, he saw Abby's face, pale against the dark juniper and deep blue sky. Her eyes never left him, the tip of her thumb clenched between her teeth.

Having her there helped some. She gave him a goal to reach, a bigger reason to hang on. She and that baby depended on him to get them out of here safely. Giving up wasn't an option.

The climb to the top seemed to take an eternity, though in reality probably only fifteen minutes or so passed. When he dragged himself over the edge at last, he lay facedown on the ground, spent and aching.

Abby rested her hand on his back, a gentle weight grounding him to the earth and to her. "Are you all right?" she asked.

He pushed up onto his elbows. "Do we have any water?"

"No."

Of course they didn't. They also didn't have a phone or radio or GPS. They had two guns, the energy bar he'd stashed in his jacket, the hard candies he always carried and whatever Abby was carrying in her pockets. They also had a baby, who was going to get hungry sooner rather than later, and no idea where they were.

He sat up and pulled out his bandanna to wipe as much mud as he could from his face and hands. The baby began to whimper and Abby gathered it into her arms and rocked it. He studied her, head bent low over the fussy child, her blond hair falling forward to obscure half her face. She reminded him of a Madonna—a particularly beautiful one.

The memory of the way she'd touched him just now lingered, but he pushed it aside. He had to focus on how they were going to find their way back to headquarters. "Do you know where we are?" he asked.

She jerked her head up. "Don't you?"

He fought the instinct to play the macho man and lie to her, but lies like that only led to trouble. He shook his head. "We arrived in the dark, so I couldn't orient by landmarks. I made the mistake of relying on GPS." He looked around them, hoping to recognize some familiar rock outcropping or group of trees.

She moved up behind him to look over his shoulder. He became aware of her body pressed to his, her warmth seeping into him. "What do we do now?" Her breath tickled the hair at the back of his neck, sending heat sliding through him.

"I'm open to suggestions."

Abby cradled the child to her shoulder and rocked her gently. "We've got to get food for the baby," she said. "And water."

"The creek has water. I can't say how safe it is to drink, but it's a start." His own mouth felt as if he'd been chewing sawdust. He couldn't let dehydration cloud his judgment.

"So we'll walk back to the creek and get water," she said. "Then what?"

"Then I think we'd better sit down to wait."

"Wait for what?"

"For the Rangers to find us—or for whoever is in charge of the camp to return."

"Do you really think they'll come back?"

"They know we're still out here. Without a vehicle, we can't go too far. If they know we have the baby, they'll realize that will slow us down, even if we had a destination in mind. So yeah, I think they'll come back. We're a problem they won't let rest until they take care of it. The trick will be for us to take care of them first." He reached back and took her hand. "Come on."

Abby's feet dragged as she followed Michael back toward the creek and the deserted encampment. She hadn't slept well last night—the vision of the rattlesnake, alive and ready to strike, imprinted on the insides of her eyelids every time she closed them. Up at four this morning, then the tension and adrenaline rush of the events of the day, plus the ground they'd covered on their hikes around the area, had all taken their toll. She was exhausted, and the baby in her arms felt like a twenty-pound bowling ball.

But she could do nothing but keep moving. Going

back to wait for the people who wanted them dead seemed foolhardy at best, suicidal even. But the move also made sense. Every survival manual she'd ever read stressed staying in one location if you were lost. Wandering aimlessly complicated the search for you and wasted precious energy. At least by the camp they'd have water, which they all needed, but Angelique, especially, had to have.

Michael looked back over his shoulder. "How are you doing?" he asked.

"I'm hanging in there."

"And the baby?"

"She seems to like the movement." She smiled down at the infant, who had fallen asleep. "She must have spent a lot of time moving around with her mother."

"It looked as if Mariposa was in charge of the cooking today. She probably spent a lot of time on her feet, gathering water, cleaning up and cooking the meals."

"What did the other people, the ones we saw eating, do?"

"They probably worked tending a crop of marijuana, or making meth, though I didn't see any signs of production around the trailer, and I didn't smell anything off. So probably marijuana."

"Are they here voluntarily?"

"Probably not. They may have crossed the border looking for work, but once they arrived here, they were prisoners."

"So they're slaves?"

"Pretty much, yeah."

"It…it's like something out of another century. Not something that should happen today in the United States."

"It happens more than people imagine—probably more than the statistics say, though the Justice Department estimates that more than seventeen thousand people a year are brought into the United States for trafficking purposes. They're forced to work in factories or on farms, and as household help. More than eighty percent of trafficking victims are sex slaves. Many of them are immigrants, though young Americans, runaways and homeless teens get caught up in trafficking, too."

"That's appalling."

"It is." He looked toward the now-deserted camp. "If these people are involved in that kind of thing, I want to stop them."

"I want to stop them, too," Abby said. "But we also need to get Angelique to a safe place. She's going to need to eat soon, and she'll need diapers." So many things they didn't have here in the middle of nowhere. Worry settled like a brick in her stomach. "How long do you think it will be before your team realizes we're missing?"

He glanced up at the sky, the color of purest turquoise. "They'll expect me to check in in a few hours, at the latest."

And it would probably be hours after that before anyone became really concerned, she thought. After all, their plan had been to spend the day in the backcountry, where it wasn't unusual to be without cell phone and radio signals. She shifted the baby to her other shoulder. They needed to find a place to settle and wait.

They had to cross a hundred yards of open prairie to reach the first cover that led along the edge of the wash to the creek. The wash itself began as a depression in the landscape, then gradually deepened and widened into the side drainage where Michael had fallen. That mini canyon was only about thirty feet deep—compared to the Black Canyon that gave the park its name, which plunged more than two thousand seven hundred feet at its deepest point.

Michael drew his gun. At least he hadn't lost it in the fall. "How do you feel about making a run for it?" he asked. "Just in case someone is out there looking for us?"

"Do you really think they left someone behind to search for us?" she asked.

"I don't know. But we shouldn't take chances."

She nodded. "What do you want me to do?"

"Run as fast as you can to that clump of trees over there." He indicated a grouping of scrub oak. "I'll cover you. Then you can do the same for me."

She studied the expanse of ground, with its scant vegetation and rocky surface. "All right." Then she took off, cradling the infant to her, her feet raising little puffs of dust as she zigzagged her way across the ground. Within seconds, she'd reached the safety of the rocks; no one had fired.

He waited until she removed the Sig Sauer from the holster at her right hip and nodded in his direction. His darted out into the open, running hard, pumping his arms and legs, taking long strides, covering the ground as rapidly as possible. Then he threw himself on the ground beside her, too winded to speak.

"You looked good," she said. "Did you ever run track?"

He nodded. "In high school." He wiped his mouth. "A long time ago."

"I never liked running," she said. "Those drills were the worst part of basic training for me."

"I'm still trying to picture a beauty queen in boot camp."

She made a face. "I didn't tell anyone I was a beauty queen. If anything, I tried to make myself as plain as possible—no makeup, hair scraped back into a ponytail."

"I'll bet it didn't work," he said. "No one—no man, for certain—would ever mistake you for homely." He stood and offered a hand to help her up. "You ready?"

"Ready." She stood, but didn't let go of his hand right away. When their eyes met, she offered a shy smile before turning away and moving toward the creek.

At the creek bank, Michael knelt to drink. Abby wandered along the bank, searching the ground.

He looked up, the cuffs of his sleeves and the front of his shirt damp from the creek water. "What are you looking for?"

"This." She held up a nearly new tin can she'd plucked from beneath a tree. She'd spotted the label earlier and it had vaguely registered as just another piece of garbage—a can that had once held corn and been discarded. "We can make a fire and boil water for Angelique," she explained. "You and I can deal with an upset stomach from anything that might be in that water, but a baby could die from the wrong bacteria."

"Good idea." He stood and pointed up the creek bank. "Let's move to that rock outcropping there. We'll be sheltered a little from the sun and wind, and we'll have a good view of anyone approaching the camp from this direction."

He led the way to a spot beneath a lone piñon that seemed to grow straight out of the surrounding rock. The stunted tree leaned crazily to one side, its branches spread like open arms, casting a pool of shade on the red granite. Michael began gathering pine needles and bark for tinder. "I had fire starters and matches in my pack," she said.

"See if you can find some broken glass around the camp. Otherwise, I can make a fire drill out of two sticks. It takes forever, but it does work."

She returned to the creek to wash out the can and fill it with water. She got a drink for herself and studied the plants that grew in or near the water. Ten minutes later, she returned to camp, feeling triumphant.

"What are you grinning about?" Michael asked.

"I found a good piece of glass." She held up what looked like the bottom of a jar. "And I found these." She opened the sling and began laying out the plants she'd gathered.

He took the glass and studied the plants. "What is all that?"

"Wild lettuce, cress and mustard. Wild onion. A few piñon nuts." She pointed to the various plants. "We can have a salad for lunch."

"If you say so."

"I'll see to the baby first, then I'll prepare some of this for us."

Using the piece of glass to focus sunlight on the tinder, Michael soon had a fire going. He fed the small blaze with more tinder, then twigs, and finally dead wood he'd salvaged from around the camp. Abby balanced the can of water on three rocks in the center of the blaze. When the liquid was boiling, she used the sleeve of her jacket like a potholder to remove it from the heat. "You still have Life Savers with you, don't you?" she asked.

"Sure." He fished the roll from his pocket.

"Let me have a couple."

He handed over the candies and she dropped them in the hot water. "They'll make a kind of sugar water for the baby."

"Clever," Michael said.

"The sugar will give her a little energy," Abby said. "And the sweet taste might make her more willing to drink." While the water cooled, she set about stripping the stems from leaves and cleaning dirt from roots she collected.

Michael moved closer. "Is all that really edible?" he asked.

"Sure. All our native salad greens started out as wild plants. People think of this as a desert, but there are really a lot of edible plants here, if you know what to look for."

"What can I do to help?" he asked.

He'd already been a big help, keeping her calm and starting the fire. His steady, capable presence reassured her. "Just keep me company while I work. Were you a Boy Scout when you were little?"

"I was. And my family went camping a lot. Every other weekend in the summer, we'd pack the car with a tent and sleeping bags and a cooler and head to the national forest. We'd hike and fish and roast marshmallows around a campfire."

"And you liked that?"

"Are you kidding? For two days, my sister and I had our parents all to ourselves. We ran around outside, ate hot dogs and hamburgers, and no one cared how dirty we got. It was great." He smiled, remembering. "Those trips made me love being outdoors. They're probably why I was attracted to this job."

"You weren't worried you'd end up in an office, reviewing paperwork?"

"There's paperwork in every job, but from the first I applied for positions that allowed me to be out and on my own more. If it weren't for the crime and the bad guys, this would be the ideal job. What about you? Were you a Girl Scout?"

She shook her head. "Oh, no. My mother would not have spent the night outdoors unless forced to do so at gunpoint. I spent my weekends at dance recitals and beauty parlors and pageant practice."

"Boot camp must have been a big culture shock."

"It was and it wasn't." She tested the water in the can. Still a little too warm. "When I was in high school, I joined the school hiking club. It introduced me to a whole new group of kids—kids who liked to camp and hike and spend time outdoors."

"And they accepted you?"

"They were suspicious at first, but after I proved myself, they saw me as one of them. I discovered how much I liked spending time in the woods. A couple of my friends in the club went into the military right out of high school. Later, when I was searching for something to do with my life, I remembered them and thought, 'Why not?'"

She settled back against the trunk of the tree and unfastened the sling, using it as a blanket to swaddle the baby. Angelique fussed and began to cry. "I know, sweetheart. You're probably hungry." She dipped her finger in the can and brought it to the baby's lips. "Let's see if you'll take some of this for me."

The little mouth latched on to her finger and Abby

felt a pull deep within her womb. She dribbled more water into the infant's mouth.

"I think she likes it." Michael had moved closer and watched the two of them with his usual intensity.

"At least it will keep her hydrated," she said. "But I hope someone comes for us soon."

"We might have to spend the night out here, but tomorrow, I know someone will come for us," he said.

The idea of a night without shelter, blankets or formula didn't thrill her, but whining about it wouldn't change anything. For now, Angelique seemed content, and that was all that mattered.

"Why do you think Mariposa gave her to you?"

She'd had plenty of time to ponder the answer to that question. "The only reason I can imagine a mother would give up her baby was because she thought Angelique would be safer with me." And Mariposa must have been desperate, to hand her child over to a stranger.

"Why didn't she give the baby to you the first day you two met?"

"Maybe she's learned some new information since then that made her fear for her safety—or the baby's safety."

"Maybe breaking up camp today didn't have anything to do with us finding that dead man," he said. "Maybe something else is up."

"Like what?"

"I don't know. But if she thought the baby was going to be in danger, she would have tried to protect her."

Anger at the thought of anyone trying to hurt this baby pushed away some of her weariness. "I want to find whoever's responsible and make sure they're punished," she said.

"I want to find them, too." He pulled out his phone and clicked over to the photos he'd taken earlier.

"Did you get anything useful?" she asked.

He squinted at the photos of the trucks lined up, ready to leave. "I can't make out the license plates," he said. "I think they've splattered them with mud."

"Who was the man you fought with?" she asked. "Do you have any idea?"

He shook his head. "Mariposa called him El Jefe—the chief. My guess is he's the boss, at least on this level."

"So there's probably someone else supervising operations above him?" she asked.

"Probably. Someone who doesn't get his hands dirty by dealing with people directly. He probably ordered them to move camp, now that we've gotten so close."

"Why didn't they leave yesterday, after the sniper fired at us?" she asked.

"I don't know. Maybe they had to get permission from someone higher up the chain of command. Or maybe they had to wait for the trucks to arrive from somewhere else."

"Yet they still had time to gift wrap a rattlesnake for me."

"If the two incidents are related. We don't know that for sure."

She leaned back against a tree trunk, the baby cradled to her shoulder. "I promise you, no one else hates me enough to send me a deadly snake."

"No jilted lovers or brokenhearted ex-boyfriends?" He kept his tone teasing, but she sensed a tension in the air as he waited for her answer.

"Not a one. I haven't been in any kind of relationship since before I joined the army. And none of them were serious. And please don't insult me with clichés like 'a pretty woman like you' or 'having so much to offer.' I get enough of that from my parents. I've been too busy—first with rehab, now with school—to worry about relationships."

"I wasn't going to say anything."

She shifted toward him. "What about you? Do you have a woman waiting for you back home—wherever home is?" Now it was her turn to hold her breath, waiting for his reply. She didn't like to admit how much his answer mattered to her.

"No. I didn't date a lot, though I always had women friends. The last long-term relationship I had, several years ago, she broke it off because she said I was too intense. I wasn't even sure what she meant."

Yes, he could be intense, a trait that both drew her to him and made her wary. "I think you're the kind of man who, when you do something, you don't give a half measure. You put everything you have into it, whether it's a job or a relationship. If someone else isn't ready for that level of commitment, that can feel too intense. It can be scary."

"Are you scared of me?"

She didn't look away from him, her gaze steady. He'd been honest with her; now it was her turn. "I'm not scared of you, Michael. But fear doesn't always—or even usually—come from other people. More often, we're scared of something inside ourselves. Of our own beliefs or emotions."

"I'm glad you're not afraid of me," he said. "I've got your back, remember?"

A hint of a smile curved her lips. "Yeah. I remember."

Chapter 10

Michael kept his eyes locked to Abby's, willing her not to look away. What was she scared of inside herself, and how could he help her let go of that fear? But he got the impression if he tried to get that personal, she'd just pull back. As with the fall of hair that kept hiding her scar, Abby liked to keep layers between her and other people.

The baby started fussing, breaking the spell between them. Abby turned away and he sat back, stifling a sigh of frustration.

"I need your bandanna," she said. "The baby's diaper is soaked."

He handed it over, and she folded it into a makeshift diaper and handed him the soaked one. "Wash this out—downstream."

He made a face, but moved off to do as she asked.

Washing dirty diapers wasn't on the list of things he had expected to do in this job, but there was something calming and grounding about the mundane, domestic chore. Yes, he was lost in the wilderness with the possibility that a killer was searching for them, but his duty was crystal clear—to protect this woman and this baby and somehow return them to safety.

The man in charge of this camp would be back. Everything in the man's attitude and posture told Michael he wasn't one to overlook a threat. He'd been outsmarting the Rangers for weeks. The urgency of moving his people might have forced him to delay the hunt momentarily, but he wasn't going to let two people who had discovered his secret get away. When he'd stolen Michael's Cruiser he'd left the couple stranded, so he could be confident they were still close by. As long as Michael saw the man before he spotted them, they'd be safe. He'd make sure of it.

He had Abby to help, too. Thanks to her, they wouldn't starve. Roots and leaves weren't steak and potatoes, but his growling stomach would be thankful for anything he fed it. And being with Abby made him feel calmer and more certain that they'd come through this all right. She was worried, but not panicking. Anyone who mistook her for a dumb blonde was delusional.

He rejoined her and she sat up straighter, her hand making a fist in her lap.

"What do you have there?" He nodded to her fist.

She flushed. "It's nothing."

He spread the damp diaper on a tree branch to dry. "It's not nothing. What is it?"

She looked away. "I've been watching and I haven't seen any sign of anyone headed this way," she said.

Message received. She didn't want to talk about whatever she was holding. "We ought to be able to see the dust from a vehicle from a long way off," he said.

"How far do you think we are from the main road?" she asked.

"About five miles, I think. Maybe a little more."

"Where do you think they were taking those people?"

"To another camp in the park—or maybe all the way to Denver. I don't know."

"What a harsh life." She arranged the shawl to shade the sleeping infant. "Who's behind this?"

He sat beside her, wrists on his upraised knees. "We don't know that, either. There are rumors drug cartels have moved in from Mexico, but they need a local connection—a sponsor who can smooth the way for them."

"Who?"

"That's one of the things we've been trying to find out. It has to be someone with money. Someone powerful. Someone who thinks he's above the law."

"Do you have someone in mind?"

"We do. But we can't prove anything." Though law enforcement might rely on hunches to guide their investigation, they needed proof to stand up in court.

"Tell me. It's not as if I'll tell anyone else."

"Have you heard of a man named Richard Prentice?"

"No. But I'll admit, I've been so busy with school I haven't paid much attention to the news."

"He's a billionaire who owns the land at the entrance to the park."

"The place with the big stone pillars and iron gate?"

"That's the one. He's made a lot of money buying historic or critical wilderness properties and selling them to the government or conservation groups for inflated prices. But the Feds wouldn't bite when he tried to sell that place, and local governments passed restrictions that limited how he could develop it. So he made it his base of operations."

"I suppose it's a good location for overseeing a drug operation within the park, but why would a guy like that bother with drugs? He's already rich."

"Some people never have enough money. But maybe it's not about the money for him. Maybe this is one more way to stick it to a government he seems to hate. Or maybe he gets a rush out of having control over so many people's lives."

"If he does have anything to do with this, I hope you can prove it and send him to jail for a long time."

"That's what we hope, too."

She shifted onto her knees. "Take the baby for a minute," she said. "I think our food is about ready." Not waiting for an answer, she shoved the infant into his arms.

The baby was heavier than he'd expected, warm and a little wiggly, too. As he tried to figure out the most comfortable way to hold her, she opened her eyes and stared up at him. She seemed so bright and alert, her gaze fixed on him, as if assessing him. "You're onto me, kid," he said softly. "I don't have the faintest idea what I'm doing."

She shifted, curling toward him with a little sigh that made his heart stop for a moment. He stared down at her, gripped by the most intense, protective instinct he'd ever felt. "I won't let them hurt you, little girl." He stroked her cheek with the tip of his finger, the skin softer than anything he'd ever felt.

"She likes you." Abby returned, holding a section of bark like a plate. "She settled right down."

"I don't have a lot of experience with babies."

"You're a natural." She set the "plate" on the ground between them. "I can take her again if you want."

"No. That's okay." The infant fit neatly in the crook of his left arm, leaving the right arm free. "I don't want to disturb her." He leaned forward to study the items she'd arranged on the bark. "What's on the menu?"

"The salad greens I talked about earlier—no dressing, I'm afraid. The little white things are mariposa lily bulbs I roasted."

He popped one of the buds—about the size of a garlic clove—into his mouth and chewed. "Not bad. A little earthy, but a little sweet, too."

"They'd be better with salt or other seasonings, but they'll keep us going until help arrives."

"Not bad at all." He crunched down on another bulb.

They finished the meal in silence. Hunger sated, with the warmth of the sun off the rocks and the profound silence of the wilderness closing in, his eyelids began to feel heavy. He sat up straighter. He had to stay awake and watch for rescue—or the return of the camp boss.

"I think the early morning and all that hiking is catching up with me," Abby said.

"You can take a nap," he said. "I'll keep watch."

"I might have to." She looked around them. "Not that all this rock is going to make for a comfortable bed."

"Come lean against me." He patted the spot beside him.

She hesitated.

"Come on. I won't bite."

"You'd better not. I bite back." But she settled beside him.

He slipped his arm around her shoulder. "Just lean on me."

Again, she hesitated, but the gentle pressure from his hand coaxed her to lay her head in the hollow of his shoulder. She settled down with a sigh, her breast and side pressed against him, one hand resting on his thigh. He felt the same protective instinct toward her he'd felt toward the baby, but underneath the protectiveness was a more primal emotion, the awareness of her as a beautiful, desirable woman, and of himself as a man who wanted her.

The wanting was nothing new. He'd been physically attracted to her from the moment she walked into ranger headquarters. That in itself wasn't that unusual. He was attracted to women every day, a passing desire akin to seeing a luscious brownie and his mouth watering.

His desire for Abby went deeper. She wasn't a passing fascination. The more he knew her, as a complex, capable, sympathetic person, the more he felt drawn to know her more fully. Intimately.

She shifted against him and he looked down to find her head tipped up toward his. "You wanted to know what I was holding earlier," she said.

"You don't have to tell me if you don't want to," he said. "It's none of my business."

"No—I want to tell you." She held out her fisted hand and slowly opened her fingers to reveal the figure of a leaping rabbit, about three inches long. "It's just a kind of good-luck charm I keep. I know it's silly, but holding it makes me feel calmer."

"It's not silly." He was feeling anything but calm himself right now, but he didn't want to scare her by overreacting. "Do you remember where you got it?"

"I don't know." They both studied the little rabbit in her palm. It was white with brown spots, four legs outstretched as if running, ears erect. "When I came to in the hospital, I was holding it."

"I wasn't sure if you remembered." He could hardly get the words out past the knot of emotion in his throat. He tried again. "Before they unloaded you off the chopper, I put it in your hand and you grasped it. It seemed like a good sign. Even unconscious, you were fighting. Hanging on."

She stared. He tried to read the emotion in her eyes and drew back a little. She looked upset. Maybe even angry. "Why did you do that?" she asked.

"My cousin gave it to me when I deployed," he said. "She said if one rabbit's foot was supposed to be lucky, she figured four feet, still attached to the rabbit, were even better. I figured you needed the luck more than I did right then."

She wrapped her fingers around the little figure again and returned it to her pocket, not looking at him. "Thank you," she said. "I always wondered where he came from."

"Did it help?"

She nodded. "It did. Whenever I was stressed or worried or needed distracting, I'd take him out and hold him. It reminded me that someone I didn't even know had been rooting for me to make it." She raised her head and looked at him, her eyes glinting with unshed tears. "Now I know that someone was you."

He couldn't speak, afraid of saying the wrong thing. Of breaking the connection between them. She sat up a little straighter, though she remained pressed against him. "I have a hard time warming up to people. Especially since I got home from Afghanistan."

"The things you went through over there—you can't really share them with others. They're like an invisible wall, separating you from everyone else who doesn't know what it's like. They can never see things from your point of view."

"But you can."

"Not entirely. But I have a better idea than some."

"Yes." She put her hand on his chest.

"Do you think that's all we have in common—the war?" He forced himself to look into her eyes, not sure he'd like the answer she gave. He hated the idea that she'd see him as just another damaged veteran with whom she could compare notes.

"I didn't mean it like that," she said. "Only that I felt comfortable enough with you to let my guard down a little. When you look at me, I feel like you see all of me—not just the beauty queen, and not just the scarred veteran, but the whole package."

He touched her cheek with his free hand. "It's a very nice package." He dragged his thumb across the corner of her mouth.

She let out her breath in a soft sigh and leaned closer. That was all the invitation he needed. He bent his head and covered her lips with his own. She returned the kiss, arching into him and sliding her hand around to clutch his shoulder. He wrapped his free arm around her and pulled her to his chest, her soft, feminine curves molding to him. He slanted his mouth more firmly against hers and she parted her lips, her tongue tracing the crease of his mouth, setting his heart racing.

She melded her body to his, urgent, needy. This wasn't a casual, flirtatious kiss, or one of tentative exploration. This kiss spoke of built-up longing, of a craving for a connection that went beyond words.

Angelique squirmed against him and began to whimper. Reluctantly, he broke the kiss and tried to comfort the baby. "I must have been crushing her," he said.

"I'll take her." Head down, hair falling forward to cover the side of her face and shield her expression from his view, she reached for the infant.

He slipped the baby into her arms, unsure of what he should say. Kissing was one thing—talking about it was another. Still, he couldn't let the moment pass as if nothing had happened. He reached out and brushed back her hair. "Are you okay?" he asked.

"I'm fine." She took a deep breath and raised her eyes to meet his. "We probably shouldn't have done that."

"Why not?"

"Because..." She bit her lower lip, then shook her head.

"Tell me." He cradled the side of her neck. "You seemed to be enjoying yourself at the time."

A warm flush crept up her cheeks—all the answer he really needed, but he held back a smile of triumph. "I don't want you to get the wrong idea," she said. "I'm not really ready...for more than kisses. For a relationship."

Her obvious distress touched him. "I'm in no hurry. No pressure, I promise." He sat back again. "If the baby's all right, you can take that nap now. I promise I won't bother you."

After a moment of hesitation, she settled against him once more, the baby wrapped in the sling and fastened around her. He stared out across the empty landscape and listened to the rhythm of her breathing slow and deepen as she fell asleep. At least with her this close, every nerve in his body aware of her, he wasn't too worried about falling asleep himself. He'd stay awake and keep watch, protecting her with his life if he had to.

Michael woke with a start and stared out at the sun, which was sliding toward the horizon, the intense heat of midday fading toward the cool of dusk. He didn't think he'd dozed long; beside him, Abby and Angelique still slept. But every nerve vibrated with awareness. In the short time he'd lost his fight against sleep, something in the environment around them had changed.

All around them was silent—too silent. No birds sang. No lizards skittered on the rocks. No flies buzzed. The hair on the back of his neck rose, and he sat up straighter and started to turn around.

Hard metal pressed against the back of his head. "Don't move or I will blow your head off," a man said, in slightly accented English. "Give me the baby and I will think about letting you live."

Chapter 11

Abby gasped and clutched Angelique to her shoulder. The infant mewled and burrowed closer to her. An unfamiliar hand tightened on Abby's shoulder and she wrenched away and whirled to face an older Hispanic man. He held a gun to Michael's head. "Give the baby to me or I will kill your friend," he said. He held out his free hand for the baby.

"Who are you?" she demanded, clutching Angelique even more tightly to her. "What do you want with this baby?"

"You can call me El Jefe. Now give her to me or your friend will die."

"Don't give her to him." Michael spoke through gritted teeth. He still sat with his back to the man, his head wrenched to one side by the pressure of the gun barrel against his skull. But his eyes remained fixed on her, calm and determined.

Abby struggled to her feet and took a step back to put more distance between her and the man with the gun. She looked from him to Michael. Michael's face was pale, but nothing else about him betrayed agitation or fear. He'd gathered his legs under him, as if preparing to pounce. "Don't do it," he said again.

"Give her to me!" El Jefe insisted, and jabbed his weapon into Michael, who winced.

"What do you want with her?" Abby asked. She wrapped both arms around the baby. "She's an infant. She cries and wets her diaper. You don't look like a man who has time to change diapers."

"I will return her to her mother. She can take care of her."

Abby stared. Mariposa would certainly know how to take care of her own baby, but would this man really return the child to her? He was one of her jailers—the man who had ordered her to fetch water. Mariposa had wanted the child to be away from him.

"Her mother gave her to me to care for," Abby said. "I can't just hand her over to a stranger."

"You will give her to me!" He shoved the gun again, but this time Michael jerked his head to the side and swung his fist up and back, jamming it into the gunman's nose. El Jefe screamed, a wild, almost girlish sound, and blood poured from his broken nose. Michael shoved him back and grabbed for the weapon.

For an agonizingly long minute the two men struggled for the gun, rolling on the ground while Abby watched, heart in her throat, tensing herself for the explosion of the gun firing. She could have pulled her own weapon, but she didn't trust herself to get off a clear shot. El Jefe swore and struggled to grasp the weapon, but Michael was bigger and stronger, and he wasn't also fighting the pain and bleeding from a broken nose. At last, the older man gave up the fight, covering his face with his hands and shouting in Spanish.

Michael stood over him, breathing hard. "Who are you?" he demanded.

The man didn't look up, though he was no longer shouting, only muttering nonstop.

"Shut up and tell me who you are," Michael said.

The baby began to wail, and Abby rocked her in her arms, trying to comfort her. "Is she all right?" Michael asked.

"She's just hungry." And she was going to get a lot hungrier if they didn't get away from here soon.

Michael turned his attention back to the gunman, changing his line of questioning. "How did you get here?" he asked. "Where is your truck?"

Abby's spirits lifted. Of course. The man must have a vehicle somewhere nearby. A vehicle that could return them to safety—if they could find a road. But even the dirt tracks that crisscrossed the area must eventually lead somewhere. They could cover more ground searching in a vehicle than on foot.

"Why should I tell you anything?" the man asked.

"Answer my questions or I'll kill you." Michael's voice was hard; Abby shivered. She believed him.

"Kill me and you'll still be stuck out here with no way to leave," the man sneered. The bleeding had slowed. He patted gingerly at his nose, wincing.

A point for the bad guy. Abby looked around, hoping she'd spot the glint of sunlight off a truck hood or windshield, or maybe even see the vehicle, sitting in plain sight. Maybe it was too much to hope that the vehicle would come equipped with a GPS and a phone, but a woman could dream, couldn't she?

But instead of a lone truck sitting on the otherwise deserted plain, she saw something even better. "Michael, I think your friends finally found us," she said.

He kept the gun leveled on his prisoner, but glanced over his shoulder at the line of Cruisers snaking across the desert. Then he pointed the weapon up and fired three shots. The baby wailed and Abby's own ears rang, but the signal had worked; the line of vehicles sped up, headed straight toward them.

"Now we'll deal— Stop!"

At Michael's shout, Abby turned. The gunman was running away, speeding over the rough ground like a jackrabbit, out of reach within seconds. Michael started across the rocks after him.

"Michael, no!" Abby said. "He's got too much of a head start. You can deal with him later."

"We may not have another chance." But he stopped and came to stand beside her. Together, they watched the Cruisers stop and park by the creek, then they walked down to meet them.

Graham greeted them as they picked their way across the creek. "What are you two doing out here?" he asked.

"Never mind that." Michael passed his boss, headed toward the trucks. "We need to try to catch up with the man who just ran away from here."

"What man?" Graham asked.

"He calls himself El Jefe. I'm pretty sure he's the guy who was in charge of this camp. If we can get him to talk, we may be able to break this case wide-open."

Graham and Michael left in Graham's Cruiser, leaving Abby with Carmen and Marco.

"Is that a baby?" Carmen stared at the bundle in Abby's arms.

"Her name is Angelique." Abby arranged the shawl to shade the infant's face. "And we really need to find some formula and feed her."

"Where did you get her?" Carmen smiled and stroked one of Angelique's tiny hands.

"Her mother was one of the workers camped here," Abby said. "How did you two ever find us?"

"We've been following the tracks of the trucks," Marco said. "We found Dance's Cruiser, wrecked and burning in a wash almost ten miles from here. We've been searching ever since."

"There was a camp of workers here," Abby said. "Four trailers—about two dozen people. Some men with trucks came and moved them this morning."

"Those must have been the trucks we were following." Marco joined them. "The tracks led right to here."

"Did the tracks lead from the destroyed Cruiser?" Abby asked.

"We found the tracks while we were trying to figure out how the Cruiser ended up in that wash," Marco said.

"But how did you two end up here without the Cruiser, and with a baby?" Carmen asked.

"It's a long story." Abby sighed. She was hot, tired, hungry and thirsty. "Right now, we need to get this child to a safe place."

She followed them to Marco's vehicle and climbed into the backseat. Angelique fussed and squirmed. "Somebody's not happy," Carmen said.

"She's hungry and her diaper needs changing," Abby said. "And she probably misses her mother." Mariposa probably missed her baby, too. Where was she now—and why had that man wanted her?

"Who's the guy Graham and Michael took off after?" Marco asked.

"He was in charge of the workers in the camp. He supervised the move. We hid and watched them hook up the trailers and drive off. I fell asleep and when I woke up, he was there, and had a gun on Michael. He demanded we give him the baby. When I refused, he threatened to kill Michael, but Michael broke his nose and took his gun. Your arrival distracted us enough he ran off."

When they reached the road and phone service, Carmen called headquarters. "Lance, I need you to run into town and buy a couple cans of baby formula, bottles and nipples, some baby wipes and a box of diapers." She looked over her shoulder at Angelique. "Size two." She grinned. "Yes, they're for a baby. Now, don't waste time arguing. We need these right away." She hung up the phone. "That's probably the oddest thing anyone's ever asked him to do. I wish I could see his face when he gets to the store and finds out how many different kinds of diapers there are. Let's hope he gets something that will work."

"You seem to know a lot about them," Marco said.

"I've got six younger brothers and sisters and half a dozen nieces and nephews," she said. "I've changed plenty of diapers in my day."

Abby cuddled the fussy baby closer. "We're going to make you more comfortable soon, little one," she said. She only hoped they'd be able to find Mariposa and reunite mother and child before it was too late.

Michael stared across the empty prairie. They hadn't found so much as a tire track that they could link to the man who had held him at gunpoint and tried to take the baby. "He couldn't have just vanished," he said.

"If he is the man in charge of the workers, he probably knows this country a lot better than we do," Graham said. He put his hand on Michael's shoulder. "Come on. Let's go back to headquarters."

"We need to go back to the campsite first. There's a bucket there that may have this guy's fingerprints on it. Maybe we'll come up with a match."

They returned to the camp and Michael retrieved the bucket from under the bush. "I'll get a team out to go over this place," Graham said.

"It's pretty clean, but maybe they'll find something," Michael said. He didn't like giving up the search for El Jefe so soon, but he doubted more time wandering around out here would bring them any closer to the man. He followed Graham back to the Cruiser.

"What happened to your face?" Graham asked.

Michael put a hand to the gash on his cheek. "I fell into a drainage. That's when I lost the phone and radio."

"Was that before or after you acquired the baby?"

"After."

"Where did the baby come from?"

"One of the workers gave it to Abby, when the bosses showed up to move them. Then we were spotted and had to make a run for it."

"But the guy in charge caught up with you?"

Michael shook his head. "That was later. Without the GPS or a phone or maps, we were lost. We needed water, so staying near the creek made sense. I knew you'd send someone to look for us when I didn't report in this evening. In the meantime, I figured the boss man might come back to look for us. I knew he'd stolen my truck, so he probably guessed we couldn't go far. I planned to get the jump on him when he returned, but it didn't work out that way." He fought down anger at himself for making such a hash of the whole day. Had his attraction to Abby distracted him so much he'd been less diligent?

"We'll find him," Graham said. "What did he want with the baby?"

"No idea. He said he would return her to her mother, but Abby got the impression the mom thought the baby would be safer with her."

"The two of you can fill us in on the details when we get back to headquarters."

At ranger headquarters, they found Carmen feeding the baby a bottle while Abby, dressed in a black task-force polo and hiking shorts she must have borrowed from Carmen, ate a deli sandwich from a tray in the middle of the conference table. She set aside the sandwich when he walked in. "Did you find him?" she asked.

Michael shook his head and sagged into the chair across from her. He glanced toward the baby. "How's Angelique?"

"She is living up to her name and being a little angel," Carmen said. She positioned the baby over her shoulder and patted her back.

"She's happier now that's she's eaten and had a fresh

diaper," Abby said. "Though I don't think you're going to want your bandanna back."

"I have more where that came from." He helped himself to a sandwich. Abby's leaves and roots hadn't tasted as bad as he'd feared, but they hadn't been very filling.

Graham pulled out the chair at the head of the table. "Tell me about this man," he said.

"I'm pretty sure he's the one who was ordering everyone else around," Michael said. "I didn't have binoculars, but he was tall and thin, and was the only one wearing a white shirt."

"And he didn't say why he wanted the baby?"

"He said he would return her to her mother," Abby said.

"Maybe he's the father," Carmen said. When the others stared at her, she shrugged. "Even criminals can love their children. Or maybe he loves the mother and she changed her mind about giving up her child, and she sent him to retrieve the baby."

"Or maybe he sees the child as a tie to him and his operation and he wants to get rid of her," Marco said.

Abby shuddered at the idea. "What harm is an infant going to do?" she asked. "She can't testify against him."

"She might share his DNA, and that might tie him to a crime we don't even know about yet," Marco said.

Abby tried to push away the thought that the man might have wanted to harm Angelique. But a man who made slaves of other people might not balk at killing a baby.

"You said you were following tracks," Michael said. "Where did they lead?"

"Nowhere," Marco said. "Once they reached the highway, we lost them."

"But now that we know what we're looking for, it won't be so easy to hide that many people and trailers," Michael said.

"Unless they dismantled everything and took everyone straight to Denver or another big city," Carmen said. "Your guy could be long gone."

Michael shook his head. "I don't think so. He wanted Angelique badly enough to come back by himself to retrieve her."

"That part doesn't make sense to me," Marco said. "He had to have others helping him when he moved the camp."

"He had at least five other men with guns," Michael said.

"Then why didn't he bring them with him to retrieve the baby?" Marco asked. "Even one other man with him would have increased his chances of success."

"Maybe he didn't want anyone to know about the baby," Abby said.

"But they already knew about the baby," Michael said. "Mariposa didn't try to hide her from the others, that I could tell."

Abby stood and went to take the sleeping infant from Carmen. Angelique hardly stirred as Abby cradled her close. "Maybe Carmen is right and he came back for Angelique because she's his child," she said. "If that's true, he might not want the others to know, or to suspect he had a soft spot for the baby."

"We don't know that," Michael said. "He might have intended to kill her."

"Then maybe he didn't want the others to know

that, either." The idea made her sick to her stomach, but they would gain nothing by refusing to consider all possibilities.

"Whatever the reason he wanted her, it doesn't really matter," Carmen said.

"Why not?" Michael asked.

"Because we know the baby represents a weakness or a secret he doesn't want anyone else finding out about," Graham said. "If you know a man's weakness or secret, you can find a way to exploit it."

"But if he's already on his way to Denver…" Abby sent a questioning look to Graham.

"I think Michael's hunch is right and he won't want to leave without the baby," Graham said. "We can use that against him."

Abby smiled down at the child, who had fallen back asleep. She'd never seen a more beautiful baby, with such long, dark lashes, and a perfect Cupid's bow of a mouth.

Aware that the room had fallen silent, she looked up to find everyone else looking at her—or rather, they were focused on the baby. "What is it?" she asked. "What's wrong?"

Graham cleared his throat. "If we spread the word around that you're keeping the baby for a while, and make you seem vulnerable, we could lure our guy out to take another chance. Only this time, we'd be waiting to capture him."

"You mean, use Angelique as bait to catch him?" She stared, sure she couldn't have heard them correctly.

Graham nodded. "You and Angelique, yes. Bait to catch what could be a very big fish."

Chapter 12

"No!" Abby and Michael spoke at the same time.

"It's too dangerous." Michael shoved back his chair and stood. "She could be hurt."

"He's right. You can't take that kind of risk with a baby," Abby said.

"I wasn't talking about Angelique." Michael moved around the table to stand beside her. "It's too dangerous for you *and* the baby." His eyes met hers and she knew he was speaking not as a law enforcement officer, but as a man who cared for her. The realization moved her, but she looked away. This wasn't a time to let sentiment cloud her judgment.

"We'd have someone from the team with you 24/7," Graham said. "And other team members stationed nearby. If our man makes a move, we'd be on him."

"It's our best chance to catch this guy," Marco said.

"If we get to him, we're that much closer to finding the person in charge of the operation. We can stop him from enslaving other workers."

"Can you help Mariposa and the others?" she asked.

"There's a good chance we can," Graham said.

Abby looked down at the sleeping infant. As much as she cared for the child, she wasn't in a position to take her permanently. The baby needed to be with her mother, as long as her mother could take care of her.

Michael's hand rested heavy on her shoulder. "Abby, don't do it," he said. "Don't risk it. We'll find some other way."

"I can't risk anything happening to Angelique," she said. "We don't know what this man's intentions are toward her."

"She's right." Carmen spoke up. "We'll need to use a decoy for the baby and move Angelique into temporary foster care."

"Agreed," Graham said. "I don't want the child to come to harm. And I don't want you harmed, either, Abby. I promise we'll protect you. But the final decision is yours."

Michael's hand on her shoulder tightened, but he remained silent. That silence—his faith in her ability to make the right decision—moved her more than any words could have. "I'll do it," she said. "As long as Angelique is somewhere safe."

"Abby…" Michael spoke so softly she might have been the only one who heard.

She turned to face him. "I want to stop these people," she said. "I want Mariposa and Angelique to have a better life. If I can do something to help them, then I have to act."

"I want that, too," he said. "But I want you to stay safe."

"I'll be safe," she said. "I know you've got my back." She deliberately repeated the words he'd told her earlier.

"Carmen, you take care of transferring Angelique to foster care," Graham said. "We'll have to manage the switch without anyone who might be watching realizing what's going on."

"They make some pretty realistic-looking baby dolls," Carmen said. "I'll get one of those and a layette. Abby will pretend to care for it as she would Angelique."

"I might as well go back to my trailer in the park campground," Abby said. "That will make it easier for this guy to get to me, and put me closer to all of you."

"I'll go with you," Michael said.

Graham gave him a hard look. "It might be better to send someone else."

"No, sir. I can do this."

Graham's expression remained grim, but he nodded. "All right. Go on to the trailer. Carmen and Marco will meet you there later to pick up the baby and substitute the doll. Randall, you and Lance can take turns watching Abby's trailer. I doubt this guy will try anything so soon, but stay on your guard."

"Yes, sir."

Abby carried Angelique, while Michael gathered up the diapers, formula and other baby supplies, along with an overnight bag from his locker. "I'll be sure to bring a car seat when we come to get her," Carmen said, following them to her Cruiser, which Michael was borrowing until his could be replaced. "Right now, you don't have far to go to the campground."

Everything at her trailer looked just as she'd left it, though Michael insisted on searching all around the outside and checking out the inside while she waited with the baby. "I don't think anyone's been here since you left," he said at last, and held the door open for her to enter.

The baby started crying before they were through the door. "I think it's time for a diaper change," Abby said.

"I'll get the stuff out of the car."

When he returned, she was still standing in the middle of the room with the wailing baby. "What's wrong?" he asked.

"I don't know where to put her. I'm not exactly set up for a baby."

Michael looked around at the compact space, then set the box of supplies on the table and began emptying it out. "We can put her in here. It's about the size of a bassinet, and she won't fall out."

"You're brilliant." She grinned at him.

"I have my moments." He grabbed a towel from the counter and used it to line the box, then slid it toward her. "Instant cradle."

"Hand me a diaper first."

While she changed the baby, he put away the formula and other supplies. She wedged the box between the dinette and sofa and settled the baby inside. Michael sat beside her on the sofa. "Now what?" he asked.

"Why don't you take a shower, then I'll grab one," she said.

"Are you suggesting I need one?" He pretended to look offended.

"No comment." She stood. "I'm going to make some tea. The bathroom is kind of small, but I think you'll find everything you need."

While she filled the teakettle and took a mug from the cabinet, she listened to the water beating against the wall of the shower and tried not to think of Michael, naked, just on the other side of that barrier. But once the image was fixed in her mind, of his sculpted shoulders and arms and muscular abs, she could think of nothing else. Her imagination filled in the rest of the picture, until desire settled over her in a languid heat.

She forced her mind away from the fantasy and savored the memory of the kiss they'd shared earlier in the day. In that moment, kissing him had seemed the most natural thing in the world—the thing she had wanted most. She'd lusted after men before, but she couldn't remember ever feeling so close to one. She hadn't been in a serious relationship in years—before she went to war. A lifetime ago, when she was a different person.

Was it only because circumstance and danger had thrown them together that she felt this way? Did she feel so comfortable with him because they were both veterans? Or because he'd saved her life when she was injured in Afghanistan? Was he right, and fate had somehow brought them together? She slipped her hand into her pocket and caressed the little rabbit figure. All these years, she'd held on to the token, feeling it was somehow important. Had the caring the gift of the rabbit represented now grown into something more—even into love?

The bathroom door opened and he emerged wearing only a pair of low-slung jeans, toweling his hair. She stared at the drops of water glinting in the dusting of brown hair across his muscular chest and her mouth went dry. Michael Dance in uniform was an impressive sight, but Michael Dance half naked was enough to make her forget her own name.

He tossed the towel aside and grinned, and she blushed, sure he had caught her staring. "I feel almost human again," he said. He moved toward her at the same time she tried to leave the kitchen area, and they collided. The trailer suddenly felt too small to contain them. She mumbled an apology and tried to slip past, and he put out a hand to steady her, freezing her in place.

He smoothed his hand down her arm and a tremor rocked her. Her skin burned where he touched her, and she fought the urge to lean into him, to lose herself in the feel of his body against hers. She looked up and realized he'd shaved, the scent of his shaving cream filling her senses.

"Tight fit," he said.

Why did her traitorous mind turn those words into a come-on, with thoughts of how well the two of them would fit together? She looked away—at the floor, the wall—anything but those sensuous lips, beckoning. If she started to kiss him now, she'd forget all about the shower, and the baby, and everything but slaking the desire that rocked through her.

"I'll just, um, take my shower now," she said, pushing past him.

"Don't you need to wait for the water to warm up again?"

"That's okay." A little cold water might be just what she needed.

The water was warm enough, though. She took her time in the shower, washing her hair and shaving her legs. *As if I was prepping for a big date*, she thought.

But this was no casual date. Michael was spending the night here in her trailer. Considering the electricity they'd managed to generate with only a brief touch, she wasn't foolish enough to believe they wouldn't act on that attraction at some point. But when—and what might happen afterward—was anyone's guess.

She slipped into yoga pants and a T-shirt and blow-dried her hair, but didn't bother with makeup. She didn't want to seem obvious or desperate. Besides, the man had seen her at her absolute worst. A little mascara and lipstick weren't going to change his opinion of her.

She opened the bathroom door and was surprised to hear humming. She froze, listening, and made out a few words. "Hush, little baby, don't say a word. Papa's gonna buy you a mockingbird."

She peeked around the door and stared at Michael, standing by the sofa, holding the baby. The infant looked impossibly small in his arms, smiling up at him and cooing as he sang softly. More priceless still was the look on his face, the stern lines and angular features softened in a smile of such tenderness it brought a lump to her throat.

He turned and saw her standing there, and the tips of his ears turned pink. "She was fussy," he said by way of explanation.

"Obviously, you've made a conquest." She joined him in front of the sofa and he tried to hand the baby over, but she waved him off. "Oh, no, she looks very happy where she is."

She sat, and he sat beside her. Angelique gurgled happily. "I've never spent much time around babies," he said.

"Then, you're a natural," she said. "You'll make a good father one day."

He was silent for a moment, both of them watching the baby, who stared back with her solemn brown eyes. "Do you think about it much—having kids, raising a family?" he asked.

"Sometimes," she admitted. "More lately, now that my life is beginning to settle down. Before, when I was in the army, and later, after I was injured, even the possibility of that kind of stability seemed so far away."

"Yeah, I haven't exactly had the kind of life that makes a wife and kids seem like a good idea."

"I have to finish graduate school and find a job—figure out what I'm going to do with the rest of my life." She leaned over and stroked the infant's satin-soft cheek. "But sometimes I wonder if those things are just excuses to keep me from focusing on all the emotional, personal things that are harder to deal with."

"I know what you mean," he said. "I can deal with the toughest situations in my job, but when it comes to relationships...sometimes that's a lot scarier."

Their eyes met, and her heart sped up, fluttering in her chest. "Do I scare you?" she asked, keeping her tone light, a little flirtatious.

"Oh, yeah." He cupped her cheek in his hand. "But I'm a big believer in the importance of facing your fears."

He lowered his head toward her, but the sound of tires on gravel made him straighten, instantly alert. "Someone's coming," he said, and handed her the baby.

He stood and walked to the window and peered out the blinds. Abby clutched the baby to her, aware that the vehicle had stopped outside her door.

"Hey, it's just us," a woman called. "We came by to see how you're settling in with the baby."

At the sound of Carmen's familiar voice, Michael's shoulders relaxed. He pulled on a T-shirt, then went to the door.

Carmen came in, followed by Lance. He carried a large cardboard box labeled Diapers.

"We brought you some more diapers and formula," he said, his voice loud in the evening silence.

He set the box on the table, made sure all the blinds were drawn, then took the top off the diaper box to reveal a realistic-looking baby doll, wrapped in a blanket identical to the one that swaddled Angelique. "It's a doll called My Real Baby," Carmen said. "Isn't it a kick?"

She lifted the doll out of the box, handling it as if it were a real baby, and passed it to Abby. "From a distance, I'm sure no one could tell the difference," she said.

Abby cradled the doll and turned to look at Angelique, who rested in the box on the sofa. "I'm going to miss the real baby, though," she said. "Where are you taking her?"

"The state put me in touch with a woman in Grand Junction who specializes in temporary foster care for infants," Carmen said. "She'll be safe there."

Safer than she would be here with her and Michael, Abby knew, but still, she hated to see her leave.

Carmen picked up Angelique and cooed at her, then transferred her to the diaper box. "I don't guess you've heard anything from our friend?" she said as she tucked blankets around the baby.

"Nothing," Michael said. "But we don't even know if he knows she's here yet."

"We talked it up in town," Lance said. "I stopped for gas and told everyone there about the baby we'd found."

"You'd think he lived for gossip." Carmen elbowed the younger agent in the side. "Everyone was all ears. Maybe some of the talk will get back to our guy."

"Maybe so."

"Call if you need anything." Lance fit the lid back on the diaper box and picked it up.

"Take good care of her." Abby curled her hands into fists to keep from reaching for the baby.

"We will," Carmen said. "See you tomorrow."

They left, and Michael shut and locked the door behind them. Abby sank onto the sofa and listened to the sound of their tires gradually fade to silence. She blinked hard, fighting tears, but they spilled over and rolled down her cheeks.

"Hey, what's wrong?" Michael hurried to her side.

"I didn't even get to say goodbye." She choked back a sob. He took her hand and patted it, but as she continued to sob harder, he pulled her to him. She buried her face against his chest. "I know it's stupid," she said. "I hardly know her, but I felt responsible for her."

"Shh. It's okay." He smoothed his hand down her hair and rocked her against him. "Of course you miss her. It's hard not knowing what's going to happen to her."

She raised her head to look at him. "You understand."

"I try." He kissed her cheek, but she turned and found his lips. She kissed him greedily, hungrily, wanting to blot out the sadness, to forget for a little while about the baby and Mariposa and a stranger who might want her dead.

He responded with the same fervor, wrapping his arms around her and pulling her tight against his chest. The tip of his tongue traced the seam of her lips and she opened to him, tasting the butterscotch candy he liked. They kissed until she was trembling and light-headed, her body humming with awareness of him, but still she wanted more.

She slid her hand beneath his T-shirt and pressed her palm against his stomach, feeling the crisp line of hair that disappeared beneath the waistband of his jeans. He kissed his way to her ear and said, his voice low and husky with need, "If you keep that up, I'm not going to be able to stop."

"I don't want to stop," she said. "I want to make love to you." As if to prove her words, she pushed him back against the sofa, her body slanted over his. He dragged one hand up, over her rib cage, and cupped her breast through her thin T-shirt, the tip a hard bead pressed against his palm. He flicked his thumb back and forth across it, sending little shock waves of desire rocketing through her. Her breath came in gasps, and her eyes drifted shut as she surrendered to the onslaught of sensation.

Then his mouth was on her, the combination of heat and moisture and the gentle abrasion of the fabric driving her wild. She let out a soft moan and fumbled to remove the shirt. He sat up and helped her, then shed his own shirt, so they were both naked from the waist up.

"You're so beautiful." He slid his hands down her sides, as if cradling something precious. "So beautiful."

She believed he would have said the same thing if her body had been scarred like her face. The words wouldn't have been a lie; she believed when Michael looked at her, he saw more than what was on the surface. He always had; maybe that was why she'd fallen in love with him.

She stood and held out her hand. "Let's move to the bed, where we'll be more comfortable."

He grasped her hand and let her pull him up and lead him to the bed at the other end of the trailer. She pulled back the covers and he started to follow, then hesitated. "What is it?" she asked.

"Just a second." He turned and slipped into the bathroom.

She took off her jeans and underwear, so that by the time he returned, she was sitting up in bed, naked.

His gaze took her in, and the wanting in his eyes made her tremble all over again. "What took you so long?" she said.

He held up a condom in a foil packet. "I had to get this from my overnight bag."

She smiled. "You think of everything."

"I was a Boy Scout, remember? Their motto is Be Prepared."

"Something tells me they weren't thinking of situations like this." She moved over to make room for him.

He stopped to shed his own jeans and her heart beat faster as she stared—while trying to appear not to stare—at his body. He was as gorgeous as her fantasies.

They lay on their sides facing each other, the dimmed reading lights on either side of the bed providing soft illumination. He traced his hand down the curve of her side, then cupped her bottom and drew her close once more. "I feel as if I've been waiting for this moment for a long time," he said. "Does that seem crazy?"

"No." She felt the same way. As if her reluctance

to go out with other men had been because she hadn't met *him* yet. Maybe those frantic moments on a helicopter over Afghanistan had forged a bond too deep for understanding. She only knew that with him, she lost the shyness and desire to close herself off and hide away. She wanted to open to him, to reveal everything, to be with him, in this moment, as she'd never allowed herself to be before.

"Make love to me," she whispered, and kissed him lightly on the lips.

He deepened the kiss, and soon they were entwined, arms and legs wrapped around each other, hands and lips stroking, exploring. He pulled away only long enough to roll on the condom, then he drew her close once more and entered her. She wrapped her legs around him, wanting to shout in joy or triumph, but then he began to move and she lost all power of speech or thought. There was only wave after wave of wonderful sensation building within her.

Her climax was the largest wave, washing over her, filling her with light and life, then releasing her, floating. Soaring. He tightened his hold on her and found his own release, crying out her name. "Abby!"

Afterward, they remained entwined, her head pillowed on his arms, her fingers stroking his chest. "I wasn't sure I'd ever feel that wonderful again," she said.

"I'm glad you don't feel you have to hide anything from me." He traced the scar on her face with the tip of one finger. With a start, she realized she lay with that side of her face to the light, her hair tucked back behind her ear. Even in sleep, she usually lay so the scar was hidden. But though this position felt a little awkward—exposed—it didn't feel wrong.

She snuggled closer to him. "You've seen me at my worst and didn't run away," she said. "I guess I really don't have anything to hide."

"I'll always be here for you," he said. "I won't let anyone hurt you again."

Michael woke early, long habit preventing him from sleeping much past sunrise. Gray light filled the trailer, and outside a bird was singing a morning chorus. Abby lay curled on her side beside him, her back to him, her face half buried in the covers. He rolled over, trying not to disturb her, and studied her sleeping form. Maybe he should pinch himself to make sure he wasn't dreaming. He'd had similar dreams often enough over the years. Sometimes he'd worried something was wrong with him; who let the memory of one woman with whom he'd never even spoken possess him so?

But it didn't matter why his attraction to Abby had stuck with him all these years, only that she was here with him now. Whether fate or chance had brought them together, he'd be her guardian and her lover. Neither of them would be alone again.

She stirred, as if feeling his gaze on her, and rolled onto her back and smiled up at him. "How long have you been watching me?" she asked.

"Only a few minutes." He moved closer; her skin was warm from sleep, so soft and smooth.

"Mmm. You're definitely awake." Smiling, she reached down to stroke him.

He resisted the urge to pull her onto him right away, and kissed her shoulder. "You're definitely nicer to wake up to than my alarm."

"Give me a second. I'll be right back." She patted

his shoulder and slid out of bed. He rolled onto his back and stared up at the ceiling of the trailer, which was only a few feet above his head. He didn't want thoughts of the world outside to intrude on this moment, but of course they did. He wondered how Angelique was doing, and if El Jefe thought she was still with Abby.

She slipped back into bed, smelling of mint toothpaste, her hair combed and the sleep washed from her eyes. "My turn," he said, and hurried to banish his own morning breath and retrieve another condom from his bag.

When he returned to the bed, she waited with open arms. He pulled her close, savoring the sensation of her breasts pillowed against his chest, the nipples already erect and hard. She draped her thigh over his, pressing close, eager. "What time do you have to report in?" she asked.

"Not for another hour or so," he said. "We have plenty of time."

"Time for what?" she teased.

He snugged her more tightly against him. "Time for me to show you more of what you've been missing."

"Or maybe I'll be the one to show you a thing or two." She untangled herself from him and sat up, then pushed him back against the pillows and straddled him.

"Oh, you think so." He caressed her waist.

"I wasn't a biology major for nothing. Hand me that condom," she said. "Class is in session."

They fell asleep again and woke to the buzzing of Michael's phone as it vibrated against the bedside table. He rolled over and snatched it up while Abby propped herself on her elbow and watched. She felt warm and relaxed and a little sore, but in a good way. She smiled, remembering how the soreness had come about. Clearly, all she needed was a little more practice with Michael to be in excellent shape.

"Nothing going on here," he said. "Did you get Angelique placed all right?…I'll tell Abby…She slept fine, as far as I know…Now, how would I know that?" The tips of his ears flushed red and Abby covered her mouth, smothering a giggle. She loved that he could still get flustered like that.

He hung up the phone and rolled onto his back. "That was Carmen. She said Angelique was settling in well when she left her last night. The woman is in her forties and has two teenagers. Angelique will be the only baby with her right now and seemed to really take to the woman."

"Thanks for letting me know. What did she say that made you blush?"

He turned even redder. "She wanted to know if I kept you up late last night—and if your bed was comfortable."

"So she knew you were attracted to me?"

"I think the whole team knew. I'm not so good at hiding my feelings."

"I guess I was the one who was slow on the uptake," she said. "At least for a while." She sat up. "And though I'd like to stay in bed with you all day, I guess we'd better get up. What's the plan for the day?"

"I guess you should be seen out and about with the baby. We want to give El Jefe every chance to find you and make his move."

"It won't be the same as having a real baby to hold, but I'll do my best."

Fifteen minutes later, they were both dressed and Abby had coffee brewing. "I'm going to go outside and look around," Michael said. He slid his gun into the holster on his utility belt. "I never heard anything last night, but you never know."

"We were both a little preoccupied last night," she said.

"True."

He opened the door and stepped out into the clear, thin light of early morning. The air still held a touch of the night's chill, and smelled of piñon and cedar. The campsites on either side of Abby's trailer were empty, and trees screened the view from any other site. Her car sat parked beside the picnic table and the empty fire ring, the borrowed Cruiser next to it. Nothing looked out of place.

He turned to survey the trailer and his heartbeat sped up. A folded sheet of paper fluttered against the door, held in place by a piece of blue tape.

He returned to the trailer and retrieved a knife from the drawer in the kitchen. "What is it?" Abby asked. She followed him to the door. "Is something wrong?"

"Someone left you a note." He slid the blade of the knife beneath the tape, detaching the note from the door. Holding it by the corner, he unfolded it and scanned the brief message.

"What does it say?" Abby stood on tiptoe, trying to see over his shoulder. "Let me see."

He held the note out to her. "Don't touch it. Just read it."

She frowned. "I can't. It's in Spanish."

He'd forgotten for a moment she didn't read the language. "It's from Mariposa. She wants you to meet her. She says she's safe and can take the baby now."

Chapter 13

Abby stared at the note, wishing she could read the words for herself. "Does this mean she managed to get away from the people who were holding her prisoner?" she asked. "How did she know where to find me?"

"She didn't." Michael tapped the note with his index finger. "This is a fake. A trick to lure you away to a place where it will be easier to kidnap Angelique and get rid of you."

Her initial excitement over the note faded. Of course he was right. "Mariposa couldn't have known I was here," she said.

"Of course not. If she did, why not knock on the door and ask to see her baby right away?"

"I can understand why she wouldn't do that," Abby said. "If she's in the United States illegally, she wouldn't want to risk running into someone who works for border patrol. I mean, your car is parked out front."

"Point taken. But I don't believe she wrote this note," he said.

"Or she wrote it because someone forced her to," Abby said. Had El Jefe convinced Mariposa it was safe for her to have her child with her again? "I wish I knew why that man wants the baby."

"Does it matter?" Michael asked. "Even if it's because he's the father and loves her, what kind of life could she have with her mother as a prisoner?"

Abby hugged her arms across her chest, suddenly cold despite the growing warmth from the sun. "What do we do now?" she asked.

"I want to show this note to Graham and the rest of the team," he said. "Let's bundle up the baby and go over to headquarters."

Abby went through the motions of arranging the doll in the sling around her body. "This feels weird," she said.

"It may feel weird, but it looks real," he said. "That's all that counts. Just keep up the charade while we're outside, in case anyone is watching."

So she cradled the doll to her and pretended to coo and fuss over it as she walked to the Cruiser and climbed into the passenger seat. Michael started the engine. "Do you really think someone is watching us?" she asked.

"That note tells me they are." He checked the mirrors, then backed out of his parking spot.

"Then, they know you spent the night in my trailer."

He glanced at her. "Does that bother you? That other people know we were together?"

"No. But won't they be suspicious? The Cruiser makes it obvious you're with the task force, even if they didn't recognize you before."

"Just because I'm with the task force doesn't mean I was on duty last night. We're allowed to have personal lives. But just in case whoever is spying on us has doubts..." He shifted the Cruiser into Park and leaned across the seat and kissed her.

She let out a small gasp of surprise, then relaxed into him, reaching up one hand to twine her fingers in his hair as he deepened the kiss, his lips firm against her own, tantalizing and once again awakening desire she'd thought long dormant. When at last he broke contact, she stared up at him, a little breathless. "I'd say that was pretty convincing."

"I wasn't acting, if you were worried about that," he said.

"No." He hadn't been acting last night, either. The connection between them had been very real—and a little unnerving, if she was being completely honest with herself. She wasn't sure she was ready to jump into a relationship, especially with a man whose life was so complicated. She'd gotten through the years since her return from the war by keeping her life simple—no ties, no long-term commitments, no lasting obligations to anyone but herself. It was a shallow way to live, but a safe one. Michael was luring her into something much deeper—and scarier.

At ranger headquarters, they found Simon hunched over a computer in the front room. He frowned at the doll Abby unwrapped from the sling. "What are you two up to?" he asked.

"Someone left a suspicious note on Abby's door last night," Michael said. "Where's the G-man?"

"I'm here." Graham emerged from his office. He looked tired, as if he hadn't slept well. Was he worried about her or Angelique? Abby wondered. Or did some new development in the case trouble him?

"This was taped to the door of Abby's trailer this morning." Michael handed Graham the note.

The captain took a pair of reading glasses from his front pocket and slipped them on, then studied the torn scrap of paper. "Do you know who left it?" He looked at Abby. "Did you hear anyone? See anyone?"

"No, sir," Michael answered, brisk and military.

"No," Abby echoed, and looked away, focused on rearranging the blankets around the baby doll, as if doing so was an urgent task she could put off no longer. She marveled at Michael's ability to keep his expression neutral, revealing nothing. For much of the time last night, the two of them had been so focused on each other there could have been a drag race on the road outside her campsite and she wouldn't have noticed.

"Weren't Lance and Randall watching the place all night?" Michael asked.

"They were," Graham said. "If they'd seen anything suspicious, they would have called it in." He laid the note on the table. "We'll dust this for prints, though I doubt we'll come up with anything."

"We got a match off that bucket that was left behind at the camp," Simon said.

"Who is it?" Michael asked.

"The woman's prints didn't pull up anything, but the man's belong to Raul Meredes." Simon turned to Michael. "Ever hear of him?"

Michael shook his head. "No. Who is he?"

"He has ties to the Milenio cartel out of Guadalajara," Graham said. "He was the chief suspect in the murder of a sheriff's deputy on the Texas border, but they couldn't make the charges stick."

"He's been operating on both sides of the border for years," Simon said. "Smuggling drugs and people."

"I don't think he wrote this note." Carmen leaned over Graham's shoulder and read the note. "The writing looks feminine to me."

"It does to me, too," Abby said. "But El Jefe—Meredes—could have forced her to write it. Or another woman might have written it."

"I don't suppose you saw any sign of a blonde American woman in the group at those trailers," Graham said.

"You mean Lauren Starling?" Michael asked. "So she's still missing."

"The Denver police are reluctant to call it a missing person. Apparently, she has a history of erratic behavior, and she pulled a disappearing act like this before. But the family is starting to make noise, so they've asked us to take a closer look—not that we have anything to go on. The car is clean—no note, map or anything indicating her intentions."

"I don't think she was at the camp," Abby said. "Everyone I saw had dark hair and looked Latino."

"Just thought I'd ask." Graham turned his attention back to the note. "What do we do about this?"

"It's a fake," Michael said. "Someone is trying to lure Abby and the baby into danger."

"The baby is safe," Carmen said. "Whatever we decide to do won't endanger her."

"We aren't going to do anything," Michael said. "It's too dangerous."

Abby froze in the act of tucking a blanket more securely around the doll. The voice was Michael's, but it could have been her father, telling her she couldn't join the army, or men in her unit protesting that she wasn't capable of leading a patrol, family members saying she couldn't go away to college, or she shouldn't study biology, or do research in remote areas. All her life, people had been telling her what she couldn't do or what she wasn't capable of. *Female* or *beautiful* or *wounded* had been labels they used against her that only made her want to dig in her heels and prove them wrong.

"We've had another new development, which may or may not be related," Graham said.

Abby stopped fussing with the blanket and turned to face the captain once more. He hadn't agreed with Michael. In fact, he'd changed the subject.

"What new development?" Michael arched one eyebrow and waited.

"Richard Prentice has blocked a park service road that crosses his land," Graham said. "It's a public road that predates the park. It's the shortest route—the only route, really—to some rare petroglyphs in the canyon. A group from the University of Denver has been studying them off and on for the past two years. This morning, they found barricades blocking the road. Prentice's lawyers filed an injunction yesterday and a judge ordered the road closed, pending a hearing."

"Why is he closing the road now, after all this time?" Michael asked.

"Because he can," Simon said.

"Or because he's doing something he doesn't want anyone getting close enough to see," Lance said.

"Something like what?" Abby asked.

Graham frowned. Maybe he was weighing the wisdom of discussing a task force case with a civilian. Abby wished she'd kept her mouth shut. Now he might send her from the room. "Abby is part of this now," Carmen said. "And she knows how to keep what we say confidential."

"Of course," she agreed, and sent Carmen a grateful look.

Graham nodded. "Sensors we planted on the public road to measure traffic into the park indicate an increase in the number of vehicles turning onto Prentice's ranch," he said. "More than we can credit to a few college students on their way to the petroglyphs, or Prentice and his various workers and visitors."

"Who do you think is going in and out of there?" Michael asked.

"We've been doing frequent drive-bys, but we haven't seen much," Randall said.

"Prentice complains loudly and long—to the press, to government officials and to anyone else who will listen—that we're harassing him," Simon said.

"We've tried taking a look from the air, but we haven't spotted anything suspicious—yet," Graham said.

"Do you think whatever is going on there has anything to do with Mariposa and Raul Meredes and the illegal workers we saw in the trailers?" Abby asked.

"We just don't know," Graham said.

"But those trailers and people had to go somewhere when they left that wash," Simon said. "Prentice's ranch makes a convenient place for them to disappear quickly. We can't find anyone who saw them after they left you two that morning, and once they hit the park road, the tracks disappeared."

"If I go to this meeting with Mariposa or Meredes or whoever, you can find out more," Abby said. "You might learn something really useful that would help crack the case."

"No!" Michael's protest drowned out whatever Graham had been about to say. Even a stern look from his boss didn't make him back down. "We shouldn't endanger a civilian," he added.

"This is what we wanted all along, isn't it?" Abby asked. "To lure him into the open so that you can capture him."

"It's too risky," Michael said. "Our original plan was to lure him here, where we have more control over everything. If you move into his territory, the control shifts to him."

Was he so worried about control over the outcome of this plan—or control over her? She tried to tell herself Michael wasn't like that, but her past experiences with the men in her life told her otherwise. After all, how well did she really know this man? He'd first made a claim on her because he'd saved her life. In the golden afterglow of lovemaking, had she misinterpreted an unhealthy obsession for love?

She forced herself to look directly at him, to try to read the true emotion in his dark eyes. But she found only stubbornness. "I'm not helpless," she said. "I've been in dangerous situations before. Much more dangerous. I'm trained to look after myself."

"You don't have an army behind you this time," he said. "Don't confuse foolishness with bravery."

The words stung like a slap. "You don't have a right to tell me what to do!" she protested.

"Abby's right." Graham stepped between them. "This could be the break we've been looking for. If we can get to Meredes, he could lead us to the person behind this whole operation."

"We might find a link between him and Prentice," Simon said.

"This might help save Mariposa and a lot of other innocent people," Abby said. "How could I not do it?"

"We'll set up the meeting for a neutral place," Graham said. "And we'll have plenty of our people watching, on guard if Meredes tries to pull anything."

"If you try to take him there, he's liable to use Abby as a hostage," Michael said.

"If we can't get to him without endangering her, we'll follow him after he leaves," Graham said.

"I want to do this," Abby said. "I want to help these people."

"I still don't think—"

But she didn't get to hear what he did or didn't think. Graham's phone rang, the old-fashioned clanging silencing them all. "Captain Ellison," he answered. He stood up straighter, shoulders tensed, expression alert. "Where?…How many?…We'll be right there."

He ended the call. "That was Randall. He and Marco think they've found the trailers from the camp, or at least some of them."

"Where?" Simon was the first to speak.

"Are there any people in them?" Carmen asked.

Graham turned to the map on the wall behind him.

He studied it for a moment, then pointed to a spot on the edge of the parkland. "There's a wash through here. The trailers are there."

Michael joined Graham in front of the map. "That's on the very edge of Richard Prentice's ranch," he said, pointing to the white area marked Private Property on the map.

"And they almost certainly crossed Prentice's land on that road he closed in order to get there," Simon said.

"How did Randall and Marco get there?" Carmen asked.

"They hitched a ride on a BLM chopper," Graham said. "Someone who owed Randall a favor."

"The bigger question is, how are we going to get there?" Michael asked. "Prentice still has the road closed."

"Then we'll have to persuade him to open it." Graham fished car keys from his pocket. "Let's go. Michael, you'd better stay here with Abby."

"I'll come with you," Abby said.

"I can't let you do that," Graham said.

"You need Michael with you, and you can't leave me here unguarded as long as Meredes is looking for me and the baby. Instead of sacrificing one man to babysit me, let me come along. I promise to stay in the vehicle, out of your way." She hesitated, then added, "Please. I need to know if Mariposa is there—if she's safe."

Graham glanced at Michael, then back to Abby. "You can come, but you're to stay well away from the action. Ride with Simon."

"Thank you," she said.

"She can ride with me," Michael said.

"No. I need you focused on the job, not her," Graham said. "Carmen will ride with you. Now let's get going."

Abby tried to arrange the baby doll more comfortably in the sling as the others gathered their gear and prepared to head out. Michael approached her. "I just want to talk to you for a minute," he said in response to her wary look. He pulled her to a corner of the room, away from the others.

"I know what I'm getting into," she said. "I don't need you to protect me."

"I'm not saying you're not smart and capable," he said. "I know you are. But I just found you." He stared into her eyes, pleading. "I don't want to lose you."

"This isn't about you. Or me. It's about doing what's right." She eased from his grasp. "If the captain thinks I can help by agreeing to meet with Meredes, then I have to do it."

Instead of telling her that he didn't like it but he understood—words she wanted, even needed, to hear from him—he turned away. He retreated to the other side of the room, arms folded over his chest, expression sullen.

She struggled to compose herself, to face the others as a strong, determined woman, not letting them see her heartbreak. One night and a few kisses didn't mean Michael had a claim on her, though the pain in her chest as she thought this warned her he might have already staked out a territory she didn't want to relinquish.

Chapter 14

"You hold on to that steering wheel any tighter it's going to come off in your hands. Might make driving awkward."

Carmen spoke lightly, making the words a joke, but when Michael glanced over at his coworker in the Cruiser's passenger seat, she was studying him intently. "You need to relax," she said. "An overbearing attitude isn't going to go over well with a woman like Abby."

He glanced in the mirror at the car behind him, which contained Abby and Simon, but the glare of the sun on the tinted windshield made it impossible to see into the vehicle.

"Leave her alone for a while," Carmen said. "Give her some space and she'll come around."

"What do you know about it?" he asked, annoyed. "Were you eavesdropping?"

"I didn't have to hear a word to know she was upset. Her body language when you ordered her to stand down told the whole story. She wanted you to back her up on this and instead, you tried to shut her down." She shook her head. "Wrong move."

"Shut up." He didn't need anyone telling him where he'd gone wrong with Abby. He'd known he was making a mistake as soon as the words were out of his mouth, but he couldn't stop himself from saying them. She needed someone to look out for her. She'd been pushing through on her own for so long she didn't know how to stop fighting. He'd tried to tell her he was there for her, but instead of reassuring her, he'd come across like some big bully. And he didn't know how to correct that impression now.

Instead, he was stuck watching while she remained determined to put her life on the line to deal with a man it was his job to take care of. His only hope was that something would happen between now and then to make a meeting between Abby and Meredes unnecessary.

Graham, leading the trio of vehicles, slowed for the turn onto Prentice's ranch. The big iron gate was open, allowing them to pass beneath the massive stone archway. "Smile, you're on camera," Michael said, nodding to the lens mounted on the side of the arch.

"And here's the welcoming committee," Carmen said as a Jeep blocked the road ahead. Three beefy men in desert camo, semiautomatic rifles slung across their chests, piled out.

"Armed guards?" Michael shifted the Cruiser into Park and pulled in alongside Graham's vehicle. "Who does this guy think he is?"

"Maybe one of the richest men in the country feels like he has a lot to protect," Carmen said.

"Or a lot to hide." He unsnapped his seat belt and climbed out of the Cruiser and joined the others—except Abby, who'd remained in the car, as ordered, as they gathered around Graham.

"I need you all to get back into your vehicles," the tallest of the trio, his white-blond hair buzzed into a flattop, said.

No one moved. Michael glared at the other two guards, who took up positions at the front and passenger side of the vehicle. They kept their assault rifles pointed toward the ground, but their manner was still threatening.

"Sir, I'll have to ask you to turn around," the tallest guard said. "This is private property."

"Captain Graham Ellison, Colorado Public Lands Task Force." Graham flashed his badge and credentials. "I'm here to see Mr. Prentice on official business."

"Mr. Prentice doesn't see anyone without an appointment." The guard's expression remained impassive, his gaze fixed on Graham. The credentials might have been bubblegum cards for all he cared.

"I think he'll want to see us," Graham said. "We've discovered what appears to be illegal activity taking place on his property and we need to bring this to his attention."

A single crease formed in the middle of the guard's brow at the words *illegal activity*.

"If you call Mr. Prentice's office, they'll put you in touch with his legal team," he said.

Apparently, one lawyer wasn't enough for this guy—he needed a whole team.

"We don't need to speak to a legal team." Graham's tone grew flinty. "We need to speak with Mr. Prentice. Call him and tell him he needs to talk to us now, or the next time he sees us, we'll have a warrant for his arrest."

The threat was a bluff. While they might find a judge to issue a warrant, they were just as likely to come up against one who was friendly with Prentice. But Graham did a good job of making the words sound like a promise. The guard hesitated. "Call him," Graham said.

The guard turned away, though the other two remained in position by the Jeep. Michael tapped his foot. If it was up to him, he'd hit the siren and drive forward, forcing the guards to jump out of the way. But maybe that was why Graham was the commander and he wasn't.

The guard finished his phone call and turned back to the car. "Mr. Prentice will spare a few minutes for you. You can follow me to the house." He pointed to Graham. "Just you. The others can stay here."

"Dance, come with me," Graham said. "The rest of you stay here."

Michael moved toward Graham's Cruiser. The guard started to argue, but Graham cut him off. "I'm not going in alone. You wouldn't."

The guard frowned, but nodded and returned to his Jeep. A quarter mile down the drive, a second Jeep fell in behind them. "These people are really beginning to annoy me," Michael said.

"That's probably the point," Graham says. "He wants to rattle us."

"I didn't say I was rattled—just annoyed." He scowled at the building that loomed in front of them. Richard Prentice's "ranch house" was a castle, complete with gray stone walls and a round tower. The three-bay garage to one side was larger than most homes.

Graham parked the Cruiser behind a black Escalade that sat in front of the door, and they climbed out and followed the guards into a dark foyer. After the bright light outside, Michael couldn't make out much about the interior of the house. A long hall seemed to lead farther into the dwelling, but the guard ushered them into a small room just off the foyer. Lined with bookshelves, this room seemed to be a library, though Michael wondered if their host had ever opened most of the matched leather-bound volumes that filled the shelves in neat, coordinated rows.

They waited a full ten minutes, Michael pacing while Graham sat quietly. Neither man said a thing. Michael was sure Prentice had the room bugged—all those books could conceal a lot of recording equipment. "He's not going to see us," Michael said finally. "I think we should go ahead and call the judge, get the warrant."

Thirty seconds later, the door to the room opened and a short man in an expensive suit strolled in. "Richard Prentice." He offered his hand. "Sorry to have kept you waiting."

Based on his reputation for outsize behavior, Michael was startled to find that the man himself was so unimpressive. The ring on his finger was probably worth more than Michael made all year, but Prentice was barely five-eight, and his hair was thinning.

"The phone call I received led me to believe you're accusing me of some illegal activity," Prentice said.

"Not at all," Graham said. "But we wanted to alert you to some illegal activity going on on your property— I know you'll want to cooperate in ge' 'ing the criminals off your land and in jail where they belong."

"Won't you sit down?" Prentice indicated a pair of wing-back chairs arranged on either side of a small table. He and Graham sat, while Michael remained standing.

Prentice perched on the edge of his chair, gripping his knees. "You'll need to explain things a little more clearly before I decide if I'm going to 'cooperate.'" He didn't exactly make quote marks in the air around the word, but Michael heard the qualifiers in his tone of voice. Prentice hadn't gotten where he was by cooperating with anyone.

"We've been investigating a possible human trafficking case on federal lands adjacent to your ranch," Graham said. "A man named Raul Meredes, with ties to a Mexican drug cartel, may be behind the ring."

Michael studied Prentice, watching for a reaction to Meredes's name. Did he imagine the way Prentice's lips compressed and the muscles of his jaw tightened? "I've never heard of him," Prentice said. "What does any of this have to do with me?"

"Our aerial reconnaissance has revealed a possible camp where we believe Meredes is holding a number of illegal aliens captive, located just outside the borders of your property."

Prentice's frown deepened at the words *aerial re-*

connaissance, but he let it pass. "Let me make sure I understand you, Captain," he said. "This isn't happening on my property."

"No, but—"

"Then, it really isn't my concern." He stepped aside. "You may leave now."

Graham held up his hand. "We have reason to believe Meredes has been using the area—including portions of your estate—for the manufacture and production of narcotics, and as a way station for a human trafficking pipeline from Mexico and South America into Denver."

"Drugs and human trafficking. Those are pretty serious charges. I think I would have noticed if anything like that was taking place around here, and I can promise you, I haven't."

"Your property encompasses over five hundred acres," Graham said. "I think it would be impossible to monitor everything that takes place on an estate that size, especially when so much of it is roadless and rugged. We believe an operation that began on public lands has spilled over onto your property."

"But you don't have proof of that." He looked as calm as if he was discussing the weather.

"If the trailers we spotted from the air are part of the illegal camp, the only way they could have reached their current location is by crossing your land," Graham said.

"I don't put much stock in speculation." He stood back, a clear signal of dismissal. "Thank you for letting me know about this, gentlemen. I'll have my men investigate the matter and I'll let you know what I find."

"This isn't a matter for civilians," Graham said.

"We'll need to conduct the investigation. That means we need access across your land to the site."

Prentice looked as if he'd bitten into something rotten. "I see where this is going. This was all a ruse to gain access to my property."

"The lives of innocent people are at stake here, Mr. Prentice."

"If, as you say, they're in this country illegally, and involved in the manufacture and distribution of drugs, then they are far from innocent."

Michael wondered if Prentice practiced that sneer in the mirror, or if it came naturally.

"All we're asking is permission to bring our crews and equipment across your land," Graham said. "On a road that until your court action was a public thoroughfare."

"The court has sided with me in agreeing that the road is private. And my property is private. I won't have you using it to harass me further."

"Mr. Prentice, this may be hard for you to believe, but the world does not revolve around you," Michael said. "This is about other innocent lives that are in danger. Any momentary discomfort for you is incidental."

Prentice glared at him. "I'll ask you to leave now." He turned to Graham. "If you do try anything, my private security force will prevent you from proceeding further. You'll also be hearing from my attorneys."

Graham took a step toward Prentice. He towered over the businessman by at least six inches, and outweighed him by fifty pounds. He didn't raise his voice, because he didn't have to. Years of command, first in the marines, then in law enforcement, had imbued him with a sense of authority. "You can either cooperate and give us access to the approach to that canyon, or I *will* obtain a warrant to search this property. We'll bring in dog teams and helicopters and CSI and everyone else we can think of. We'll search every inch of this place. And I'll make sure the press knows why."

Sweat beaded on Prentice's upper lip, though his expression didn't change. "That's an invasion of privacy."

"Yes, it is. But one that would be necessary."

Michael could practically hear the man's teeth grinding, but Graham had him backed into a corner, and he knew it. He might successfully stall for a while, but if Graham carried out his threat—especially if he got the media involved—Prentice would have no peace for weeks, even months. "You don't really give me any choice, do you?" he said.

"Not really," Graham answered.

Prentice stepped back. "Fine. Use the road. But my men will be watching, and if you travel too far afield, you will need that warrant."

Graham nodded. "Thank you. We appreciate your cooperation." He moved past the businessman; Michael followed.

They'd reached the front door when Prentice's voice rang out behind them. "What will you do with Meredes?" he asked.

Graham looked back. "We'll arrest him and question him. We don't believe he's acting alone. We believe he has someone in Colorado—someone with money and power—who is funding his operations. Possibly a large landowner with a history of antagonism toward the government."

Prentice's face reddened. "What are you saying?"

"I'm not saying anything, Mr. Prentice. Merely answering your question." He nodded. "Goodbye."

Michael waited until they were back in the vehicle before he spoke. "I don't trust him," he said. "He's hiding something."

"He's probably hiding a lot of things," Graham said. "Whether it's anything we're interested in or not, I don't know."

Right. What did they care about Prentice? "What next?"

"Now we see what Randall and Marco uncovered."

They returned to the others, who stood in a cluster around the two Cruisers, Abby with them. Their eyes met, hers full of questions. He resisted the urge to go to her; now wasn't the time. "We have Mr. Prentice's permission to use the road," Graham said.

"We'll escort you," the guard said.

Graham shrugged. "Do you know where we're going?"

"We'll follow you." The guard looked toward the others.

"Don't even think about suggesting they stay behind," Graham said.

They returned to their vehicles and formed a caravan, this time with the guards' two Jeeps bringing up the rear. "What happened in there?" Carmen asked as Michael guided his Cruiser behind Graham's.

"About what we expected—he pretended all of this has nothing to do with him, that his private property rights trump any other concerns. I don't trust him."

"We've never trusted him," Carmen said. "That doesn't mean he's guilty of anything. Maybe he really did close the road after noticing an uptick in traffic. He might not have anything to do with Meredes."

"Then why not cooperate with our efforts to stop him?"

"He's made his reputation out of not cooperating with the Feds on anything. What does he have to gain by doing so now? And he did cooperate in the end. How did Graham manage that?"

"He promised to come back with a warrant and a search team to tear the whole place apart. That worried Prentice enough to give in. But I'm sure we'll be hearing from his lawyers."

"And probably a few journalists. I've noticed he likes to make his case in the press, and they eat it up."

He didn't care about the press. "I wish now Abby had stayed at headquarters."

"Then you would have had to stay, too. Meredes might have decided that was the perfect time to swoop in and take her and the baby."

"You could have stayed with her." Not that staying with Abby was a hardship, but he had a job to do. Staying out of the fray when people needed help struck him as wrong.

"Uh-uh. You signed on for bodyguard duty, not me. Why would I want to sit out the action?"

"I know Spanish. A lot of these immigrants don't speak any English."

"I know Spanish, too, amigo."

They stopped at the edge of the wash. Graham climbed out of his Cruiser and the others joined him. "Randall and Marco said they think the trailers are down here," he said.

"In the bottom of the wash?" Simon looked skeptical.

Graham walked to the edge the ravine and took out a pair of binoculars. "I see something." He passed the glasses to Michael. Sunlight glinted off metal at the bottom of the wash.

One of the guards had out his own binoculars. "Looks to me as if the rancher who owned this before used it as a dump site," he said. "People did that back then—when a ravine was full of junk cars and metal, they'd haul in a load of dirt to cover it up."

"There's no rust on that metal," Michael said. "It hasn't been sitting there for decades."

Graham reached into the Cruiser for his pack. "We'd better go down there."

"We'd better hurry," Carmen said. She'd taken out her own pair of binoculars. "I see movement." She focused the glasses closer. "It's a woman, and she's waving something. I think she's signaling for help."

Chapter 15

Abby stood on tiptoe, trying to see what was happening in the ravine, but here by the Cruiser, she was too far away from the action. Apparently, they'd found some people alive down there, but she had no idea who. She wanted to be helping, instead of stuck up here with this hot, heavy baby doll strapped to her torso. She was tempted to stick the doll in the back of the Cruiser and join the others at the ravine. Who would even notice? Prentice's guards ignored her, their attention focused on the action below.

Michael emerged from the trail that led into the canyon and she started toward him, eager for news. Despite the tension between them earlier, she was sure he wouldn't shut her out.

"Send every ambulance you can spare. And hurry."

He spoke not to her, but into his phone, as he hurried toward her.

"What's going on?" she asked, meeting him in front of the vehicle.

"Hey. Are you okay?" He squeezed her arm and looked into her eyes.

"I'm fine. But what's happening down there?" She nodded toward the canyon. "Who's hurt?"

He released her and moved to the back of the Cruiser and began pulling out emergency gear—a first-aid kit, blankets and water. "It's pretty bad down there," he said. "Maybe a dozen wounded. Some dead." He crammed supplies into a pack as he spoke.

"But how?" Abby tried to take in this news.

"Looks as though somebody—Meredes and his men, probably—pulled the trailers up to the edge of the ravine and pushed them over—with all the people locked inside."

She stared at him, unsure she'd heard him correctly. "Is Mariposa there?" she asked, afraid to say the words.

"I haven't seen her yet, so maybe she wasn't there or she got away."

She hugged the baby closer, as if she could take some comfort from the doll. "Why do something so horrible?"

"I guess they weren't useful to the operation anymore. They were a liability, so he got rid of them."

Nausea rose in her throat. The man responsible for this was the same one who wanted Angelique. Thank God the baby was safe. "What are you going to do?"

He shouldered the pack. "We're going to go after him," he said. "We're going to make him pay for this."

"I have to meet with him," she said. "If that's the best way to draw him out, I have to do it."

He grasped her hand and gave it a gentle squeeze. "I know," he said. "I don't like it, but I understand. I'm sorry I came on so strong before. It's just... I don't want anything to happen to you."

"I'll be okay." She managed a brief smile. "I have a lot to live for."

He glanced over his shoulder at the ravine. "I'd better get back down there."

"What can I do to help?" she asked.

"Nothing right now. Stay up here. Out of the way."

When he was gone, she felt even more useless and worried. The sun beat down with searing intensity. Still cradling her fake charge, she moved into the shade, the shouts of those below drifting up to her as they worked to save the injured and dying. She felt numb, the way she'd felt in Afghanistan after encountering tragedy, the horror of the events too much to take.

She leaned against the tree and closed her eyes, willing herself not to fall apart. This wasn't about her. The others didn't need anyone else to look after right now. She had to keep it together.

Something tugged at her arm and she jerked upright, eyes wide, mouth open to scream, but a hand clamped over her lips silenced her. "Don't make any noise, senorita. While the others are busy, you will come with me." She stared into Raul Meredes's eyes, fighting panic, as he covered her face with a cloth and the world went black.

Abby came to in the backseat of a vehicle, wedged between the door and the body of a man who sat with a rifle resting across his knees. The vehicle hit a bump and her head knocked against the door. She grunted, the only sound she could make against the gag that all but choked her, and the man turned to look at her, then said something in Spanish to whoever was driving.

Her arms and shoulders ached from where one of her captors had tied her hands behind her back, and the bandanna in her mouth tasted of cotton and dust. Her captors hadn't bothered covering her eyes, though all she could see from here was the back of the seat in front of her, and the profile of the man beside her. He wore fatigues and dusty boots, and the hands that cradled the rifle were dirty, the nails bitten.

This man wasn't Meredes. She wondered if he was driving. Was there another guard in the front passenger seat? She and Michael had seen at least three other men with guns when they came to move the trailers, but for all she knew, Meredes had a dozen at his command.

She couldn't see the baby. They would have figured out quickly that it was a fake. They must have been watching, and seen that the others were preoccupied with the goings-on in the canyon. Or maybe Prentice had called Meredes to warn him of the task force's discovery. He couldn't resist the opportunity to snatch the child. Was he furious at being frustrated in his efforts to obtain the baby? Would he take that frustration out on her? A man who would callously push imprisoned people to their death in a canyon wasn't likely to have qualms about hurting a woman who had crossed him.

She wondered how long it would be before Michael and the others realized she was missing. They ought to be able to follow the trail of this vehicle over the rough terrain, but then what? If Meredes planned to use her as a hostage and bargain for the baby, she might have a chance to escape. But what if he wanted to send a different kind of message—by killing her and disposing of the body?

She shuddered and pushed the thought away. That kind of thinking would get her nowhere. In the army, she'd been trained to focus on escape and survival. If she could do the first, she knew how to do the second. She could find food and shelter in the wilderness. All she needed was an opportunity to slip away from Meredes and the man beside her.

The vehicle jerked to a stop, the brakes squealing. The guard got out, then came around to her side of the vehicle, opened the door and took hold of her bound arms and dragged her out of the car. A hot breeze buffeted her as she steadied herself, and she squinted at the surrounding landscape. They'd stopped at the edge of the canyon—Black Canyon, the one that gave the park its name. This must have been part of the gorge that wasn't in the national park, away from tourists and traffic.

She'd correctly guessed that Meredes was driving. He walked around the vehicle and stood in front of her. Though not a big man, he was tall, and wiry. He wore his sideburns long, but was clean shaven, his white shirt stiff with starch, his jeans precisely creased. It seemed odd to find a dandy here in the middle of the wilderness.

He said something in Spanish and the guard pulled a large knife from his belt. Her terror must have shown on her face. He laughed and waved the knife in front of her nose, then bent and cut the restraints from her ankles.

The passenger door of the vehicle opened and Abby received another shock to her system as Mariposa stepped out. The other woman frowned at her. What was she thinking? Was she upset that Abby hadn't brought the baby? Had she known about the plan to kill her coworkers by pushing the trailers into the ravine, or was she an unwilling pawn? What was her relationship to Meredes? Was he her lover? Her captor? Both?

The guard shoved Abby toward the edge of the canyon. Her heart hammered in her chest and she dug in her heels. Did they intend to throw her into the chasm and leave her to die, as they'd done with the workers in the trailers?

Her guard said something in Spanish and Meredes addressed her. "Follow me," he said, and indicated a narrow trail that led along the side of the canyon.

The barrel of the rifle pressed to her back told her she had no choice in the matter. She fell into step behind Mariposa, the guard behind her. Meredes led them along the canyon rim and then down into the canyon itself, the trail cut into the canyon wall. They descended about twenty feet, to a narrow ledge where someone had built a cabin. The stone-and-wood structure hugged the side of the gorge, blending perfectly with its surroundings. It would be invisible from anyone who didn't already know it was there.

Inside, the cabin was furnished simply but comfortably, with a double bed, a sofa and a table with four chairs arranged around an iron woodstove. The guard knelt before the stove and began building a fire. Despite the heat on the canyon rim, the air here in the shadowed chasm held a chill. Meredes shoved Abby into a chair. Mariposa filled a kettle from a water barrel by the door and set it on the stove to heat.

Meredes faced Abby and removed the gag. "What have you done with Angelique?" he asked.

"She's safe," Abby said. She watched Mariposa as she spoke; the woman's shoulders sagged with relief.

"You were stupid to think you could fool me," Meredes said. "Do not make that mistake again."

She said nothing, only glared at him. "Where is the child?" he asked.

"She's somewhere safe," Abby repeated. "She's in a good home." She hoped Mariposa knew enough English to understand the words.

"She belongs here."

"Why? So you can make a slave of her the way you have these other people?"

He slapped her, a hard, stinging blow that snapped her head back and made her ears ring.

"That is not your concern." He shoved her into a chair, then settled onto the sofa. Mariposa brought him a mug; Abby caught the aroma of coffee. He sipped the drink and settled back against the cushions, a man comfortable in his home.

"Why did you murder those people?" she asked.

His expression didn't change. "What people are you accusing me of murdering?"

"The people who worked for you. The ones in the camp. You locked them in their trailers and pushed the trailers into the ravine."

Crockery rattled, and they both turned to look at Mariposa, who quickly turned away. Had she not known about the fate of her fellow immigrants? "I don't know what you're talking about," Meredes said, though his eyes told a different story. The hatred she saw there made her shiver.

"Some of them survived," she said. "The Rangers

rescued them. They'll be able to identify you as the one who held them prisoner, then tried to murder them."

"They cannot identify someone who was not there," he said.

"I don't believe you," she said.

"It doesn't matter to me what you believe," he said. "Once I have the baby, you will be no use to me anymore."

"Do you think you're going to trade me for the baby?" she asked.

"Trade?" He sipped his coffee. "That is what I will let the Rangers think, but I promise you, senorita, you will never leave here alive."

Michael helped load the last stretcher into the waiting ambulance. The man strapped there had borne the rough ride up from the canyon floor in stoic silence, only occasional grunts betraying the pain from his broken leg and ribs. "You're going to be okay," Michael said in Spanish, and patted the man's shoulder. The man stared back at him, one unspoken question in his eyes—*why?*

Michael had asked himself the same question a dozen times in the past two hours. Why would someone do this to innocent people who worked for him? "If Meredes had no use for them anymore, why didn't he just turn them loose in the nearest town to make their own way back to the border or to find work elsewhere?" he asked Carmen as they headed back to his Cruiser. "Why go to so much trouble to harm them?"

"Maybe he wanted to make a point," Simon said. "To let word get around about what happened to anyone who crossed him. Fear is power to a man like that."

"Maybe he's just a psycho who gets off on hurting people," Randall said.

And this was the guy they were willingly going to let Abby face? Michael shuddered, and looked around for Abby. Just seeing her would make him feel better.

"Where's Abby?" he asked.

The others looked around. "Is she in the car?" Carmen asked.

"She's not here," Simon said from beside his Cruiser.

Heart racing, Michael ran to the clump of trees where he'd seen Abby last. He stared at the scuff marks in the dirt, not wanting to believe what he was seeing. "Randall, get Lotte over here," he said.

The young ranger looked up from adding a bottle of water to the dog's dish. "What is it?" he asked.

"Just bring her over here. Now."

"Lotte. Come."

The dog obediently trotted along beside Randall, to where Michael crouched next to the scuff marks. "Abby's gone," he said. "I think this is where they took her. She struggled. I need Lotte to help us find her." He struggled to keep his voice calm and dispassionate, though inside he wanted to scream.

"We don't need a dog to follow this trail." Simon pointed out across the desert. "The tire tracks are easy enough to see in this terrain."

Michael stood and clamped Randall on the shoulder. "Come on," he said. "Maybe we have time to catch up with them."

"Wait just a minute." Graham's command stopped them. He joined them in studying the tire tracks headed into the desert. "You can't go tearing off without a plan."

"Meredes probably isn't alone," Carmen said. "If you corner him, you put Abby in danger."

"She's already in danger," Michael said. "The man's a murderer."

"He took her alive." Graham pointed to the ground. "There's no blood. He probably plans to use her to trade for the baby."

"Which we can't give him," Carmen said.

Michael took a deep breath, struggling to control his emotions. "So we follow him, but we don't make any rash moves. We find out where he's taking Abby and scope out the situation. Then we formulate a plan to rescue her."

"All right." Graham nodded. "Carmen, you go with them. Keep me posted about whatever you find."

Michael pulled out his keys. "Come on," he said.

They piled into the Cruiser, Carmen in the front with Michael, Randall and Lotte in the back. Carmen rolled down her window and leaned out. "It should be pretty easy to follow the tracks through here," she said.

"He must have some kind of hideout," Randall said. "Either that, or he knows a shortcut back to the main road."

"Get the map from the console and tell me if you see any likely hiding places," Michael said. He hunched over the steering wheel, following the faint depressions made by the vehicle's tires across the prairie. He wanted to tear out across the empty expanse, but the rocky ground forced him to reduce his speed to scarcely above a crawl.

The stiff paper of the map crackled as Randall spread it out. "There's half a dozen side canyons branching off from the main gorge in this direction," he said. "Careful you don't drive us into one."

"Do you see any place that would make a good hideout?" Michael asked.

"Dozens of places," Randall said. "There's the canyons, old buildings left from the days when this was a ranch. And he could pull a trailer in anywhere. No roads, though, so he's probably not headed to town."

"Just keep following the tracks," Carmen said. She leaned forward, squinting out the windshield. "And keep your speed down, so you don't kick up dust. We don't want him to know we're tailing him."

"He's far enough ahead he can't see our dust," Michael said, but he forced himself to ease off the accelerator.

He guided the Cruiser along a dry creek bed, around an outcropping of rock. The remains of an old corral appeared on their left, ancient fence posts sticking up from the eroded land like broken teeth. "The map indicates some old ranch buildings around here," Randall said. "Keep an eye out for vehicles."

"I see something." Carmen grabbed his wrist and he braked to a halt. She pointed to the ruins of an old log cabin. "There's a car parked there."

He peered closer and could make out the front bumper and headlights of a vehicle. "Looks like an older Jeep," Randall said.

"Let's get out and take a look." He backed up and parked the Cruiser in the shadow of the outcropping they'd just passed, out of sight of the old Jeep. Michael looked through the gap between the boulders out on what must have been an old bunkhouse or line shack, the roof caved in, glassless windows showing grass and piñons growing up from the dirt floor. The vehicle, an older Jeep Cherokee, had been parked against the remains of a log wall, partially hidden from view.

He settled into position behind the right-hand boulder and took a pair of binoculars from the pack.

"See anything?" Randall asked.

"Just the Jeep. It wasn't one of the vehicles Abby and I saw at the camp. Maybe it's been parked there awhile. It doesn't look as though anything but coyotes have been out here for years."

"The maps designate the ruins as a historical structure," Randall said. "Part of the ranch that operated here before the park."

"Doesn't the park date back to the thirties?" Carmen asked.

"Something like that," Randall said. "Amazing how long things last in this dry air." He snapped the leash on Lotte. "She'll tell us if anyone's been here recently, and where they've gone."

Moving quickly and quietly, they shouldered day packs, and Michael picked up the assault rifle he'd removed from the gun safe at headquarters that morning. The memory of that first day Abby had walked into headquarters, when they'd been pinned down by that sniper, still burned fresh. He could still recall the feel of her body beneath his, and the fierce protectiveness he'd felt for her even then. Multiply that anxiety by twenty now.

They approached the Jeep from an angle, spreading out and putting Lotte in front. The dog remained relaxed, tail up, ears erect, nose alert. "She'd tell us if anyone was around," Randall said. "Whoever parked there is long gone."

"Not too long." Michael pressed his palm against the hood of the vehicle and felt the heat of the engine.

Carmen dropped to one knee at the front of the Jeep. "The pattern on the tires looks the same as the ones we've been following," she said.

He scrutinized the landscape around them, alert for any sign that someone was near. But he didn't have the sense that anyone was watching. A hot wind buffeted them, bringing the scents of sage and piñon. The only sounds were the scrape of their boots on rock and the occasional creak of a pack strap or the clink of the rifle stock against the pack. Whoever had driven this Jeep seemed to have disappeared.

He pulled a pair of thin latex gloves from his pocket and slipped them on, then carefully opened the driver's door. The brown cloth seats were worn, a rip in the back repaired with duct tape. The cup holder was empty, as was the center console and the glove box. No dust collected on the dash. "It looks like they wiped it clean," he said. "But we'll get someone to check for prints anyway."

He moved to the backseat. More of the same. He might have been looking at a used car for sale on a dealer's lot. He started to close the door when the glint of something on the floorboard caught his attention. He bent to get a closer look and his heart stopped beating for a moment. Carefully, he reached down and picked up the little ceramic figure of a brown-and-white rabbit.

"What have you got there?" Carmen came to stand beside him.

"It's Abby's," he said. "She was here." He folded his hand around the good-luck charm and looked at the seemingly empty prairie around them. A few hundred yards away, the ground fell away, into yet another canyon. Abby had been here, maybe only moments before. But where was she now?

Chapter 16

"Please, make yourself comfortable." Raul Meredes motioned to the chair across from the sofa in the little cabin.

"I can't be comfortable with my hands tied like this," Abby said. She'd never be comfortable as long as she was held prisoner here, but she saw no sense in pointing that out to a man whose whole livelihood revolved around imprisoning people against their will.

In answer, he reached into the pocket of his neatly pressed jeans and pulled out a large knife. He pressed a button and a blade sprang out, sharp and gleaming. Abby shrank from it and he laughed, then grabbed her shoulder and turned her around.

Having her hands free again felt wonderful, then it felt awful, as blood flow returned and with it sharp pains like needles, up and down her arms. She massaged her forearms and wrists and looked at Mariposa, who had watched the exchange without a word. The other woman turned away, her attention on the kettle on the stove.

"Sit," Meredes ordered, and Abby did so, perched on the edge of the chair as if poised to run at the first opportunity. But she had nowhere to run, with the deep canyon on one side of the cabin and guards all around it. She wanted to ask what he intended to do with her—but she wasn't sure she really wanted to know the answer to that question, or that Meredes would tell her the truth.

She focused again on Mariposa. The stove made the cabin uncomfortably warm, even with the windows open. Standing next to it, Mariposa must be burning up, but she showed no signs of discomfort. She spooned instant coffee into two cups and added boiling water, then took one cup to Meredes. He smiled and caressed her hip, then pinched her bottom. Her expression never changed, though when she turned away, Abby thought she read disgust in the woman's eyes.

Mariposa brought the second cup to Abby. *"Gracias,"* Abby said. She sipped the brew to be polite, though she wasn't a fan of instant coffee; this concoction tasted particularly nasty.

"What happened to your face?"

The question startled her, both because she hadn't expected El Jefe to talk to her, and because most people—most adults anyway—were too polite to ask about her scar.

"I was injured in the war," she said.

"You should have plastic surgery to fix it," he said. "Without the scar, you would be beautiful."

Her hand tightened on the cup. She wanted to hurl the hot liquid into his face, but she wanted more to keep living, unharmed, so she simply said, "Some things can't be fixed."

"This is what happens when women try to fight," he said. "They are too sentimental to make good warriors. And they make the men around them soft."

She'd heard similar opinions from some of the men she'd served with in the army. But the majority of her fellow soldiers had respected her and trusted her skills and training.

"Do you have other injuries from the war?" he asked.

Everyone she knew who'd fought had injuries, even though many of them weren't visible. "I don't see how it matters to you," she said.

"I was making conversation. Passing the time." He looked offended.

She sat back in the chair, determined to appear relaxed, even if she wasn't. "How long do you intend to stay here?" she asked.

"As long as necessary," he said, which was no answer at all. She was sure he was purposely trying to frustrate her, so she said nothing.

"I will offer to trade you to the Rangers for Angelique," he said after a moment.

"If Mariposa wants her baby back, she can petition the court to return her to her." Though Abby wasn't sure how the court would view an illegal immigrant who had willfully handed over her infant to a stranger.

"Why would I waste my time with courts and judges? My way is much faster, and more effective."

He sounded so sure, but she doubted the Rangers—

even Michael—would hand over the child in exchange for her. "Why do you want the baby?" she asked.

He scowled. Clearly, he didn't like being on the receiving end of nosy questions. She braced herself for an angry retort. Instead, he sipped more coffee, then said, "Mariposa is sad without her. I don't like to see her sad."

Mariposa, bent over something in the sink, hunched her shoulders.

Abby looked back at Meredes. "Are you the baby's father?"

His scowl made deep lines, like gullies, on his sun-damaged face. "Does that surprise you?" he asked. "Do you think a man like me would not value a daughter? One of the things that makes something valuable is rarity. With my wife in Tamaulipas, I have four sons. But I have only one daughter. She will be a great beauty."

Of course. Beautiful women were the ones who counted. Hadn't she been hearing that all her life?

She stood. "I'll help Mariposa in the kitchen." Surely he would think that was an appropriate place for a woman.

He made no objection, so she moved to the sink and began drying the cups the other woman washed. *"Gracias,"* Mariposa whispered, her voice barely audible.

Abby had so many questions she wanted to ask: *Why are you with this man? Has he hurt you? Why did you give your baby to me?*

But Meredes's looming presence, not to mention the language barrier, prevented them from communicating with anything beyond looks.

As she stacked the dried dishes on the shelf above

the counter, she looked for a knife or other weapon. But even if she found one, what good would it do? One knife was no match against Meredes and his guards. She could see one of the men out the kitchen window, pacing back and forth, weapon slung across his chest, a cigarette pinched between his lips.

Michael and the others would be looking for her. The Jeep tracks wouldn't have been too difficult to follow across the prairie, provided they'd discovered them and linked the tracks to her disappearance. Meredes hadn't tried to cover the tracks—maybe because he'd known that once they reached the remote canyon, locating the cabin would be more difficult. A visitor had to be practically on top of the building before it was visible, and the guards would see any intruder long before he'd be aware of them.

If he planned to trade her for the baby, he'd likely arrange some kind of meeting. That would be her best opportunity to escape. Until then, she'd remain alert and bide her time.

The dishes done, Mariposa indicated that Abby should sit once more. Abby reluctantly turned to the chair across from El Jefe. Mariposa started to sit at the table, but El Jefe held out his hand to her. *"Sentarse conmigo,"* he said, and pulled her into his lap.

Abby looked away as he stroked his hand up and down Mariposa's thigh. The other woman looked miserable, but she didn't try to fight him. Maybe she'd learned doing so was futile. And maybe he was only fondling Mariposa because he sensed it made Abby uncomfortable. She assumed a disinterested expression and tried to think of some way to distract him.

"Did Richard Prentice supply this cabin?" she asked.

His hand stilled and something flickered in his eyes—was it anger, or fear? But he quickly recovered. "I do not know this Richard Prentice," he said.

"You don't know the largest landholder in the county?"

"Maybe I have heard of him, but I do not know him."

"You're practically on his land. Maybe you *are* on his land." She tried to remember the layout of the map Michael had shown her. The park boundary must be near here.

"I am on public land. There is a great deal of public land in Colorado, free for anyone to use. So much of it is empty. No one ever visits. This suits our purposes well."

"What is your purpose here?" she asked.

His expression transformed to a sneer, but he remained silent.

"What happened to those people we saw at the campground?" she asked. "Who were they? What were they doing?"

"There were no people," he said. "No campground."

"But I saw them. There were four travel trailers and all of these people. You moved them away with trucks." *And pushed them to the bottom of a ravine.* She swallowed hard, wondering if she dared confront him again with what she knew he'd done.

His eyes met hers, and the look in them made her feel cold in spite of the summer heat. "Senorita, if you know what is good for you, you will accept that you never saw such people," he said.

* * *

"Lotte tracked Abby right to the edge of the canyon, here." Michael pointed to the place on the map on the wall of ranger headquarters. "She was there, I'm sure of it." The frustration of being so close and not being able to reach Abby gnawed at him.

"Meredes must have some kind of hideout nearby, but it's well guarded," Randall said. He rubbed his shoulder where a fragment of rock had nicked him after the guards started firing. One minute, the three of them and Lotte had been standing on the rim of the canyon, peering down. The next they'd been forced to retreat to the Cruiser. Even Michael had reluctantly agreed they needed reinforcements.

"That's almost at Prentice's boundary." Graham traced the blue line on the map that marked the edge of park lands.

"*Almost* only counts in horseshoes and hand grenades," Randall said.

"Don't tell me a man with ties to a Mexican drug cartel is hiding out that close and Prentice knows nothing about it," Michael said.

"It's what he'll say," Simon said. "And we can't prove any different."

"Then, find me some proof that links him to Meredes," Graham said.

"What do the workers we pulled from the rubble in that wash say?" Graham asked.

"Simon and I interviewed a couple of the victims at the hospital," Marco said. "But they're terrified to say much. The man they know as El Jefe promised them work—jobs paying more than they'd been told they could earn working for the farmers or ranchers in the area. When they agreed to do the work, he brought them here and made them prisoners. During the day, they worked growing marijuana. They traveled to and from the grow sites under armed guard. At night they were locked into the trailers and more guards kept watch."

"They can't tell us where the grow operation is," Simon said.

"Do you believe them?" Graham asked.

"I do," Marco said. "It's easy to get turned around out there in the wilderness, and the guards didn't take them over any recognizable roads. They moved around a lot, to avoid detection."

"What about the woman—Mariposa?" Carmen asked. "Where does she fit in all this?"

"She didn't work in the fields with the others," Marco said. "She did most of the cooking and cleaning. El Jefe singled her out. She wasn't exactly his girlfriend, but she had special privileges."

"So he might be the baby's father," Carmen said.

"We didn't ask about that," Simon said. "We were more interested in determining how the organization is structured."

"They all said they had never seen a man who looked like Richard Prentice in their camp," Marco said. "But they didn't get many visitors of any kind— just El Jefe and the guards."

"Prentice wouldn't dirty his hands mingling with the workers," Michael said.

He paced the conference room, unable to sit. Abby had been in or near that canyon, with Meredes, he was sure. She'd definitely been in that Jeep, and left the rabbit behind. Had she accidentally dropped it, or had she left it on purpose for him to find? "We need to go back there, find Meredes and rescue Abby," he said. "Go in there with everything we've got."

"We're not going to do that." If Graham shared Michael's rage toward the Mexican, he didn't show it. "We've got a potential hostage situation. We're going to approach this cautiously and minimize the risk to everyone."

"But those people are killers." Saying the word out loud made him shake.

"That's why we won't rush in."

Graham's calm only increased Michael's agitation. *Get a grip*, he told himself, and walked away, fighting to keep his composure. Everything the captain said made sense. But his emotions where Abby was concerned didn't always respond to logic.

"You got it bad, don't you?" Randall joined him in the corner of the room and spoke softly.

"I care about her."

"Just don't let it mess with your judgment."

"My judgment is fine." But even as he said the words, he wondered. By focusing on Abby, was he losing sight of the bigger picture, the reason he was doing this job in the first place? He wasn't here to protect just one woman, but to make life safer for many people—visitors to the park, the illegal immigrants who fell victim to the drug dealers' scams and the people whose lives could be ruined by the drugs they imported. So much more was at stake than his relationship to one woman.

When had she become so important to him? He couldn't identify a single moment when she'd changed from someone who'd made a strong impression on him in the past to the woman he loved. When she'd walked back into his life that afternoon at ranger headquarters he'd been impressed by her strength and bravery, touched by her compassion, and yes, physically attracted to her. All that had come together for him sometime over the past few days. They'd clicked, and last night at her trailer, he'd been sure she felt the same.

Then he'd blown it by coming on too strong.

A ringing phone shook the tense silence of the room. Carmen answered. "Public Lands Task Force."

Her expression of calm dissolved into one of agitation. "Just a minute." She held the phone out to Graham. "It's for you. Raul Meredes."

Graham took the receiver and punched the button to put the call on speakerphone. "I have something you want." Meredes's voice, heavily accented but clear and precise, filled the room. "Since you also have something I want, I think we should make a trade."

Graham said nothing, but nodded to Simon, who went to the computer and began trying to trace the call.

"Are you listening, Captain?"

"I'm listening."

"You will bring the baby to the old water tank by the old ranch corral at eight o'clock tonight. The women and I will be there, waiting."

"We can't meet that soon," Graham said. "The baby isn't close and we have to get her. We can meet you in the morning."

Michael took a step toward the captain. Was he serious about leaving Abby with a killer overnight? Randall took his arm. Michael tried to shake him off, but the younger man held tight.

"You will bring her this evening." Meredes's words were clipped—an order, not a request.

"We can't," Graham lied. "She's in Denver. Even if we chartered a private plane and left now, we couldn't get her back here by eight." The captain's gaze found and held Michael's, sending the message to keep quiet and trust him.

Michael remained tense, but he nodded to Randall, letting him know he didn't have to restrain him anymore.

"In the morning, then. 6:00 a.m."

"How do we know Abby is safe?" Graham asked. "We don't have a deal if you've harmed her."

The thought that Abby might be injured—or worse—made Michael's stomach roil. He balled his hands into fists and waited for Meredes's answer.

"If you want to see her safely, you will bring the baby to me in the morning," Meredes said.

Before Graham could reply, a woman's breathy gasp replaced the Mexican's gruff voice. "Captain, is that you?" Abby's words were high-pitched and strained.

"Yes, it's me. Abby, are you all right?"

"Do as he says, Captain," she pleaded, on the verge of tears. "Please."

With a click, the call ended, the hum of dead air filling the room.

Randall patted Michael's back. "We'll take care of him, don't worry," he said softly.

"Oh, we'll take care of him, all right," Michael said. He blinked, trying to clear his vision of the angry red haze. He straightened and nodded to Randall to show he was all right. Rage wasn't going to get Abby back.

He turned to Graham. "What's the plan?"

Chapter 17

Meredes lifted the blade of the knife from Mariposa's throat and Abby let out a gasp of relief. One moment he'd been talking on the phone with Graham and the next he had jerked Mariposa to him and pressed the knife to her throat. "Tell them to do as I say or I will cut her," he'd growled.

Mariposa, eyes wide with terror, had whimpered as a trickle of blood had formed along the edge of the knife. Meredes had thrust the phone into Abby's shaking hand. "Tell them," he'd commanded.

She'd forced the words past the fear in her throat, terrified that Meredes would kill Mariposa right in front of her.

He'd brought the women with him out of the cabin and up onto the canyon's rim. He'd refused to say where they were going, but when he'd stopped only a short distance away and pulled out his phone, she'd realized he'd only been moving to where he could get a good cell signal.

He replaced the knife in the sheath on his belt and took the phone from her. "He says the baby is in Denver. Is this true?" he asked.

The last she'd heard, Angelique was with a woman in Grand Junction. But maybe she'd been moved to put her farther from danger. Or maybe Graham was putting off Meredes to buy time. Maybe he had a plan to rescue her. "I don't know where they took her," she said. "But the offices for the state child welfare services are in Denver, so it makes sense they'd take her there."

The answer didn't seem to please him, but he said nothing more on the subject. "Come." He motioned for her to move ahead of him, then took hold of Mariposa's arm and dragged her after them. She held one hand over the cut on her neck and stared at the ground. Abby thought of dogs who cringed at their master's abuse, yet continued to follow after them. Did Mariposa seriously care about Meredes, or did she simply think she had no other choice but to try to stay in his good graces?

Inside the cabin once more, she followed Mariposa to the sink. "Let me," she said, and took a cloth and wet it under the faucet, then pressed it to the cut. Mariposa winced, then tried a wavering smile. *"Gracias,"* she whispered.

"Leave her," Meredes ordered.

Abby ignored him. He still needed to be able to show her to the Rangers when they arrived if he had any hope of retrieving the baby. As long as he thought that, he wasn't going to do her any serious harm.

"Do you want me to cut her again?" he asked. "I said, leave her."

Mariposa understood his harsh tone of voice, if not his words. She pushed Abby away from her. Reluctantly, Abby returned to the chair across from Meredes. "As a former soldier, you should understand the importance of obeying orders," he said.

"I pledged to obey my commanders in the army," she said. "I never made that kind of promise to you."

"I am more powerful than you," he said. "That is all the authority I need."

She couldn't argue with his assertion that he had power over her for the moment, but she held on to the hope that that would change. Michael and the others would come to rescue her. But she had a long night ahead of her first.

Night came early to the little cabin. The canyon walls blocked the sun and cast the dwelling in twilight in early afternoon. The shadows continued to lengthen until full darkness shrouded the hiding place. Mariposa moved to the kitchen and began taking cans and packages from the cabinet. "Can I help?" Abby asked.

Mariposa glanced at her, then at Meredes, who sat by the woodstove, cleaning his nails with the blade of the knife. He looked up when Abby stood and moved into the kitchen, but made no objection. Mariposa handed her a can of beans and an opener, and pantomimed that she should dump the contents of the can into the large pot she'd set on the stove.

While Abby opened cans, she stared out the window over the sink. She could no longer see much of the landscape, but she already knew that the window looked out into the canyon itself. If she tried to climb out it, she'd only fall to her death, hundreds of feet below. The two guards watched the front of the little house; occasionally she heard them talking in Spanish, or smelled the smoke from their cigarettes. The back of the house rested against rock. El Jefe had chosen his hideout well for its protected position.

She glanced up at the low ceiling, then quickly away. The gunshots she'd heard earlier must have been the guards firing at the Rangers. They'd retreated for the moment, but she didn't believe they'd give up so easily. They'd wait until dark, and come in with reinforcements.

With canned vegetables and some spices, Mariposa made a soup that was more delicious than Abby would have thought possible. Though nerves stole her appetite, she forced herself to eat a little. She needed to remain strong for whatever ordeal lay ahead.

After the women washed the dishes and put them away, Mariposa went to the bed in the corner and lay down, her back to them.

"Is she all right?" Abby asked. The other woman's sudden retreat alarmed her.

"Leave her," Meredes said. "She misses the little one."

"She must have thought the baby would be safer with me than staying here with you," Abby said.

"It wasn't me she was worried about, it was Denver. She's afraid of cities."

"Denver?"

"I told her I was taking her and the baby to Denver. She should have been happy to leave this desolate place."

"What was she going to do in Denver?"

He shrugged. "Nothing difficult. I would set her up in a house there. Occasionally, she'd entertain some friends I would send to her. Nothing difficult."

Abby watched Mariposa as he spoke. Her back stiffened, then she smothered a sob. Understanding washed over her in a sickening wave as she remembered what Michael had told her. She forced herself to look at Meredes again. "You wanted her to be a prostitute."

"It's easier work than any she'd have found if she'd stayed in Tampico. And she could have kept the baby with her."

Except Mariposa wanted more for her daughter than a life of slavery. So she'd given her away. Abby swallowed the emotions that threatened to overtake her.

"She wants the baby back now, so I told her I'd get her for her," he said.

"How thoughtful of you."

He must not have missed the sarcasm in her voice. "She'll work better if she's happy," he said.

But how could anyone kept a prisoner be happy? She had to do something to help her new friend, and to help herself in the process. But what? She returned to her seat on the sofa and tried to think, but her thoughts spun in circles. After a while, lulled by the silence and weary from the stressful day, she dozed.

"The water tank where Meredes wants to meet is here." Graham indicated the dot on the map labeled Historic Structure.

"And the Jeep was parked about here." Randall pointed to a second dot, several hundred yards from the first.

"And we were fired on from here." Marco indicated a spot on the edge of the canyon. "So the hideout is probably very near there. The shorter distance he has to travel to make the exchange, the less chance of our intercepting him or Abby making a run for it."

"Would she do that?" Carmen asked. "Make a run for it, I mean?"

Michael realized she'd addressed the question to him. "How should I know?" he said. He'd make a run for it, but Abby was a woman, and he was clearly no expert on the female sex.

"You know," Carmen said. "You've spent more time with her than anyone. Is she the type to be paralyzed by fear, or would she save herself?"

He thought back to how Abby had handled herself that first day, when they'd been trapped by the sniper. Even fighting flashbacks to the war, she'd held herself together. She'd faced her fears. And when they'd been lost in the backcountry, she hadn't panicked or blamed him, or any of the things other people might have done under similar circumstances. She'd looked after the baby, found food for them to eat and settled in to wait. "She wouldn't panic," he said. "She's the type who assesses a problem and tries to find solutions. And she'd fall back on her military training. In the army, they train you to focus on escape if you're captured, so she'll be looking for opportunities to get away from Meredes. And she'll fight back with everything she's got if she's in danger."

"That's good," Graham said. "We can count on her to help us when we get to them."

"How are we going to get to her?" Randall asked. "From what Lotte told us, they're down in the canyon."

"That's why we're going in at night," Graham said. "I'm counting on catching them unawares. And I want to take Meredes alive. We need him to tell us what he knows about the operation."

The others nodded, but Michael kept silent. He understood the importance of Meredes to the investigation, but when it came to protecting Abby, all bets were off. He hadn't saved her life once to lose her now.

Abby woke with a start, unsure at first what had roused her, then the noise reached her ears again: a low thump, like something—or someone—landing on the roof. She stood, heart pounding. Meredes looked up from the book he'd been reading. "What is it?" he asked.

Was it possible he hadn't heard? She clutched her stomach. "I have to use the bathroom," she said. "Something in the soup didn't agree with me." Earlier in the afternoon, she'd made a trip to the outhouse perched on the edge of the canyon. A guard had waited outside the door, then escorted her back to El Jefe, who had waited for her in front of the cabin.

He frowned at her now. She bent double and moaned, loud enough to cover what she was sure was the sound of footsteps on the roof.

He went to the door and opened it, and called something in Spanish. Gunfire from in front of the cabin cut off his words as plaster rained down from the ceiling overhead. Abby looked up in time to see the blade of an ax pierce the ceiling. The ax struck again and again, then Michael dropped down through the resulting hole, landing a few feet from her.

"Are you all right?" he asked.

"I'm fine. I knew you'd come."

Meredes whirled to face him, one hand on the gun at his side. "Give it up, Meredes." Michael leveled his pistol at the Mexican. "You're surrounded. We already took care of your guards outside."

"You won't take me." Before she or Michael could

react, Meredes lunged for Abby. He wrenched her to him and pressed the barrel of the pistol against her temple. "One move and I'll blow her head off," he growled.

He was as rigid as a statue, the hand clamped around her arm digging in like an iron restraint. He smelled of sweat and fear—of desperation. He pressed the gun to her head as if trying to bore a hole. She gritted her teeth against the pain and, trying to rein in her own panic, looked to Michael. His gaze burned into hers, equal parts anger, determination and caring. "Let her go, Meredes," he said. "You'll never get away from here alive if you don't."

"She'll be the one who dies if you come any closer." He moved toward the door, dragging her with him. "Call your bosses. Tell them I want a helicopter here in half an hour."

"There's no way—"

"Tell them!"

Gaze still locked to her, Michael pulled the radio from his belt. "He's got Abby," he said. "He wants a helicopter and safe passage out of here or he'll kill her."

And when he got those things, he'd kill her anyway, Abby thought. Would he push her body out of the helicopter in the United States, or wait until he was safely over the border? She had to do whatever she could to avoid getting onto that helicopter with him.

"Tell them to stand back and give me room," Meredes said.

Michael repeated the instructions. "He's coming out," he added.

Would they have had time to position a sniper in the rocks along the canyon? Abby wondered. Did they have night-vision goggles to make the shot possible?

Maybe Meredes wondered the same thing. He hugged Abby to him, his arm pressed tightly beneath her breasts, his head positioned behind hers. Even an expert would have trouble getting off a safe shot now.

Outside, the moon was a silver sliver of light amid a glittering array of stars. Dark shapes stood at a distance—other agents of the task force. "I've radioed for the helicopter." Graham's voice spoke from the darkness. "They'll be here in forty-five minutes."

Three-quarters of an hour to stand in this man's cruel embrace. Would either of them be able to endure it?

"Don't come any closer." Meredes backed away from the agents. Where was the drop-off into the canyon? She tried to remember how much room they might have, but the darkness made it difficult to orient herself. With no electric lights in the cabin and no light pollution from a nearby town, not to mention the canyon walls closing in on either side, the darkness was like a physical shroud, thick and unyielding.

"Let her go," Michael said from somewhere to their left. "Take me instead."

Meredes's laughter abraded her raw nerves like fingernails on a chalkboard. "How chivalrous of you. But you are worthless to me."

He took another step back and Abby cried out in protest. "Careful," she said. "We must be close to the canyon."

He stiffened and stretched one foot carefully behind him. Abby wondered if she could trip him, then throw herself forward, to the ground. But his grip on her was too strong. If he fell over the edge, he'd be sure to drag her with him.

"Over to the cabin," he said. "We'll wait on those rocks."

He dragged her toward the boulders piled against one corner of the cabin, then leaned against the rocks, keeping her tight against him, cradled between his legs. Her head and heart pounded in unison, a drumbeat of fear and adrenaline.

Light blinded them, a white glare that hit them full-on. "Cut it out!" Meredes shouted, enraged.

"Shut it off!" Graham ordered, and they were plunged into darkness again, blinded now, spots dancing before her eyes.

"We'll have to turn on lights to guide the helicopter in," Graham said.

"Then, wait until it arrives," Meredes said. "I still have the gun to her head, even if you can't see it." As if to emphasize his point, he dug the barrel in harder. She felt a trickle of blood run down the side of her face and flinched. He moved his free hand to cup her breast, his fingers digging in. "Just holding on tight," he murmured.

She forced herself not to react, to remain rigid in his arms. She wouldn't give him the satisfaction of knowing how afraid she was. She wouldn't let him see any weakness. He was used to people being afraid of him, of using weaker women like Mariposa. She wouldn't be another victim for him to gloat over.

Mariposa. For the first time in minutes, she thought of the other woman. Was she still asleep on the bed in the cabin? Surely she hadn't slept through this chaos. Maybe she'd followed them out and was safe with one of the Rangers, invisible in the dark. Abby hoped so. She hoped Mariposa could be reunited with her baby, and safely returned to her home, wherever that was.

Something scraped on the rock behind them, along the side of the cabin. El Jefe jerked upright. "If anyone tries anything—" he shouted. But the words died in his throat. Mariposa landed on top of them. Meredes fell to his knees and Abby kicked out against him, scrabbling away from him even as a gun exploded, deafening her. She screamed and rolled away, then Michael was pulling her up, into his arms. Light blared around them, blinding her.

"Are you okay?" Michael smoothed the hair back from her face.

"I'm fine." Her head still throbbed, and she'd have a few bruises tomorrow, but she was alive and safe. "What happened?"

"Mariposa crept up from behind and tried to stab Meredes with a kitchen knife."

She twisted around. "Is he—?"

"He's dead." Michael pulled her closer and together they watched Carmen help Mariposa from the ground and gently pry the knife from her hand. The Mexican woman was sobbing and staring at the man on the ground in front of her, blood pooling around him.

"She didn't kill him," Michael said.

Abby stared at the body of the man on the ground. "I don't understand."

"A sniper shot him." Randall joined them. "As soon as you moved out of the way, they fired. They must have been watching, waiting for a chance."

"I wondered if you'd position a sniper," she said.

"It wasn't one of ours," Randall said.

She frowned. "Then, who?"

"Someone else wanted him dead," Michael said. "Before we could question him."

Mariposa's sobbing broke the silence. The pitiful

sound tore at Abby's heart. "What will happen to her?" she asked.

"We'll question her, but I doubt there will be any charges filed," Michael said. "We'll want to know whatever she can tell us about Meredes's operation. Then we'll try to find her relatives in Mexico and arrange for her and the baby to return there."

"I hope she can find a place where she can be happy and safe," she said. Wasn't that what they all wanted? She studied the man on the ground again; he looked so small and harmless in death. Yet he'd destroyed so many lives. He'd almost destroyed hers.

"I'm not sorry he's dead," Michael said. "But I'm just sorry we didn't get the chance to question him."

"You want to know who's backing him?" she asked.

"He's only one small part of the operations in the area," Michael said. "Our guess is, he was in charge of the labor force. Other people must be overseeing production and distribution."

"What about the people you found in the canyon earlier today—the workers from the camp?" she asked.

He smoothed his hand along her shoulder. "Three of them died, and some of them are seriously injured, but will probably live. We'll question them, but it's unlikely they know much. They probably never saw anyone other than Meredes and the guards. They'll be processed through ICE offices in Grand Junction and sent back home."

She looked at El Jefe's still body once more. "He got off too easy," she said.

"Forget about him." Michael gently turned her away from the dead man. "I have something that belongs to you," he said. He opened his hand to reveal the little ceramic rabbit.

Seeing the familiar token was like being reunited with an old friend; she felt a surge of relief. "I wondered what happened to it." She took it from him. "Thanks for saving it for me. I'm not sure I really believe in luck, but I like having it around."

"I thought maybe you'd left it for me to find."

"I didn't think of that." She glanced up at him. He radiated caring and concern, two emotions she'd spent a lot of time warding off, as if letting people worry about her made her somehow weaker. Michael had helped her to see things differently. Other people's compassion could make her stronger. "Besides, I knew you'd come for me."

"You did?"

"You haven't let me down yet."

He put his arm around her. "Come on. I want a paramedic to take a look at that cut on your head."

"It's nothing." She touched the tender spot and felt the blood matting in her hair.

"Humor me."

"All right. I'll let someone clean me up and slap on a bandage. Then what?"

"Then maybe we'll stop by your trailer and you can pick up a few things."

"Why do I need to do that?"

He turned her to face him and cradled the side of her face in his hand. "Because I want you to come stay with me."

"Do you think I'm still in some kind of danger?" she asked.

"No. I want us to be together."

There her heart went, racing again. So much for playing it cool and not letting him see how much this mattered to her. "For how long?"

"For as long as you like. Though forever would be fine with me."

She put her hand over his and took a step back, wanting to see him more clearly—to see all of him, not just his eyes regarding her so intently. "What are you saying?"

He swallowed. "You're going to make me spell it out, aren't you?"

"Yes."

"All right. I love you. I want to be with you. Always. I want to marry you, but if you think it's too soon for that, I'm willing to wait."

"It seems to me you've already been waiting awhile now," she said. "Five years."

"But part of that time, I didn't really know what I was waiting for."

"Neither did I." She moved into his arms once more and tilted her head up to kiss him. Here in his embrace felt like the safest place she'd ever be. As long as he held on to her, she'd be capable of anything. "I don't want to wait any longer," she said. "I don't want to waste any more time."

"Are you saying you'll marry me?"

"Now who wants everything spelled out?" She smiled. "Yes. Yes, I'll marry you. I love you and I want to be with you." Here was a man she could trust to love her, not for what she looked like, but for who she was. When a woman found that kind of gift, she'd be smart to hang on and never let go.

* * * * *

HARLEQUIN
PLUS

Try the best multimedia
subscription service for romance
readers like you!

Read, Watch and Play.

Experience the easiest way to get
the romance content you crave.

Start your **FREE TRIAL** at
<u>www.harlequinplus.com/freetrial</u>.